THE MENTOR

Before becoming a thriller writer, Steve Jackson was a journalist, musician, recording engineer, guitar tutor and riding instructor. Originally from Scotland he now lives with his partner in St Albans.

For more information about Steve Jackson visit www.steve-jackson.net

Visit www.AuthorTracker.co.uk for exclusive updates on Steve Jackson.

STEVE JACKSON

The Mentor

HARPER

Harper
An imprint of HarperCollins*Publishers*
77-85 Fulham Palace Road,
Hammersmith, London W6 8JB

www.harpercollins.co.uk

This paperback edition 2007
5

First published in Great Britain by
HarperCollins 2006

Copyright © Steve Jackson 2006

Steve Jackson asserts the moral right to
be identified as the author of this work

A catalogue record for this book is
available from the British Library

ISBN-13 978 0 00 721211 8
ISBN-10 0 00 721211 9

Set in Meridien by
Palimpsest Book Production Limited,
Grangemouth, Stirlingshire

Printed and bound in Great Britain by
Clays Limited, St Ives plc

For Karen, with love.

Acknowledgements

A big thank you to the following:

Betty Schwartz opened the door, and kept it open long enough for me to get a foot firmly wedged inside. What can I say? You're a star!

My wonderful agent, Veronique Baxter, is without a doubt the hardest working agent in the business. Thanks for wading through all those early drafts . . . you must have the patience of a saint! Your insights and enthusiasm have been invaluable.

The fabulous Wayne Brookes, editor extraordinaire, did a spectacular job of steering this novel through the stormy waters of the publishing world. You've made the dream real. Thank you.

My family and friends have been there for me through the highs and lows. In particular I'd like to thank my mum and dad; my sister, Anne; my brothers, Mike and Paul; Kenny and Maureen Studsrud; Candice Williams, Ken Crouch and Nikki Searle.

Prologue

Fifteen minutes till showtime.

Waiting doesn't bother me, never has. It comes with the territory. Killing time . . . yeah, I'm good at that. The room is oppressive and smells of disinfectant and piss, rented by the hour rather than the day and not much bigger than the bed. There are no Gideons in the bedside drawer, no mints on the stained pillows. The mattress is lumpy and covered with a dirty grey sheet. No duvet. The headboard is screwed to the plasterboard wall to stop it banging, the screws going in at all angles. Paper-thin curtains hang raggedly across the window, the hint of a floral pattern barely visible; tracings in pink, red and green. A garbage-strewn alleyway can be glimpsed through the crack. There's no wardrobe, no chest of drawers, no point, really. You come to a place like this to fuck or die.

I've rented the room for two hours and paid in cash. The desk clerk was caged behind the wire mesh and I wouldn't be surprised if he had a baseball bat or a gun hidden back there. A shock of electrified white dreads hung halfway down his back and a fat joint was clamped between his bluing lips. Late sixties or early fifties, difficult to say. He was staring through the sweet-smelling smoke at a black and white portable, screwed-up bloodshot eyes taking it all in. On the screen, Arnie was waving a big gun. Half man, half cyborg . . . come with me if you want to live! The clerk took the money and shoved a key through the slot without turning from the TV.

'Uhm,' I said. 'A friend . . . a female friend. She'll be, er, turning up shortly. Could you send her to my room?'

The clerk turned slowly, took a long drag on his joint and gave me a look as if to say *what the fuck do you think this is? The motherfuckin' Hilton?* He exhaled and grinned through the smoke, his teeth yellow and gold. 'Sure thing, mon,' he said. Still grinning, he turned back to the TV. He'd looked at me for all of two seconds; looked but didn't see. The man on the other side of the mesh was already forgotten. Just another horny white businessman indistinguishable from the dozens of horny white businessmen he sees each and every day.

A glance at my watch. Eight minutes to go. Further down the hall, a whore is earning her next fix. Moaning and groaning and on the home straight now, telling the punter what he needs to hear: he's a bad, bad boy . . . and *sooo* big. I ignore the noise, boot up the laptop. A click and a purr as the fan spins to life. I type in the password, fingers click-clacking across the keyboard. Hacking into London Underground's main computer system, I quickly access the security cameras. The screen shows a grainy CCTV image of a crowded platform: Leicester Square. It's a realtime feed, the picture coming via satellite through my mobile, into the laptop. There are three cameras positioned to give a complete view of the platform, and with a single click I can bounce between them. It's amazing what you can do with technology.

Rush hour is in full swing, the station crowded with suits. White faces, black faces, yellow faces. The colours vary but the expressions are the same: tired, stressed and bored. A train pulls in and the crush on the platform momentarily eases. The doors shut, then open again to let another couple of businessmen squash inside. I'm not sure who the lucky ones are. Those whisked away by the train or those left behind.

Within a minute the platform is crawling again. I scan the faces, searching for the girl. Everywhere I look little dramas unfold . . . haikus of humanity. A Pakistani in a crisp suit is standing near an exit, briefcase in hand, laptop bag slung over one shoulder. His tongue subconsciously moistens dry lips, eyes making love to every square inch of the woman in front. She senses something, turns suddenly. His head jerks away too quickly and a slender smile slides across her lips. She runs a hand through her short mannish hair, secretly flattered by the attention. I click to another camera. A backpacker is moving through the crowd like an astronaut, in slo-mo, the gravitational pull of the platform sucking him down. A rucksack is strapped to his back; greasy hair tumbles over his shoulders. He's wearing cut-off denim shorts; there are piercings in his ears, nose and lip. The one word logo on his T-shirt says it all: LOSER.

The deal was for the whole sum up front, all two million of it, the fee non-refundable. It's the only way to do business. That half now, half later nonsense is strictly for amateurs. It crosses my mind she might bottle it. Wouldn't be the first time an op had gone tits up at zero hour. I tell myself to be patient.

Seconds tick by, slowly turn into minutes. I know what they call me behind my back: a dinosaur. They mean it as an insult, but I don't see it that way. The word dinosaur has its origins in Greek. Deinos meaning terrible; sauros meaning lizard. Terrible Lizard. People should choose their words more carefully.

I click between the cameras, scanning the crowd, checking the faces against the photo lying next to the laptop. A heavily pregnant Arab woman is standing beside the chocolate machine. She's glowing, radiating a righteous light. Her head moves from left to right, searching for the best place to stand. She presses towards the middle of the platform. The crowds part to let her through, like they know she's something special. She treads carefully, hands resting on her bump, moving with the waddle of a woman whose waters could break any second. She's smiling at the businessmen as they move out the way, smiling at women who are obviously mothers. They keep giving her sympathetic glances. *Poor thing! Pregnant in this heat, that can't be any fun!* She shrugs and smiles. *What can I do?* A telepathic conversation taking place between the members of an organisation every bit as mysterious as the masons.

She stops near the yellow line and her eyes flick to the digital display hanging from the roof. The next train is due in one minute. She turns her head and for a brief moment she's staring directly into the lens. Even in monochrome she looks glorious. Barely out of her teens with long dark hair and exotic skin. There's no tension in her face, no regret in those dark, smoky eyes; she's perfectly at peace with herself. Her lips are moving as she silently recites verses from the Koran to herself. **STAND BACK TRAIN APPROACHING**, flashes the sign. The train pulls in, the doors slide open. A tidal wave of bodies spews onto the platform and I lose sight of her. A heartbeat later the screen becomes a blizzard. If I didn't know better I'd suspect a technical fault.

If I didn't know better.

PART ONE

Dead Flowers In
Her Hair

We laugh at honour and are shocked to find
traitors in our midst.

C.S. Lewis

1

Paul Aston slammed the phone down and kicked back in his chair. 'Shit, shit, shit,' he muttered under his breath. What was her problem? So he was working late. News flash: long hours came with the territory. She already knew that, so why was she acting like it was a big surprise? The phone went and he tried to ignore it. Probably Laura ringing back to tell him to go to hell. Conditioning got the better of him and he snatched it up, said a cautious hello.

'Hey, Paul.'

'Thank God, a friendly voice.' Georgina Strauss was most definitely a friend first and a work colleague second, and that was unusual; in this business you tended to cultivate contacts rather than make friends. They'd gone through the Intelligence Officer's New Entry Course together, the IONEC in MI6 speak. MI6 loved its acronyms, as Aston had quickly discovered. When he first started it had been like learning a new language.

'Look, Paul, got to be quick. A bomb's gone off in Leicester Square tube.'

'Shit,' he breathed into the mouthpiece. He checked his watch. The middle of rush hour. 'How many dead?'

'No idea. Too fucking many.'

'What happened?'

'Our guess is that it was a suicide bomber. They marched onto the platform and blew themselves to bits.'

'Jesus.'

'Didn't I say it was only a matter of time before something like this happened again? For once I hate always being right. So what about all those lessons that were supposed to have been learnt after 7/7, eh?' She sighed and Aston could imagine her sitting there shaking her head. 'This is so fucked up, Paul.'

'Fucked up . . . that doesn't even begin to cover it.'

'You owe me,' George said, and then she was gone.

Aston hung up and took the Batphone from his shirt pocket. The Batphone was always on, always charged; he wasn't allowed to go anywhere without it. Before he could flick it open, it started vibrating and chirping. He didn't need to check the caller ID. Only one person had this number.

Mac jumped straight in without so much as a hello. A barrage of questions to make sure he'd heard the news, testing him out on the whats and wheres, and then he let rip.

'Okay, so what the fuck are you sitting there with your thumb jammed up your arse for?'

'You caught me on the way out the door.'

'I hope you're not trying to bullshit me.'

'No, sir.'

A snort that could have meant anything, then: 'I want you there straightaway. I want to know everything that's happening. You got that? Everything.'

Aston made a face at the mobile. 'Yes, sir.'

'And Aston.'

'Yes.'

'Don't use the journalist alias.'

Aston hit the street running; by the time he'd jogged over Vauxhall Bridge his shirt was soaked through with sweat. The evening was humid, the air heavy and moist. He stopped on the other side of the river to catch his breath and glanced back at MI6's HQ. The elaborate architectural style had more than a touch of the Middle East about it; it was easy to see why the media had christened it Babylon-on-Thames. The cost of the building had run into nine figures and from the outside it wasn't apparent where the money had gone. It was the things you didn't see that cost the money. The elaborate anti-bugging devices, the bombproof walls, the triple glazing. The fact that five floors of the building were hidden beneath ground level.

The city was in chaos. All tube services had

been suspended, so everyone had headed to the surface to get a cab or a bus. The roads were grid-locked and the air was alive with sirens, horns, arguments. Everywhere Aston looked he saw panic and confusion. Nobody had a clue what was going on. The PM had been assassinated, Buckingham Palace had been nuked . . . the mutterings Aston heard as he headed for Leicester Square ranged from the sublime to the ridiculous. He stopped running, sweat trickling down his back. If he ran to Leicester Square in this heat he'd have a stroke. There had to be a better way.

The cyclist was dressed in a suit and the crash helmet made it look like he had a metallic blue alien skull grafted onto his head. He was riding along the gutter, squeezing between the kerb and a convertible BMW. The driver had killed the engine, resigned to being there for the long haul, fingers tapping anxiously on the steering wheel as he listened to a news bulletin. The cyclist drew level. Aston grabbed his arm and pulled him from the bike, sent him tumbling to the ground. He picked up the bike, jumped on and charged along the pavement, shouting at people to get out of his way.

He'd just passed the National Portrait Gallery when he saw his first survivor. The girl was in her mid-twenties and covered from head to toe in dust, as if frosted with grey icing sugar. She was sitting on the kerb with her knees hugged tight against her chest, rocking back and forth, focusing on nothing. Aston cycled on, passing more survivors. All of them had the same dead eyes, that same thousand yard stare. Some were crying, some were injured. They were cut and bruised, confused. Blood stained their faces, their clothes. An icy feeling settled in Aston's stomach as he realised these were the lucky ones.

Then he heard the screams. Cries of anguish mingled with cries of pain, a full-on symphony of suffering that got louder the closer he got. He wanted to block his ears, wanted to turn around and ride as fast as he could in the opposite direction, anything to get away from that terrible noise. Instead, he let his training kick in. From here on he was Detective Inspector Stuart Bromley. One of the Met's finest. There was no way DI Bromley, hardened by years of seeing the worst humanity could dream up, would run away. Aston got off the bike, propped it up against a lamppost, brushed the creases from his clothes. Handling the fear was easier when you were pretending to be someone else.

He turned a corner and stepped into a living nightmare. All the usual suspects were there. Cops, firemen and paramedics were beavering away on one side of the hastily erected barriers. Journalists, TV reporters, photographers, cameramen and rubberneckers were trapped on the other side. It was like stepping onto a movie set . . . except this was no Hollywood fantasy. His senses overloaded, slamming into the red. Colours, sounds and smells seemed sharper, more defined. Vehicle engines revving, orders being barked out, the screams and cries of the injured, red and blue lights throbbing on top of ambulances and police cars like a migraine, the excited voyeuristic murmur of the crowd, that dirty London smell coated with a thin layer of puke and cinders.

Aston pushed through the crowd, moving as if he owned the place. He almost smiled when a couple of the more seasoned hacks started firing questions at him. *No comment*, he fired back. That was the thing with cover. As long as you believed – really believed – you could fool almost anyone.

A PC manning the barrier stopped him, told him he couldn't come through. Aston didn't say a word. He drew himself up to his full height, pulled out his ID, flipped it open and thrust it an inch from the PC's nose. Indignity personified. There was no way the ID wouldn't pass inspection. Central Facilities had got it from the same place the Met got theirs. The PC muttered an apology, shifted the barrier and let him through. The media was still trapped on the other side. Mac had been right. The journalist alias wouldn't have got him very far. He turned away from the barrier and marched towards the station entrance, dust kicking up from the heels of his shoes.

2

An old man wearing a neck brace was strapped
to the gurney, a bright red blanket covering his
body. His wrinkled face was twisted with pain,
grime and blood filling the age worn crevices,
ivory hair streaked black and crimson. He was
calling out a name, over and over – 'Helena,
Helena, Helena!' – his voice surprisingly strong
considering his condition. There was the hint of
an accent, something Mediterranean. Was Helena
one of the dead? The paramedics pushed on three
and the wheels folded away as the gurney slid
inside the ambulance. They jumped in behind,
pulled the door shut. The ambulance shot forward,
siren wailing, and within seconds another had
rolled up to take its place. Two paramedics were
already waiting at the kerb with the next victim.

Aston did a quick 360 degrees. For the moment
this was the medics' show; the survivors took
priority and everything else could wait. The police
were nothing more than glorified security guards;

15

there to keep the newshounds at bay, to keep the peace. The DI Bromley alias had got him this far but it wouldn't take him much further. The only people going in and out of the station were paramedics and firefighters. He did another surreptitious 360 degrees, looking for the angle. There was always an angle. Aston made a mental note of where the PCs were. Uniformed police didn't worry him: easy to spot, easy to bullshit. CID was a different story. Detectives were born with the curiosity gene and the last thing he needed was to find himself answering a load of awkward questions.

A huddle of suited detectives had set up shop by a news stand opposite the station entrance. They were acting big and talking animatedly, hands emphasising the more important points. Aston walked off in the opposite direction, putting some distance between them, all the time looking for that angle. Another ambulance screamed past, siren wailing. It pulled into the middle of the road to go around the line of fire engines parked at the kerb, the driver thumping at the horn and scattering a couple of firemen out the way. Aston stopped, watched for a second. All the action was centred around the lead fire engine; nobody was paying any attention to the one at the back.

Walking as though he was born to be there, Aston passed the firemen, passed the first three engines. He stopped level with the last one, glanced back at the firefighters. They were all looking the other way, paying no attention to him. He pulled the door open and jumped up into the cab. Had to be quick. No telling how much time he had. There was a ton of gear in the cab: bright yellow helmets, face masks, bulky jackets, axes, respiration equipment, all the good stuff he'd need to pull this one off. Heart pounding, Aston grabbed one of the jackets, pulled it on. A little long in the arm but it would do. He pulled on a pair of trousers, found some boots, took a torch from the shelf and stuffed it into the deep jacket pocket. A sound outside. He stopped dead, listening; said a quick prayer that whoever was out there would stay out there. The scratch of a match, a long, deep inhalation, an even longer sigh. Aston twisted his head so he could see into the tall side mirror. The boy was no older than nineteen, tall and gangly like a baby giraffe. The uniform looked all wrong on him. It was too big, as though he still had some growing to do before it fit properly. The boy had taken off his helmet and placed it by his feet. Head pitched down, staring at the floor, he brought a cigarette to his lips, fighting to keep his hand still. And then he threw up, vomit splattering his boots. Jesus, was it really that bad down there?

Aston timed his departure with the second bout of retching. While the boy was busy losing his lunch, he quietly let himself out the other side, climbing down onto the pavement and gently pushing the door closed behind him. He put on the helmet, glanced in the side mirror to check he looked the part. Almost, but not quite. He bent down and scooped up some dirt from the gutter, smeared it on his face. Walking was tricky to begin with, but he soon got the hang of it. Now he knew why firefighters walked with that macho swagger; it was the bulky trousers that did it. A deep breath as he drew level with the lead fire engine, praying he wouldn't be challenged. His luck held. Everyone was too busy with their own problems. Confidence growing, he headed for the station entrance, passing a couple of policemen who didn't even give him a second look. Like Mac said, pulling off a disguise was all about getting into someone else's shoes; getting under their skin.

The station foyer had been turned into a triage ward, dozens upon dozens of stretchers covering the cold, hard floor. Halogen lamps flooded the area with their sterile glare, generators thud-thud-thudding in the background. Aston looked around in disbelief. It was like something from the First World War. Doctors in bloodstained butcher's coats flitted from patient to patient, assessing each one, categorising them, making life and death decisions in the blink of an eye. They worked on the ones with the best chance of survival; those who didn't make the grade were quickly stretchered away to make room for those who did. Nurses flitted around like some rare breed of ivory butterfly, settling down momentarily to fit an IV, to give an injection or a painkiller, to offer some words of comfort. They worked efficiently, their movements economical and precise, their fear hidden behind training and procedure. The sounds and smells from outside were more intense in here, as though reality had been ratcheted up another couple of notches. The noise worked into Aston's brain, shredding synapses, putting his teeth on edge. Screams echoed off the tiles, the volume creeping past ten. Underpinning this was a lower pitched rumble that was somehow worse – *moans groans crying voices pleading for help whispering voices begging for an escape from the pain please please please anything to take the pain away* – a bass counterpoint to the hideous melody. The stink was worse than the noise. The stench of shit and puke dominated, stealing what little oxygen there was from the heavy air. There was another smell too, a clean smell that seemed completely out of place: the antiseptic aroma of hospitals. The combination made Aston want to throw up. It was all too much, all too real. The hopeless cases had been moved next to the ticket booth, where a priest in a grey cassock was trying to provide comfort to people past hearing or caring. He was clutching his crucifix so tightly his knuckles were shining. His salt and pepper hair, usually so neat for Mass, was standing on end, a nervous hand pushing it in all directions. Aston watched the priest kneel beside a stretcher. It was difficult to tell if the victim was male or female, young or old. The face was ruined: ugly, moist and black. The priest's lips moved, mouthing incantations in Latin. Dead words in a dead language for someone who would never see another sunrise. He crossed himself then leant over and closed the corpse's eyes. A look of disgust spread across his face and he frantically wiped his hand across the front of his neat grey cassock, leaving a nasty dark smear. He jumped to his feet, visibly shaken, spun around to see if anyone had noticed. Aston looked away quickly, leaving the priest alone with his embarrassment, and as he turned he caught sight of the body bags. They were piled up in a dark corner, hidden in the shadows. There had to be a couple of dozen of them. Probably more. And this was just the start.

'Jesus Christ,' Aston whispered to himself. He'd expected it to be bad, but nowhere near this bad.

Feeling shaky, he headed for the escalators, his lunch sitting heavily. He took a couple of deep breaths to steady himself. Three of the ticket barriers had been ripped out and dumped to one side, creating a thoroughfare between the make-shift ward and the platforms below. Aston moved aside to let a couple of medics through. He couldn't help looking at the stretcher as they passed. Car crash curiosity. Aston didn't fancy the woman's chances. He turned a corner and almost collided with a firefighter.

'Watch where the fuck you're going!' The explosive consonants of someone used to barking out orders; a tone of voice Aston knew only too well. He looked up, saw a Viking masquerading as a fire-fighter; the sooty black marks on his face could have been painted on by a make-up artist. The man glaring down at him was hitting fifty, well over six foot with a perfectly trimmed ginger moustache. Aston muttered an apology, all the time telling himself that he was meant to be here, praying his cover wasn't going to be blown, not when he was this close. He had the uniform – and most people didn't look any further than that – all he had to do was keep his cool. Mac would throw a shit-fit if he screwed up now. And Mac was a damn sight scarier than this guy.

'Who the hell are you?' The firefighter gave Aston the once over, moustache twitching.

'Paul Hester.' It was the first name that came into his head.

'Haven't seen you before.'

'I'm based in Watford,' Aston said. 'Brought in to help out.'

'One of Blackie's boys.'

'That's right.'

Aston didn't have a clue who Blackie was, but if the Viking wanted to believe he was one of Blackie's boys then that was fine with him. There was a long silence, long enough for Aston to think the Viking was testing him and he'd just screwed up big time, then: 'Okay Hester, some of the lads are clearing a cave-in on one of the exit tunnels for the westbound platform of the Piccadilly Line. They could do with an extra pair of hands. Do you think you can find them okay or do you want me to draw a map?'

21

'I'll find them,' Aston said.

'Good lad.' The Viking marched off through the barriers and Aston breathed a sigh of relief. That had been way too close for comfort.

He reached the long escalator and stared down into the depths. The bottom was there somewhere, hidden in the gloom. Light bulbs had been strung up along one side, their weak glow reaching for the far wall and not quite making it. He chose the escalator nearest the bulbs, picking his way carefully from step to step, moving through alternating patches of light and shadow, his heart hammering in his chest. He half expected the escalator to suddenly burst into life, calliope music huffing and puffing through the gloom and multicoloured lights flashing luridly, like something from a fairground House of Horrors.

The further down he went, the hotter and stuffier it got. Aston unzipped the bulky coat, wafted it a couple of times, but it made no difference. He sucked in a long, whistling, asthmatic breath, grabbing what little oxygen he could. How the hell did firefighters deal with this day in and day out? Maybe it was one of those things you became acclimatised to.

At the bottom of the escalator, he pulled out the industrial-sized torch, clicked it on. There was even less air here and Aston fought back the panic, stomped it down with rationality. Walking through the tunnels was a surreal experience; the darkness made them unrecognisable. The occasional advert would catch in the torch beam – a book, a movie, a London attraction not to be missed – glimpses of the familiar, but, for the most part, the landscape was completely alien. Every now and again a face would come at him out of the dark. Paramedics mainly, stretchering the injured and the dead to the surface. Aston jumped each time it happened. Although he knew differently, it felt like he was the only person inhabiting this strange universe.

Half a dozen firemen were working on the cave-in, using their hands to remove the rubble piece by piece. They worked in silence to conserve energy; they worked methodically in case they came across a survivor trapped in a debris cave; they worked carefully, the possibility of another collapse hanging over them like the sword of Damocles. A halogen lamp had been set up, its beam bouncing off the blockage. Muddy water from a burst main sluiced around Aston's feet. He followed the lead of the nearest firefighter, the two of them working side by side. They made a pile of rubble behind them, the larger chunks they carried together. Within no time Aston was drenched in sweat. It trickled down his forehead, into his eyes, blinding him. Every five minutes or so one of the firefighters would shout for everyone to stop. Another would use an infra-red scanner to probe the debris and everyone would hold their breath, praying for a miracle.

The sight of the doll's leg poking out from the rubble broke Aston's heart; somehow it brought home the full horror of what had happened here. The people who'd died today had been innocents, none more so than the children. Sweating and groaning, he'd hefted a large slab out the way, and there it was, a glimpse of dirty pink cotton. Aston dropped to his knees, his lungs suddenly packed with ice despite the heavy heat down here. He knew what he was seeing, but the rational part of his brain wouldn't let him admit the truth. Do that and he'd have to get out, start running and keep going until he reached the surface. It wasn't that he was weak, it was just that sometimes you needed a little denial to keep you functioning. Aston concentrated on his breathing, forcing the hot, filthy air into his chest, melting the ice – in, out, in, out – then he went to work. With the utmost care he excavated the doll, working in silence, totally absorbed by the task. He had no awareness of anything going on around him. The sounds of the firefighters working, their harsh breathing and tense shouted whispers, the cold- ness of the water, the sharp stab of the halogens, none of this registered. Down on his hands and knees he dug into the rubble, dirt and grime grinding into his baby-soft skin; his hands were conditioned to the smoothness of plastic, tele- phones and computer keyboards, not the grim reality of manual labour. The sharp grit got onto his skin, into his skin, under his skin, abrasive right down to the bone. He looked at his hands, and barely recognised them. They were pruned from the water and the damp dirt, black as a miner's. There was red mixed in there, too. Blood. He couldn't feel any pain, couldn't see any cuts; his hands were numb, the injuries belonging to someone else. Aston began digging again, carefully, reverentially. Through the dirt and sweat he saw the pink Babygro with *Mummy's Little Princess* on the front. Saw the mangled bloody face. He lifted the doll out, knowing that once upon a time she had been alive – breathing, laughing and loving – but unable to admit this to himself. Not yet. Not ever. So, even though the limbs felt like they were made from jelly rather than plastic, he told himself again it was just a doll, and although he knew differently he kept telling himself it was a doll, only a doll, because that was the one thing keeping him sane right now, the one thing keeping him from falling apart. But denial could only carry you so far, and Aston could feel reality creeping in. He tried to push it back, but it was too late. Fingers moving as though they had a mind of their own, he reached out and fussed her hair, stroked her cheek. Flesh instead of plastic. No point lying to himself anymore. The full horror crashed in on him all at once and he was powerless to stop the flood. He was a lone figure holding his hands up to pacify the raging torrent; there one moment, and then washed away and destroyed the next.

Aston cradled the baby in his arms, the tiny broken face resting gently against his chest, and moved deeper into the tunnel, away from the harsh halogen glare. Still holding her tight to his chest, he slid down a wall. Then the tears came and he wept. He knew that from this moment on nothing would ever be the same.

3

There were seven missed calls on the Batphone when Aston got back above ground. He steeled himself then hit redial.

'Where the hell have you been?' Mac demanded. 'Why haven't you called?'

Aston explained that he'd been a couple of hundred feet underground and it was difficult to get a signal. He hadn't meant to sound sarcastic, but that's how Mac took it. When Mac calmed down, Aston attempted to fill him in. He didn't get far.

'Shut up and listen. You think I've just been hanging around with my dick in my hand waiting for you to call? Is that it?'

'No, sir.'

'Too bloody right. If I spent my life waiting for you, I'd never get anywhere. While you've been off gallivanting I've been working my arse off trying to figure out what the hell's going on.'

Gallivanting, Aston stopped himself from saying.

'If you've got anything you think might be useful,' Mac added in a voice heavy with sarcasm, 'bung it in a report.'

'Yes, sir.'

'And if it's not too much trouble I'd like that on my desk first thing in the morning. And it'd better fucking well be there.' With that the line went dead.

'Cunt,' Aston whispered at the mobile.

Miraculously the bike was where he'd left it; any other day it would have been nicked in two seconds. He cycled back to Vauxhall Cross through near-deserted streets, the wind pushing past him a welcome relief after the suffocating tunnels. It was almost midnight and still humid; the night was a thunderstorm waiting to happen.

He banged away at the keyboard for almost an hour, taking no notice of what he was typing. His hands were sore, fingers weary. The injuries were superficial – minor scratches and cuts, an abrasion on his left palm – certainly nothing requiring hospital treatment. Some antiseptic and an Elastoplast . . . job done. All he could think about was the dead baby. He typed faster . . . if he could somehow get his brain to work quicker then maybe he could outrun those nightmarish images. Fine in theory, but all that happened was he made more typos. He didn't bother reading the report through when he finished. If it read like it was written in Chinese he didn't give a shit. He e-mailed the report to Mac's secure account and headed for home.

His mother had warned him he'd end up in the poor house, and for once she'd been right. The poor house in question was a three-storey red brick building in Pimlico that had been constructed in the late 1800s by a philanthropic mill owner. It had lain derelict until 1995, when it had been restored and converted into 'studios and apartments' . . . estate agent doublespeak for 'bed-sits and rabbit hutches'. Aston had bought a one-bedroom hutch on the first floor, which the estate agent had assured him was money well spent. The area was up and coming, he was investing in the future, in ten years' time the apartment would be worth double. Whatever. All he knew was that a large chunk of his paycheque disappeared each month just to keep his toes from slipping off the first rung of the property ladder.

It was pushing two by the time Aston got home. He was physically and mentally exhausted. Laura was crashed out on the black leather sofa, as innocent as an angel. She was wearing grey jogging bottoms and a tiny tight red T-shirt with BABE written in spangly pink letters on the front. She was snoring lightly, even though she swore blind she never snored. Aston had considered recording her so he could present her with irrefutable evidence of her crime, but she'd find some way to wriggle out of it. When it came to arguing she was as slippery as a Southern lawyer.

The fallout from her evening lay across the laminated floor. Aston knew the danger signs. Used tissues were scattered like so many crushed lilies; a box of Milk Tray was within reaching distance; she'd demolished half a tub of Häagen-Dazs. An empty DVD case sat open on the floor in front of a hi-tech stack containing all the latest gizmos. Mission Control was his one indulgence. He always had to have the latest toys. It was a boy thing. He picked up the DVD case. *Breakfast at Tiffany's*. Not good. She only watched that when she was on a serious downer. The TV was on and tuned in to BBC News 24, the sound a low mumble.

Aston perched on the edge of the sofa, carefully so it wouldn't squeak. He brushed her fringe from her face, gently pushing the black strands away with his fingertips. God, she was beautiful. He wanted to wake her; didn't want to wake her. After the day he'd had he needed to feel her arms around him, an affirmation of life to get rid of the stench of death that still clung to him even though he'd scrubbed himself raw in the shower back at Vauxhall Cross. Right now he needed that more than anything. But she looked so peaceful sleeping there, it didn't seem right. He leant in close, kissed her forehead. She stirred but didn't wake. Aston went to the bedroom, got a duvet, draped it across her, then fixed a drink – a JD and coke. He settled into the TV chair, the bottle close to hand, leant back and the footrest came up. He took a sip, ice cubes rattling, and stared at the box, too wired to sleep.

They'd been living together for almost six months, seeing each other for about a year. Laura was the first woman he'd lived with and looking back he wondered how long she'd been planning her assault. First the electric toothbrush appeared. It turned up in the bathroom cabinet one day and sort of stayed there. Next a change of clothes turned up. Made sense. If she was staying over, which she was doing more often than not, then she needed fresh clothes. Before he knew it there was a battered old teddy living at the bottom of the bed, a box of Tampax on the bedroom windowsill, and he was having to fight for wardrobe space.

Laura still didn't know what he did for a living. She thought he worked for the Foreign Office over on King Charles Street in Whitehall; a lie he'd told so often to so many people there were days he almost believed it. It was one of the first things they taught you on the IONEC. You don't work for us, you work for the Foreign Office. The I'm-A-Spy conversation was one he'd been meaning to have. It was on his mañana list. He felt he owed her the truth, but how did you start a conversation like that? *Hi honey, hope you had a good day; by the way, I'm a spy.* Then there was the fact that he'd have to apply to personnel for written permission. Probably in triplicate. It was much easier to live in denial. He hadn't planned on becoming a spy. When he was little he wanted to be an astronaut; at secondary school he told the career's officer he was going to be a movie star. By the time he got to the sixth form common sense had kicked in. He got four grade As in his A levels and ended up studying business at Oxford.

Growing up, the subject of his real father was a big no-no. Whenever Aston asked, his mother would get twitchy and quickly move the conversation elsewhere. In the end he gave up asking. He'd overheard her talking with his stepfather once. They'd thought he was asleep but he'd got up to ask for a glass of water and heard them on the other side of the lounge door. When he realised what they were talking about, he'd pressed his ear against the wood, not daring to make a sound. All he learnt was that his father was a lying son of a bitch who should be strung up. Strong words from a woman who considered 'damn' a dirty word. His mother was birdlike and anxious, a professional housewife who always worried what other people thought. If the Browns got a new car then she wanted one, too. But it had to be bigger, and better, and newer.

His stepfather wasn't a bad person, just terminally boring. He was a financial analyst, which, as far as Aston was concerned, said it all. His mother had married Brian when Aston was four. Brian owned a big house in the sleepy little village of Great Bedwyn in Wiltshire and commuted to London each day, which meant that Aston hadn't seen him much, and that was fine. There were no stepbrothers or stepsisters and that was fine, too. Brian had tried. He'd brought him up as his own, done all the usual Dad things, like taking him to football matches and teaching him to shave. But no matter how hard he tried, Brian wasn't his father.

Brian and Aston's mother had split up a couple of years ago and this had shocked Aston. For a woman so sensitive to other people's opinions, this was totally out of character. Aston had thought Brian and his mother would go to the grave together. He certainly hadn't expected her to run off with Roy, the small, balding lead tenor from the church choir. The gossip must have spread around the village like wildfire. His mother still lived in Great Bedwyn – in sin – and seemed happier than he'd ever seen her.

There had been little love between his mother and Brian, and his mother's motivation to marry had always struck Aston as pragmatic rather than romantic. A single mother in the Seventies, she'd simply done what was necessary to survive. Aston didn't blame her. He'd had a pleasant middle-class upbringing, lived in a comfortable house, never wanted for anything. Things could have been very different.

Aston was first 'approached' a couple of days after his Finals. He knew Professor Charles Devlan by sight and reputation; most students did. Devlan was a computer genius, although according to his students Computer God was more accurate.

He had a long grey ponytail, dressed in jeans and T-shirts, and was about as un-Oxford as it was possible to get – eccentric in ways that left his colleagues scratching their heads. Aston could never work out why he was a lecturer when he could have been earning millions in the private sector.

'Mind if I walk with you for a bit?'

Aston was on his way to the library to drop off some overdue books. He turned and saw Devlan beside him, a big smile lighting up his boyish face. Aston shrugged and said he didn't mind, thinking it a bit strange.

'Aston, isn't it? Paul Aston?'

'Yes, sir,' Aston replied, wondering how he knew his name. He'd never attended any of Devlan's lectures; there was no reason he should know who he was.

'So, Paul, have you thought about what you're going to do when you leave?'

'Well, I was planning on taking a year out, do some travelling. After that, I'm not sure. My stepfather has a job lined up for me at Barclays but I don't know if that's the route I want to take.'

'Ah, I see.' Devlan paused. 'I don't suppose you've ever considered working for the Government?'

'Not really.'

'No, I don't suppose you have. Maybe you should think about it, Paul. I've got a few contacts. I could point you in the right direction. Anyway, must dash.' And with that he was gone.

It was one of the most peculiar and intriguing conversations Aston had ever had. In particular, the emphasis Devlan had placed on the word 'Government' had left Aston in little doubt of what he was getting at.

The offer appealed to the Walter Mitty in him and three weeks later he was flicking through a copy of *The Economist* in the reception hall at 3 Carlton Gardens, an elegant old building in SW1 that overlooked St James's Park. A secretary appeared and Aston fought the urge to cock an eyebrow and call her 'Mish Moneypenny'. He followed her across the marble floor, up the stairs to the mezzanine.

Mr Halliday was a bear of a man who topped off well above the six feet mark. His brown striped suit was years out of date and made him look like a bank manager from the Forties. He even had a pocket watch, the silver chain dangling from his waistcoat. His hair was snow white, clipped in a neat short back and sides, Brylcreemed in place. He offered a hand and Aston braced himself for a bone crushing. Halliday's grip was surprisingly gentle. He pointed Aston to a seat, then sat down on the other side of the mahogany desk and pushed a sheet of paper and pen across the burgundy leather blotter.

'Before we get started,' he said, 'I need you to read and sign that.'

TOP SECRET was printed in red across the top of the sheet and the words sent electricity shooting up Aston's spine. Underneath the extract from the Official Secrets Act was a space for his signature. He made his mark, pushed the sheet back across the desk.

'Excellent.' Halliday reached into the desk drawer and pulled out a green ring binder. 'Now I'd like you to read this.' He put his hands behind his head, rocked back in the chair, and didn't say another word until Aston finished.

There were more than thirty pages in the folder, each one tucked safely away in a clear pocket. The first part gave a history of MI6 and set out the service's aims and objectives. The second part was an A to Z of life in MI6: six months on the IONEC; a couple of years manning a desk at HQ; after that, alternate three-year home and overseas postings until compulsory retirement at 55. What it amounted to was the next thirty-odd years of his life being mapped out for him. This didn't sit well with Aston. He did the interview on autopilot, his mind already made up. *Thanks but no thanks.*

The year he spent travelling was a blast, the three years working for Barclays a prison sentence. His escape came in the form of a chance meeting with Professor Devlan in Camden Market one rainy Saturday afternoon. Aston was browsing through a second-hand book stall, turning the pages of a Stephen King novel he couldn't remember if he'd read or not, when someone said his name. He looked up and recognised the professor straightaway. The ponytail was a bit whiter, but the boyish face hadn't aged at all. They got chatting, and on hearing that Aston's career wasn't everything it could be, the professor suggested he reconsider working for the Government. Aston said he might just do that. The next day he wrote a letter and mailed it to 3 Carlton Gardens. At the time he didn't find anything suspicious about his chance encounter with Devlan. Lots of people visited London. In retrospect, it had obviously been a set-up. Ten days later Aston was once again following Mish Moneypenny up the marble staircase to Mr Halliday's office.

Halliday had changed considerably since they'd last met. He'd lost almost six stone, and, more impressively, had shrunk by a good five inches. His eyes had changed from brown to a piercing ice blue; they twinkled as if he was sharing a joke at the universe's expense. If asked, Aston would have placed this incarnation of Halliday in his mid-forties, however, there was something he couldn't put his finger on that led him to believe he was in his fifties. His hair had once been blonde and had now faded to the colour of sunbleached corn; if there was any grey it had been hidden by chemicals or plucked. They shook hands then went through the same rigmarole as before: the signing of the OSA form, the reading of the green folder. This time Aston considered each question carefully before answering. Halliday wanted to know everything, from his inside leg measurement to his political leanings, from his family history to his criminal record. Aston left Carlton Gardens feeling as though he'd been buggered by the Spanish Inquisition, convinced that he'd screwed up the interview.

Halliday must have thought differently, because two weeks later Aston found himself in Whitehall where he spent the day undergoing a gruelling series of civil service tests and interviews. The following week he was back at Carlton Gardens for a grilling by a panel of MI6 officers. Halliday mark II was hovering in the background, no doubt listening for any inconsistencies in his answers.

The final stage was the security check, an extensive excavation of his past where every cupboard was checked for skeletons. Aston's juvenile conviction for shoplifting presumably didn't count because a couple of months later the acceptance letter dropped onto the doormat.

The IONEC passed in a blur with weeks alternating between London and MI6's training facility at The Fort in Portsmouth. Aston quickly discovered that alcohol was the oil that kept the cogs of MI6 turning smoothly . . . not that this was a problem. He also discovered his love affair with booze was shared by George; one of the many things they had in common. They were equally competitive, always trying to upstage one another, and the IONEC soon turned into a two-horse race. In the end Aston pipped her at the post. George ended up with a 'Box 2' on her staff appraisal form – above average. Aston got a 'Box 1'. Of course, this was another excuse to go out and get pissed.

With a mark like that Aston wasn't surprised to find himself assigned to Production and Targeting, Counter-Proliferation. The PTCP had been set up to stop countries like Iraq and Iran getting hold of weapons of mass destruction. What he didn't expect was to end up working as Mac's assistant. Mac had asked for him personally – something he got a buzz from pointing out to George. Robert Macintosh was a legend, one of the unsung heroes of the Cold War. He'd been H/MOS, the head of the Moscow station, when the Soviet Union disbanded. After that he'd been appointed H/VIE. The Vienna station was one of MI6's biggest, not because Austria was of any interest, but because the country was ideally situated to spy on Russia and the Middle East, the arms trade, and the International Atomic Energy Agency.

On his first day Aston turned up bright and early, eager to make a good impression. Mac turned up even earlier.

'You're going to have to do better than that if you're going to get one over on me.' The man behind the desk smirked, sharp blue eyes twinkling.

It was Halliday mark II.

Aston flicked between the 24-hour news channels. There was only one story; that there were no ad breaks showed how big it was. All the reporters were giving Oscar-winning performances, all of them acting as though they'd seen the horrors up close and personal. Black ties and suits pulled out of mothballs for the occasion, they were shocked, appalled, sickened. Aston tried to reconcile what they were saying with what he'd witnessed in those claustrophobic tunnels, but couldn't get the two to match. Their words and pictures fell pathetically short of the mark. Depending on the news channel the death toll ranged between two hundred and five hundred. But these were just numbers – cold, hard statistics that meant nothing. A person couldn't be reduced to a number. The people who'd died had been husbands and wives, sons and daughters, children. They had loved and they had been loved. And now they were dead, and for those left grieving nothing was ever going to be the same again. Those reporters didn't have a fucking clue.

'Hey, you're back,' said a husky voice from the sofa. Laura sat up and pushed a hand through her rats' tails, dragging the strands away from her sleepy face. 'What time is it?'

'Almost three.'

Laura tiptoed over, careful to keep her heels off the cold wood, dragging the duvet behind her.

She curled up on Aston's lap, all eight stone and five foot five of her, pulling the duvet across them, snuggling into his chest. She fitted perfectly. He shifted to help her get comfortable, kissed the top of her head. She lifted her face and they kissed properly.

'Where have you been, Paul? I tried to phone but I kept getting your voicemail. I couldn't get you on your mobile, either. I've been worried.'

'I'm sorry. By the time I got your messages it was too late to phone. Work's been manic today.'

She noticed his hands, picked them up and examined them, frowned as she rubbed her fingertips over the Elastoplast. 'What happened?'

'Would you believe it, I tripped and fell. How's that for clumsy?'

'Looks painful.'

'I'll live.' Aston smiled at her, saw the tears. Without thinking he wiped them away with his thumb. 'Hey, what's up?'

Laura used the edge of the duvet to wipe her face. Even though it wasn't cold, she pulled it more tightly around them. 'You remember my friend Becky?'

He tried to place the name, and shook his head.

'We went through teacher training together. She was at Trish and Simon's wedding.'

41

A spark went off in his head. 'Yeah, I remember. She's okay, isn't she?'

'She's fine. It's her brother, Martin. He gets the tube from Leicester Square. Same time every night. She hasn't heard from him . . .' her voice faltered.

'Oh Jesus, Laura.'

'Poor Becky. She doesn't know what to do with herself. I would have gone to see her. But there was no way I could get there . . .' Laura rambled on, words and sobs mingling together. Aston let her talk and when she finished he held her close, felt the dampness seeping through his shirt.

'How was work?' Laura asked.

She was changing the subject, and that had to be a good thing. While she'd been talking his mind kept flashing up pictures of the dead baby. So he told her about the problems they were having in New Zealand, and how it was a complete bastard dealing with anyone over there because of the time difference, how you either had to hang around till nine in the evening or get up at some ridiculous hour of the morning. It no longer surprised him how easily the lies came. All part of the job. He took it for read that he'd open his mouth and the lies would all be lined up waiting to spill out. He occasionally wondered how healthy all those lies were for their relationship.

'. . . a complete nightmare of a day,' he

concluded, and at least that much was the truth.

'Poor baby,' Laura muttered into his chest. She was almost asleep. A light rain began tapping on the window pane; far in the distance came the first rumble of thunder.

4

It only took a couple of hours for the media to christen the atrocity. Sky News, the tabloid of the TV news stations, did the honours. During the seven o'clock round up the anchorman referred to the Leicester Square bombing as 18/8, and the name stuck. The tabloids used it the next day, and it didn't take long for the broadsheets to follow suit. Of course, BBC News and CNN weren't far behind. 18/8 HUNDREDS DEAD, was the screaming headline on the front of the *Sun* the next morning, the typeface so large it took up the whole page. The story stretching across a dozen pages was big on sensational pictures – bodybags being carried out of Leicester Square, shocked survivors looking dazed and confused, grim firefighters with dirty faces – but light on words. At least, light on any words of substance. There were inches galore of speculation, eyewitness accounts, tales of bravery, but not much in the way of facts. Even now there was little to say on the subject, and certainly nothing that hadn't been said a thousand times already. Almost two weeks had passed since the bomb attack. Autumn was rapidly approaching, the evenings closing in and the days getting cooler, and they were still no closer to nailing the bastards responsible for the atrocity. Sitting at his desk on the fifth floor, staring at his computer screen, Aston was painfully aware of this.

Fact: The bomb detonated at 5.21 p.m. on Friday, August 18th.

Fact: Another woman had died overnight, pushing the official death toll up to two hundred and sixty-two.

Fact: The manpower working on this one was unprecedented. MI6 had pulled every spare man, MI5 had done the same, so had the Met.

Fact: Two weeks on and they didn't have shit.

It was so bloody depressing. Not to mention stressful. The internal phone rang and Aston picked it up with a sense of foreboding.

'Get your arse in here now,' Mac barked.

Before Aston could say anything the line went dead. Sighing, he picked up his notepad and pen and walked the dozen steps to Mac's office, a distance as long as any last journey to Old Sparky.

Mac was pacing; wearing out rug, as he liked to put it. He'd been wearing out a lot of rug recently. As head of the PTCP he'd been right in the firing line. Under normal circumstances, Mac was as cool a customer as you were ever likely to meet. However, these circumstances were far from normal and he was definitely showing the stress. There were a few more lines, wrinkles that enhanced the rugged lived-in look of his face; his neat hair had a few loose telltale strands that could only come from nervous fingers. And more than once Aston had caught his boss with the top button of his shirt undone and the tie pulled down a fraction of an inch; something unheard of in the days before 18/8. The signs were subtle but they were there if you knew where to look.

And it wasn't just Mac who was under pressure. They all were. The attacks had come from all angles. The media had crucified MI6, laying the blame for the tragedy squarely at the feet of The Chief, who'd promptly shared that blame around as best he could. Then there'd been the questions raised in the House of Commons, a hundred and one little questions which all amounted to one big question: how could MI6 allow this to happen again? To make matters worse, the PM had come out smelling of roses. He'd pulled out his smartest black tie, feigned the right amount of sympathy, made all the right noises, and the media had lapped it up. Overnight he'd become the public face of the country's grief, and in doing so his approval rating had soared. There was nothing like a good disaster to get the public on your side. What the public failed to realise was that the Government was responsible for funding MI6, and year after year those budgets had been getting tighter and tighter. And maybe if MI6 had the funding they had asked for then all this could have been prevented.

'Bastard,' Mac said.

Aston wasn't sure which particular 'bastard' Mac was referring to. The PM was a favourite candidate, but there were a number of likely suspects: MPs, reporters, colleagues at MI6. Over the last fortnight Mac had raged about all of them. The only person who'd escaped was Grant Kinclave, The Chief, and Aston guessed that's because Mac and The Chief were best friends. They went back a long way, had both earned their stripes during the Cold War – probably had matching school ties hanging in their wardrobes.

Aston slipped into the chair on the tradesman's side of the desk, flipped open the notepad, and waited to be spoken to. When Mac was in this sort of mood it was best to agree when called upon to agree, make the right face shapes as appropriate, but for the most part it was wise to just shut up.

The office was furnished with utilitarian precision and dominated by a neat, uncluttered desk: the in- and out-trays were always kept at a manageable level, and the desk tidy was stocked with sharpened pencils and pens that actually worked (one of Aston's duties; God help him if his boss ever reached for a pencil and found it blunt). Fish swum merrily back and forth on the flat screen monitor. The only personal touch was a small framed photograph next to the door. It had been positioned so you could see it from the desk. The picture had perplexed Aston to start with, but when he finally placed it, it all made sense. Orson Welles had made his famous 'cuckoo clock' speech in front of this big wheel in *The Third Man*. Not that Aston thought the Orson Welles connection was relevant. No, the connection was that the wheel was in Vienna, and Mac had been head of station there during the early Nineties, a posting that was the highlight of his career. This had surprised Aston. He'd never had Mac pegged as the sentimental type.

Mac stopped pacing and turned to Aston, seeing him as if for the first time. 'Guess what they've gone and done now?'

Aston said nothing and waited for Mac to continue. 'They' could be anyone. The Government, the media, terrorists.

'They've only called for my resignation . . . again. Bastards!'

Well, that narrowed it down. This was political, which meant he was here for one reason. To sit and listen while Mac blew off some steam. Aston flipped the notepad closed and settled back, all ears. If Mac was venting in that particular direction, then at least he wasn't here for a bollocking. All that could turn in a heartbeat, though; Mac was a man of changeable weather. And to think, when he'd been assigned to work for Mac he'd actually gone out and celebrated. Working for the legendary Robert Macintosh, what an honour. If only he'd known then what he knew now.

'Of course, it isn't going to happen,' Mac said. 'And do you know why it isn't going to happen?'

Before Aston could say 'no', before he even had a chance to shake his head, Mac was off again.

'Because they can't get rid of me. It'd be like getting rid of the ravens at the Tower of London. I go and this whole fucking building will crumble to dust, mark my words.'

The devil on Aston's shoulder suggested that now might be a good time to point out that MI6 was bigger than one single person, that it was an organisation, which by definition meant it existed by virtue of the combined efforts of all those people in London and around the world who worked for it. The angel on the other shoulder vetoed this on the grounds that his next staff appraisal was imminent and a black mark from Mac wouldn't do his promotion prospects any good. Promotion prospects, that was a laugh! If Mac had his way he'd have him working in servitude for the rest of his days. Face it, he was here for life.

'Who the hell do they think they are? What do they know about the intelligence game? Absolutely fuck all, that's what.' Mac took a deep breath. Calm, calm, calm. Then he grinned the sort of grin that could charm the pants off a nun. The grin became a good-humoured laugh, the sunshine after the rain. 'Storm in a teacup is what it is. By tomorrow they'll be looking for someone else's bollocks to nail to the wall. Okay, Aston, what's new? Go on, impress me.'

Aston felt his heart sink and his stomach rise to meet it. Whatever he said next, it wouldn't be impressive. How many different ways could you say you didn't know shit?

5

The Farriers was buzzing, the after work commuter crowd twisting each other's arms to have one more for the road. Nobody needed much persuading. Aston pushed between two stockbrokers – the bright red braces and loud ties were a dead give-away – and waved a tenner to catch the barmaid's eye. She was a pretty little thing in her early twenties, wearing a black thong that peeked out from the top of her hipster jeans, and a Little Miss Mischief T-shirt that stuck to her body like a second skin. She finished dealing with a businessman who had the shiny skin of one facelift too many, and an indecent amount of gold dripping from his hands and wrists. Aston waved frantically and she made her way over.

'What can I get you?' The accent was East European. Hungarian or Slovakian. Another 'language' student over here looking for her golden ticket. Aston didn't blame her. The collapse of the Soviet Union had created a clusterfuck that would take decades to sort out . . . if it ever got sorted out. He ordered two JDs and coke and squeezed out from the bar.

Two neatly dressed middle-aged women at a table near one of the windows were finishing their drinks. Aston sidled up, ready to pounce. Their clothes were designer, and it wouldn't have surprised him if each outfit was worth more than his entire wardrobe. Laura had tried to educate him on the difference between Prada and Gucci, but he didn't get it (and had no particular desire to, either; you'd have to be out of your mind to spend a couple of grand on a dress just because it had a fancy name on the label). Still, these two obviously knew the difference. The women placed their wine glasses back on the table, stuffed their Marlboro Lights into tiny handbags that were no doubt worth their weight in platinum. As soon as they got up Aston was in there, just ahead of the stockbrokers. He raised his glass, flashed them a better-luck-next-time smile. The stockbrokers shrugged and went off to lean against the jukebox.

His mobile vibrated. Two sharp buzzes. Probably George replying to his whr th fck RU? text. He pulled it out, flipped it open:

soz hon gotta wrk L8 :(

CU in abt an hr

lol george xx

No surprises there; they were both working stupid hours at the moment. It had been touch and go whether he'd get away, but Mac had left early tonight and he'd made the most of the opportunity. Aston settled into his chair and took a long pull on his drink. He could think of worse places to waste an hour. The Farriers was just off Soho, one of their favourite haunts. There was something elegantly shabby about the place. Wonky floors and squiffy right angles; the worn wood surfaces preserved with a couple of centuries' worth of beer, tobacco and dirt that mingled into an aroma that was warm and comforting. George had once described The Farriers as 'well matured', and Aston thought that pretty much covered it.

Thursday night was their night, a tradition dating back to their training days. A couple of drinks followed by a curry, then a few more drinks to wash the curry down. During the IONEC they'd always gone for the diviest bars they could find, the divier the better. The first prize had gone to a nightclub called Bubbles. Even by Portsmouth's standards Bubbles was in a league of its own. The carpets were so sticky it was like wading through treacle, the clientele ninety-nine percent male . . . all Navy. No mistaking what profession the three women at the bar belonged to. They'd had to step over the bodies in the stairwell and dodge between the ambulances and police cars to escape.

Alcohol was indeed the oil that kept MI6's wheels running smoothly. If you wanted to find out what was really going on at Vauxhall Cross then the best place to head was the in-house bar. Another plus was that, unlike civilian boozers, the opening hours were somewhat more flexible. They'd been sent to The Fort to learn about spycraft, but boozing was an important part of the curriculum, too. Funnily enough, this was the subject the training officers seemed most keen to teach. Aston and George had passed this part of the course without trying.

Aston drained his drink and picked up George's. He raised the glass in a toast to absent friends, took a sip. Waste not, want not . . .

'Mind if I sit here?'

Aston looked up with the intention of politely telling whoever it was to piss off, and almost choked on his drink.

The man smiling down at him was in his early fifties and had the immaculate grooming of a politician: the Savile Row bespoke suit, Italian leather shoes, manicured nails. His hair was dyed black, the smile filled with perfect white teeth. He was average height, average weight, and the clever grey eyes didn't miss a thing. Legend had it that Grant Kinclave lived in a gilded cage on the top floor of MI6's HQ, a penthouse suite with sweeping views of the Thames. His private bathroom had gold fittings, marble floors, and a throne fit for a king. Every day he bathed in champagne and was scrubbed down by a dozen virgins. Or something along those lines.

'Be my guest,' Aston managed to say. He indicated the empty seat opposite, his heart frozen in freefall.

Kinclave sat down, slid a beer mat closer, made sure the writing was the right way round, that the edge of the mat was parallel with the edge of the table, then placed his G&T slap bang in the centre. Satisfied everything was just so, he turned his attention to Aston, studying him with those clever grey eyes.

'So, Paul, how are things going?'

'Can't complain,' Aston replied non-committally. Here they were, two old friends meeting up for a drink at the end of another long day. Nothing unusual about that . . . except one of them was MI6's Chief, one of the most powerful men in the country, someone who was accountable to no one, not even God. There had been moves in the Nineties to change this. The Cold War was over and this was a new era, which meant a new way of doing business. It was a nice line to feed to the media, but the truth of the matter was that MI6's doors were closed as tightly as ever. Aside from a few token nods towards accountability, gestures that were light on substance, it was business as usual.

Aston had only seen The Chief up this close once before. During orientation on his first day, the door of the conference room had swung open and a man strode in, moving as though he was the centre of the universe. Aston had shared a look with George: it was obvious she didn't have a clue who this was, either. However, from the grand entrance, and the way the two training officers jumped to attention, it was apparent he was someone important. Unsure what to do next, the six trainees had followed suit, rising uncertainly, bewildered expressions passing between them. The man smiled thinly and indicated they should sit. When everyone had settled, Kinclave introduced himself and welcomed them to MI6. He spoke for the next ten minutes in the stirring tones of a Baptist preacher, stressing time and again how important the work they did here was, how secrecy was paramount. While he spoke his eyes moved constantly, scanning the room, scanning faces. More than once, Kinclave's gaze settled on Aston, and it was an effort not to look away. Afterwards The Chief went around the table shaking hands and wishing the candidates well. Aston wasn't sure – and he'd replayed the scene in his mind a thousand times since – but Kinclave seemed to take more interest in him than the others. Holding his hand longer, picking him apart with those eyes. Maybe it had been the same for everyone. After all, it was one of those life moments where every single detail, no matter how trivial, takes on extra significance.

Pokerfaced, Aston sipped his drink and said nothing, curiosity eating away at him. Now he'd got over his initial shock, he wanted to know what was going on. Your drinking partner suddenly has to work late and the head of MI6 happens to wander in, plonks himself down at your table and wants to chat about the weather. The whole thing smacked of a set-up. Aston took another sip, eyes surreptitiously wandering around the pub. No way would Kinclave be on his own. And he wasn't. Aston counted three of them. The man by the door wearing a long leather Matrix coat was a definite; too conspicuous, wanting to be seen. He had the air of someone who knew how to take care of himself. Probably carrying. The man was trying to look bored but he kept glancing over at Kinclave, like Daddy Bear protecting its cub. The other two shadows were at the table near one of the windows. They'd been there when he arrived. From their body language, the uncomfortable way they touched hands, he'd assumed they were having an affair, out in public and worried about being caught. Now he knew different. It was so obvious he could have kicked himself. He'd played the same game with George on numerous occasions.

'Anything new on 18/8?' Kinclave asked.

Aston shrugged. 'Not really.' It was a redundant question, something to fill the uncomfortable silence. The Chief already knew everything happening there, undoubtedly knew a hell of a lot more than Aston did. All he could add to the official story was that the nightmares in which he was cradling the dead baby were as terrifying as ever, that he would give anything for a decent night's sleep, that he was drinking way too much and picking stupid fights with Laura, but he didn't think The Chief would be interested in any of that.

Kinclave lifted his glass, turned it in his hand, momentarily fascinated by the reflections and smudges. He took a drink, straightened out the beer mat, placed the glass back dead centre. 'Of course, I can depend on your discretion,' he said.

Aston nodded. 'Of course.'

Kinclave leant in closer and spoke so quietly Aston had to strain to hear. 'This is difficult . . . but have you noticed anything, well . . . *odd* about Mac recently?'

'Odd?'

'You know,' The Chief said, 'is there anything about the way he's been acting that strikes you as unusual?'

Aston thought carefully before answering. Mac was no more eccentric than usual, no more grouchy, no more of a pain in the arse. 'No,' he said.

'We're worried about him. Very worried,' The Chief said. 'You see, ever since his wife died . . .'

Aston was aware of those piercing grey eyes crawling across his skin, burrowing into secret places.

'Ah,' Kinclave said, 'you didn't know about his wife's illness.'

Didn't know about her illness? Aston thought, *I didn't even know he was married.* Obviously this was a day for surprises. Almost three years he'd been working for Mac and he didn't know he had a wife.

'It's so sad,' Kinclave said. 'They'd been together for over ten years, you know. He met Sophia while he was heading up the Vienna station. I thought Mac was a terminal bachelor. Just goes to show, eh? And the fact they managed to stay together all that time . . . well, I don't need to tell you how hard it is to keep a relationship together in this business . . .'

For a second, Aston was convinced that Kinclave was commenting directly on his relationship with Laura. A crazy notion. The Chief had better things to do than be concerned with the trivialities of his personal life. Kinclave sipped his drink, momentarily lost in thought. He straightened the beer mat, placed the glass back dead centre.

'Sophia had motor neurone disease,' he continued. 'Such a terrible disease. The body slowly shuts down but the brain is still as sharp as ever. Can you think of anything worse? Imprisoned by your own body. Absolutely horrendous. And she was so young. Only forty-seven. We tried to persuade Mac to take early retirement so he could look after her, but he wouldn't hear of it. You can imagine what he had to say about that.' Kinclave gave a thin smile and Aston nodded. Mac had often joked that they'd have to fit his coffin with a telephone and fax machine.

Another sip, another straighten of the mat. The Chief cleared his throat. 'Sophia died at the end of July.'

Aston did the maths. It didn't add up. 'But Mac's been at work,' he said. 'He didn't take any time off. I didn't notice any change in him.'

'That's Mac,' Kinclave said simply. 'Getting up and getting on with it.'

'But his wife *died*. I work with him, I should have seen some change, some indication.'

A wistful smile from The Chief. 'You never knew Mac when he was working in the field. By Christ, he was good. One of the best undercover operatives we ever had. Actually, I'd go so far as to say the best. Such a talented actor. He could become anyone. No, what you've seen these last couple of months is Mac playing a role. I've known Mac for more than thirty years. Take it from me he's hurting.'

'Even still—' Aston began.

'Paul,' Kinclave interrupted, 'if Mac wants you to believe everything's A-okay, then everything's A-okay. End of story. You know how persuasive he can be.'

Aston lifted his glass and drained it. He put it back on the table and looked over at The Chief. 'If you don't mind me asking, why are you telling me all this?'

'Ah . . .' Kinclave paused. 'This is a bit – how should I put it? – a bit delicate. We're worried about Mac. On the surface he appears to be holding up, and if you ask him he'll tell you he's doing fine.'

A light went on in Aston's head. 'You want me to spy on him, don't you?'

'I'd rather not use the word "spy", if it's all the same with you,' Kinclave said smoothly. 'Far too many negative connotations. No, what I'd like is for you to keep an eye on him. If you notice anything unusual about his behaviour, then you report it directly to me.'

Aston didn't know what to say. Spying on Mac . . . what next?

The Chief fixed Aston with those clever eyes. 'There's one other thing I'd like you to do, Paul,' he said. 'Now, I'm meeting Mac for dinner tonight. That means you'll have a three-hour window. In the left-hand pocket of your jacket is a key, an address, and a number you can contact me on. I just want you to have a quick look around, check everything's in order, that sort of thing.'

'What?' Aston choked out, convinced there was something wrong with his hearing. 'Let me get this straight. You want me to break in to Mac's house?'

'Now, now, Paul, let's not get all holier-than-thou. I've seen your file. I read all about that little stunt you pulled during training.'

Checkmate. There were a number of things he'd done in the name of MI6 that he wasn't particularly proud of, and although that particular stunt had earned him a ton of Brownie points, that was one of them. 'But this is Mac we're talking about,' he offered. It was a token argument that wasn't fooling either of them.

'Exactly,' The Chief said. 'And at the end of the day it's Mac we're doing this for. Don't forget that. The old bugger's much too stubborn to ask for help, so, if he does need a shoulder to lean on, then we've got to first establish that, and second, work out the best way of providing it.'

'Why not ask him? You know, talk to him?'

The expression on The Chief's face soured, suggesting this was the most ridiculous thing he'd ever heard.

'Okay,' Aston admitted. 'That was a stupid question.'

'Remember, Paul, we look after our own,' Kinclave said. 'Always have done, always will.'

6

'Mind telling me what the fuck is going on?'

'Nothing's going on,' Aston said. He was heading up Tottenham Court Road to Goodge Street tube station with his mobile glued to his ear, hurrying to beat the rain. The evening was cold and grey, summer already a distant memory. He kept an eye out for a taxi, but it wasn't going to happen. Taxis in London were like gold dust at the best of times, never mind when the weatherman was promising rain. The other option was to go by bus, but he didn't have all night. There was only one thing to do. Take a deep breath and just go for it.

'You're such a crap liar, Paul.'

'There's nothing going on,' Aston repeated.

'Excuse me,' George fired back. 'There I am getting my coat on, thinking that's it for the day. But before I can escape my boss is calling me over and telling me he wants me to go and buy a left-handed screwdriver. So off I go and as soon as I get outside guess what the first thing I see is? Wild fucking geese. Hundreds of the little bastards. And I have this overwhelming urge to go chasing after them.'

'George—'

'If you tell me one more time there's nothing going on I'll break your bloody legs. I swear to God I will.'

Aston sighed into the mobile, well aware he was fighting a losing battle. 'Look, we can't talk over the phone. Can you meet me at Highgate tube station?'

'No problem. I'll be there in half an hour.'

'Twenty minutes,' Aston said.

'Okay, twenty.'

Aston clicked the phone shut. The Chief hadn't said anything about going to Mac's on his own, and he hadn't asked for clarification on that point. Aston was glad George was coming along; some moral support wouldn't go amiss. He dipped a hand into his pocket, fingers finding the jagged edges of the key. It felt cold, slightly sinister. He'd worked out when the drop had taken place. On his way to the bar he'd passed the woman from the jukebox couple. She'd been heading towards the ladies and brushed against him. They'd connected for only the briefest of seconds. A quick apology then she'd disappeared into the toilet. Nicely done.

The rain started as he reached the station. Aston jogged the final few steps and brushed the dew from his hair. He paid in cash for a ticket and reached for the change with a shaky hand. Already his breathing was faster than usual, his heart rate rising, and he wasn't anywhere near the platform yet. Aston walked down the escalator, resisting the urge to turn and run. This was the first time he'd used the Underground since 18/8. Up until now he'd got by using cabs, buses and his own two feet. Still, he had to face the fear sooner or later. Best get it over and done with. The deeper he got the quicker he wanted to move, as though he could somehow outrun those black memories. At the bottom he forced himself to walk to the platform. According to the digital display the next train was due in three minutes. Three minutes! He paced up and down the platform until the train arrived. As soon as he sat down he closed his eyes and imagined himself on a beach on a tropical island – the sun warm on his skin, sand gently scratching between his toes, the waves swishing rhythmically against the shore – just like George had told him to. Amazingly for one of George's wacky ideas, it actually worked. He could feel the panic letting go: muscles loosening, pulse slowing, his breathing regulating.

George was waiting at the ticket machine. As soon as she saw Aston she walked over and hugged him. And this wasn't a fleeting kissy-kissy hug, either. She grabbed him and held him close and tight, so close he could feel her heartbeat. 'How was it?' she whispered in his ear.

'Could have been worse.'

She let go and held him at arm's length, gave

him a quick once over. 'Well, you're a bit pale – but apart from that . . .' She linked her arm through his and led him towards the exit.

George's most striking feature was the mop of black frizzy hair she constantly bitched about. At the moment it was cut to shoulder length and tied back with a red scrunchy; she'd had it long, had it short, but hated it whatever length it was. At university she'd had a crew cut, a number 1, sandpaper instead of hair. Her mother had been mortified, said it made her look like a lesbian and she hadn't brought her little girl up to wear Dr Martens and dungarees. More than once she'd told Aston she was the ugly duckling who never quite made it into a swan. Aston told her she was talking shit, but she wasn't listening. George wasn't supermodel gorgeous, but she was a long way from scaring the kiddies. She had the most beautiful brown almond shaped eyes, olive skin, and she scrubbed up quite nicely when she could be bothered, which wasn't very often. Most of the time she dressed down: plain clothes, sober colours, nothing too revealing, nothing that would get her noticed. Perfect for a spy. George didn't have any trouble attracting men but keeping hold of them was a different matter. They were either too old, too young, or too married. Her love life was a soap opera Aston long ago stopped trying to keep up with.

The address was written in a careful copperplate script: 23 Farley Road, Crouch End. Underneath was a mobile number. They shared an umbrella that was too small to cover both of them, George jiggling it about to keep them dry. A young couple heading home after a long day. It was an act they'd got down to a fine art. They could do everything from the young lovers cruising through a hormone OD and desperately in need of a room to the long-married couple who wanted to stab each other. It wasn't hard. From the word go they'd been comfortable with one another, so comfortable that every now and then the MI6 rumour mill would crank out a story. Officially their relationship was strictly platonic; unofficially there'd been one blip.

The incident was never talked about. To celebrate the end of the IONEC they'd gone out with the intention of getting annihilated, and reached their objective in style; even by their standards it had been a big night. Next morning Aston had woken up in bed with a mega hangover, and George lying next to him. They were both naked, and from the hazy flashbacks Aston kept getting, the state of the bed, and the fact his dick felt like it had been pounded with a mallet, it was apparent they had done more than sleep. Aston couldn't put his finger on why it felt wrong. It just did. Like sleeping with your sister or something. When he closed his eyes all he could see was an albino boy with bad teeth playing the banjo. George felt the same. After an awkward discussion they decided the best way to deal with the situation was through denial.

While they walked, Aston told George about his meeting with Kinclave. 'You know,' he said in conclusion, 'I've been working for Mac for – what? Almost three years? Not only did I not know he was married, until tonight I didn't know where he lived. Shit, I don't know anything about him.'

'Not true,' George said. 'You know what he wants you to know.'

It took fifteen minutes to get from Highgate station to Farley Road. The rain was hammering down now, slick on the pavements, rivers raging along the gutter. Number 23 was a red-bricked Edwardian semi-detached with bay windows on both floors. The front garden had been concreted over and a brand new X-type Jag was parked there. All the curtains were closed.

'I don't like this,' George said as they walked up the narrow path.

'Join the club,' Aston replied.

Underneath the porch, he shook the loose raindrops away while George collapsed the umbrella and brushed the rain from her frizzy hair.

'Why do I let you talk me into shit like this, Paul? Answer me that, eh?'

'I didn't exactly twist your arm.'

'Just open the bloody door, Paul, before I bottle it and go home.'

Aston slipped the key into the lock and turned it. The door opened easily on well-oiled hinges.

'If it's all the same with you,' George said, 'let's stick together. None of this "let's split up so we can get the place searched twice as quickly" crap.'

'Fine by me.' Aston wondered if he looked as wired as George. Probably. His stomach flip-flopped as he entered the house, his heart felt too big for his chest. He pushed the door shut, locking them in, flicked on the hall light. This wasn't the first time he'd broken into a house, but that didn't make it any easier. He swallowed involuntarily.

'What exactly are we looking for?' George asked.

'Search me. The Chief was a bit vague on that score. "I just want you to have a quick look around, check everything's in order, that sort of thing".' Aston gave a reasonable impression of Kinclave's Etonian drawl.

There were three closed doors leading off the hallway. Aston pointed to the door at the end of the hall. 'Right, we'll start there.'

The door led to a cosy, tidy farmhouse kitchen. There was slate on the floor and lots of oak: dining table and chairs, a large Welsh dresser filled with knick-knacks and crockery. A sign above the Aga proclaimed that the kitchen was the heart of the house. Maybe once it had been, Aston thought. It was easy to imagine this kitchen full of life and laughter and sunshine. The big window over-looking the tangled, overgrown garden faced east and would have caught the rising sun, holding onto it until well past midday. Yes, once this had been the heart of the house. Not anymore, though.

Whatever life had breezed through these four walls was long gone.

'Notice anything strange?' George asked.

'Like what?'

'You know, Paul, for a spy you can be pretty unobservant at times.' She pointed out the bowl of furry, moist fruit sitting on one of the work surfaces, the flowers decomposing in a vase on the kitchen table.

'No one's currently living here,' she said. 'This kitchen hasn't been used for Christ knows how long.' George marched over to the fridge and yanked the door open. The smell of rancid milk floated heavily through the kitchen. She lifted out the carton and read the sell-by date on top. 'My guess is that he hasn't been here for the best part of a month.'

'That'd be around the time Sophia died.'

'So where's he staying?'

'More to the point, why isn't he staying here?'

'Too many memories, perhaps,' George suggested.

'Perhaps,' Aston agreed, unconvinced. And now that George had mentioned it, he could sense the emptiness that filled the kitchen. There was an air of neglect, a whispering sense of things lost never to be found again. And it wasn't just the kitchen. He'd noticed it when he'd stepped into the house; noticed subconsciously but it hadn't registered because he didn't have a name for it. And now he did: abandonment. Like a sunken ship, this house had settled into the silent dark loneliness.

The next door along the hall led to a small study. This was obviously Mac's domain. There were no pictures on the walls, no personal touches whatsoever. The room was as anonymous as its owner. A thin layer of dust had settled across the room, coating the top of the filing cabinet and clinging to the screen of the monitor. Aston went over to the filing cabinet and pulled open the top drawer. Empty.

'I'm going to try the next room,' George said. 'The sooner we get out of here the better. I'm getting really creeped out now.'

Aston thought about reminding her of the 'let's stick together' speech and decided not to. She was a big girl. He stared into the empty drawer, hand on the handle. Strange. He heard George's anxious footsteps moving down the hall, heard her open the next door, the click of the light switch.

'Paul,' she shouted. 'Get in here now. You've got to see this.'

The filing cabinet drawer clanged shut and he ran along the hall. George was blocking the doorway, and he stopped behind her, placed his hands on her shoulders.

The front room was really two rooms separated by a wide archway to create a large open space. Before Sophia's illness had taken over this had been the lounge and dining room. High ceilings, worn wooden floorboards, colourful paintings on the white walls, trinkets and ornaments arranged on the black painted mantelpiece, a multicoloured rug in front of the fire, framed photographs lining the bookcase. The room was filled with dozens of personal touches. Female touches. If the kitchen was the heart of the house, this room had been its soul.

An upright piano was pushed up against one wall and covered with a white sheet. The piano must have belonged to Sophia. Aston couldn't imagine Mac tinkling the ivories; cracking his knuckles before launching into a Mozart concerto, or bashing out some barroom blues. No, he couldn't see that one at all. Bedpans and packets of pills sat on top of the piano. A vase of mummified roses jostled for space, the heads brittle and black and scarred with a memory of crimson.

The large metal-framed hospital bed dominated the room, neatly made up with clean white sheets. A shower cubicle with waist-height doors had been built into one corner. It was wide enough for the lightweight plastic wheelchair that sat forlornly next to it. The Chief was right, thought Aston, it was impossible to imagine what it was like. One by one all those things you take for granted stolen away: unable to wash or feed yourself, the indignity of wearing nappies. And the worst part was that your brain worked as well as ever, throwing up memories of how things used to be, monitoring the decline, that slow slip-slide towards the grave. Motor Neurone Disease was worse than any curse. Nobody deserved to die like that. *Please*, Aston thought, *when it's my time make it quick.* His attention was drawn to the piano again. How insensitive was that? Why hadn't Mac moved it out of the room? That would have been the decent thing to do. Instead it was just sitting there, a constant reminder of one more thing Sophia had lost.

On the table next to the bed was a water jug and a small framed wedding photograph. Aston picked up the photo, called George over to take a look. Mac was smiling in the photo. Actually smiling. He wasn't grinning, or doing that sanctimonious smirk of his. No, this was an honest-to-God million-dollar beamer. For once in his life Robert Macintosh looked happy. Time had been kind to this incarnation of Sophia; in her younger days she must have been stunning. She looked radiant in the photo, glowing with health, and Aston wondered when it had been taken. A few years ago, judging by the suit Mac was wearing. There was no hint of the disease that would ravage her. She was wearing a simple blue silk dress and carrying a posy of flowers that exploded with colour. Simple countryside flowers, dandelions and daisies mostly, were woven into a small tiara that sat on top of her long golden hair. A fairy princess on her wedding day.

George took the photo, held it up to the light and studied it carefully. 'She was pretty.'

Aston looked curiously at her for a moment. On the surface George's comment had sounded like a compliment, but it had seemed forced, like she was saying it because it was the expected thing to say. Then again, they were both strung out, and he was probably overanalysing.

'What?' George said. 'Why are you looking at me like that?'

'No reason.'

'If you've got something to say, then say it.'

Aston plucked the photograph from George, put it back where he found it. 'Someone got out of bed on the wrong side today.'

George sighed. 'Sorry, Paul. It's just that being here in Mac's house like this . . . well, it doesn't feel right, know what I mean?'

'I know exactly what you mean.'

They climbed the stairs together, side by side, neither willing to take the lead. The haunted house vibe had infected Aston, got him on edge. Every creak elicited an uncomfortable extra fraction of a heartbeat to add to his already racing pulse, every pipe groan got him sweating a little more. They reached the landing and worked methodically through the rooms. The first door on the right was the bathroom: gleaming white porcelain, an old-fashioned bathtub supported on four spindly legs, and a brass shower head. The next door led to a spare bedroom: functional furnishings and little in the way of personality.

His fingers brushed the handle of the door at the end of the landing and that was enough to get the electricity crackling. The hairs went up on the back of his neck, on his arms. A quick glance at George told him she felt it, too. He was rational, they both were, but sometimes you had to admit you couldn't explain everything away with science and logic. And right now his thoughts were anything but logical. They were the thoughts of a child who needed the wardrobe checked one more time for monsters despite the fact it had been checked half a dozen times already.

The door swung open, and in the light sneaking past them he saw the silhouette of a woman. His first thought was that it was Sophia's ghost. An irrational thought, but that didn't make it any easier to shake off. Behind him, George let out a tense gasp. He quickly flicked on the light, convinced it must be an optical illusion – ghosts didn't exist; there had to be a rational explanation – but the woman didn't disappear in the glare. If anything she became more solid. As Aston's eyes adjusted, and he was able to see what was going on, he gave a nervous laugh. It wasn't Sophia's ghost, but what he saw wasn't any less disturbing.

'This is totally fucked up,' George muttered, taking the words from his mouth.

Mac had turned the bedroom into a shrine. What Aston had thought was a ghost was a mannequin. He moved in for a closer look, George at his side. The mannequin was dressed in the same blue silk dress from the wedding photo; the wig was made from real hair, the soft, fine strands wound into a shoulder length French plait. There were dead flowers in her hair, and Aston guessed this was the same tiara Sophia had worn to her wedding. The dandelions and daisies were crisp and fragile, the colours dulled by the passing years.

Every spare surface was covered with candles, some in holders, some in saucers, but most welded in place with melted wax. The wardrobes and drawers still held her clothes, and Aston swore a hint of her perfume remained in the air. An ivory handled hairbrush and hand mirror sat gathering dust on the dressing table, where perfume bottles were lined up like soldiers, all the labels facing out. The bed was immaculately made up: razor sharp creases in the linen, the pillows fluffed up and placed with military precision. One wall was covered in photographs, all Blu-tacked neatly in place; a scattering of pictures had fallen off and lay on the floor. The pictures had been taken all over the world, the light and architecture changing from photo to photo. Here, the bright sunshine and tall skyscraper backdrop of Singapore. There, the dull light and severe Tsarist palaces of Moscow. Japan, Italy and Austria. New York and Paris. And in all of them Sophia was smiling and happy, radiating health and without a care, completely unaware of the disease waiting to strike her down, not knowing that she was living on borrowed time.

'Well, they certainly got around,' George said, gazing over his shoulder at the photos. 'Seems Sophia had money as well as looks.'

'Who's to say Mac didn't pay for all the travelling?'

'You're kidding, right? You've seen what we're paid. You don't get into this line of work for the money.'

Aston stooped down and picked up one of the photos from the floor. It was older than the rest, and Mac was in it, too. Behind the smiling couple, an antiquated big wheel loomed, the same big wheel from the picture in Mac's office. Aston had always assumed that he had it there as a souvenir of his time in Vienna. Holding the photo he realised there was probably more to that picture than he thought. They made a good-looking couple. Sophia had a soft, innocent face and slim body, a feline beauty that complemented Mac, who, with his corn-coloured hair and piercing blue eyes, had more than a touch of the Robert Redfords about him.

'So what do you make of all this?' George asked.

'Pretty fucked up,' Aston said, echoing her earlier sentiments.

'Pretty unsettling, too,' George said. 'Makes you wonder what's going on in his head, right now. You know him as well as anyone. Any ideas?'

Aston shook his head. 'Wouldn't even like to hazard a guess.'

'Seen enough?'

'Yeah,' Aston said, but George hadn't bothered to wait for an answer. She was already halfway along the landing. Aston backed out of the room, but before he hit the light switch he took one last look at the mannequin, one last look at the tiara of dead flowers in her hair. The dummy stared back with blank indifference, which unsettled him even more. He pulled the door closed and headed downstairs. At the bottom he passed the open door to the study and the grey filing cabinet called to him. He stopped dead. 'Hang on,' he shouted to George.

'What is it now?' She was standing by the front door, hand on the handle.

'There's something I need to check out.' He disappeared into the study. Through the open door he heard George sigh, her footsteps getting closer.

'This better be good, Paul.'

Aston didn't reply. He stared at the filing cabinet for a moment then walked towards it and pulled the top drawer open. Empty. Something wasn't right here. He went through the other two drawers. The folders in the middle drawer contained household bills and bank statements. Nothing exciting. The bottom drawer contained a couple of software CDs, a small guillotine and a portable document shredder. There was something wrong with this picture. Aston took a step back, looking at the cabinet, seeing it in the context of the study. It was a big filing cabinet for the size of room, yet it wasn't really being used. That didn't make sense. There was no way Mac would do that. Aston focused on the space around the cabinet and suddenly saw it. He got down on his hands and knees and ran his hands across the carpet. There were two shallow parallel grooves in front of the cabinet, barely visible. His hands ran frantically across the cold steel, pulling open drawers, clanging them shut, searching. The lever was at the back. A sharp tug and the wheels creaked into place. The cabinet slid forward easily. Aston got back on his knees and rolled the carpet away. He checked the floorboards until he found the loose one. He pulled it up and reached into the dark, fingers finding smooth plastic. The rattle of a handle. Aston lifted out the laptop case and handed it to George.

7

Words float across the table, but there's no substance to the conversation. It's all part of the act. Words to pad out the silences, words to create the illusion that everything's A-OK. After all, this is something we do once a month, schedules depending. Just two old friends getting together to chew the fat. As usual there's the occasional stroll down memory lane, trips to places and events history turned a blind eye to, some shop talk. And as usual I smile when I'm supposed to smile, nod when I'm supposed to nod, let loose with the occasional laugh. My skin is prickling, the hairs on the back of my neck itching. And all the time I'm watching, taking everything in.

He reaches over the table, candlelight shadows streaking his face. As he grabs the bottle and tops up our glasses, he jokes about the cost of the wine. 'At least we're not picking up the tab, eh, Mac?' I laugh with him. He's nervous but hiding it well. Suspicious of silence, he's anxious to keep the conversation going, working hard to avoid any awkward pauses.

The waiter brings our main course and presents my plate with a flourish. His stink is offensive, sweet and cloying; a caterpillar moustache crawls across his top lip. He steps back smiling. *Can I get sir anything else*? 'No, thank you,' I say, turning on the charm and firing a sunny smile right back at him. His smile widens and he's *so* pleased that I'm pleased. He flutters back to the kitchen, weaving between tables positioned far enough apart to ensure privacy. All are occupied. Usually there's a wait of a month to get in to Carmichael's, but not for us. The maître d' gets a monthly retainer. For what we're paying it's the least he could do.

I recognise some of the faces. Tabloid fodder for the most part. There are soap stars and pop stars, MPs and models. In a quiet corner a young movie wannabe is being entertained by a grey-haired man who's old enough to be her grandfather. He's got sagging jowls, piggy eyes and a stomach straining to get free from its black silk prison. A fat Hollywood cigar steams away between thick ring-encrusted fingers. The little poppet's perfect in a little black dress. She's got the perfect body, the perfect skin, the perfect teeth. Beauty and the Beast. I don't recognise him. He looks important – a big shot director, perhaps. She's hanging on his every word, desperate to get onto that A-list, giggling at his stories. Her fingertips brush the back of his hand; champagne touches, light and bubbly.

And he's buying the act. What does Mr Big Shot think? That she's after him for his looks? I watch her take a dainty sip, a little Dutch courage so she can deal with the next bit. Enough alcohol and she'll be able to blot it out: the sweaty whale blubber slimy against her skin, his bulk burying her deeper and deeper into the mattress.

God, I hate this place. I hate the falseness, hate the sycophancy, most of all I hate the desperation of the wannabes. But Kinclave loves it here, so I smile and endure. He's always been blinded by the glitter and glam, gets a kick from rubbing shoulders with the Beautiful Ones.

My knife slices easily through the steak. Rare, only the briefest acquaintance with the flame. The butterflies in my stomach have stripped my appetite, but I chew and swallow and make like it's the best steak ever. Kinclave is banging on about the old days, eyes misty with remembrance and too much wine. He always gets maudlin when he's been drinking. His voice washes over me as he launches into another Russia story, an old favourite. I tune him out, tune into the burble of the restaurant. I catch snatches of conversation from all directions, odd words that merge into surreal sentences. Cutlery scratches against crockery and glasses tinkle. There's classical music playing gently in the background, a string quartet. I clocked the couple at the table by the door straightaway. Always make sure your arse is covered. After all, isn't that the MI6 way? I drink my wine and chew my steak and wait for him to make his move.

His mobile hums a tune and he pulls it out, checks the display. 'Sorry, Mac,' he says, 'Duty calls.'

'No problem,' I say.

Kinclave gets up, folds his napkin neatly and places it on the chair. I can't see it but I know the edges will run parallel to the edge of the chair. He moves towards the toilet with the phone pressed to his ear, keeps his back to me. He doesn't want me to lip-read. The conversation is short, the news worse than he thought. He hides it well, though. His shoulders sag briefly before he catches himself. The back straightens, his shoulders fill the corners of his neat Savile Row suit again. He hangs up and makes a call, then returns to the table.

'Everything okay?' I ask.

'Everything's fine,' he lies.

He prompts himself back into his story with a 'Where was I? Ah yes . . .' I switch off and concentrate on pretending to enjoy my steak, making the appropriate noises wherever necessary.

'My God, Mac, some of the things we got up to, eh?'

'You said it,' I agree, not sure what I'm agreeing to and not particularly caring.

'Were we ever that young?'

I give an appropriate smile, an appropriate shake of the head. 'Where have the years gone, eh? It's hard to believe I retire in less than six months.

Only seems like yesterday I arrived at Century House for the first time.'

Kinclave picks up his glass, swirls the wine then takes a sip. 'Don't worry about that resignation nonsense,' he tells me.

'I wasn't.'

'That's the spirit. Far as I'm concerned you're far too valuable to lose. All that experience . . . no, it would be ridiculous.' His voice slinks to a whisper. 'I don't care what the PM says. Anyway, I'm not having some jumped-up careerist telling me how to run my shop.'

I'm probably the only person in the world he'd confess these innermost feelings to. But you know what? I don't care.

'So, Mac, given any thought to what you're going to do when you retire?'

'I'll probably take up fishing.'

'That'll be the day. Seriously, though, if you want to come back as an SBO, the offer's there.'

That's rich. SBOs oversee operational security in the Controllerates, sad cases who won't let go. Far as I'm concerned they're nothing more than glorified security guards.

'The money's good,' Kinclave offers.

'To be honest with you, since . . . well, since Sophia died I haven't given it much thought.'

I deliver the line frostily, driving the conversation into a silence even Kinclave can't circumnavigate. He's saved by the waiter, who flounces over and scoops up our plates, asks if everything was to our satisfaction and would we like to see the dessert menu. Why not, Kinclave tells him, grabbing that lifeline and making the waiter's day at the same time. The waiter is still beaming when he brings the menus. The couple by the door are on their coffees and brandies now. The girl is especially talented, innocent and elegant, acting the airhead. She's positioned so she can see our reflection in the window. Very cute.

It was raining the day of the funeral, a freak grey day sandwiched in the middle of a week of gorgeous summer sun. We pulled up outside the crematorium under a battleship sky, the rain streaking the window of the Daimler. I took the front right corner of the coffin; the other three corners were taken by workers from the funeral house, serious men with serious faces and black suits. At Sophia's request I was the only mourner. She wanted as small a funeral as possible. She hadn't even wanted me there, but that was one argument I actually won. My memory of that day is fragmented; I did the whole thing on autopilot, my heart and soul numb. Pachelbel's Canon played softly as we carried the coffin to the altar. A few empty words from the vicar, then a prayer and a hymn I can't remember the title of. I was invited to say a few words, and this I did, but not aloud. I stood behind the coffin with my hands clasped in front of me, eyes locked on the small posy of wild flowers that had been placed on the lid. Lips tight and without uttering a sound, I told her all the things I'd miss about her, how much I loved her, said goodbye. Tender words for her alone. The vicar patted me gently on the shoulder and muttered some banal observation as I made my way back to the empty pew. Another hymn, another prayer, then the conveyer carried the coffin into the flames. Later that day I drove down to the coast and hired a boat, and under that same battleship sky I scattered her ashes into the choppy white waves.

'. . . I can't imagine what you've been through,' Kinclave is saying.

I slip back into the here. He's staring at me and shaking his head. His eyes are full of pity. I don't need his pity.

'I know things seem bleak,' he says. 'But you can get through this. The important thing to realise is that you're not on your own.'

I've heard it all before. I didn't believe it then; don't believe it now.

He shakes his head and sighs. 'You really should talk about it, you know. It can't be doing you any good keeping everything bottled up . . .' Another flash of pity. 'Look,' he says. 'I've got it all arranged. I've found this little place in the country. Five star. Spa, swimming pool, massages. Some time out to get some perspective will do you the world of good, Mac. They'll have you back to yourself in no time.'

'You want to send me to a health farm?'

'Only if you want to go.'

'You think a week in the country drinking

vegetable smoothies and eating lettuce is going to solve anything?'

'Well, it can't do any harm. Alternatively you could take some leave – you're due a ton, go on a trip somewhere.'

'That's really going to cheer me up, Grant. Next you'll be sending that twitchy psychiatrist to see me so we can have a good old chinwag about all the things I'm repressing.'

'Mac, I'm only trying to help. You must be going through hell at the moment.'

'Grant, I don't need your help or anyone else's. I don't need a shrink and, before you say anything else, I don't need a doctor, either. If you so much as mention Prozac, I'm out of here.' A gentle, engaging smile. 'Now, how about we forget this conversation ever took place and order dessert?'

8

'Paulie, Paulie, Paulie . . . and what brings you to my little corner of the world? Mac got you working late again?' Mole took a long drag, tapped the dead ash into the beat-up tobacco tin balancing on his lap. He clamped the roll-up between his lips and wheeled himself forward.

'Kind of,' Aston said as the door slid shut and a blast of cool air caressed his face. It was pretty late, almost eleven on a school night; however, he'd guessed Mole would be here. A pretty safe bet. Mole turned to dust when the sun came up, only reconstituting when darkness fell. The air was sweet with patchouli, and there was a trace of BO. A Doors CD was playing softly, the hypnotic groove loose and intense. *The End*. Morrison and the boys at their stoned best. Aston recognised this particular track from the six months he spent as a wannabe Bohemian when he was seventeen. He'd written a ton of crap poetry, drunk too much cheap red wine, talked a lot of bollocks, and then he'd woken up one morning and it was time to move on to the next fad. Computer fans buzzed in the background, the different pitches creating a smooth harmony. The only illumination came from the monitors dotted around the room and it took a second for Aston's eyes to adjust. Various screensavers – colourful bouncing balls and inter-stellar space journeys – cast sneaky shadows; flick-ering, swimming kaleidoscopes of light. Mole preferred it this way, said he felt more at home existing in the Unreal.

Mole stopped the wheelchair in front of Aston and leant to the side, peering past him. 'And what have we here? Is that the Gorgeous George skulking back there? Come on out, sweetheart. Don't be shy. I don't bite . . .'

George stepped out from behind Aston. 'Hi, Mole. How are you doing?'

'All the better for seeing you. I don't get many visitors down here, and I rarely get any as pretty as you.'

If proof was needed that MI6 was serious about dealing with the new world order, then Aston reckoned Mole was that proof. In his battered Levis, tatty old Aerosmith tour T-shirt, and a pair of Nikes that were only a few short steps from trainer heaven, Mole was no 007. He was in his mid-thirties and unhealthily overweight. He had flabby jowls and fish eyes that bulged behind thick bottle-bottom glasses. His long hair was tied in a ponytail that came halfway down his back, greasy grey streaks running through black. Before being press-ganged into joining MI6, Mole had amused himself by cooking up viruses and hacking into systems that were supposed to be hacker-proof. His masterwork was a virus called Revelations 2001 that had crashed the Web and cost businesses across the globe millions. Police on both sides of the Atlantic had gone after him, expending huge amounts of time and resources, and eventually tracked him down to a council estate on the outskirts of Sheffield where he lived with his mother.

It was Mac who realised that Mole's particular talents would be wasted in prison. MI6's computer eggheads were good, he argued, but what they needed was someone who wasn't afraid to venture into the uncharted territories on the edge of Cyberspace, someone who would go to that edge and beyond. Mole was that person. Strings were pulled, a deal cut, and Mole escaped prison on the condition that he went to work for MI6. It wasn't exactly a hardship for the hacker. For his sins he had one of the most impressive computer systems in the world to play with.

Mole's eyes locked on the laptop bag dangling from Aston's left shoulder. His face suddenly changed, hardened, the little-boy-lost smile replaced with a hungry grin. The hacker stubbed out the roll-up and snapped the lid back on the tobacco tin. 'So what can I do for you?'

Aston unzipped the laptop bag, pulled out the

computer. Mole grabbed it and wheeled himself back to his desk. He turned it in his hands, examining it in the light given off by three huge flat screen monitors that were arranged like dressing-table mirrors. 'What's the story?'

'We need to know what's on there,' Aston said. 'Everything that's on there.'

'You haven't tampered with it, no? Switched it on and had a go at breaking the password? Opened it up even?'

Aston shook his head. For years the spy world had been using computers to move information. E-mail was ideal for sending anonymous coded messages; the forgotten areas at the edge of the hard-drive were perfect for hiding information. As technology progressed, the security had become more extravagant. Hit a wrong key and that was it. Game over. All those secrets wiped.

Mole finished his visual inspection and shifted the mouse to make room on the desk. He put it down gently, hand resting on the lid, fingers tapping out code on an invisible keyboard. He stared at Aston through the magnifying glass lenses. 'Okay, mind explaining what this is all about?'

'I just need to know what's on the computer.'

'I heard you the first time,' Mole said. 'See, the thing is I remember every computer I build. They're my babies. And before I kick them out the nest I give them a mark. Something I can recognise them by. Don't look at me like that. I know that sort of thinking is alien to you, but I'm not a spy. I'm a hacker, and hackers have egos the size of the sun. How do you think they caught me? I was signing my work with foot high letters. Thought I was so fucking clever.' Mole picked up the laptop. 'Appears to be an off-the-shelf IBM Thinkpad, doesn't it?' He carefully turned the computer over and pointed to the first two digits of the serial number. A six and a nine. 'Childish, I know. But there we go.' He smiled at George. 'This laptop belongs to the honourable Robert Macintosh. Which begs the question: Why do you want to break into Mac's computer?'

'Need to know,' Aston said, enjoying the way the words sounded. He'd lost count of the number of times he'd been fed that particular line. It made a nice change to deliver it.

'Well, if I don't need to know,' Mole said, 'then we're wasting each other's time.'

Aston noticed Mole was in no hurry to hand over the laptop. His hand was resting protectively on the lid, fingers tapping. Mole was as curious to find out what was on the computer as he was.

'Would it make any difference if I told you I was working for The Chief?' Not quite the truth; not quite a lie.

Mole raised an eyebrow.

'If this is one of yours,' George nodded to the laptop, 'I take it you can get in? Without it self-destructing, I mean?'

A roll of the eyes. 'Do you really expect me to

answer that? Of course I can get in.' Mole ran his fingers underneath the laptop and there was a tiny click. 'There we go,' he said with a self-satisfied smirk.

The hacker linked his fingers, stretched them out like a concert pianist, and switched the computer on. ENTER PASSWORD blinked up on the screen. His fingers flew over the keyboard, hammering plastic. The screen flickered and changed, characters and symbols as mysterious as hieroglyphics flashing past in the blink of an eye. As Mole typed faster, Aston noticed the hacker frowning. The frown became more defined and he almost asked what the problem was, but he knew better than to disturb Mole when he was working. He'd done that once before and it hadn't been pretty.

Thirty seconds passed. A minute. Two minutes. Mole suddenly stopped and reached for his Pepsi Max. He took a long slug, belched, wiped his mouth with the back of his hand. 'Naughty, naughty,' he muttered, smiling to himself.

'What's wrong?' George asked.

'Wrong?' Mole swivelled round in the wheel-chair. A pre-rolled ciggie had magically appeared between his lips. He flicked a lighter and leant into the flame. 'Why, nothing's wrong. Well, nothing I can't handle.'

'So something's wrong?' George pressed.

A long drag. Smoke tumbled from Mole's nostrils. 'You know about backdoors?'

'Yeah,' George said. 'They're put in programs so the programmer can access a system without having to worry about passwords and stuff.'

'Well, Mac's had the backdoor I put in locked up nice and tight.'

'You can't get in, then?' Aston said.

'Oh ye of little faith,' Mole said with a little shake of his head. The hacker hit a key and the desktop page appeared. He grinned at Aston. 'What do you think? That I only put one backdoor in? A little more credit please.'

Aston smiled. 'I'm impressed. So what have we got?'

'Not so fast. Whoever took out the backdoor knows his stuff. Obviously he's not in the same league as me, but he is competent. That backdoor wasn't easy to deal with. I had to make it tricky enough so that if it did get found nobody would suspect a second one.' Mole took a Godfather-sized tug on the roll-up and waved it at Aston. 'If it's okay with you I'm going to keep hold of this and give it a thorough going over. I don't want to hurry in case there are any nasty surprises lurking in there.' A pause before adding: 'You sure you don't want to tell me what this is all about?'

'Positive.'

A drag and a long sigh. 'I suppose I come to you if I find anything.'

'Me or George,' Aston agreed. 'Or The Chief, I suppose.'

'Nah, you're alright there.' Mole laughed from behind the cloud of smoke. 'I'll leave the brown-nosing to you.'

9

Like I guessed, the news was worse than Kinclave thought – bad enough for him to get the girl to tail me when I left the restaurant. And like I thought, she was talented. It took a while to lose her, but only because I was enjoying myself. I eventually gave her the slip in the myriad tunnels that snake through Piccadilly Circus tube station.

With my jacket pulled in tight to ward off the chill, I head down to the river, walking with purpose, owning the streets. I lean against a wall and block out the brown river stink. The water swirls below me, dark and mysterious and poisonous. For a while I watch, transfixed by the movement, the gentle waves rolling, rolling, concentric circles merging and separating in the murky dark. Rain runs across my face and drips from my nose.

My father was in MI6 back in World War II. I can remember him sitting on my bed telling me stories of the things he got up to. He'd sit with his back against the headboard, his long legs and stockinged-feet stretching almost all the way to the other end, the comforting smell of aftershave and pipe tobacco surrounding him. The tales he told were real *Boy's Own* adventures, and I lapped up every word. There were stories about missions behind Nazi lines, ops filled with danger and excitement. And he'd finish each story with a tap on the nose and a wink and a 'Remember, Rob . . . Need-To-Know'. I'd give him a tap and a wink back. 'Need-To-Know' I'd whisper. He'd ruffle my hair and tell me to sleep well, and then he'd turn off the light and leave me dreaming about killing Nazis and blowing up bridges.

When I hit my teens I realised he'd made it all up. There was no way he did those things. It was only when I started working for MI6 myself and managed to get hold of his file that I discovered that, although he had made it all up, the things he had done were no less spectacular. What's more, I discovered how highly he was respected within the organisation. His record was spotless and for a while he was being touted as a possible future Chief.

The official report stated that it was a 'regret-table accident', but it wasn't. It was murder, plain and simple. I was ten and my father was stationed in Moscow. Walking home one night he spotted a woman being mugged. Without thinking, he ran to help her and was stabbed. The mugger was never found, not that the authorities tried very hard. This happened way back in the early days of the Cold War. For whatever reason, the KGB had wanted my father taken out of the game, and that was that. Case closed. Of course, there was an inquiry, lots of bureaucratic nonsense that wasn't worth a damn.

We were told about his death by the head of station, Giles Meredith, a loose-fitting man who seemed to bumble his way through life. To me, he was always a slightly comical figure, but my father seemed to respect him (and now, with thirty plus years of experience, I can appreciate that what you see isn't necessarily what you get). My parents had been to Meredith's house a couple of times for dinner parties, but this was the first time he'd come to ours. He took charge of the situation straight away, guiding me and my mother through to the living room, ignoring my mother's increasingly frantic questions until we were both sitting on the sofa. When he told us what happened it didn't sink in at first. I thought there must be some mistake, they'd got the wrong person. I kept expecting the living-room door to clatter open and my father to walk in, pipe steaming, a sly smile on his lips. My mother fell into a long silence and then she started screeching. It was the most hideous noise I'd ever heard. I wasn't sure what to do. I felt I should probably be crying, but I couldn't. So I sat on the sofa while Meredith tried to console my mother, hands on lap, staring into the middle distance and wondering what was going to happen now.

My mother didn't die as such, she sort of faded away; after Father was murdered she became less and less substantial until she ceased to exist altogether. First to go was her mind. I got home from school one day to find my grandmother there. There was gin on her breath and disappointment in her eyes. Without an iota of compassion she informed me that my mother had been locked up in the nuthouse, and I was going to live with her because families looked after each other and wasn't that just fucking marvellous? When I told her there was no way I'd ever live with her she called me an ungrateful bastard and hit me so hard I was sent spinning to the floor with bells ringing in my head. From the get-go I was under no illusions of the way things were going to be. I saw my mother twice more, once in the flesh and once in a casket. The week before my mother died, my grandmother took me to the asylum. She dragged me through the screaming corridors to a dark windowless room. There were four beds in there, each containing the mummified remains of something that might once have been human. This was most definitely the last stop. My mother was in the bed nearest the door. Around her sunken eyes and collapsed cheeks, I could make out the shape of her skull. Her skin was loose yellow parchment hanging from her bones and she weighed next to nothing. With each inhalation there was a moment of suspension at the top of the breath where there was no movement, moments that seemed to go on forever, and each time I thought that was it she'd exhale and hitch in another rattling gulp of air. Thankfully, her eyes stayed shut.

It was only natural I should want to join MI6, but it wasn't easy. With no help from my grandmother, who spent most of her time either pissed, comatose or beating me, I got a place at grammar school. While there I discovered I had a knack for drama. Playing different characters gave me a temporary escape from the real world, and how I needed that escape. I won a scholarship to Cambridge where I studied psychology, and during my final year I was approached.

The rain eases and the circles in the river shrink, loosen, then disappear altogether. I could go anywhere, be anyone, start all over again. I've got the aliases established, got the necessary skills to pull them off. I could be an engineer, an academic, a financier, you name it. Everything's stashed away in a safe place. Full documentation: passports, driving licences, NI numbers, complete histories, the works. Nobody knows about Stewart Graves or Graham Webster or Harry Mortimer. It would be easy to sneak out the country. The safest way is to head to Ireland, make my way to Dublin and catch the first plane out. But I won't do that. Not yet, anyway.

I head back to my hotel, an anonymous no-star

affair in a part of town that won't be featuring in the travel guides anytime soon. London's the perfect hiding place: nobody sees anyone, nobody sees anything. The occasional glance to make sure I'm not being followed, more out of habit than necessity. The streets get narrower, the shadows deepen. The Invisible Ones are huddled in doorways with blankets pulled around them, one hand protecting their few meagre belongings, the other wrapped around a tin of Special Brew or Woodpecker or meths. A scrawny Jack Russell yaps, and a slurred voice growls for it to shut the fuck up.

'Got any spare change?'

The voice is behind me, off to my left. I turn slowly and see a dark figure hovering in the shadows.

'Come on,' the voice says, 'you've got cash to spare.'

'Fuck off,' I tell him.

He steps into a streetlight and I get my first good look at the Ratman. His face is long with eyes sunk deep in their sockets, black coronas surrounding them. He's got that junkie stare, rotting teeth and skin the colour of old marble. His clothes are held together by dirt: three jumpers and a coat, odd shoes that are way too big, hair hidden under a dirty fur-lined Cossack hat. He uses the back of his fingerless glove to wipe away the snail trails under his sharp nose.

'Just a quid,' the Ratman says. 'Just a quid and I'll fuck off and never bother you again. Promise.'

'You'll fuck off now,' I tell him.

'For a fiver I'll do whatever you want. Anything.'

Smiling, I walk towards him. He gulps and his throat is so scrawny it looks as if he's swallowing a golf ball. The Ratman looks around uncertainly, takes a step back, out of the light and into the shadows, looking for safety where there's no safety to be found. He backs up to a wall and comes to a standstill. I motion him forward with a wiggle of my index finger. He looks left, looks right, searching for a way out, but in the end all he can do is walk towards me. As he steps back into the light I study his face carefully. The sodium distorts it, and as I stare it starts to change, morphing into all the faces I've grown to hate so much over the years. I can feel the anger rising, spreading through me from tip to toe, and I do nothing to hold it back. So often in life we are forced to suppress our real emotions, those primal desires that originate in the most ancient parts of the brain. And sometimes we are given the opportunity to let them loose and for a few glorious moments we know what it means to be truly alive. A deep breath, adrenaline coursing through my veins, heart doing double time.

'What did you say?'

The Ratman doesn't reply, just stands there paralysed, wearing a terrified expression.

A step forward. 'You're a worthless piece of shit, do you know that?' In that sentence I hear echoes of my grandmother; my brain conjures up memories of her alcohol-soaked breath.

'Sorry,' the Ratman manages. 'I didn't mean to—'

'Shut the fuck up, okay? I've had enough of your whining and your whimpering. You're pathetic, do you hear me? You make me sick.' Up close the Ratman's stink is overpowering, the smell of decay and piss and hopelessness. 'Do I look like a queer?'

'No,' he says, then adds a shaky: 'Sir.'

'No, sir, is right,' I tell him.

Without warning I head-butt him full in the face. He stays upright for a second, blood spurting from his nose, then folds to the ground. The Invisible Ones stir in the shadows but nobody comes to help. When you're this far down you are really and truly on your own. I rip off the Cossack hat, grab him by the hair and pull him to his feet, punch him twice in the face. Two sharp jabs. Steam rises from the front of his trousers and tears streak his dirty cheeks.

'Don't kill me,' he whimpers. 'Please don't kill me.'

I'm so close I can smell the fear, the heat coming off his face. I want to kill him, I really do; I've never wanted anything so badly in my life. I let go and he drops to the ground. He's trembling all over, nothing but a pathetic bundle of rags. I hunker down, crouching at eye level to get a better look. His sunken eyes are big and wide, the tiny spark in the pupils might be hope. His eyes lock with mine and the spark flickers, fades then disappears. He's convinced I'm going to kill him.

I stand up and walk away. Behind me, The Invisible Ones are leaving the safety of the shadows, cautiously making their way towards their fallen comrade. I don't need to turn around to confirm that help is the last thing on their minds. Even this far down there's someone worse off than you, someone you can take advantage of, even if it's just to steal a pair of odd worn shoes and a battered old Cossack hat.

10

'Come on, Paul, wake up.'

Aston wished the voice away and rolled over on the sofa with a cold leather squeak. Shivering, he pulled the thin jacket in tight and buried his head under a cushion. A hand grabbed his shoulder and tried to drag him back around. He buried himself deeper into the sofa, resisting the insistent pull, telling himself this wasn't happening.

'Don't you dare turn your back on me, Paul. We need to talk.'

A shiver ran up Aston's spine. *We need to talk.* Those four words always spelled trouble. And lately that's all she seemed to want to do . . . talk. Laura sure knew how to pick her moments. It was way too early to deal with this.

'Stop pretending to be asleep. I know you're awake.'

The hand became a fist that pounded against his arm. The blows weren't hard and he swiped blindly, swatting as though they were mosquitoes.

'You're going to sit up now. And you're going to talk to me. I don't think that's too much to ask.'

'Leave me alone,' Aston mumbled into the sofa. 'Need more sleep.'

Laura stopped hitting and started shaking again, using both hands this time, gripping hard enough for Aston to feel her fingernails digging into his arm 'Okay, okay,' he said. 'Let me get my act together, eh? I don't think *that's* too much to ask. What time is it anyway?'

'Just gone half seven.'

'And you want to talk now? Jesus, Laura, can't this wait?'

'No, it can't wait, Paul.'

Aston rolled over and lay on his back for a moment, psyching himself up. It was all coming back to him. Slowly. After leaving the laptop with Mole, George suggested they find a late bar. Aston hadn't needed much persuasion. Making up for lost time, they'd started with doubles then hit the trebles. It was around this point that everything became a bit hazy. Aston opened his eyes and sharp sunlight pierced his brain, making his head spin and his stomach churn. He was still fully dressed: his tie a loose noose around his neck, the tail trailing over his shoulder; shirt and trousers wrinkled and smelling like a wino's. His jacket was a crumpled mess and nowhere near thick enough to deal with the morning chill. There was a half empty bottle of JD by the side of the sofa. Presumably he'd carried on drinking when he got home, drank until he'd passed out. He sat up and rubbed at his face. Wishing that the demons in his head would stop clattering around, he attempted a smile. 'Don't suppose you'd be a sweetheart and get me a coffee and a couple of aspirin?'

Laura shook her head, disapproval all over her face. 'Do you have any idea how rough you look?'

'Thanks. Love you, too.' Aston rubbed his bristly chin. He knew what he looked like, didn't need Laura reminding him. Bloodshot eyes, tired skin, too many wrinkles. The worn face staring back from the bathroom mirror these days was no stranger.

'Seriously, Paul, you've got to cut back on the drinking.'

'So, I enjoy a drink every now and again. What's the big deal? Everyone does.'

Laura cleared a space on the coffee table and perched opposite Aston. She paused for a second then let out a long sigh and locked eyes with him. 'What's going on, Paul? The last couple of weeks you've been acting really strange.'

'Strange?'

'Yes, strange. You've been drinking more than usual . . . a lot more than usual. And you've been so distant.' A snort. 'You're not the easiest person to get close to at the best of times, but lately it's like you've moved to Antarctica or something.'

'I've got a lot on at work, that's all.'

'And the best way to deal with that is to get pissed every night and freeze me out.'

'It's not every night.' Even as he was saying this, Aston was doing the calculations. His last alcohol-free day had been almost three weeks ago, the Sunday before 18/8. Jesus, that was a sobering thought. And it was true, he had been hitting the bottle harder than usual. But was it any wonder after what he'd seen down in those airless tunnels?

'Well, it certainly seems like it's every night to me.'

'It's no big deal.'

'No big deal! Yeah, you're right, Paul, getting annihilated every night isn't a big deal. Getting so pissed you can't remember what you've done, yeah, that's no biggie either. In fact, it's perfectly normal. Like you say, everyone does it, so what's the problem? Have you started drinking during the day, yet? You know, a little hair of the dog to stop the shakes?'

Aston sat up straighter, hoping this would make him look more together than he felt. 'That's so fucking typical of you. Blowing everything out of all proportion. You're making it sound like I'm an alcoholic.'

'Well, you're currently doing a good impression of one.'

Laura held his gaze and the silence was tense and unbearable. Aston broke away first, rubbed his eyes and felt the bristles on his chin. He needed a coffee bad, something to shift this headache. He was in no fit state to have this conversation. One wrong move and it would be Armageddon. Aston stared out the window at the dull morning sky while he wrestled his anger under control. He was a hair trigger away from losing it completely. Laura was really pushing all the wrong buttons. Like she never drank. Like she'd never had a hangover. Heaven forbid that Little Miss Perfect would ever get a bit tiddly and do something silly. Like *that* never happened. Aston took a deep breath and smiled as sweetly as his hangover would allow.

'Say something, Paul.'

'Like what?'

'Well, how about you convince me that you're not an alcoholic. That'd be a good start.'

'I'm not an alcoholic,' Aston said dryly.

'Jesus, Paul, I'm being serious here. I'm worried about you.'

'So am I. I'm not an alcoholic. I've always enjoyed a drink. It goes with the territory. How many teetotal civil servants do you know?'

'For Christ's sake, Paul, this really isn't the time for jokes.'

Aston sighed and shook his head. 'I say again: I enjoy a drink, big fucking deal. That doesn't make me an alcoholic. Anyway, I'm not the only one around here who gets pissed, am I?'

'Don't you dare,' Laura warned. 'Don't you dare turn this around onto me.'

'Why not? I've had to put you to bed more

than once after a night out. People in glass houses and all that.'

'The difference is that I'm not getting into that state every night. Once in a while, fine. But do it every night and it becomes a problem. Deny that it's a problem, and that's when you're in big trouble.'

'Jesus Christ, Laura, give me a break.'

Laura stared deep into his eyes, holding his gaze again.

'I am not an alcoholic.'

'Maybe not yet, but carry on like this and that's where you're heading.'

Aston shook his head. 'You're way off the mark.'

'Okay, I'm off the mark. In that case, maybe you could tell me exactly what you were up to last night.'

'Can't we talk about this later?'

'When exactly?' Laura said. 'Paul, we never see each other anymore. For the last couple of weeks you've been working late every night. I'm asleep when you get in. You're asleep when I get up. Not much of a relationship, is it?'

'We're spending time together now.'

'I'm talking about quality time.'

'I took you out to dinner. Remember? We went to that little Italian place you like.'

'That was three weeks ago.' A long sigh. 'You really don't get it, do you, Paul?'

'Obviously not.'

'You were with her last night, weren't you? You were with George.'

'So what if I was? It was a Thursday. I always go out with George on a Thursday. You know that.'

'And you couldn't even miss one Thursday, could you?'

'Why should I? When we started seeing each other we decided that we should make a conscious effort not to lose contact with our friends. If I remember rightly, your idea.'

'But there are times when being a couple takes priority,' Laura said. 'What was the date yesterday?'

'August 31st. Why?'

'And that date doesn't mean anything to you?'

'No. Should it?'

'Obviously not.'

For a terrible moment, Aston thought he'd missed Laura's birthday – a hanging offence – but that was in February. 'I'm going out on a limb here, but I'm guessing it means something to you.'

'To *us*, Paul.'

'What are you talking about?'

'It was our anniversary. One year we've been together. I didn't expect to be whisked off to Paris or anything like that, but a bunch of flowers would have been nice, or a romantic meal, or just some small indication that maybe I actually mean something to you. I don't think that's too much to ask, really. But no, you'd rather go out on the piss with your friend. You know, Paul, that makes me feel so special.'

There was no anger in her voice, just quiet resignation, and somehow that was worse. So that's what this was all about. This was the real reason she was so pissed off. If it was so bloody important to her why hadn't she dropped a hint or two? Something along the lines of 'it's our anniversary on Thursday, how about I cook a nice meal and we can spend the rest of the evening shagging each other silly' would have been subtle enough. Surely she realised that blokes were crap at remembering those sorts of things. Birthdays and anniversaries just weren't as important to men as they were to women; it was a genetic thing. Not that it would have made any difference. The Chief of MI6 ambushes you in a pub and tells you to go and break into your boss's house, then you drop everything and jump to it. Aston had a feeling that wasn't what Laura needed to hear right now.

'Sorry,' he said.

'Something's happened to you over the last couple of weeks, Paul. Something that's changed you to the point where I don't recognise you anymore. The fact you won't talk to me makes things worse. I'm not sure how much more I can take,' she added quietly. 'I really don't.'

'We're talking now, aren't we?'

'No, Paul, I'm talking while you act all defensive and do everything possible to avoid any sort of meaningful discussion.'

Aston rubbed at his face again, his headache

getting worse with every passing second. 'Okay, Laura, what do you want me to say?'

'Jesus, Paul, I don't want you to say anything. I just want you to talk to me.'

Aston shrugged and stared out the window. Where did you start . . . ?

'Paul, I'm not a mind reader. If you'd tell me what's going on, then maybe I could help.'

'And maybe I don't need your help.'

A long sigh and a longer silence. 'Okay, fine,' Laura said in a low voice. 'I've tried to be understanding, but obviously I'm wasting my time. I think we both know what's *really* going on.'

'Okay,' Aston said carefully. There was a look on Laura's face he didn't like one bit. 'Now you've lost me.'

'I knew it,' Laura muttered to herself. 'I fucking knew it. I tried to tell myself that you were different.'

'Look, Laura, what's this all about?'

She turned towards him, eyes blazing with hurt and anger. 'You're fucking her, aren't you?'

'Fucking who? What are you talking about?'

'George. You're fucking George, aren't you?'

Aston surprised himself by laughing. It was out there before he realised it was the wrong thing to do. 'Laura,' he started to say, but she cut him off.

'Yeah, that's right. Hysterical, isn't it? I bet the two of you are having a right laugh at my expense.'

'Laura, I am not fucking George. We're friends. End of story.'

'And I'm supposed to believe that. Just take your word for it. Well you've got to be fucking someone because you sure as hell aren't fucking me at the moment.'

'Look, I'll say it again: there's nothing going on between me and George.'

Laura snorted and said nothing. She sat on the edge of the coffee table, arms folded, body coiled tight as a spring.

'There's nothing I can say to convince you, is there?' Aston said.

'It's the only explanation that makes sense,' Laura said quietly.

'Okay, I'll admit that maybe I've been a bit preoccupied lately, but that's because work's been a complete nightmare.'

'So the reason you're not having sex with me is because you're stressed, is that it?'

Aston shrugged.

'Bullshit!' A pause. 'And that's another thing. What exactly is it you do again? Because I'll be buggered if I know. Isn't it amazing, we've been together for a year, a whole fucking year, and whenever anyone asks what you do I uhm and ah and change the subject because I don't actually know.'

Aston stood and headed for the door. 'I'm going to take a shower. We'll talk later. When you've calmed down.'

'That's right,' Laura shouted after him. 'Run away. That's the way you deal with everything, isn't it?'

Aston froze with his hand on the handle, turned slowly. He walked back to the sofa and sat down on the arm. 'You want to know what I do? Okay I'll tell you. You want to know why I've been a bit stressed these past couple of weeks. Yeah, I'll tell you that as well. Why the fuck not?'

'Oh, this I've got to hear,' said Laura.

'I work for MI6,' Aston said matter-of-factly. 'And the reason I've been stressed out is because I was at Leicester Square. Actually down in the tunnels while it was all going on. I watched them carry the bodies out. And I dug up a dead baby with my bare hands. Satisfied?'

Silence stretched between them. Neither moved, neither breathed. Aston stared at Laura, daring her to speak.

'You know, Paul, for a while there I actually thought you were going to tell me the truth.' Laura stood up and headed for the door. 'How fucking sick can you get? You know Becky's brother died at Leicester Square . . .' She opened the door, turned to face him. 'I won't be back later, Paul. And I'd appreciate it if you weren't here at the weekend so I can move my stuff out.'

Aston watched Laura slip through the crack, watched the door close gently behind her. His head was pounding worse than ever. What a perfect way to start the day. Absolutely fucking perfect.

11

Aston swiped his card, typed his four-digit PIN into the keypad and pushed against the security door. It wouldn't budge. He glanced down, saw the LED was still on red. Brilliant, just brilliant. Even the machines were ganging up on him today. Someone behind grumbled and he fought the urge to turn around and give them a mouthful. The fight with Laura had left him raw and hyped; any excuse to burn off some of that anger. And what the hell was that all about anyway? They both knew she'd be back. She always came back. She'd go out on the piss with her mates over the weekend, have a good old moan, convince them he was a complete and utter bastard. Sunday evening she'd breeze into the flat like nothing had happened.

'Modern technology, eh?' said a plummy voice to the left. 'Fine when it works, a complete bugger when it doesn't.'

The man pushing through the next door was

typical MI6: aristocratic nose, striped suit, RAF moustache. Ex-military with a public school tie hanging up in the wardrobe. The man smiled a sorry-old-boy smile and disappeared inside.

'Come on, come on,' said a voice behind. 'Some of us have work to do.'

Aston didn't need to turn round to check out the person behind. There were plenty of his sort lurking in the corridors of Vauxhall Cross, too. Civil servants with degrees in toadying. Mac reckoned they should all be locked up in a small room and left to bore each other to death . . . a point of view Aston subscribed to. He swiped the card again, typed in his PIN, but the LED stayed stubbornly on red. 'Don't need this,' he muttered. 'Really don't need this.'

On the third attempt Aston swiped slowly, making sure the card went all the way through, double-checked each number of his PIN: 5-7-3-4. He looked around and saw two guards standing by the VIP entrance, watching him. He held up his card. 'There seems to be a problem with this,' he mouthed, emphasising each word; the guards wouldn't be able to hear a thing through the bombproof glass.

One of the guards motioned towards the VIP entrance and Aston hustled through the backlog towards it, the other worker bees moving out of his way to let him past. Their silence was unnerving; the fact no one would meet his eye even more so. He'd already been tried and found guilty. And to make matters worse he had no idea what his crime was. Anxiety swirled in his empty stomach and his head pounded worse than ever. The VIP door slid open and Aston stepped into the narrow capsule. The pressure pad on the floor confirmed there was only one occupant and the door at the far end opened. The guards were waiting for him, the bigger of the two stood in the open doorway, blocking his way. The smaller guard had greasy black hair, a Hitler flick, and a Napoleon complex. From his body language – the stiff shoulders, straight back, the way he puffed out his chest to make himself bigger – he obviously outranked his partner and wanted everyone to know it. Aston held out his pass card. 'It was working fine last night,' he said.

Napoleon took the card and gave it a thorough going over. Turning it in his hand, looking for any indication it might be a forgery. He handed the card back and Aston took this as a good sign. There were no guns being shoved into his back, no cuffs being snapped onto his wrists.

'Come with us, sir,' Napoleon said.

'What's this all about?' Aston asked.

'I'm afraid I can't answer that.'

'Can't or won't?'

Nothing from Napoleon.

'Okay, here's an idea,' Aston said, 'and I realise I'm going out on a limb here. But I get the idea that you've been doing this job for a while, which

123

means you must have seen this sort of thing before. So what I'm thinking is that maybe you could speculate. You know, throw a few ideas out there, see if any of them stick.'

'I don't do speculation,' Napoleon said, completely deadpan.

'No, I don't suppose you do.' Aston sighed and made an after-you gesture.

Flanked by the two guards, he walked through the lobby, moving smoothly across the marble floor, heading for the two massive columns that dominated the cathedral-like space. High-speed elevators buzzed up and down inside the columns, sunlight snuck in through the tall light-well in the roof. Aston could feel the stares of the people they passed burning into the back of his skull, but whenever he turned around they'd be looking elsewhere. Although he knew he'd done nothing wrong, he felt like a criminal. It was the same feeling you got when you were pulled over by the police. You knew you weren't speeding, knew your papers were all in order, but you still managed to convince yourself that the next stop was prison. Guilt was part of the human condition, he reasoned, and there was fuck all you could do about it.

The elevator whirred, red numbers blinking on the digital display. Aston stood near the back watching the two security guards in the mirrored walls. His nerves were jangling, hairs on his arms charged. The two guards stared straight ahead, refusing to meet his eye, giving nothing away. They passed the seventh floor and his apprehensiveness gave way to anxiety. By the time they stopped at the top floor he'd tipped over into full-blown paranoia. He'd never been this far up before.

The guards escorted him to a massive office with a wide window that gave a sweeping view of the London skyline. Looking around the office, Aston had a pretty good idea where a large chunk of the building's quarter of a billion price tag had gone. So this was how the other half lived, eh? The shagpile carpet was deep enough to get lost in, the paintings on the walls originals rather than prints. There was a closed door to his right, presumably leading to that fabled bathroom with its gold fittings and imposing throne. Whether there were a dozen virgins in there remained to be seen.

The Chief sat behind a wide oak desk that was obsessively free from clutter, his back to the panoramic window. Kinclave didn't appear to have had much sleep. There were dark smudges under his eyes, the crow's feet more defined. He was still neatly turned out – a perfect Windsor knot and razorblade creases – however, his overall appearance was a little more worn than usual.

'Please take a seat, Paul.'

The Chief motioned to the two chairs on the other side of the ocean of desk. One chair was already taken. Katrina, MI6's resident shrink, turned and said a cheery good morning, her fizzy smile no doubt fuelled by top-grade caffeine. She was the last person he expected to see here. Aston sat down in the deep leather swivel chair and tried to get comfortable.

'Let's get straight to business, shall we?' Kinclave said.

Let's, Aston thought.

'Bad news, I'm afraid,' said The Chief. 'Mac's disappeared.'

'Disappeared! What are you talking about?'

Kinclave smoothed the sides of his hair. 'After your call last night, I thought it prudent to have Mac followed when he left Carmichael's. I was hoping we could find out where he was staying. After all, if he hasn't been staying at home he must be staying somewhere. Can't imagine Mac roughing it in a cardboard box under Waterloo Bridge, can you? Anyway, Mac, gave his watcher the slip. And just to complicate matters further, he hasn't turned up for work this morning.'

'Maybe he's running late,' Aston suggested.

Kinclave raised an eyebrow but didn't say anything. Didn't have to. Mac was always at his desk by seven. Aston looked from The Chief to Katrina. 'You think he's cracked up, don't you? Had some sort of breakdown. That's why you're here.'

The caffeine smile widened into something bordering on patronising. 'Paul,' she said. ' "Break-down" is such a redundant term. It's bandied around

126

far too frequently to be even remotely useful. Let's face it – everybody's either had, or is having, a nervous breakdown these days.'

Her voice was an anorexic whisper, but there was a soothing, confiding quality to it which, given her occupation, was only to be expected. You can tell me anything, the voice promised; your secrets are safe with me. 'Robert's under a lot of stress,' she said, and Aston wondered what Mac would make of the idea that the 'twitchy bitch from shrinksville', as he called her, was on first name terms with him.

'The loss of a loved one is perhaps the most stressful event we can ever experience,' she went on. 'We need to find Robert before he does anything silly.'

'Define "silly",' Aston said.

'Paul,' Kinclave said, and both Aston and Katrina turned to face him. 'What Katrina's saying is that she thinks Mac is suicidal, as you well know. Now, time's pressing. Sensible questions only, please.'

Aston sunk into the leather chair, feeling suitably chastised, wishing it would swallow him up.

'You were at his house last night. What were your impressions?'

He thought for a second, then said: 'It was obvious he hadn't been there for a while, probably about a month or so.'

'Yes, yes,' Katrina said, nodding encouragingly. She jotted something onto the pad that had appeared on the edge of her chair. 'That would be about the time Sophia died. A classic sign of denial . . . wanting to run away from the source of the pain. That would be a perfectly natural reaction.'

Don't I know it, Aston thought, but didn't say anything.

'And?' Katrina prompted.

Aston paused while he searched for the words to describe the bedroom. 'He's built a shrine to her.'

This got Katrina's attention. She sat up in the chair, completely alert, as though she'd been chewing through an electric cable and had suddenly hit copper. 'A shrine . . . what makes you say that?'

'Because that's what it was,' Aston said, irritated by her questions, doubly irritated by his hangover.

'Can you describe what you saw?' Katrina asked pleasantly.

So Aston told her about the wall covered with photographs, and the candles, and the way that the room carried the ghost smell of her perfume. He left the best part till last.

'He dressed the mannequin up in his late wife's wedding dress,' Katrina mused. 'Interesting. Very interesting. And how did this make you feel?'

'Completely creeped out,' Aston said, then realised he'd played right into her hands. She'd caught him off guard, got him to tell her things he'd rather keep to himself.

Katrina smiled that caffeine smile. 'It makes for a powerful image. I wonder what Robert is trying to say here.'

'Your job isn't to wonder,' Kinclave said. 'Your job is to come up with answers. I want to know what's going on in that head of his.' A sigh before adding quietly: 'Basically I want to know if he's going to do anything "silly".'

'It's possible,' Katrina admitted.

'Of course it's bloody possible,' The Chief snapped. 'Anything's bloody possible. I want to know how likely it is.'

'At this stage all I can tell you is that it's a distinct possibility,' Katrina answered, completely unfazed. 'Of course I'll have to investigate further. I'd like to see Robert's personnel file.'

Kinclave nodded. 'I'll make it happen.'

'And I think it might be a good idea to take a look at the house for myself.'

Another nod. 'Okay, anything to add?' Kinclave aimed the question at both of them.

Shakes of the head all around.

'Good,' Kinclave said. 'Paul, if Mac contacts you, or if you have any sudden inspiration as to where he might be, I want to hear about it straightaway.' The Chief turned to Katrina. 'I expect a complete evaluation on my desk by lunchtime.'

'Yes, sir,' they said in unison.

'That'll be all.' Kinclave spun around in his chair and stared out at the Thames below. Picking up on this cue to leave, Aston led the way to the elevator.

'And how are you doing, Paul?' Katrina asked as they waited for the lift.

'I'm doing fine.' Aston could feel her eyes on him, picking him apart. He stared at the numbers, willing the elevator to hurry up. His head was pounding worse than ever.

'Well, if you need to talk, you know where to find me.'

'I'll bear that in mind.'

The elevator arrived, the doors slid open and Aston got in, Katrina scuttling behind. They descended in silence, the hum of machinery above their heads the only sound.

12

Aston finished his drink in one gulp. It didn't even touch the sides. He called the barman over, ordered another. Sometimes you drank for pleasure, sometimes you drank to forget, and sometimes you drank for the pleasure of forgetting. It didn't matter how far he ran, how fast, he couldn't get away from those dark memories of 18/8. They seemed to be there constantly, lurking in the shadows, stalking him. Alcohol helped, providing him with a layer of insulation, time out from reality. But it wasn't a cure. The rational part of his mind knew that; unfortunately the rational part wasn't running the show at the moment.

'Fancy some company?' said a familiar voice from behind.

'Knock yourself out,' Aston said without turning. The barman put his drink down and Aston rummaged in his back pocket for his wallet and handed over a tenner. 'The same for the lady,' he said.

'Very presumptuous. What if I'm not thirsty?' George said.

'That'll be the day.'

The barman brought over the drink and handed Aston his change. 'Cheers,' he said, raising his glass.

George tapped her glass against his and took a sip. 'So what's up with you? You look like the world's about to end.'

'Nothing. Just enjoying a quiet drink after a hard week at work, that's all.'

'And how many drinks constitutes a "quiet drink"?'

'A couple,' Aston said.

'You don't think you might want to slow down a bit there?' George suggested.

'Don't you start,' Aston slurred, the words coming out louder than he intended. A couple of businesswomen at the other end of the bar shot disapproving looks. Aston raised his glass to them, slopping a little over the rim. 'Hey, if you're interested, why not come over and join us, eh? We could have ourselves a party. Go hit the clubs. It's Friday night, after all. And everyone knows that Friday night's party night.'

A whisper passed between the women and they went back to their drinks, avoiding eye contact, doing their best to ignore him.

'That's enough, Paul,' George whispered as she grabbed his arm and led him from the bar.

He went willingly, albeit a little unsteadily. It

was still early, not quite seven, and the Red Lion was quiet, the staff gearing up for the Friday night rush. George found a quiet nook and guided him into a seat. He thumped down hard, took a slug of his drink. Technically, he should still be at work – his hours were currently 24/7 – but you can only bang your head against a brick wall for so long. Around five he'd thrown up his hands and admitted defeat. He hadn't been able to get out of the office fast enough. He'd walked the streets for a while, taking turns at random, not caring where he was going. He knew where he wasn't going, and that was back to his empty flat. The last thing he needed was to spend the evening staring at four walls, his only entertainment being the groans and squeaks of the couple upstairs, an in-your-face reminder of his own fucked-up love life.

When Aston had got bored of walking he'd sloped into the nearest pub and started downing doubles. Somewhere between the third and fourth drink he'd phoned George and ranted at her for a bit, and when he eventually paused to take a breath she'd managed to ask where he was. The barman had been able to help out on that one and she'd told him to stay put till she got there. She could have saved her breath. There was a bar full of booze to keep him occupied and he wasn't going anywhere.

'What's going on?' Aston said into his glass. 'Why me, eh? What did I do to deserve this?'

'It's not that bad.'

'And how do you work that one out, George? Laura's left me and there's a good chance I'm having a nervous breakdown.'

'You're not having a nervous breakdown, Paul.'

'Well, that's what it feels like.'

'Do you want to talk about it?'

Aston emptied his glass. 'It's the nightmares I find hardest to deal with. It's driving me mad, George. Waking up in the early hours dripping in sweat and feeling like I'm suffocating. Then you're wide awake, counting the numbers on the bedside clock, and those hours before dawn can be so fucking long.'

'It sounds awful.'

'Drinking helps. If I was sober I don't think I could cope with it.'

'Are you sure that drinking isn't making it worse?' George waited till she had his full attention. 'Paul, I know you don't want to hear this, but maybe you should see a doctor.'

'No, no doctors.'

'Hear me out,' George said. 'At the very least they can prescribe you some sleeping tablets. If you start sleeping properly again then perhaps that'll enable you to get some perspective.'

'Yeah, I'm sure the doc will sort me out in no time,' he said with all the drunken conviction he could muster. 'Magic pills to fix these bloody nightmares. Shit, he's probably got some magic pills that'll help me sort out my love life, too.

After all, they've got miracle cures for everything these days.'

'Now you're pissing me off,' George said. 'Listen to yourself, Paul. This feeling sorry for yourself business is so boring. Shit happens . . . deal with it.'

'Thanks for your concern.'

'All I'm telling you is the exact same thing you'd be telling me if the roles were reversed.'

'Enough talk,' Aston said, waggling his empty glass. 'Now, I might be pissed, but I'm not so pissed that I don't realise it's your round.'

'Yeah, yeah,' George said as she took the glass and headed for the bar.

'And make sure it's a double,' Aston shouted after her.

George came back with a glass and a tall coffee mug. Aston reached out for the glass and George handed him the mug.

'What—' he began.

'You've had more than enough,' George cut in. 'A coffee might help sober you up a bit.'

'One more drink isn't going to hurt.'

'Paul, it's just gone seven and you're already wasted. I don't care what sort of day you're having, that's not good. Now, what you're going to do is drink up your coffee like a good boy.'

Aston lifted his mug in a toast and sipped the strong, hot coffee. 'You're a hard woman, Georgina Strauss, a hard woman indeed.'

George lifted her glass to her mouth, paused. 'Okay, why don't you tell me about Mac? You mentioned something on the phone, but I wasn't able to make much sense of it because you were slurring.'

Aston pressed a finger to his lips and shushed. 'Need to know,' he whispered.

George smiled. 'And I need to bloody well know.'

Aston told the story as well as he was able to, filling George in with the details of his meeting with Kinclave and Katrina. When he finished he gave her the low-down on his fight with Laura. It wasn't easy. He had trouble getting his tongue around some of the words. From time to time George would tell him to keep the volume down, and occasionally she'd have to pull him back on track again. Maybe the coffee hadn't been such a bad idea.

'So he's vanished,' George said when he finished.

'Mac has well and truly left the building,' Aston agreed. 'Totally ran circles around the poor girl Kinclave sent to tail him. By all accounts Kinclave crucified her, which was probably a bit unfair.'

'I hope he's okay.'

'The old bastard can look after himself,' Aston slurred.

'And how can you be so sure? Paul, his wife's died, there's no telling how that's affected him.'

'Now you're sounding like that psychotic psychiatrist.'

'Well, maybe she's got a point.'

'She doesn't know shit.'

'You've been working with Mac too long. His prejudices have worn off on you.'

'Whatever,' Aston slurred again.

'I wonder where he is.'

'He'll turn up,' Aston said, then added with a sarcastic grin: 'Maybe he just needs some time out to get a little perspective.'

'Fuck you, Paul,' George said, but she was smiling. 'Okay, if I'm not going to get any sense out of you on this, how about we turn our attention to the next item on the agenda? Namely, sorting out your love life.'

'If you're going to tell me there are plenty more fish in the sea, save your breath,' Aston said. 'I'm really not in the mood.'

'Actually,' George said, 'what I was going to say before I was so rudely interrupted is that she'll come back. She always comes back. We both know that. I mean, you two having a fight – yeah, that's a new one. Like that doesn't happen at least once a week. What do you see in her anyway, Paul? She's so high maintenance.'

'You've seen her . . .'

'Beauty's only skin deep, Paul.'

'Who says I want to go any deeper?'

'You are so shallow.'

A shrug. 'I've been called worse.'

'I can't believe she thought we were having an affair.'

'It's ridiculous.'

'Completely ludicrous,' George agreed as she got to her feet. 'Okay, I think we should get you home.'

Aston got up, linked his arm in hers. 'Lead the way.'

The alcohol hit him the second he stepped into the fresh air. He staggered slightly, took a tighter hold of George's arm to steady himself. It felt as though someone had whacked him around the head with a sock full of snooker balls.

'You alright there?' George asked.

'Fine,' he slurred. 'Absolutely fine and dandy.' He could feel a goofy grin spreading across his face; there was nothing he could do to stop it. *Should have known better than to drink on an empty stomach,* he thought. He tried to remember when he had last eaten; a conundrum up there with working out the meaning of life. He became aware that George was staring at him, had probably been staring at him for a while, waiting for him to say something. She had a bemused expression on her face. 'What?' he muttered.

'Nothing,' she said.

'I'm fine.'

'Yeah, I heard you the first time. Absolutely fine and dandy, wasn't it?'

'Fine and dandy,' Aston repeated.

'Come on,' George said, linking her arm through his. 'Let's get you home.'

The journey passed in a blur. One second he

was standing dazed and confused outside the pub, the next he was sitting in his favourite armchair telling George how wonderful she was, how she was his best friend, an absolute diamond . . . the words kept coming and he was powerless to stop them. Thankfully they'd managed to get a cab; as anaesthetised as he was he didn't fancy another tube trip . . . not yet anyway. He'd closed his eyes in the back of the taxi, heard the driver telling George that if he threw up there'd be a charge, heard George assuring the driver that there wouldn't be a problem, hoped that she was right. The next thing he knew, George was shaking him awake and telling him he was home. It was so much less traumatic than travelling by tube.

He looked down at his hand. The half finished bottle of JD he'd cracked open last night had appeared there. Aston glanced from the bottle to the coffee George had made him, back to the bottle again. He picked up the mug from the coffee table, took a long gulp. It scalded his mouth but he hardly noticed. He put the mug down, unscrewed the bottle, topped up his coffee with an inch of whisky, took a sip. His first thought was to hide the bottle from George, but that's what alcoholics did. Yes, he was more pissed than he'd been in years; however, pissed and full-blown alcoholism were completely different things. He put the bottle on the table.

The toilet flushed, footsteps tapped down the hall. The door opened and George came in. She saw the bottle and marched straight up to him, hand held out, fingers beckoning. 'Give me,' she said.

Sheepishly, Aston handed her the mug. She sniffed it, took a sip. 'Okay, this one's mine.' A nod to the other mug on the table. 'That's yours.'

Aston shrugged and reached for the mug.

George gave a long sigh. 'I hate seeing you like this, Paul.'

He paused for a second, letting her words sink in. 'I'm sorry,' he said eventually. 'Sorry, sorry, sorry.'

'And don't apologise. It makes you sound pathetic. The one thing worse than a drunken arsehole is a pathetic, drunken arsehole.'

'I don't deserve you. Really I don't.'

'Jeez, Paul, give it a rest.'

'No, let me talk a minute.' Aston looked at her. Both of her. 'You're the best friend anyone could ask for. The absolute best. Really you are.'

'You know something, Paul? You're going to be so embarrassed when I remind you about this tomorrow.'

'No I won't.' Aston took George's hand, made circles on the back of it with his finger. He tugged hard and spun her onto his lap. He wrapped his arms around her waist, pressed his face against her back. Her heartbeat thumped in his ear and he could feel her warmth. George tried to move but Aston kept hold of her. She started to struggle and he held on tighter.

'What the hell are you doing, Paul? Let go!'

The more she struggled, the tighter he held on. His hand shifted upwards, moving as though it had a mind of its own. All of a sudden there was pain everywhere and he was rolling on the floor holding his groin and gasping for breath, wondering how the hell he'd got there. He looked up and George was glaring furiously at him, towering above him. 'Try anything like that again and I'll fucking kill you,' she hissed; and then she was gone, slamming the front door hard enough to rattle the pictures. Aston waited for the pain to subside then reached up to the coffee table and grabbed the bottle. He carried on drinking until nothing mattered anymore. Laura, Mac, MI6, George, they could all go to hell.

13

Taking my inspiration from the Invisible Ones, I spent the afternoon in the charity shops, picking up an odd assortment of clothes, things I wouldn't normally be seen dead in: flared brown nylon trousers, a thick multicolour wool jumper, fingerless gloves, and an old aviator hat. Then it was back to my no-star hotel for the fun part. With scissors and dirt I distressed the clothes, made them look as if it had been a decade or two since they'd last made the acquaintance of a washing machine. And then the *pièce de résistance* . . . I dumped the whole lot in the sink and pissed on them, sprinkled them with a little of that authentic street perfume. It's the details that separate the amateurs from the pros.

I dress slowly, reverentially, taking my time so that I can become the part I'm about to play. Someone else's skin . . . someone else's shoes. I rub some dirt into my face and mess up my hair, then I'm good to go. I'm no longer Robert

Macintosh. To pull off a disguise you have to truly *become*, you have to live and breathe your new identity. Nobody from the other world would recognise me. Kinclave could walk past me on the street without so much as a second glance.

The old boy on reception doesn't look up, just keeps on reading his paperback Western. Not that it would matter if he did. He's got that 'seen it all before' aura about him, the eyes of an alcoholic. All he cares about is finishing his shift, getting paid and getting down to the nearest pub.

The trainers are a bit on the tight side and hurt my feet. And that's good. I can use that. The tight shoes slow me down, encourage me to move with a distinct street shuffle. Stanislavski eat your fucking heart out. My first stop is Mayfair, and even amongst all that opulence I blend in perfectly. That's the beauty of this disguise: I can go anywhere and no one sees me. Nobody ever sees the Invisible Ones. I don't stop when I get to the old-fashioned red postbox, don't have to. The white chalk mark is easy to spot. The single line tells me where the drop is taking place. We have two drop sites – one white line and two white lines – simple is always best.

Back in the cheaper streets, I settle down in a doorway to rest my feet. These trainers are killing me. Thinking about the world I've left behind, it's hard to believe I was once a part of it. I close my eyes for a moment and all I see is Sophia. She's crippled and desperate and begging to die, and it breaks my heart. I try to think about happier times, but those thoughts won't come. They're in there though, locked in my head. I want to let them out but they're buried too deep. I open my eyes and close them again. Makes no difference. I can still see her lying on the bed, gasping for breath. I'm on top of her, straddling her. The pillow is duck feather, the case freshly laundered and smelling like a summer breeze, parallel creases run down either side. And she's smiling. For fuck's sake, she's actually smiling. And I have to do it because I can't let her suffer anymore. Afterwards I just wanted to kill myself but I wasn't strong enough to do that. I tried. God, did I try. I dreamt up a hundred and one ways to end it, but I didn't have the guts. I lay in that bath for almost three hours, topping up the hot water, staring at the razor blade, unable to take the final step.

A policeman moves me along and I can tell he doesn't want to get too close in case my misfortune is contagious. I shuffle along the streets with a can of Woodpecker clutched in my dirty fingerless mitt. The can is empty. The cider was sweet and sickly, but I drank it down anyway, telling myself it's the little details that make the difference. I pass a couple more policemen who look straight through me, some Friday night party people who won't even give me the time of day. There are still a few commuters at Paddington, heading home after another soul-destroying day. I watch people disappear down the stairs to the Underground and there are a few anxious faces. It happened once, could happen again. You can tell yourself lightning never strikes twice . . . believing is another matter.

I swap the can for a coffee, paying in silver and bronze, and wrap both hands around the cardboard. I take a sip, making it last. Collapsing onto a seat, I breathe my fumes over the lady next to me, tell her how pretty she is, ask her if she's got any change. She doesn't bother to hide her disgust, just glares at me, grabs her briefcase and stomps off. Good. It was her seat I wanted. Holding the coffee in one hand, I take a sip. The fingers of my free hand brush the underneath of the seat, a movement so smooth no one would have noticed. I unclip the magnetic holder and my heart speeds up. It's got nothing to do with the coffee, either.

Those bastards are going to love what I've got planned next.

PART TWO

The Third Choice

It is a man's own mind, not his enemy or foe, that lures him to evil ways.

Buddha

14

It's been years since I've been down this way and it takes a while to find the right place. Tall buildings stretch up on both sides of the narrow cobbled street, crooked and dirty and grey. I stop at a shop halfway along, a building that's a monument to neglect. Nothing's changed since I was last here. The same red paint is smeared on the doors and the window frames, cracked and chipped and blistering, the wood underneath turning black. The same rusty sign hangs above the door, creaking in the breeze. I can just about make out the shop name. Faded gold letters on black:

Fogarty's Fancy Dress
Established 1975

The door has swollen over the years but I get it on the second attempt. One short, sharp push and it falls open, the bell jangling above my head. I step into the preserved atmosphere, a world of mothballs and dust and stale tobacco smoke. Butterfly colours sparkle in the shop's dim light. The costumes take up every square inch, crammed together on rails, each one offering an escape from the mundane. This is the Land of Illusion, a place where you can be anything you want: a pirate, a clown, a caveman. There are elegant ballgowns for the ladies, DJs for the gents; four identical grey mop-top suits from The Beatles' early days dangle together, lined up and ready for the next John, Paul, George and Ringo. Hats and shoes are squashed in wherever there's a space. There's something sad about all those empty costumes, though, something slightly sinister.

'We're closing for lunch in five minutes,' a voice calls from the depths. 'If you want something, make it quick.'

A click as the lock releases. I flip over the closed sign and head towards the voice, squeezing through the narrow gap between the rails, hunching slightly so I don't bang my head on the low beamed ceiling. My trainers glide across the well-worn boards, heels padding. A radio is playing with the volume down low, tuned to Classic FM. Rich harmonies and fiery melodies, notes flying everywhere, a virtuoso performance from the pianist . . . a Rachmaninov concerto if I'm not mistaken. Fogarty is behind the counter, hunched over a sewing machine, his face a study of concentration, eyes narrowed behind black-rimmed spectacles, pins clamped between thin lips. A final buzz of the machine and he pulls the dress out. Sequins glimmer and shimmer, catching the light. He slips the dress onto a hanger, places it carefully onto the rail, then swaps the pins for a B&H. He takes a long satisfying drag and breathes out a plume of smoke. A cough, and then he swivels around in his chair and looks straight at me. He doesn't see me, though. All he sees are the rags, the filthy face under the stubble.

'For heaven's sake,' Fogarty says. There's a touch of Irish brogue in there. Only a touch. It's been many a moon since his boat landed on these shores. 'How do I get rid of you people, huh? For the last time, I don't have any old clothes I want to get shot of.'

'That's no way to treat an old friend,' I reply in my gravelly street voice.

'I don't know who you are, but you're certainly no friend of mine.'

I switch to my normal voice. 'Are you sure about that?'

Fogarty looks me over again, more closely this time. He smiles, and the smile soon morphs into a deep smoky laugh. A spark of recognition lights his face.

'Well, well, well,' he says. 'Mac, as I live and breathe. Fuck me it's been a while.'

'A couple of years,' I agree.

'A couple of years, my arse. Got to be closer to ten.'

'Doesn't time fly?'

Fogarty's around the front of the counter now, the cigarette clamped between his lips. He grabs my hand in both of his and pumps it. Up close I can appreciate how long it's been. He's put on weight, a ton of it, and his hair is pure white. There are deep trenches running across the landscape of his face. None of us are kids anymore.

'So what's the story, Mac? Haven't you been paying your tailor? I mean, those clothes are way past their sell-by date. Way past.'

'If I told you, I'd have to kill you.'

Fogarty laughs and coughs at the same time. Dragon jets of smoke stream from his nostrils. 'Still the same old Mac, eh?'

'I'm serious.'

'Yeah, yeah, course you are,' Fogarty says.

I head for the other side of the counter and sink gratefully into the swivel chair, make myself right at home. It's good to get the weight off. I spin around to face the ancient sewing machine. It's from the ark. Spin back around and gaze at the sea of costumes. 'This place hasn't changed a bit,' I tell him. 'It's still a shithole.'

'Maybe so,' he says, 'But it's my shithole. Tell you what, let me get locked up and I'll go fix a couple of drinks. What do you say?'

'Way ahead of you,' I say. 'Thought it'd be nice to have a chat, catch up on old times, so I locked up on my way in. Wouldn't say no to that drink, though.'

An eyebrow goes up. 'What's this all about,

Mac? Just happened to be in the neighbourhood, eh?'

'Later. Just get the drinks. Can't you see I'm dying of thirst here?'

Fogarty crushes out the cigarette and gives me another once over, grinning. 'This I've got to hear,' he says.

A shake of the head and then he's gone, the bead curtain rattling back into place behind him. I give it a second then get up, part the curtain with the back of my hand. I can just about make him out. He's in a small office, the white hair bobbing in and out of view. I listen hard, making sure he's not making any inappropriate phone-calls. All I can hear is him rummaging through a cupboard, presumably looking for a bottle. Satisfied he's not about to grass me up, I let the curtain gently sway back into place and sit down again.

Fogarty returns with a bottle of brandy, places two large balloon glasses carefully on the counter and pours out a couple of healthy measures. The brandy goes to work straightaway, warming from the inside. I sink a bit deeper into the swivel chair and close my eyes.

'So,' Fogarty is saying. 'What's going on, Mac?'

I open my eyes and he's staring at me through his black-rimmed glasses, looking like a wise old owl, looking worried. He reaches for his cigarettes, lights one.

'Why does there have to be anything going on?

Is it against the law to pay a visit to an old friend nowadays?'

Fogarty takes a drag and gives me a wise old owl smile. 'We could dance around in circles all day, or we can cut to the chase.' He pauses, looking intense, and I nod for him to go on. Fogarty was always a smart one. 'You're here because I owe you one, and you've decided it's time to call in the favour. Am I right or am I right?'

'Got it in one.'

'Thought so. Okay, what do you want?'

'I need somewhere to stay for a while. No questions asked.'

'No problem. And? I hear an "and" in there.'

'And I need a new face.'

'No questions asked?'

'No questions asked.'

'And that's us square?'

I nod. He raises his glass and I raise mine. They clink together and a single crystal note rings out loud and clear. A done deal.

'A pleasure doing business,' he says.

15

Aston was awoken by the telephone and answered on autopilot. Big mistake. His mother's high-pitched voice drilled into his head, serious GBH of the earhole. It didn't matter how many times he told her, she couldn't get her head around the idea that you didn't have to shout. As far as she was concerned the only way the person on the other end was going to hear was if you BELLOWED INTO THE MOUTHPIECE, like an Englishman abroad trying to get the natives to understand. He glanced at the bedside clock, experienced a confused moment or two when he couldn't work out if the twelve referred to midday or midnight . . . when was the last time he'd slept past noon? He rolled over and hit the handsfree button, rolled back and pulled the pillow over his head. Thankfully, his mother didn't need anyone else in order to have a conversation; all she needed was a sounding board. While she ranted, Aston assessed his condition. He could move his fingers and toes, and had a raging hard-on, which was a good start. His head was a different story. Whenever he opened his eyes it felt as though someone was using his brain as a pincushion. Best keep them closed. The darkness was soothing, a balm to ease the pain.

He got the gist of his mother's rant without really listening; her current agenda had been fixed by the events of 18/8. She was convinced that the country was at war, that the Terrorists – and whenever she talked about them they always merited a capital 'T' – had invaded. Even in Middle England they were at large, planting bombs in phone boxes, planning to kidnap her, committing all sorts of atrocities. The sleepy little village of Great Bedwyn was next on their target list. Obviously. Terrorists the world over were all lining up to take potshots at a tiny corner of Wiltshire nobody had heard of. If you wanted to grab a headline, where else would you attack? New York? LA? Paris? Aston had given up trying to convince her that her life wasn't in danger, that she had more chance of winning the lottery than being caught up in a terrorist attack. The odds for winning the lottery were in the region of 14,000,000-1; the chances of being blown to bits in a terrorist attack in Wiltshire were double that . . . shit, make that treble. To start with he'd been understanding. He realised she was genuinely frightened. 7/7 had scared people half to death, but the fear had faded; time not only healed, it created distance and built walls to hide the fear behind. With every passing week, the atrocity slipped further back in your memory; life slowly returned to normal. Yes, it had happened once, you told yourself, but lightning didn't strike twice . . . except it had, and with this latest attack that wall had come tumbling down and left everyone wondering what was going to happen next. Because something else had to happen. A natural reaction, Aston supposed, and one the terrorists (and he wasn't going to encourage his mother by referring to them with a big fat 'T') wanted. He'd patiently explained that by acting this way she was playing into their hands. Terrorism was based on fear, he told her. The terrorist act was secondary to the psychological effect. Terrorists wanted to scare people, to stop them in their tracks and get them thinking: *My God, this could happen anywhere, at any time.* And as soon as you started thinking like that, the bad guys had won. They wanted to cause chaos and disruption; they wanted flights turned back in midair because a passenger has a couple of wires hanging from her jacket and it might be a bomb; they wanted people looking over their shoulders wondering if they were going to be next.

Of course his mother hadn't listened to a single word. The Terrorists were out to get her. End of story.

Aston laid in bed, head pounding in time with the rhythm of her words, wishing she'd go bother someone else. He loved her, but this was too much. He had the hangover from hell and she really wasn't helping. His subconscious picked up the word 'London' and he tuned in, alarm bells clanging, a cold sweat creeping from his pores. Not good. Surely she wasn't planning a visit. Dealing with her at the end of a phone was one thing, dealing with her in person was another matter altogether. If she came to stay there'd be no escape. He listened intently, carefully piecing her words together. Not easy when her words were rattling around like a scattering of jigsaw pieces in the bottom of a box; put them together right and you got to see the big picture, otherwise you'd be left scratching your head. The last piece dropped into place and he breathed a sigh of relief. She wasn't planning to invade. From what he could make out, Roy had managed to get tickets for the Last Night of the Proms. And the reason for the call, the thing she had interrupted his hangover for . . . she wanted to know if they were going to be safe from the Terrorists.

When he finally got rid of her, he pulled the phone out of the socket and closed his eyes. Five minutes later, too wired to sleep, he got up and stood in the shower. His head was filled with unpleasant images of the previous day's events, flashbacks that made him cringe. Things he'd done; things he'd said. Laura was right. Not about him being an alcoholic, but carry on down this road and he'd end up with a liver made of stone and burst veins erupting from his nose. Was that what he wanted? To finish his days lying in a hospital bed with skin the colour of old parchment, his internal organs shutting down one by one? It wasn't a pretty picture.

And he wouldn't be the first spy taken down by booze. MI6 was littered with casualties. And it wasn't just MI6. MI5 and the boys in blue had their fair share of casualties, too. It was easy to pass the blame. They were working in a high-stress environment, putting their lives on the line. They needed a release and alcohol was perfect. Down a couple of beers and let off a little steam. Or how about this one? It was a part of the job. They'd drilled that into them at The Fort. Hard days of training during the day, followed by harder nights of drinking, the instructors goading you on to have just one more because they got a kick out of seeing you hungover the next morning. But boy could you hold your drink by the end of the IONEC. Then there was the macho element, the idea that because you could drink more than Smithy in the Far East Controllerate or Gary over in I/Ops that somehow made you better at your job. Yes, he could find dozens of justifications, little things he could tell himself to feel better, but it was all bullshit. The bottom line was that you either chose to drink, or you chose not to drink. You chose to be weak or chose to be strong.

Aston let the water pound at him, jagging his skin. He turned up the heat and watched his skin turn red, pitched his face into the spray. Another flashback. He had a hold of George and she was struggling, trying to get loose. Jesus, had he really sunk that low? He felt his face heat up by another couple of degrees, and this had nothing to with the water temperature. What a twat! How the hell was he ever going to make it up to her? He banged the shower off, reached for a towel and dried himself. The first thing to do was to knock the booze on the head, at least for the foreseeable future. Then the hard bit . . . apologising to George. That was one hell of a slice of humble pie he was going to have to swallow. Look on the bright side, though. Okay, so today hadn't got off to the best start – the rant from his mother he could have done without, and this hangover was fierce – but there was absolutely no way it could be any worse than yesterday. Nothing could match that.

Fingers crossed.

16

I follow Fogarty up to the flat above the shop. The sign on the front door stating he's been called away on a family emergency will ensure we're not disturbed. The fact that he has no family is irrelevant. The stairs are narrow, no carpets, the floorboards shined to a high gloss over the years. Halfway up, Fogarty's out of breath. He rests for a moment, hand on the banister, and coughs a lump of phlegm into his handkerchief. He turns to me with apologies in his eyes.

'The fags'll kill you,' I tell him.

'No shit.' He checks out the hankie then stuffs it back into his pocket and carries on climbing.

It makes me appreciate what good shape I'm in. We're about the same age, give or take a couple of years, but he looks much older. He's overweight, smokes, a stranger to exercise. There's cholesterol as thick as cheese squeezing through his veins. Basically, he's a heart attack waiting to happen.

The door at the top has three locks: a heavy

combination padlock, a five-lever mortice and a Yale. Fogarty covers the padlock with his hand and spins the tumblers. He unclips a bunch of keys from his belt loop. The five-lever mortice gives way with an audible click. He rattles the final key in the Yale and we're in. The flat is cosy, the living room big enough to swing a small cat with a short tail. The place could do with a lick of paint: yellow nicotine stains circle the light fitting and there are light patches on the walls where pictures have been moved. There's an old man smell mingled with the dead smoke of a million cigarettes. The air is worn out. I glance through at the kitchen and can't help noticing there are tins everywhere. They're piled up in crates on the work surfaces, on the floor. Tins of soup, beans, meatballs, you name it. My stomach grumbles. The last time I ate properly was at Carmichael's, and that was a lifetime ago.

'Make yourself at home,' he says.

'I will.' A nod towards the kitchen. 'What's with all the cans? You know something I don't? Preparing for the next World War or something?'

Fogarty looks at me like I'm the mad one. 'These are dangerous times we're living in, Mac. You saw what happened at Leicester Square. It's going to happen again. Mark my words. And next time it's going to be worse. Much, much worse. You've got to be ready for anything. I don't care what the Government says about how they've got everything under control. That's bullshit. I mean, what the fuck can they do? They can't protect us! No way! Christ, I wouldn't trust that useless bunch of bastards to find their arses with a map.'

'You're serious, aren't you?'

'Dead serious.'

And I can see that he is. His eyes are wide and bright behind the glasses, and that makes him look even more like an owl, but now a baby owl that's lost its mother. 'Fair enough,' I say, drawing the words out, playing with him. 'But what if next time, what if, I don't know, let's say they decide to put some nasty shit in the water supply? Some superbug that's going to wipe out London?'

'I only use bottled water,' Fogarty replies, quick as a flash.

'Okay . . . what if they decide to use nerve gas. Crack open a canister of Sarin in the underground, like Tokyo a couple of years back?'

Fogarty cracks a checkmate grin and reaches down the side of the sofa. He pulls out a battered cardboard box and removes the lid. The gas mask has to date back to the First World War, and was probably nicked from one of the soldier costumes downstairs. It's all I can do to keep myself from laughing. 'I've got to hand it to you. You've got it all worked out,' I say.

Looking pleased with himself, he lights another B&H. 'I like to think so, Mac. It's all about being prepared. Being ready.' Fogarty takes a drag and lets loose with an emphysemic cough. Another drag to settle his lungs then: 'You really don't smell too good, you know. If you want to grab a shower, the bathroom's through there.' He points to the door on the far side of the room. 'Down the hall, first on the right. I'll look out some clothes for you.'

'That'd be good,' I tell him.

'No problem,' he says. 'You know, Mac, it's good to see you again.'

'Yeah, likewise.'

The shower is old and knackered, like Fogarty. It runs hot and cold and the water falls limply, dripping rather than spraying. It's good to get rid of the street stink, and by the time I've finished I'm feeling almost human again. I raid the cabinet for a razor, scrape the stubble away, admire my reflection. I'm a handsome old bastard really. There's a pile of clothes outside the bathroom door. Jeans, a plain white T-shirt, a navy sweatshirt with a light blue sailing ship on the left breast. From the musty smell I guess he's got a load of old clothes stored down in the basement or something. One thing's for sure, they don't belong to Fogarty. It's been a hundred years or more since he was this size.

Back in the living-room Fogarty asks: 'When do you want to get started?'

'Ready when you are.'

I follow him down a hallway, past the bathroom, and into a small box room. The thick black sheet hanging across the window has silver gaffer tape along the edges to keep the day out, and the light from the hall carves shadows from the gloom. He marches across to the make-up table and flicks a switch. The light is blinding and immediate, spilling from the bulbs lining the mirror. There are four on each side, another three across the top. Big bare bulbs. For the briefest of seconds I see her sitting in front of the bright mirror and my heart freezes. She's dabbing mascara onto her thick lashes and I'm leaning in, my lips whispering down the line of her long elegant neck. Her perfume fills me up. She turns her head and our lips meet. My God, she's beautiful. An angel in a red velvet dress.

'You alright, Mac?'

'Yeah,' I say distantly. I feel suddenly empty.

'You sure? You don't look it.'

'I'm fine. Let's get started.'

He spins the barber's chair, motions for me to sit down, turns it so I face the mirror. I look deep into the glass. She's in there somewhere, hidden in the glacial depths.

'What's it to be?' Fogarty asks, sounding oddly like a barber.

'Don't care, so long as I'm completely unrecognisable when you've finished.'

'Old or young?'

It's tempting to have a few years carved off to turn back the clock. 'Older,' I say. 'The older the better. Nobody gives a shit about the elderly.'

A smoky cynical laugh from Fogarty. 'Ain't that the fucking truth!'

As Fogarty goes to work I stare hard into the mirror, practically hypnotising myself. Suddenly I catch a swish of red velvet in the corner of my eye. I focus on it, focus hard, not wanting her to get away again. And there she is. She's smiling out from the glass, smiling for me. I shut my eyes, lost in memories, lost in time.

17

Vienna, 1993

It was a perfect Hollywood moment. The camera zoomed in for a close up and everything else blurred into soft focus. People and objects merged into a background wash, the noisy barroom clatter reduced to mumbles and whispers. The briefest of smiles and a soft look, that was all. But it was enough for now, because it had been meant for him and him alone. In that moment no one existed except the angel in the red velvet dress. She was burning fiercely, eclipsing everything around her. Nothing mattered except the here and now. Nothing at all. Yes, it was a perfect moment from Tinsletown's Golden Era, up there with Bogie and Bergman in Casablanca.

Bollocks, *he thought*, save it for the poets. *But even as he thought this he was grinning away to himself. Truth be known, he'd been coming here every night for the last week, hoping that by some miracle she'd notice him, and knowing that was as likely as Arnold Schwarzenegger being elected Governor of California. Quite simply, she was the most gorgeous creature he'd ever seen: blonde haired, with the elfin features of Audrey Hepburn and the most perfect body. He guessed she was in her mid-thirties, but age was irrelevant. She was one of those timeless beauties, someone who would turn heads no matter how old she was. And now she had noticed him all he could do was stare at the empty space she'd just vacated, a red bloom rising in his cheeks. If any of his colleagues saw him now they'd be calling for the men in the white coats. Rendered speechless and stupid by a woman . . . come on, pull the other one, they'd laugh. Part of him wanted the ground to open up and swallow him. At the same time, he was more than happy to sit here staring like a simpleton.*

Slowly the room came back into focus. The Hollywood fairy dust was replaced by gritty reality: the harsh stink of foreign cigarettes mingled with the earthy medicinal smell of alcohol; the dark wood and dusty floorboards; the flickering from the candles on the tables scattered around the room. Gradually, the low mumble rose to a muddle of conversations, most taking place in a language he was still trying to get to grips with. He was already fluent in German; however, the Austrians spoke with an accent that was tricky to understand. To complicate matters further, the Viennese had their own dialect. He had a gift for languages and was almost there; on a one-to-one he could pass as a native. Making sense of a barroom full of babble was the ultimate test. When you could do that, you'd cracked it. Trying to play it cool, he poured a glass of red wine and settled back in his seat. His eyes followed her surreptitiously as she worked her way around the room, delivering fresh drinks, picking up the empties, being gorgeous.

This was new territory for him. Stranger things had happened, the few logical brain cells that were still operating told him, but not much stranger. A whole host of new emotions were bubbling inside, emotions he was having difficulty labelling. The only feelings he could positively identify were confusion and uncertainty. At any other time that would have been a catastrophe; there was no place in his world for uncertainty. He'd built his reputation on his ability to make split-second analyses of problems; he could extract the fact from the fiction in the blink of an eye and come up with the ideal solution.

Everybody – well, anyone who mattered – had known that he was being groomed for the Big Chair. He was the only choice because he'd worked fucking hard to make sure he was the only choice. He'd had it all planned. When he became The Chief there'd be big changes. He'd drag MI6 kicking and screaming into the new Millennium. Not an easy task in an organisation staffed by people who would do anything to hold on to the safety blanket that was the status quo. The world was changing fast, and in order to survive MI6 needed to change, too. The Berlin Wall had been reduced to dust and souvenirs, and the Bear had finally been slain. The Cold War was over. This had sent most of his colleagues into a state of collective panic. The Russians were MI6's raison d'être and without the commies to fight they'd all be out on the streets, P45s in hand, heading for the nearest job centre. They'd been running scared because they couldn't see the big picture. Conquer one enemy and what do you do? You go find another enemy to conquer. Ask Genghis. Ask Alexander. The Chinese were being lined up as the next bad guys, but the real threat was from the Middle East. Terrorists and religious fanatics working in small cells to cause a whole lot of hurt. The USSR had been big and unwieldy and, ultimately, that had been its downfall. There was a new enemy on the horizon and that required a new way of thinking. And new ways of thinking were his speciality.

Unfortunately, it would seem that talent didn't count for anything these days. For the last six months he'd been H/VIE, the top dog at the jewel in MI6's crown, the Vienna station. He should have been on top of the world, but he wasn't.

It had come as no surprise when he'd been summoned to the top floor of MI6's HQ at Century House in Lambeth. As the lift buzzed upwards he'd psyched himself up to savour every single second. This was it. The moment he'd been working towards for more than twenty years. He'd guessed something was wrong as soon as he stepped into the office but his smile didn't falter, not for a second. For the eternity the meeting lasted he was the consummate professional, a stiff upper-lipped civil servant who would sooner slit his own throat than show his true feelings. To pull off the act he had to dig deep, calling on the experience gained from all those years working in the field. He was humble and gracious, everything they expected of him, and all the time he was thinking about what he would do if he had a machine gun.

Kinclave was the first to offer his congratulations, which was probably fitting since he was the Brutus in this particular production. And even as he endured the hearty handshake and the backslapping his smile didn't falter. 'It's a wonderful opportunity,' Kinclave had told him, and despite only being Chief for all of two seconds he'd already perfected that air of regal indifference. 'I know you're going to excel in your new role. Just like you excel in everything you do.' And then Kinclave had flashed that polished, politician's smile and it was all he could do to hold back from driving his fist into those perfect rows of white teeth.

That had happened six months ago and even now he still couldn't believe it had gone so wrong. On paper he was far superior to Kinclave. Unfortunately, MI6 was no longer about spying. It was about budgets and targets, and all the rest of that corporate crap. That's where Kinclave came in. He was a civil servant, not a spy – able to smarm and brown-nose with the best of them. The Powers That Be had decided MI6 needed a figurehead rather than a leader . . . it wasn't fucking fair. All that hard work, and for what? A pat on the back; a thanks-for-all-the-hard-work-here's-the-consolation-prize. Fuck them. Fuck all of them.

Heading up the Vienna station was a prestigious post, but it didn't compare to being Chief. And he'd seen it for what it was straightaway. An attempt to appease. Throw the dog a big, juicy bone and he'll be happy. Unfortunately, this bone wasn't near big enough, nor juicy enough. The reality of the situation was that his career had stalled. He'd do his three years in Vienna and then it would be back to London for a series of high-profile positions, which would see him through to retirement. But as for being Chief – well, he'd missed that particular boat.

Could have been worse, *he told himself as he sipped his wine,* could've ended up in charge of a station in a tiny corner of Africa no bugger had ever heard of. *At least Kinclave had spared him that particular hell. Mind you, if the positions had been reversed, he wouldn't have thought twice about shipping Kinclave off to the back of beyond. In fact, he'd had a suitable station already picked out.*

He was being careful with the wine: only sipping, closely monitoring the level in the bottle. He already felt light-headed and giddy, and that was after one glass. If he didn't watch out he'd be stripped of his ability to speak, and that wouldn't do. He'd already decided that tonight was the night he would talk to her. There was no way he was going to screw that up by being drunk. Even thinking about talking to her had doubled his heart rate and made his palms clammy. How crazy was that? Here was someone who could make life and death decisions reduced to a quivering jellyfish.

And all he was going to do was talk to her, he told himself for the umpteenth time. That's all. Just talk. What was so wrong about wanting to find out a bit more about her? Where she was from, what she enjoyed doing, that sort of thing. The plan was a simple one . . . as all the best plans were. Like the good spy he was, he'd already ascertained that she wasn't married. No ring on her wedding finger; no marks where the ring should be. That would make life easier. A husband would complicate matters. If there was a boyfriend . . . well, he'd cross that bridge when he came to it. First off, he would chat to her, and when he judged the time was right, he'd ask her out for dinner. Nothing heavy, like a date, just dinner for two people who perhaps had a few things in common . . . Yeah, right. Who was he trying to kid? The bottom line was that he wanted to fuck her every which way and then, when he'd exhausted his repertoire, invent a few new moves.

He watched her glide between the tables, stopping to talk to the punters, a smile and a few words for each one, graciousness personified. She stepped up to the bar and someone bought her a drink, a tall man with glasses and receding ginger hair. She lifted the drink to her lips, sipped, the fingertips of her free hand briefly touching the sleeve of Ginger's jacket in response to something he said. A joke perhaps, judging by the way she giggled into her hand. She turned from the bar and he watched her walk across the room, enjoying the way her hips swayed from side to side inside the red dress. That had to be one of the sexiest walks he'd ever seen. He carried on watching, wondering where she was headed, who the lucky person was, then gradually it dawned on him that she was heading for him, that he was the lucky one, that she was now watching him as intently as he was watching her. She sat down without being invited and placed her drink on the table. It was in a long glass. A waft of coconut drifted over the table. Malibu and coke.

'My name is Sophia,' she said. Her German was

good, but she was no native; it was schoolbook German, sterile and lacking the twists and turns the Austrians used to make the language their own. There was an accent there he couldn't quite place. Usually he was good at accents, but he was having trouble thinking straight. From a distance she'd been gorgeous, but up close, so close that he could smell that she was wearing his favourite perfume – Opium – she went way beyond gorgeous.

Later, when he had time to think through what happened, he would keep coming back to this moment. This was the moment he realised that he wanted more than a quick roll and a 'thanks for a great time, I'll call . . .', which tended to be his usual way of doing business. For the first time in his life he wanted the earth to move, wanted the fireworks, the happy ever after. He'd built his life on logic and rationality, and the emotions he was currently experiencing were so illogical he didn't know how to begin analysing them. Whichever way he examined the situation there was no getting away from the fact that he was head over heels about this woman.

Much later, when he was able to look at things with a more rational eye, the question he kept coming back to was whether or not he would have done anything differently. Whether, if he'd been able to see into the future, he would have just got up and walked out of that bar and never looked back. It was one question he never managed to find a satisfactory answer for. But anyway, the question was irrelevant. The second she sat down, placed her glass on the table and told him her name, it was a done deal.

And much, much later, in the bleak minutes before dawn, lying awake and staring into the darkness, he would think that in some warped way they had deserved each other.

18

'Sorry,' Aston said in a small, pathetic voice. His face appeared from behind the huge bouquet: lilies, roses, carnations, an explosion of colour and smell. He smiled broadly, trying to ignore his aching head.

'Piss off, Paul. I don't want to talk to you.' George was peering through the crack in the door, fingers playing with the brass intruder chain, face darker than thunder.

Aston shuffled on the doorstep, holding the bouquet at arm's length. 'Please take it,' he said. 'I chose it myself. Went into the shop and everything. You know how those places play havoc with my hay fever.'

'You don't get hay fever.'

'Don't be like that, George. I've said I'm sorry. Bought you flowers. What more do you want?' Another forced smile. Someone was hammering nails into his skull. He stretched the smile as wide as it would go, pushing through the pain barrier.

'Do you think a bunch of flowers makes up for what you did? Do you think it even comes close?'

Aston gave it his best little-boy-lost look. 'Look, George, I am so very, very sorry. But I wa—'

'If you're about to tell me you were pissed, then I'm going to take that bunch of flowers and plant them where the sun don't shine. Being drunk is no excuse for what you did.'

'I know.' Aston stared at his feet. His arm drooped to his side, the heads of the flowers brushing the doorstep.

'You're lucky I only elbowed you in the bollocks. Have you got any idea how close I came to castrating you?' George narrowed her eyes and unconsciously fingered the intruder chain.

'Look, George. I really am sorry for what I did. Really I am. Now are you going to let me in or are you going to keep me standing out here for the rest of the day? Because I'll stand here all day if that's what it takes. Stand here all weekend if necessary.'

George shook her head, the tight black curls trapped in the scarlet scrunchy waving from side to side. The door closed, the chain rattled. She opened it and stood to one side. Aston moved quickly before she changed her mind. He handed her the flowers and headed for the lounge, doing some fancy footwork to get through the junk in the hall. There were cardboard boxes every-where, a bicycle, an old chest of drawers. If he hadn't known better he would have thought George was moving out. The lounge wasn't any tidier, and Aston had to gather the clothes scattered on the sofa into one big pile to get a seat. 'A coffee and some aspirin wouldn't go amiss,' he called out.

'Don't push it, Paul,' George shouted back from the hall. 'You're still on probation. The flowers were a good start but you've still got a ton of sucking up to do yet.'

'Come on, George. Give me a break. I'm dying here.'

Aston heard her stomp off in the direction of the kitchen. Cupboards banged and mugs rattled. She returned with coffee and painkillers, handed the tub to Aston. He shook out a couple of tablets and knocked them back with a slug of sweet, black coffee. 'Thanks,' he said.

'Don't mention it.' George lifted a pile of books from the armchair and looked around for somewhere to put them. They ended up on top of the telly, the flat's last free surface. Aston wasn't the tidiest person in the universe – Laura reminded him of this on a regular basis – but his untidiness was nothing compared to George's. Junk was piled up in every corner, against every wall. One box was filled with doll parts: heads, legs, arms, torsos; a macabre collection that would have kept a psychiatrist busy for a year. There were piles of books, yellowing newspapers, magazines dating back to the beginning of time.

'You knew Mac better than most, Paul. If you were him, where would you go?'

Aston thought for a moment then shook his head. 'I wouldn't even like to hazard a guess. If there's one thing I've learnt over the last couple of days, it's that I never really knew Mac.'

'You keep saying that, but I disagree. I think you know him a lot better than you realise. He's got to be somewhere, Paul.'

'Obviously.'

'Unless . . .'

Aston picked up on the implication straight-away. 'Not Mac. He wouldn't do that.'

'That's not what Katrina thinks.'

'And I'm telling you there's no way Mac would top himself.'

'Okay, back to my original question. Where the hell is he?'

'Fucked if I know.' Aston shrugged and sipped his coffee, both hands wrapped around the mug. He drifted into silence, woolgathering. It was nice just to sit here and relax. That was one of the good things about their relationship. They'd reached that level of friendship where they could sink into silence and it wasn't an issue. George was pretty special. A one-off. He took another sip so he could hide his grin in the mug. That was drunk talk, and for once he was sober. It was over twelve hours since his last drink. On current form that had to be some sort of record.

'I've decided to give up drinking,' Aston blurted out.

'And where did that come from?'

Aston shrugged. 'Just seems like the right thing to do.'

'Uh-huh,' George said. 'So you're giving up drinking. Again. Call me cynical, but . . .'

'This time I mean it, George.'

'Course you do.' George shook her head and laughed. 'Paul, I've lost count of the number of times you've gone on the wagon. And it always seems to happen when you've got a particularly bad hangover. Funny that, isn't it?'

'At least *pretend* to be supportive.'

'Why bother? We both know it's not going to happen. The first excuse and you'll be partying like it's 1999.'

'Okay, maybe I won't give up forever,' Aston admitted.

'That's better. Much more honest.'

'But for the time being I've got to stop. I need a clear head. If I'm not careful it's going to start interfering with my work. It's not doing me any favours, George.'

'You can say that again.'

Aston took another sip of coffee, forced it down. His stomach gurgled unpleasantly, and he suddenly felt shaky and weak. The cold sweats and heart palpitations came next, all of this happening in the space of a few seconds. God, he hated it when he got like this.

'You okay, Paul? You don't look so good,' George said, her face and voice full of concern.

'Never felt better.'

'Yeah, right. You're white as a sheet.'

'I'll be fine in a second.' He took a couple of deep, steadying breaths. 'I'm fine,' he said quietly.

'How long has this been going on, Paul?'

'What do you think?'

'Leicester Square?'

Aston didn't need to say anything. The answer was written all over his face.

George got up from the armchair. She gathered the clothes from the sofa and tipped them unceremoniously over the side. Sitting down, she shuffled closer, took his nervous hands in hers, held them until they steadied. 'It wasn't your fault, Paul. It was just one of those shitty, fucked-up things that happen. There are some nasty people out there. Jesus, in our line of work, we know that better than most. Right?'

'Like I don't fucking know that,' Aston snapped.

'Hey, I'm only trying to help.'

'George, I've done all the rationalisation, rationalised until I'm blue in the face. It doesn't make any difference, not in the long run.'

'It will, Paul, you've just got to give it time.'

'And how long is it going to take? A month? A year? Ten years?'

'You've got to let go, Paul. If you don't it's going to eat you up. Destroy you. And I can't stand by and let that happen. I care about you too much.'

'If only it was that easy,' he said. 'Look, George, you have no idea what it was like down there. It was fucking awful.'

'I can imagine.'

Aston smiled an ancient smile. 'That's the thing, George. You *can't* imagine. No one can. You had to be there. You know, when I got home that night, Laura was asleep on the sofa and the TV was on, tuned into a news channel. All those reporters were going on and on and on, talking like they'd been there, like they'd actually seen it all for themselves. They didn't have a clue.'

'Still having nightmares?'

'Sometimes. That's where alcohol does help. It really screws up your REM sleep.'

'So you drink to stop the nightmares?'

'You got any better ideas?'

George squeezed his hand, looked him directly in the eye. 'Drinking yourself into a coma every night is not the way to go.'

'I think we've already established that.' Aston attempted a real smile. 'I'm not doing the Alcoholics Anonymous thing, though. I draw the line there. Can you imagine? Me in a draughty church hall, sitting in a semi-circle with a load of drunks. "Hi, my name's Paul and I'm an alcoholic". No fucking chance.'

'I think you've got a way to go before we have to go down that route.' Another squeeze of the hand. 'Okay, Paul, if you need someone to talk to, a shoulder to lean on, whatever . . . well, you know where I am.'

Aston pecked George on the cheek. 'Thanks.'

George pulled him towards her until their foreheads touched. She draped her arms round his neck, stroked his hair. 'What am I going to do with you, eh?' Aston rested his head on her shoulder, lost for a moment in the warmth of her touch.

Another long silence, then George unwrapped herself, sat back and said: 'Why did you do it, Paul?'

'Do what?'

George raised an eyebrow. 'What do you think?'

Aston thought for a moment. 'I'm not sure. It was like someone else was pulling the switches.'

'You scared me.'

'I scared myself.'

George looked at him, shook her head. 'I tell you, I'm so glad I'm not you. Your life's well fucked up at the moment. So what are you going to do, Paul?'

'Well, giving up drinking's the first step.'

George smiled. 'See, you're talking like you're on the old "twelve step" already.'

'Ha bloody ha!'

'Okay, you give up drinking, then what?'

Aston shook his head. It was a good question. How did he start sorting out the fuckfest that was his life? 'No idea.' Aston grinned without meaning to. 'I suppose I'll just have to take it one step at a—'

He stopped mid-sentence, distracted by the mobile vibrating in his pocket. Aston pulled it out, saw it wasn't flashing and gave it a puzzled look. Another vibration hit him and his heart went cold. He pulled out the Batphone. It flashed merrily in his hand.

'What?' George said.

'It's Mac,' Aston whispered, although he had no idea why he was whispering.

George crowded in close. 'Well, what are you waiting for?'

Aston connected the call, pressed the phone to his ear. 'Hello.'

Nothing but static for a second, then a voice crowed in his ear: 'Paulie, Paulie, Paulie . . .'

Aston let out a long sigh, unaware he'd been holding his breath. 'For fuck's sake, Mole! How did you get this number?'

'Full of surprises, ain't I?' Mole said. 'You're obviously forgetting that I'm omnipotent. You'd be surprised at the things I can do.'

'You've got something!' Aston said.

'That'll be the understatement of the century.'

'Tell me.'

'Not over the phone.'

'No problem. Where do you want to meet?'

'How about your place? Thirty minutes okay with you?'

'No problem.'

'Your lift works?'

'Yup.'

'I'll catch you in thirty,' Mole said, and then he was gone.

19

'Jesus, Mary and Joseph,' Fogarty says. 'Your own mum wouldn't recognise you, and that's the truth.'

I admire myself in the gilt-framed mirror over the blocked-up fireplace, checking out my reflection from all angles, and I have to admit he's got a point. I look eighty, ninety even. Fogarty found some old-people clothes down in the shop: a mangy brown jumper with leather patches on the sleeves, beige slacks that were ill-fitting and baggy around the crotch, a long overcoat, a battered trilby and a walking stick. I stare into the mirror, still trying to get used to the new face, turn the walking stick over in my hands, tap it against my palm. It's heavy, knobbly and knotted and varnished to a smooth shine.

'I'm impressed,' I tell him. 'You've done a class A job. Then again, you always were a talented son of a bitch.'

'Thanks,' he replies, all bashful.

'We've got a bit of a problem, though.'

'A problem?'

'You see, I'm working undercover at the moment.'

'I guessed that, Mac.' Fogarty chuckles. 'The disguise is a bit of a giveaway.'

I tap the walking stick gently against my palm. 'When I say I'm working undercover, I'm talking deep undercover.'

'I'm not sure what you're getting at, Mac.'

I can hear the first traces of uncertainty in Fogarty's voice. Good. It's time to establish boundaries, show him who's boss. 'The thing is, nobody can know I'm here.'

'Well, I'm not going to be telling anyone, Mac.'

'And how can I be sure of that?'

'You've got my word.'

'And that's supposed to reassure me?'

Fogarty's eyes narrow behind the glasses. 'When I give my word, I keep it. Always have, always will.'

'And that's admirable,' I tell him. 'Okay, down on your knees, hands behind your back.'

'You what?'

'You heard me.'

'You're taking the pi—'

Without warning, I swing the walking stick into the big gilt-framed mirror, smashing it into a thousand pieces and sending a shower of sparkling glass shards tinkling down across the fireplace.

'Jesus Christ, Mac. What the fuck?'

'Do I need to ask again?'

Fogarty gets down onto his knees, using the side of the sofa for support. He puts his hands behind his back, gazes up at me like I'm the Antichrist.

'I'll need some rope.'

'In the kitchen. The drawer next to the sink.'

'Don't move,' I warn him as I head for the kitchen.

'Don't worry. With these knees it would take me a week to get up.'

There's a ball of parcel string in the drawer. I rattle a couple of the other drawers open until I find some scissors, head back. Fogarty's where I left him, hasn't moved a muscle.

'How long have you known me for?' His voice is a mouse whisper. 'You can trust me.'

That's worth a laugh. 'Trust,' I say as I start binding his hands together. 'You're joking, right? Do you think I've lasted this long by trusting? Come on, Fogarty, I had you down as having a bit more nous than that.'

'What's happened to you, Mac?'

'Look,' I say, all calm reassurance. 'I'm sorry, but this is the only way. If it's any consolation you're going to be due a bumper pay-day when I'm done.'

His eyes light up at that. 'How big are we talking about?'

'Will five zeroes do you?'

'Depends on the number at the front.'

'And that depends on how co-operative you are,' I tell him. 'Okay – let's have your legs.'

Fogarty puts his legs out, a lot more eager to please now there's a whiff of cash in the air. I bind him at the knees and ankles, tie the knots tight and snip off the loose ends. I apologise about the gag, but he seems to understand. 'Be good,' I tell him as I head for the door.

It takes a while to get used to the disguise. The latex is clammy and heavy and I want to scratch my face. Problem is I can't get to it. To start with I'm moving too fluently, so I force myself to slow down, work some rust into my joints. *Think Stanislavski*, I tell myself, *think old and feeble*. Down on the tube, a woman gets up and offers her seat. I accept gratefully with a croaky mumble. She smiles from ear to ear, her good deed done for the day. Sanctimonious bitch. The train suddenly stops and all the lights go out. There's a scream from the far end of the carriage, a prayer whispered to my left. Someone else is singing a hymn and a woman near me joins in. A male voice picks up the melody, adding a low rumbling bass harmony. Suddenly everybody's got religion. It's a regular convention of Born-agains. I want to laugh. It's so fucking predictable. God doesn't get so much as a second thought until they need something. Says a lot about the world we live in. Where's the giving? Where's the love? If I was God I'd send a plague down *tout de suite*, wipe the slate clean and start again.

It's only been fifty seconds, maybe a minute, but it feels much longer. The hymns and prayers are still going, more quietly now, like the Born-agains are slowly winding down; a couple more tocks and they'll be frozen in time, petrified like the Pompeians. Everyone on board is convinced this is it. Death is marching through the tunnels with a canister of Sarin in one hand and a bag of grenades in the other. There's breathing all around me, shallow and stolen, each breath taken as though it was the last. A woman is hyperventilating a few feet away and desperately trying to keep her terror in check. A small boy asks if he's going to die, the question straightforward and honest. He has no idea of the implications. When you're dead you're dead, I want to tell him. That's it. There's no celestial light at the end of the tunnel, no heaven, no hell. Death is the end. The lights flicker back on. Ghost white faces are caught in the harsh fluorescents, some wet, all terrified. The relief is palpable. Shoulders relax, smiles appear, there's false bravado all around. Then the clapping and cheering starts up and it's so pathetic. A screech, a creak, a jolt and the train clanks forward. I stare out the window at the carbon walls. A plague would have been nice, but what did I expect? God is dead. How much more evidence do I need?

I get to Richmond in good time and it's a relief

to be away from the city stink. The air is thinner out here and it's easier to breathe. I take my time crossing the road just to piss the motorists off. What do I care? I'm antiquated, a truculent old bastard. Someone lets rip with three impatient blasts of their horn so I stop in the middle of the road and turn ever so slowly, really labouring the point. I wave my stick and mouth an old person curse. Reckon I could probably teach old Stanislavski a thing or two.

I arrive at The Mermaid thirty minutes early, order a half and go outside. The lunchtime rush hasn't kicked off yet and I find an empty table overlooking the river. A child's sun is painted into the azure splendour and there's not a single cloud to spoil the view. Sophia loved it here, especially on days like this. We'd usually come on a Sunday; have a roast dinner then drink the afternoon away. Those were good times. Even near the end I'd still bring her. She wouldn't drink, wouldn't eat; couldn't stand the indignity of it. She let me feed her in private, but that was out of necessity. And I know she hated that, too. Hated me seeing her that way, hated being in a wheelchair with her head rolling onto the support, her hands twisted and useless. Mostly she hated the way people would snatch a glance then pretend they hadn't. That was the ultimate insult, a real heartbreaker. So I brought her here because she asked me to, because I loved her and would have done anything for her, and when she stopped asking to come and started asking me to do the other thing, I did that for her, too. Because I loved her and always will. I stare across the river, my heart and head heavy with memories.

As usual, Christopher arrives bang on time; you could set your watch by him. He takes up his usual position: standing casually, one hand resting on the white painted railing, a glass of soda water in the other. I've lectured him on how dangerous it can be to get stuck in a rut, but he doesn't listen. His gaze settles on a rowboat. It's cutting through the still water, the cox shouting instructions, a v-shaped wake spreading out behind. He sips the soda water. Christopher is lean and clean and handsome, black hair cut short, his dark Mediterranean skin glowing healthily in the sun. He's five years younger than me and doesn't appear to have aged a day since I first met him all those lifetimes ago. It wouldn't surprise me if he's found the secret of eternal youth. He's dressed casually in jeans and a black cotton shirt, eyes hidden by a pair of Secret Service sunglasses.

I sidle up and strike a similar pose. Glass in one hand, the other resting on the railing. He looks at me, looks right through me, then turns away, giving me the cold shoulder, his body language yelling at me to piss off. I don't move. Instead, I drink my beer and watch the rowboat disappear around a bend.

'Hello,' I whisper in my usual voice.

His head snaps round, eyes narrowing. 'Mac?!?'

'Well, I sure as fuck ain't Elvis now, am I?'

'What are you playing at?'

'Trying to teach you a little lesson, that's all. What have I told you about routine? Next time we'll meet somewhere else, okay?'

He answers with an imperial shrug.

'Let's walk,' I say. 'We can walk and talk at the same time. And remember, I'm supposed to be old. Keep the pace nice and slow.'

I follow Christopher down the steps that lead to the river, carefully, taking them sideways and gripping onto the rail for dear life. Christopher gives me a look, shakes his head. A breath of wind scoots across the water, ruffling the surface. The sun is far too warm for this coat and my face is sticky and uncomfortable under the latex. A jogger with a black lab trailing on a leash is heading towards us; further along the path a couple of kids are snogging on a bench.

'What's with the disguise?' Christopher asks. He keeps glancing back, giving me a funny look.

'You can never be too careful,' I say with a dismissive shrug.

'Fair enough,' he replies. 'It's good, though. Fooled me. Incidentally, my associates are pleased with the last job you did.'

' "Pleased",' I say. 'I should imagine they were turning fucking cartwheels.'

'It was impressive,' he concedes. 'A day to remember.'

'Front-page headlines across the globe. Twenty four hour a day television coverage. Impressive doesn't even begin to cover it.'

'You did well.' A pause. 'We've already asked much of you, but there's something else you might be able to help us with.' Another pause to make sure he's got my full attention. 'Of course, you'll be well paid.'

I zone out while he goes into his spiel. He pauses as we pass the kissing couple but he needn't have bothered. They're oblivious, octopus arms everywhere, zits and cheap perfume. They're way too young to be playing grown-up games. The boy has his hand inside the girl's jeans, delving deep. As we pass the girl groans, making the sorts of noises she's heard on TV. There's no hiding the disapproval on Christopher's face.

Out of earshot, he carries on, his sentences peppered with Allah this and Allah that and Allah be praised. I want to ask him why Allah doesn't do his own dirty work if he's so bloody clever. But I don't. I get the general drift. He's looking for a ground-to-air missile, something clever enough to bring a Jumbo down. Or a 737. He's not particularly worried which, so long as it's filled with Infidels.

I stop, turn to face him. 'Come on, you can do better than that. I mean, bringing down a plane . . . No,' I tell him, 'what you need is something that'll really grab the headlines. Something that'll completely eclipse the Leicester Square bombing.'

'I take it you've got something in mind?'

The question is tossed off casually, but I can hear the curiosity burning beneath the surface, the excitement. His smile widens as I tell him. He's licking his lips, but I doubt he realises.

'You can do this?' he asks when I've finished.

I nod.

'How?'

'That's not important.'

'When?'

'I expect delivery any day now.'

'That soon?'

'Yup, that soon.'

'How long have you been planning this? I mean, you don't arrange something like this overnight.'

'A while,' I say. He's fishing, and I'm getting bored.

'How much?'

I pluck a figure from the air, something big and dirty. 'Thirty million.'

'Euros or Sterling?'

'Fuck off,' I tell him.

'I'll need to consult my associates.'

'It's now or never. I need ten million wired to me by the morning. You have till the end of the week to get the rest sorted out.'

'Okay,' he says, beaming. Then in a whisper: 'Allah be praised.'

'Allah be fucking praised, alright,' I mutter back.

20

Vienna, 1993

'You don't talk much,' she said in her flawless textbook German. 'I don't even know your name.'

She was right. Since she sat down he hadn't said a single word. 'Macintosh . . . Robert Macintosh.' He dangled an arm over the table, fingers limp and pathetic. The hand was already out there before it occurred to him how stupidly formal he must look. She saved him from further embarrassment by taking the hand. Her skin was peachy, nails manicured and painted scarlet.

'How about we make life easier and speak in English?'

'Fine by me,' he said. Translating was a little tricky right now; she was far too much of a distraction. It was only a matter of time before he told her that her 'lobsters were looking particularly blue tonight', or something equally stupid.

'So what do I call you? Mr Macintosh?' There was a funny little half-smile on her lips. She was taking the piss – not in a harsh way, just mocking him gently.

'Mac. Everyone calls me Mac.' It was an effort to get that much out. He told himself to relax, forced himself to take a deep breath. What the hell was the matter? This woman had got him as nervy as a teenager on a first date.

She considered his answer for a moment. 'No,' she said, at last. 'I really don't see you as a "Mac".' She studied him closely. 'And you're definitely not a "Robert". That would be too formal.' And now she was staring deep into his eyes, hypnotising him. 'I know, I'll call you Robbie. Yes, that's it from now on you're Robbie. You don't mind, do you?'

'Not at all,' he heard himself say. 'Call me whatever you want.' He cringed. So much for playing it cool. Any second now she was going to remember an important engagement elsewhere and he'd only have himself to blame. He was so wrapped up in his thoughts that it took a moment to notice her hand was lying on top of his. She was reaching across the table, waiting for him to notice. He looked from her hand to her face then back again.

'You are sooo cute!' She laughed. 'It's okay, Robbie. I don't bite. Honest.' She whipped the hand away, grabbed the wine bottle, held it up to the candle to see how full it was. 'What's this? Not thirsty? Well, we can't have that, can we now? That would be such a waste.' She knocked back her Malibu and coke, half-filled the long tumbler with wine and gave him a top up. 'Cheers,' she said as she lifted her glass.

He followed suit, touching his glass gently against hers. 'Cheers.' He took a mouthful, reasoning that drunk or sober he couldn't be any more of a prat. 'So, how did you end up working here?'

'I needed work, they needed a waitress. It was as simple as that.'

'That wasn't what I meant. Why Vienna?'

'Why not?' she said, then added: 'My grandmother on my mother's side was Austrian. When I was little she was always telling me stories about Vienna. She made the city sound like a fairy story.'

'And is it?'

'So far, so good. Then again, I haven't been here long enough for reality to get the better of me.'

'So you just packed up your bags one day, hopped on a plane, and here you are?'

'Something like that.'

'Where's home?'

'Everywhere and nowhere.'

There was a touch of sadness in the admission, which he picked up on. 'No fixed address, is that it? Just going where the wind carries you?'

'Where the wind carries me,' she repeated. 'I like that. Yes, that pretty much covers it. I hate the idea of being tied to one place.'

'Perhaps you haven't found a good enough reason to stay in one place.'

'And do you think you're that reason, Robbie? Isn't that a bit presumptuous?'

He felt his face hot up, felt her hand on his again. When he looked up she was smiling that adorable little half-smile. 'That's not what I was getting at.'

'Don't look so serious,' she said. 'I'm playing with you, that's all. Just having a little fun.'

A sip of wine to give himself time to recover. 'So how long are you planning on staying in Vienna?'

'Until I get bored.'

'And how long will that be?'

'Well, that depends . . .' she said with a flirtatious twinkle, and left it at that.

'Where are you from? Originally, I mean. I can't place the accent.'

'All over,' she said. 'My father was in the army and as a result my accent is a little confused, to say the least. I was born in Cyprus. Spent a lot of time in Germany.'

'That's why your German is so good then.'

'The only way to learn a language is by living there. You can't learn out of books. It doesn't work.'

He opened his mouth and she shut him up by placing a finger on her lips. 'My turn. I'm beginning to feel like I'm being interrogated here.'

He grinned. 'Sorry.'

'So, Robbie, how long have you been in Vienna for?'

'About six months, give or take.'

'And what do you do?'

The question was to be expected and he trotted out his cover story flawlessly, as he'd been trained to do. He was a diplomat working for the Foreign Office and currently stationed at the British Embassy on Jauresgasse in the Landstrasse district. There were some beautiful old buildings in that part of the city, and of course there was the St Marxer Friedhof where Mozart was supposed to be buried, although nobody could say for sure whether this was true or not since he'd ended up in a pauper's grave, and had she managed to get out that way yet?

No, she'd replied, but maybe you could give me a guided tour some time . . .

The lies came easily, smoothly, and for the first time since she'd sat down he began to relax. It was always easier to deal with a difficult situation when you were pretending to be someone else.

'Your job sounds fascinating,' she said.

He leant across the table, caught a whiff of Opium. 'Between you and me, it's boring as shit.'

She laughed and it was one of the most gorgeous sounds he'd heard. 'I've finished for the evening,' she said, leaning towards him, fingers circling the back of his palm. 'How about we go somewhere a little quieter?'

'What have you got in mind?'

'Well . . .' she let the word hang, suspended by its implications. 'I'm currently staying at a pension not far from here. The woman who runs it is a nightmare, but if we're quiet I'm sure I can smuggle you in without her noticing.'

'Oh, I can be quiet,' he said. 'So quiet you won't even notice I'm there.'

21

They got to Pimlico in good time, Aston checking his watch every thirty seconds and feeling like a kid on the night before Christmas. Something had got Mole all fired up, and it took a lot to get the hacker excited about anything. For Mole, life wasn't just mellow, it was real *smooooth* . . . laid back didn't even begin to cover it. Aston wanted to know, right now, what the hacker was salivating about.

'Stop it,' George said as they passed through the ticket barriers.

'Stop what?'

'The watch thing. You're starting to get on my nerves. Relax. We'll get there when we get there and not before.'

'Still on that Zen Buddhist trip, I see.'

'Maybe you shouldn't be so dismissive.'

A mobile went, two sharp insistent beeps. They both reached for their phones like gunslingers. Aston was quickest, pulling out both his phones in a split second.

'Looks like I'm the popular one,' George said, smiling smugly, thumb flicking over the keypad. She read the message and the smile vanished.

'What?' Aston asked. 'What's the matter?'

'It's my mum. She's been rushed into hospital. I've got to go.' George thrust the mobile into her pocket, turned and headed back towards the ticket barrier.

'George!' Aston called after her. 'Do you want me to come with you?'

'No. Go meet Mole. Phone me later and let me know what's happening,' she shouted over her shoulder.

Aston watched George disappear. He'd done enough to fulfil the friend-in-need part of the contract. He'd had no intention of going with her. He knew that; she knew that. Still, they had to do the dance. Life was a game, alright. Like Mac kept telling him. In a lighter moment he'd said to Mac: 'What? Like snakes and ladders?' Mac had run a hand through his soft, hay-coloured hair, then pinned him to the spot with his sharp gaze and said in a serious whisper: 'More than you could ever fucking imagine.' Aston stood in the station foyer for a moment, hands in pockets, then headed for home.

There was no sign of Laura when he got back, which was a relief. The last thing he needed was another row. Perhaps he should call it a day, he thought, not for the first time. The problem was he'd miss the sex, miss those blowjobs. And it wasn't like they were always fighting. No, they were going through a bad patch, that was all. Every relationship went through rocky periods; it was to be expected. Anyway, you needed a little friction to keep the passion sparking. Most of the time they got on fine, and when things were good between them – well, they tended to be very good indeed, particularly between the sheets. Of course, there was more to their relationship than sex. Much more. Unfortunately, at that precise moment he couldn't think what that 'more' might include. Aston laughed out loud, and the demons in his head jigged about and stuck some more pins into his brain. He went into the bathroom, got a strip of paracetamol from the cabinet, popped a couple into his hand and swallowed them dry. Next, he did a quick check of the flat to see if Laura had moved any of her stuff out, to make sure all his clothes were still intact. Everything was how he'd left it that morning. No surprise there. Her threat to move out had been as hollow as he'd thought. *Tomorrow night*, he told himself, *she'll be back tomorrow*. She was so bloody predictable.

The kettle hadn't even had time to boil before Mole turned up. Aston buzzed him into the building and went downstairs to meet him. He noticed the smell halfway down the stairs and picked up his pace. Shit, his neighbours were going to love this one. He was still trying to placate them after the party Laura had thrown – without bothering to tell him – a couple of months ago. The hall was absolutely reeking with the sweet smell of marijuana, and Aston hurried over to the elevator where Mole was punching the button in time to a tune he was humming under his breath. Mole turned, his face alight with a shitfaced grin, the huge spliff poking between his finger spewing out pyroclastic clouds.

'Jesus, Mole, put that thing out.'

'What, this?' Mole waved the spliff in front of Aston's face, took a massive drag. 'Nah, don't think so. I'm celebrating . . . and when you see what I've got, you'll be wanting to celebrate, too. Hell, I might even be able to persuade you to have a little toke. Who knows, eh?'

The lift door concertinaed open and Mole wheeled himself inside, hit the button for the first floor. 'Sorry, only room for one,' he said as the door closed. 'See you up top.'

Aston shook his head and made for the stairs. He jogged up to the first floor and came around the corner to see Mole struggling to get out the lift; he hadn't got enough clearance for the left wheel. Aston resisted the urge to rush over and help. Mole hated it when people played the pity card. The hacker backed up and tried again. No problem this time.

'Fucking things,' Mole muttered and took another toke. He held his breath for a long second then exhaled, smoke pouring from his nose, a Michelangelo expression on his face.

Further up the hall, Aston heard a lock rattling. 'Inside! Now!' he hissed, pushing the front door

open, willing Mole out of sight before his neigh-
bour appeared.

'You've really got to—'

'Next person who tells me to relax or chill out,
I'm going to kill. I mean it. I've got the worst
hangover of my life and I'm not in the mood. Got
it?'

Mole rolled into the hallway. As he passed Aston
he waved the spliff, grinning. 'Sure you don't want
any of this?'

Aston made a funny noise that was part growl,
part exasperation. He pushed the door shut and
followed Mole into the lounge.

'Nice place you've got,' Mole said, looking
around, giving Mission Control the once over.
'Cool stereo system. An Arcam. Tasty! You've got
all the toys, don't you?' His head stopped, eyes
locked on the computer set up on a desk in the
corner of the room. 'What the fuck is that?'

'What?'

'That!' Mole pointed at the computer. 'They
stopped making them a hundred years ago, a
thousand years ago. The last time I saw one of
those was in a fucking museum.'

'It's not that old. I only got it last year.'

'That's what I'm talking about. It's an antique.
You are on the Internet? You know, the world
wide web? Tons of porn, and honeys in chatrooms!'

'I know what the Internet is.'

'Broadband?' Mole shook his head. 'Forget I
asked. I think I already know the answer.'

'Actually, I *have* got Broadband.'

'Fuck me! Wonders never cease.'

'Are you quite finished?'

'Getting there.' Mole rolled forward and studied the front of the computer. 'So where's the handle you crank to start her up?'

Aston leant over and hit the 'on' button.

'Well, fuck me, it actually works. Amazing! Absolutely amazing! Now, while I piss around with this abacus, what say you go get me a coffee. Black, two heaped spoons of coffee, four sugars.'

'Two spoons of coffee! You sure about that?'

'Look outside and tell me what you see. That's right. Daylight! I should be counting the Z's right now, catching up on my beauty sleep. I haven't slept since you dumped that laptop on me. When was that? Two days ago? Three? I tell you, I'm so sleep-deprived I'm starting to hallucinate.' Mole took a drag, squinting sideways through the smoke. He tapped the ash into his hand, looked for something to use as an ashtray. When he couldn't find anything, he turned his hand over and shook it clean.

Aston watched the ash flutter down onto the laminate flooring. 'Jesus Christ, Mole, no wonder you never get invited anywhere.'

Mole wheeled around to face the monitor and started typing. In the hacker's world Aston had ceased to exist, anything that couldn't be defined by a one or a zero no longer mattered. When Aston got back from the kitchen, Mole was sitting staring at a blank screen and looking pleased with himself. He placed a coffee mug on the hacker's left, a saucer he could use as an ashtray on his right.

A final toke then Mole crushed the spliff into the saucer. He took a long slug of coffee, oblivious to the fact that it was boiling hot, and licked his thick lips. 'Right, you ready for this?'

Aston nodded.

'This is really going to fuck your head up. You have been warned.' Mole leant forward and hit enter.

To start with Aston wasn't sure what he was looking at, or why, but he kept watching, searching for the relevance. A CCTV image, the picture grainy and cold. There were people, lots of people, a whole crowd standing around waiting for a train. The camera zoomed in on a man, got bored then focused on a woman. And still he couldn't see the relevance. Who were these people? What was so important about a bunch of commuters waiting for a tube train? And that's when he got it. A sharp intake of breath as the view switched to a new camera. The name of the station was obscured by bodies, only a few letters were showing, but he didn't need any more than that. The camera flicked from person to person before eventually settling on a heavily pregnant Arab woman. Her eyes were burning and her clothes hung baggily, lips moving. There was no question about her condition. Except there was. A big question. She wasn't pregnant. Aston could see through the deception. He could see the explosives moulded into the shape of a bump and strapped to her body; could see the hand in her pocket, the finger stroking the trigger. She was moving towards the middle of the platform now. Moving to where the greatest concentration of people would be (and this alone was enough to freeze his heart; the calm way she was going about her business, the fact this had all been thought out in advance, planned down to the last detail). People were stepping aside to let her through, and Aston wanted to shout at them to stop her. But it was too late – this was history. What was done was done and couldn't be undone. So he forced himself to watch, knowing exactly where this was headed. He couldn't turn away, wouldn't turn away. He'd been a witness down in the claustrophobic dark, and now he would be a witness again. In some strange way he owed it to the victims to keep watching. And then she turned and faced the camera. Only for a moment, but it was long enough for him to see how young she was, to understand how foolish she'd been, how misled.

And then the train pulled in and the screen went blank.

Silence for a long second, then Mole said: 'Hell of a snuff movie, ain't it?'

Aston was speechless. This went beyond shocking. All those people dead. One second there, the next gone, like some sick magic trick. It reminded him of the footage from 9/11, those pictures of the people jumping from the burning towers. This had the same surreal quality, yet it was somehow more horrendous. And the reason for that was because you could see the actual faces. The jumpers had been specks, little black ants; you could tell yourself they weren't real, and it was a lie that was believable because it had to be; the reality was too much to take in. Unfortunately the lie didn't work here.

Then there were the wider implications, and that was one place he couldn't go right now. Wouldn't even contemplate going.

'You going to say something?' Mole asked.

Aston snapped out of his trance. 'Who else has seen this, Mole?'

'No-one.'

Aston ducked under the computer desk and came up holding a blank CD. 'I'm going to need a copy. Can you do that?'

'No problem,' Mole said. 'But before I do, there's something else you should see. The fact it was so tricky to get at indicates it could be important. I have to be honest, though, it means nothing to me.' He hit a couple of keys and a new screen flashed up on the monitor.

Mole was going on about how he was sure that there was other stuff on the laptop, how he was *this* close to retrieving it, but Aston didn't hear. He was staring at the text on the screen. The message was meant for him, of that he had no doubt. He read it, re-read it. Mac had always loved playing mind games and this time he'd taken it to a whole new level. He read the message again:

**HERE'S WHERE YOUR REAL EDUCATION BEGINS
HIGH TIME WE FOUND OUT HOW
GOOD YOU REALLY ARE**

22

'It means something to you then?' Mole was saying.

'Maybe.'

'Maybe, shmaybe. It's written all over your face. Word to the wise: don't play poker. You'll get taken to the cleaners.'

Aston moved away from the computer and paced, distracted fingers pushing through his fringe. Right now he would kill for a drink.

'You gonna tell me or do I have to guess?' said Mole.

'Would if I could, but I need some time to get things straight in my mind first.'

'Told you it was a headfuck, didn't I?'

'Yeah, it's a headfuck alright,' Aston was still pacing, desperate to burn off the anxiety that was strangling his heart.

Mole reached inside his denim jacket for his rusty, battered baccy tin. There was a scratched painting of a unicorn on the front, hippy art in rainbow colours. The hacker popped the lid, took a long, hard sniff. He dabbed the edge of a Rizla with his tongue, stuck a couple of the papers together, a third one across the middle to add strength, smoothed them flat on the inside of the lid. Thirty seconds later he had a spliff up and burning.

'Do you have to smoke that shit in here?' Aston said.

'I'll go outside on the landing if you want.' Mole took a huge hit and held it in. Eyes closed, he exhaled, an angelic expression spreading across his features. 'So who would have thought it. Mac involved in the Leicester Square bombing. There's going off the rails and there's going off the rails . . .' Mole whistled and shook his head; stared intently at Aston through the thick bottle-bottom lenses. 'That's some heavy duty shit he's got himself involved in.'

And there it was. Out in the open. The one thought Aston had been circling away from since seeing the film. And he still couldn't comprehend it. More than anything he wanted to find some other explanation, one that made at least some sense. 'We don't know Mac's involved.'

'*He . . . llo!*' Mole said in a singsong voice. 'What do you think's going on here?'

'All we've got is circumstantial evidence. Mac's as straight as they come. He wouldn't be involved in something like this, *couldn't* be.' Aston's voice lacked conviction. The other night he'd told George he never really knew Mac. Not true, George had said, you know what he wants you to know. Until now he hadn't appreciated how prescient those words were.

'Circumstantial evidence!' Mole was saying. 'This isn't the Old Bailey. We don't need to prove anything beyond reasonable fucking doubt. I think we can safely conclude that Mac is up to his eyeballs in this.'

'Yeah,' Aston conceded. 'You're right. It's just that . . .' Just what? There was nothing he could say to help make sense of this. And, God, he needed a drink. Needed one bad. Needed one now. That mischievous little monkey had crawled right up onto his back and was digging its claws in, hanging on for dear life and deafening him with its shrieks. Aston went into the kitchen and got a bottle of JD from his stash at the back of the top shelf in the tall cupboard. He came back into the lounge and placed the bottle on the middle of the coffee table, stared at it.

'Not sure this is a good idea,' the hacker said. 'You've got this funny look on your face, and I have to tell you, you're starting to scare me a little.'

Aston carried on staring at the bottle. All that mattered was the bottle. Crawling inside the glass and getting himself a first-class ticket to oblivion. In no time he would be stripped of reason and accountability, drifting in a place where every hour was happy hour . . . and how good would that be?

The bottle felt cold and smooth in his hand. A crack as he broke the seal. The woody smell of Mr Daniel's finest filling his nose.

What the fuck am I doing? Slowly, he screwed the lid back on. Then he launched the bottle across the room, throwing it with all his strength. It sailed through the air and exploded with a loud crash against the Picasso print above the mantelpiece, glass fragments cascading in a crystal shower, streaks of whiskey dripping down the wall, golden brown puddles pooling on the laminate floor. The fog in his brain lifted and he came back round to see Mole edging towards the door.

The hacker froze, hands on wheels. He plucked the spliff from the corner of his mouth. 'I really think I should be going now.' There was a tremor in his voice.

'It's okay, Mole,' Aston said in a monotone.

Mole took a nervous toke, cracked a nervous smile. 'We're really sailing through the seven stages, aren't we? We've had denial, we've had anger, what's next?'

'I'm fine.' And this time he sounded more like his normal self.

'That'll be acceptance, then,' Mole said quietly, and tried for another smile.

Aston shrugged. 'Something like that.'

Mole took several nervous little puffs. 'I tell you, my heart's doing about 200 a minute. Feels like it's about to blow a gasket.' Another toke, deeper and more controlled. Then he exhaled a stream of smoke and curses, thumped the armrest of the wheelchair. 'Fuck, Jesus and shit! You're a fucking psycho! Out of control! Completely out of control. You totally scared the shit out of me. D'you know that?'

'Sorry,' Aston said.

'Yeah, well next time you go Hiroshima give me plenty of notice so I can get to a safe distance.'

Aston pulled out his mobile and scrolled through the numbers till he got George's. The phone rang once, then diverted to her answering service. Must still be in the hospital. Aston left a message for her to call ASAP, and wondered, not for the first time, why they were funny about mobiles in hospitals. It was the same with planes. What was that all about? If mobiles were that dangerous terrorists wouldn't need bombs. Why bother when all you had to do was buy the latest Nokia and an airline ticket, hit the big blue and play Tetris till the plane plunged into the ocean.

'No George then?'

'She must still be with her mum.'

'That's got to be a killer. I know how much it'd screw me up if anything happened to my mum.'

'Never had you pegged as the sentimental type, Mole.'

'You telling me you wouldn't be gutted if anything happened to your mum?'

'Suppose.'

'No suppose about it.'

Aston sat on the arm of the black leather sofa.

The place stank like a Jamaican distillery, the smell of whisky and grass completely obliterating the potpourri in the bowl on the windowsill and the air-freshener plugged in the wall behind Mission Control. Laura was into her nice girlie smells. She'd have a shit fit if she turned up now . . . a thought that gave Aston a sadistic buzz. Booze and blow, what would she make of that aromatic combination?

So what was the next move? The only thing he knew for certain was this was one buck he wanted to pass as soon as possible. But who to go to? The police was one option, but he doubted those jokers would have a clue what to do with this. The only guarantee was that they'd find some way to fuck it up. No, for now this had to stay in-house. And there was only one place to go with it. Right to the top. Mac's message was still on the screen:

HIGH TIME WE FOUND OUT HOW GOOD YOU REALLY ARE

Okay, so maybe he could pass the buck, but he had a feeling this was one buck that was going to bounce right back.

'What you thinking?'

'I'm thinking I might have to pay Mr Kinclave a visit. This is way too big to deal with on my own.'

'And you think Kinclave's your best bet?'

'Not really, but if I take this to anyone else, first thing they're going to do is take it straight to Kinclave. Might as well cut out the middle man.'

'Good luck.' Mole took three tokes in quick succession and killed the joint in the saucer. 'Did I ever tell you I hate that cunt?'

'Frequently.'

'Well, I hate that cunt.'

'So, my next problem,' said Aston, 'is that I need to track him down. What's the likelihood he's at Vauxhall Cross?'

'You're kidding, right? Kinclave working on a Saturday? On a weekend? Get real!'

Aston sighed. 'That's what I thought. Don't suppose you've got his home number, do you?' He noticed Mole grinning mischievously at him. 'What, you do?'

'Nah, something better. What would you say if I told you I could give you Kinclave's exact location? And we're talking to the nearest millimetre here.'

'I'd say you're a genius. Then again, you already know that. Or, to be more accurate, you never tire of making sure the rest of us know it.'

'And don't you forget it.'

'Okay, Mole, impress me.'

Mole spun the wheelchair around and faced the monitor. He spread his fingers across the keyboard, like a pianist preparing to perform Beethoven. 'Well, my friend, watch and learn, and prepare to be amazed.'

The hacker's fingers thrashed the keyboard and Aston watched in fascination as page after page appeared on the screen. The homepage for The Royal Sovereign Hotel flashed up for a couple of seconds, and then it was gone, replaced by a list of names and numbers. Aston had no idea what he was watching, but it was certainly impressive.

'Okay, here's the deal,' Mole said, turning from the screen. 'Kinclave is currently residing at the Royal Sovereign Hotel, just off Mayfair. He's booked into room 112 under the name George Kennedy—' Mole tutted, shook his head. 'Fucking amateur. Do you know how many people use their own initials when they choose an alias? Incidentally, he's not alone. Mrs "Kennedy"'s with him as well.' A quick roll of the eyes. 'Make of that what you will, but my guess is this is an away game. Can't see his wife being too chuffed, can you? Impressed?'

'Okay, Mole. I'm impressed.'

'Nothing to it, really,' the hacker said. 'Basically, I tracked him through his mobile. Those things are like beacons. I won't bore you with the science, but if you want to remain incommunicado, first thing you do is get rid of your mobile. Or at least take the bloody battery out. It's not rocket science. Not that I'd expect anything less from Kinclave. His ego wouldn't let him turn his phone off, just in case the PM needed to contact him or something. How the fuck did he get to be Chief? That wanker doesn't know the first thing about the spy game.'

'Probably licked a lot of arse on the way up.'

'Must've done,' Mole said. 'Anyway, I tracked him down to the Royal Sovereign, and the rest was easy. Put it this way, if I can get into Langley's computers then some poncey hotel isn't going to cause me a problem. A little click here, a little click there, and I'm in the register. Then it's a case of going through the names and looking for the likely suspects. A quick check of the credit card details and job d—'

'You have Kinclave's credit card details?'

Mole coughed into his hand and looked away.

'There's something you're not telling me here.'

Mole whistled to himself, flipped the lid off his baccy tin, pulled out a roached packet of Rizlas and started skinning up.

''Fess up,' Aston said.

Mole looked around the room as though it was the most impressive room he'd ever seen.

'You already knew he was at the Royal Sovereign, didn't you? Already knew the alias he'd be using? Knew that he wouldn't be alone?'

'Okay, okay,' Mole said. 'Enough of the third degree. Let's say I had my suspicions and leave it there.'

'You've been cyber-stalking him, haven't you?'

Mole laughed and fired up the spliff. ' "Cyber-stalking". Where did you come up with that one?'

'So what would you call it?'

'Okay, so I've been keeping tabs on Kinclave. Where's the harm? You never know when that stuff might come in handy . . . Like now, for instance.'

'And who else have you been keeping tabs on?'

A long toke, an imperial wave of the spliff, then: 'Ask no questions . . .'

23

It's a pleasant slice of suburbia: tree-lined pavements, leafy and green, SUVs and modern-day Minis parked at the kerb. There are a few people around – a couple pushing one of those trendy three-wheeled baby buggies; a quartet of giggling girls dressed in their party glam who haven't quite made it home yet – nobody who's going to cause me any problems. Why would they? I'm an old fart. No trouble to anyone.

Walking past the house, I glance quickly, checking it out. The curtains are drawn, no one's at home. I consider how much time I've got to play with and decide I've got enough. That's the thing with time – it stretches and contracts to fill whatever space needs to be filled. The house opposite will suit my needs. There's no garden, just a cracked slab of concrete with weeds coming through and a vintage red Merc parked there. The car has been well cared for; the bodywork is immaculate, gleaming, no stranger to chamois leather and wax. I know from previous visits that Clive lives alone. Hopefully he hasn't got himself a girlfriend since we last chatted. Unlikely. It was a windy day in the ugly forest the day Clive was born. No matter how much he spends on flash cars and flash clothes, I can't see any woman being quite that desperate. I know a fair bit about old Clive. He's in his late thirties, terminally single, works in advertising, originally hails from Newcastle, and unless he's lucky enough to be out he'll be dead within the next couple of minutes.

I wait until the street's clear then make my way to Clive's. I place the old-person shopping bag behind the Merc, out of sight of the street in case someone with sticky fingers passes by and decides to get greedy. I climb the three steps leading up to the front door, jam my thumb on the bell, keep it there. Even above the hectic rattle I can hear Clive's heavy footsteps. The door swings open and I stand there gasping for breath, a panicked look on my face, one hand over my heart. My other hand is in the pocket of the long coat gripping the scalpel handle. 'Please help,' I moan. 'Help me . . . My heart . . . !'

Clive takes one look, makes an immediate decision. Like I guessed he would. He's a mover, a shaker, used to making quick decisions. It's good to know that even in London there are still some Good Samaritans.

'Let's get you inside,' he says, and he's already got an arm around me, leading me into the hall.

I lean against him, letting him have my full weight, hear him groan under the strain, feel his muscles quivering. He gets me into the lounge, sits me down on the sofa, turns to pick up the phone.

'Just hold on. I'll get you an ambulance. Hold on, okay?'

There's panic in his voice. This is all too real for him, a complete shock to the system. The lounge is cold and sterile, designer this and designer that. There are hi-tech boy's toys everywhere: the plasma widescreen TV, surround-sound speakers and a tall gadget stack. Sony, Technics and Wharfedale. One bookshelf is filled with DVDs rather than books, another lined with CDs. Tasteful monochrome prints hang on the white walls, placed with the precision of an interior designer; dry, dead flowers sit in a vase in the empty fireplace; a single armchair with a flip-up footrest faces the TV; the sofa looks like it's never been used, pillows perfectly positioned and puffed. A quick look-see fills the blanks in this particular biography. I can imagine Clive sitting here, defining himself through his possessions; it's an empty existence given meaning through credit card indulgences. He's probably so far in the red it would take a dozen lifetimes to pay it all off. It's a lonely old life that Clive leads. My arm snakes around his throat, the scalpel slips easily between the vertebrae at the top of his neck. He folds to the floor, a puppet *sans* strings. A little blood, hardly any fluid, a clean kill. There's awareness in his eyes. He's puzzled, can't understand why his limbs won't work, doesn't get it at all. I watch the life drain away. A disembodied voice calls from far away, telling me over and over to 'please replace the handset and try again'. I pick up the telephone receiver and drop it into the cradle.

I've killed before, but this is different. With Sophia I was setting her free. And depending on the way you look at it I suppose I could be held accountable for all those deaths on 18/8. I don't see it like that, though. Was Mr Colt responsible for all those people taken out with his handguns? I don't think so. Like the old cliché goes: guns don't kill people, people kill people. It wasn't me standing there on that Underground platform with all that Semtex strapped to my belly. I was just the delivery boy . . . what happened after the delivery, well, that's not really my problem, is it? Anyway, every war has its casualties. Like poor old Clive. Wrong place, wrong time, that was his only crime. Why should I feel guilty? Why should I feel anything? Clive was in the way, now he's not. Another casualty of war. End of story.

I carry the shopping bag carefully. It's difficult not to. Certain things demand respect, and this definitely falls into that bracket. I position myself a little way back from the window and train my binoculars on the house opposite. It's a red-bricked Victorian affair, bay windows and black wood-work. At some point in the recent past it's been converted into flats. I get myself comfy and then

I wait. Waiting has never bothered me and I doubt it ever will. I've lost vast chunks of my life hanging around waiting, time I'll never get back. Time lost staring at the walls in another humourless hotel room; time lost in the black hole of another airport departure lounge. But it's not something I regret. You make your choices and you live and die by them. That's the way it is. Nothing I can do to change that; nothing anyone can do.

People parade past the window. I see them but they can't see me. Not that your Average Joes notice much. Blinkered and blind, they wander through life, oblivious to everything except that which affects them directly. Makes you wonder why they bother. I shake off my coat and drape it over Clive's head. Not out of respect – I just can't bear to look at the ugly bastard.

After leaving Christopher, I'd made my way to Shepherd's Bush, stopping at a Pound Shop on the way to get the OAP shopping bag. The lock-up is down a desolate back street and costs a small fortune to rent. There's nothing to connect me to it. Someone called Henry Ashford rents it on behalf of a company that trades under the name Greenfire, a company that exists on a letterhead and has its head office in the Virgin Islands. Not that the landlord gives a shit who Henry Ashford or Greenfire is. So long as he gets his money each month he's happy. If anyone thought it odd that an octogenarian was wandering around on his own down there, they didn't say anything. Don't you just love this city? Mind you, if people were more vigilant it would make life a lot more complicated. I waited until the coast was clear then heaved up the heavy metal door. It was stiff, creaking and squeaking. I flipped on the light, banged the door shut. The Ford Escort van had been extensively modified by a chap who didn't agree with paying duty on the cigarettes and booze he regularly brought in from the continent. It has the same amount of miles on the clock as it did on the day Mr Henry Ashford Esq. acquired it on behalf of Greenfire. The bag of sugar I put in the petrol tank and ran through the engine ensures that won't change. It wouldn't be a good idea for anyone to be driving this around town. I went through the van's hidey-holes, grabbed a couple of grand in notes that disappeared into the inside pocket of my heavy coat, got the bits and bobs I needed and packed them carefully in the shopping bag, laid a plastic carrier over the top to keep them out of sight. The next stop was a small computer shop where the greasy child behind the counter couldn't have been any more patronising if he'd tried. He ended up selling me the most expensive laptop in the shop, two of them, and a webcam. He didn't blink an eye when I paid in cash, probably figuring that someone as old as me wouldn't have a clue what plastic was. We both ended up winners. He got the warm fuzzy glow that comes from fleecing an old fool, and a big wad of cash which will no doubt be conveniently forgotten when he fills in his next tax return. I got a state-of-the-art computer that does everything I need and more, no questions asked.

Clive's leaking shit and a few other fluids I'd rather not think about. Not a nice smell. I squint through the binoculars at the house opposite, scan the street. And here she comes. About bloody time. I watch her fumble in her pocket for her keys, select the right one and push it into the lock. She squeezes inside, pushes the door shut behind. Another scan of the street to make sure there's no one lurking out there who shouldn't be. Looking good. I check my watch, decide that half an hour should do it. I know those thirty minutes are going to crawl by, but I want to be sure we're alone. This is where things start to get interesting and I'm not going to spoil it by making some rookie mistake.

Anyway, waiting doesn't bother me. Never has, doubt it ever will.

24

Outside, tourists bustled through the wide streets of the Innere Stadt, heading back to hotels and pensions, heading for another bar. It was a little after midnight and he wondered how it had got so late. Last time he'd looked it had only been nine, and that had been a couple of minutes ago. She knew exactly where she was going, and he tagged along behind, following her past the grand solid stone buildings; past the bars and restaurants with their colourful facades. The night was warm enough to wander around in just a shirt; it was the middle of summer and the people of Vienna had obviously been righteous that year. She took him down a thin alley that led into a cobbled courtyard. Four buildings crowded around on each side, and in the middle was a statue of a small boy.

'This is where we've got to be quiet,' she whispered.

She took his hand and led him into the nearest building. They tip-toed past the antiquated elevator with its rickety metal accordion gate, headed up the stairs.

She unlocked the door quickly and they fell inside, laughing in whispers. The room was simple: a double bed with a patchwork throw, a pine chest of drawers and wardrobe, a tiled floor with a plain blue woven rug. The only attempt at decoration was a large ornate crucifix hanging above the bed; and this was definitely a Catholic Jesus, racked with pain and guaranteed to elicit guilt from anyone who gazed upon Him. She clicked the door closed, pushed him against it, lips pressing against his. He went willingly, pulling her close, his tongue exploring her mouth.

'I'm not going too fast for you?' she whispered, the words tickling his ear.

'Are you kidding?'

'I was hoping you'd say that!'

She dragged him to the bed, tugging at his shirt, unbuttoning it, trying to wrench it over his head. He lifted his arms and it slipped off. She was already attacking his trousers, unbuckling the belt, popping the button, unzipping him. They danced across to the bed, twisting and turning, hands everywhere. She pushed him onto the mattress, grabbed the legs of his trousers and yanked them off. His hands reached out for her and she slapped them away.

'No,' she said. 'We're doing this my way.'

'Okay,' he said, and he scooted up the bed towards the pillow.

'Did I say you could move?'

He froze to the spot, breathing hard, not daring to move.

'That's better.'

She hitched up the long red velvet dress, high enough to give a glimpse of the top of her stockings. She knelt on the bed and slowly worked her way towards him, straddled him. Her thumbnail dug into his chest and she dragged it down towards his stomach, leaving a nasty red weal. He bit his lip and made to say something, and she shut him up with a slap, the sound ringing off the bare whitewashed walls. She grabbed his face, thumb and fingers squeezing into his cheeks, squeezed hard. 'My way,' she hissed. 'Remember that. Okay?'

He nodded.

'Good boy,' she said, then grabbed his hair, pulled his head to one side and kissed him gently. She made her way to the bottom of the bed and stood where he could see her. A ripping sound as she unzipped. She flicked the dress off one shoulder, then the other, let it drift to the floor. Standing in her underwear – black bra and panties, black suspender belt and stockings – she smiled her funny little half-smile. 'So, you want to fuck me, then?'

All he could do was gawk and nod. Her body was amazing, toned and taut from working out – perfect breasts, perfect everything.

'Like you haven't been thinking about fucking me all night, eh? I saw you watching me earlier, saw you undressing me.'

Slowly, she peeled off one stocking, then the other, resting each foot on the bed as she rolled them down. She walked around the side of the bed, grabbed his arm, forced him to move. Her grip was firm and insistent, the *nails digging into his skin. The pain was exquisite. Kneeling by his head, she took his hands one at a time and bound them to the headboard with her stockings. He gasped as she pulled each knot tight. She slithered off the bed, told him to look at her, demanded that he look at her. He turned his head and she undressed for him. Bra first, then the suspender belt; finally she pushed her panties over her hips and let them fall to the floor. She stepped out of them and climbed back onto the bed, knelt over his face. She ground down and he lapped hungrily. Even though he could hardly breathe he kept licking, feeling as though he might pass out any second, hoping he'd pass out because that would be such a kick. And then he was inside her and he had no idea how it happened. One second he was drowning under her, the next she was riding him. His head flipped back and all he could see was Jesus glaring down at him, condemning him. She shifted slightly, one hand pressing on his chest, the other pushing the sticky blonde strands from her face, and it was all he could do not to come. She seemed to know instinctively which buttons to press, teasing him to the point of orgasm then pulling back, teasing and pulling back until he thought he was going to explode. And then the pièce de résistance. She reached over and, like a magician, produced a silk scarf. The scarf looped around his neck, once, twice. Holding both ends, she rocked back and forth, increasing the tempo. Twisting the scarf around her wrists, she pulled tighter, tighter and his face reddened to a deep shade of crimson, hips bucking in time with her thrusts. Exorcism through intercourse. He could see death, see life. They merged and separated, merged and separated, a heartbeat between them. Timing was everything now. The orgasm ripped him in two and for a split second he knew what it was to be God.*

Rational thought was impossible, common sense and logic had both taken a long vacation. The alarm bells should have been ringing, but they weren't. At the time it never occurred to him there might be a reason why she knew just what turned him on, a reason she seemed to know all about those dark, secret places he thought he'd kept so well hidden. Those realisations came later. And, of course, by then it was too late.

25

'Can I help you, sir?'

Aston was miles away, currently distracted by the woman coming out of the revolving door, wondering which film he'd seen her in. She sailed through the Royal Sovereign's plush lobby, oozing film star arrogance, perfectly at home amongst the rich golds and reds, the expensive marble and bright chandeliers. A male model was draped over her arm, a trinket who looked like he'd probably have trouble spelling his name. Then again, when you looked like Adonis and could pull a movie star, who cared. Aston would have traded his First from Oxford for a roll with Cameron Diaz, any day. He'd been standing in this bloody queue for what seemed an eternity and had zoned out when the woman in front started arguing about her bill. She was French; loud and annoying with a tenuous grasp of English, and it was obvious from the way the concierge was handling her that he wished she'd go away and be distasteful elsewhere.

A polite cough into a hand, then: 'Excuse me, sir, can I help?'

'I hope so.' Aston pulled out the small wallet and pushed it across the desk. As the concierge studied the ID card, Aston said: 'Is there somewhere we can talk? In private?'

The concierge handed the wallet back and motioned Aston towards a small back office with a 'this way, please, sir'. Aston negotiated the desk, holding his laptop bag up to stop it banging, and followed him inside. The concierge had to be pushing seventy, every single year marked out on his tired face. He was thin as a rake with a sharp nose, prominent cheekbones and slicked back white hair. His bright red uniform was immaculate, creases in all the right places, not a speck of dust. The office was small, devoid of any personal touches. There was an old desk that looked like it had been here forever, a computer, a filing cabinet, and that was it.

'I remember you,' the concierge said. 'You work for Mr Macintosh.'

'I'm impressed. It must be three years.'

'I never forget a face.'

Aston silently thanked Mac for being so thorough. MI6 paid monthly retainers to the concierges and head waiters at London's top hotels and restaurants. Most of what they came up with was gossip, nonsense the glossies would have paid a fortune for . . . mildly interesting in a salacious sort of way, and filed away in case it was ever needed, but certainly nothing that would effect the fates of nations. Every now and again, however, they'd come up with a gem that wouldn't have come to light otherwise. It was amazing the things they were privy to. Shortly after Aston started with Mac, the two of them had spent the best part of a week wearing out shoe leather visiting these hotels and restaurants. Mac wanted him to meet 'the folks who work beneath the stairs'. The object of the exercise: to teach Aston that the spy business was a people business. Yes, you could do the job via phone or email, but that was no substitute for going face to face. It was only when you were standing in front of someone you got a true measure of them. Back then, he'd thought it a waste of time. Now he had to concede the old bastard had a point.

'This is a bit delicate,' Aston began.

'Yes.' A slight raising of the eyebrows, a nod of the head to go on. Little tics that gave the impression that discretion was his middle name.

'You have a guest,' Aston continued. 'Mr George Kennedy. I believe he's staying in room 112 . . . with his "wife" . . .'

'Ah,' the concierge said.

'I need to speak to him.'

'Well, I can get a message to him. That wouldn't be a problem. No problem at all.'

Aston made a face, shook his head. 'You see . . . I'm sorry, I've forgotten your name.'

'Harold.'

'You see, Harold, the thing is I need to speak to him in person.' A pause before delivering the next line. He dropped his voice to a confidential whisper to give it the gravity it deserved. 'It's a matter of national security.'

'Ah,' the concierge said, nodding knowingly.

'Somehow one of the tabloids has found out that Mr Kennedy is here . . . with his "wife",' Aston said. 'I don't need to tell you how embarrassing that could be.'

'No, not at all.'

'So, if I could just borrow your master key for a few minutes . . .'

'I'm not sure I could do that. Regulations, you know. Couldn't I just phone his room? Warn him that way.'

Aston shook his head, lowered his voice another notch. 'Wouldn't work. We're pretty sure they've got your phone system tapped.'

'Impossible.'

Aston said nothing, just gave a look that said 'come on, we're both men of the world'.

'Really?'

The concierge was desperate to do the right thing. A nudge in the right direction was all it would take.

'I'm really not sure about this,' Harold said. 'I could get into a lot of trouble.'

'A matter of national security . . .' Aston dangled the words in front of the concierge, giving him the get-out. And now to close the deal: 'Of course, it goes without saying that there will be a nice fat bonus for you next month.'

Harold looked at Aston. 'National security, you say . . . well . . .' He reached into his pocket and pulled out a credit-card-type key and handed it over.

'Thank you,' said Aston.

'Drop it back to me at the main reception on your way out.'

'Remember: I was never here.'

'My lips are sealed,' said Harold.

Aston took the elevator to the first floor and turned left when he got out. He stopped outside 112. There was a *Do Not Disturb* ticket hanging on the handle. He took a moment to compose himself. This could be interesting. He didn't bother knocking, didn't bother pretending he was from room service, that tactic beloved by movie-makers. He just pushed the card into the slot, waited for red to turn to green, and marched straight in.

Mr Kennedy was lying back amongst a tangle of silk ivory sheets wearing nothing but a smile. An open bottle of Bolli was on the bedside table; two half-filled champagne flutes sat next to it. And next to that a thick wad of tens and twenties. There were some nibbles on a plate, caviar and crackers by the look of things. The room was elegantly furnished, tasteful and expensive. Oil paintings on the wall, thick crimson blackout curtains over the windows. There were fresh flowers in tall vases: orchids and lilies in white, purple and blue. Aston got all this in a split second.

Mrs Kennedy was in her early twenties, as pretty and delicate as the orchids. Soft pink skin, silicone tits, and high chiselled supermodel cheekbones. She was sucking Mr Kennedy's cock like it was an Olympic sport, putting her heart and soul into the act, soft bleached hair rustling in time with her bobbing head.

Kinclave's smile vanished the second he saw Aston. He pushed the girl away and pulled himself upright, his penis already shrinking. He dragged the silk sheet across himself and glared, looking both furious and guilty at the same time. The girl's face was pretty and vacant; if she was bothered by the intrusion it didn't show.

'What the *fuck* do you think you're playing at?' Kinclave fired the words out, spittle playing on his lower lip. His face, usually so serene and unreadable, was twisted with rage.

'We need to talk.'

'This really isn't the time.'

'We need to talk *now*, sir.'

'Well, why the hell don't you use the phone like everybody else? Or arrange a meeting? Barging in here like this. I mean, what the hell were you thinking?'

A good question. What the hell had he been thinking? Aston was starting to wish he was anywhere except here. He shifted his weight from foot to foot, embarrassed. When he'd played this scene through in his head it hadn't panned out quite like this. Aston's stomach dropped as he realised that he'd probably be working in some tiny office in the middle of nowhere for the rest of his career. Any chance of a promotion had just gone out the window.

'Well?' Kinclave shouted. 'Are you just going to stand there looking like a complete prat, or are you going to explain what the fuck this is all about?'

Aston glanced over at the girl. 'Not in front of her.'

'She has a name,' the girl said.

'Shut up,' Aston said.

'Sweetie,' the girl keened, drawing out the vowels. 'Are you going to let him talk to me like that?'

'Put some clothes on,' Kinclave said, without taking his eyes from Aston.

The girl slid off the bed in one fluid movement, graceful and agile. She grabbed her clothes from the floor, dressed quickly, picked up the pile of cash from the bedside table. She stopped at the door, turned her hand into a phone, held it up to her ear. 'Call me,' she said to Kinclave and slipped out of the room.

There was a white bathrobe with the Royal Sovereign's logo embroidered in red and gold on the chest draped across a chair. Aston picked it up and tossed it to Kinclave. 'I'm sorry to disturb you,' he said, 'but this really can't wait, sir.'

For the briefest of moments Kinclave had a strange expression on his face. It was the look of a man who'd been living with a secret for a long time and had finally been found out. And as quickly as it appeared, the expression vanished, replaced by a hard poker face. Kinclave pulled on the robe, got out of bed and closed in on Aston. He stood toe to toe, a couple of inches taller, a stone or two heavier, trying to intimidate him with his sheer physical presence.

'I'm going to nail your balls to the wall for this, Aston. Do you hear me? You're finished.'

Aston almost blurted out that he wasn't the one shacked up in a hotel room with a prostitute while his wife was at home oblivious to what her hubby was up to . . . and maybe she'd like to find out. The devil on his shoulder was telling him to do it. What did he have to lose? His career was as good as over, anyway. Kinclave had just said as much. He stopped himself in time. Inflaming the situation wasn't the way to go. 'It's about Mac,' he said.

'I don't give a shit. You could be telling me that Jesus Christ himself was back in town, preaching down at Hyde Park Corner, and it wouldn't make any difference.'

'Please, sir, I just need a couple of minutes of your time. If this wasn't important I wouldn't be here. Believe me.'

'I think it's probably best if you leave now. The sooner you leave the more likely I am to forget that you ever existed.'

'For fuck's sake!' Aston shouted. He had to get Kinclave to listen. A deep breath to regain his composure. 'All I'm asking for is a couple of minutes.'

A long pause, then: 'The last person that spoke to me like that is still pushing a pen in deepest, darkest Africa.' His voice was calmer, more reasonable. 'Okay, Aston, this better be good. If it's not then come Monday you're looking for a new job. Do I make myself clear?'

'Crystal.'

Aston perched on the edge of the bed, unzipped his laptop and booted up. He reached into his leather jacket for the disc Mole had made, plugged the disc in and let the film roll. Then he sat back and wondered how long it would take The Chief to work it out.

The film finished in a wash of static and Kinclave said: 'You said this was about Mac. I don't see the connection.'

Aston rewound to the part where the station sign minus most of its letters flashed up. Blink and you'd miss it. He paused the film. 'Take a good look.'

'Oh,' was all Kinclave said.

'I thought you'd want to see this straightaway, sir.'

'And this is what I think it is?'

'Afraid so.'

'Where did you get it?' Kinclave said, still staring at the screen.

'Mac's laptop.'

'And where did Ma . . .' His voice trailed off. He looked from the screen to Aston. 'Oh shit,' he whispered.

26

My eyes ache from squinting through the binoculars and my face aches from being stuck behind the latex. I can't wait to get back to Fogarty's and get the bloody thing off. A check of my watch and another quick look-see. I've got a good view from Clive's, a hundred yards or so in each direction. Can't see any cops skulking behind the trees and walls, no suspicious cars cruising the neighbourhood. My gut's telling me it's not a trap, and as an early warning system my gut has served me well over the years. In fact, I can't remember a time when it's let me down. I gather my stuff together, carefully pick up the shopping bag and head outside. I fight the urge to jog across the road, telling myself that I'm a fossil, and fossils don't jog. Shuffling along is fine, but jogging is a definite no-no.

I place the bag on the doorstep, get the spare key from its hidey hole underneath Mr Rabbit, the stone bunny that guards the scrap of dirt she calls a garden. In my book, a straggly rose bush and a scraggy collection of weeds does not constitute a garden. The lock is stiff and I have to rattle the key to get it in. There's a knack to it, but I've had plenty of practice. A flick of the wrist and I'm in. She's standing at the end of the hall, gaping at me as though I'm a complete stranger – which, thanks to Fogarty's magic fingers, I am – wondering what the hell I'm doing in her flat.

'Careful, you might catch a fly,' I tell her.

She closes her mouth, opens it again. 'Mac . . . ? Is that you?'

'Expecting someone else?' I pick my way through the junk in the hall, past the cardboard boxes, the rusty old bicycle, the chest of drawers. She takes a step back when I get to her and I wonder how much she knows. Her clothes are baggy, hiding her glorious curves, and providing plenty of hiding places for a weapon. I've tried to persuade her to wear tighter clothes, more revealing clothes, and from time to time she indulges me, but only when we're alone.

'What have you done to your face?' she asks.

'Do you like it?' She's close enough to touch me, but doesn't. She stands staring, arms pinned rigidly to her sides. Normally she would have dragged me into the bedroom by now. I'd be flat on my back, trousers around my ankles, whether I liked it or not. She's a howler, someone who doesn't mind the neighbours hearing. Not the best

I've had, not the worst, either. What she lacks in artistry, she more than makes up for in enthusiasm.

'So,' I say, 'are you going to stand there gawking all day or what?'

She comes to me, hugs me. A quick peck is all I get; there's no passion in the kiss. I take the opportunity to work my hands up and down her body, slowly, sensually. There are no guns, no knives, no cans of Mace. I inhale deeply, my fingers twisting her thick black ringlets, toying with the scarlet hair band. I love the smooth moist feel of her hair, love the smell of coconut.

She pulls away, a disgusted expression on her face. 'I'm sorry, I can't do this. The make-up . . . it's too freaky.'

A nod towards the bedroom. 'Sure you don't want a bit of old man loving? Just because I look like this, doesn't mean I can't get it up.'

'Mac, be serious.'

'I am being serious.'

'I think we need to talk, don't you?'

Without waiting for an answer she heads for the lounge. I pick up the shopping bag and follow. As per usual the place is a bombsite. She's on the sofa, watching me.

'Have you any idea how pissed off I am with you?'

'Good to see you, too.' I place the bag by the side of the armchair and sit down.

'Well, what the fuck do you expect, Mac? You

can't just go off disappearing like that without a word.' Her face is creased, ugly with anger.

'I can and I did.'

'Where the hell have you been anyway?'

'Around.'

'Jesus, Mac! You're fucking impossible, do you know that? I've been worried sick about you.'

I spread my arms in good-humoured benevolence. 'Well, here I am. Safe and sound.'

'Fuck you.'

It's quite sweet, really. She wants to look after me. I reach into the pocket of the old-man coat. There's not even a hint of concern or suspicion on her face. Probably thinks I'm getting a hankie. I point the taser at her and, before she has a chance to register what's happening, I squeeze the trigger. The two needle tipped darts stick into her stomach, the copper cable trailing behind. She bucks and jerks as fifty thousand volts hit home, instantly paralysing her. I watch her twitch on the floor for a while, then pick her up and carry her through to the bedroom.

27

The Batphone vibrated and squawked, and Aston pulled it out, flicked it open. 'Okay, Mole, mildly amusing first time around, but the joke's wearing a bit thin.'

Nothing but static.

Aston took the phone from his ear and checked the display. The signal bars were all up. The battery was fine, too, half a tank of juice. Bloody things were more trouble than they were worth.

'Hello,' he said half-heartedly, not expecting an answer. 'Hello hello hello.'

More white noise from outer space, then: 'How's it going?'

Aston stopped dead and did a quick 360 degrees. Shit! A wide street, a thousand windows overlooking it. He was completely exposed. Tourists and natives jostled past, catching his elbows, giving him looks. Aston ignored their muttered complaints and did another 360, looking for the best place to stage an ambush.

Could be anywhere. He glanced down expecting to see a red laser dot pinned to the front of his black leather jacket, expecting the bullet to slam into his chest any second. His heart and lungs were filled with nitrogen; a surge of adrenaline had pushed his senses into overdrive making everything ultrareal. Colours were blinding, sounds deafening. He heard every single conversation, saw every single face. Smells assaulted him from all angles: petrol, exhaust fumes, Gucci Rush perfume, Old Spice, BO, garlic. Every detail was sharp and vital. A red double-decker flew past, the pressure wave rocking him on his heels. And slowly, slowly came the realisation that there wasn't a gun trained on him. Mac didn't do business that way. A quick stab from a poison-tipped umbrella carried by an assassin dressed in a pinstripe suit and a bowler . . . that was more Mac's style. A quick prick, barely an insect bite, and before you knew it you'd be rolling in the gutter with your internal organs dissolving.

'What's the matter? Not like you to be so quiet.' Even through the mobile's earpiece there was no mistaking Mac's rich baritone voice, nor the accompanying laugh.

'Where are you?'

'Like I'm going to tell you that. Come on, play the game.'

'What do you want? I'm assuming this isn't a social call.'

'And I've taught you better than that.' He

adopted the voice of a weary professor. 'Now, why do we never assume?'

'Because when you assume you make an ASS out of U and ME.' Aston trotted the line out, deadpan.

'Found the computer?'

'What computer?'

'Good boy, never admit anything,' Mac said. 'So have you found it? Bet you have.'

'Like I'd tell you if I had.'

'What's this?' Mac said. 'I'm out of the office for a couple of days and you get all cocky. You're not playing the game. Now what I want you to do is take some time to think about things. I'll call back in five, and you'd better be ready to play.'

The phone suddenly went dead and Aston took it from his ear, stared at it, then released a volley of curses. A woman trailing a small boy by the hand gave him a dirty look as she walked past. The boy stared with big green eyes, head twisting like the girl in *The Exorcist*. Mum picked up her pace, getting as much distance between her son and the bad man as possible. Aston glared and cursed at the phone some more. Could he have handled that any worse? *But I was caught off guard.* Not much of an excuse, and certainly not an excuse Mac would have accepted. No, Mac was probably out there right now, laughing his tits off because he'd managed to get one over on him again.

So, what now? Wait for Mac to get back in touch? No, too passive. *You're not playing the game,* he'd said. Fair enough, he'd take the game to him. He pulled out his other phone, found Mole's number, hit dial and prayed he wasn't going to get fobbed off onto Voicemail. Mole answered on the second ring with a cheery 'Watcha!'

'Where are you, Mole?'

Mole hesitated, then said: 'Well, I'm kind of still at your place. See, it's like this . . . when I saw that widescreen TV all I could think of was that it'd be perfect for watching porn on. And that surround system you've got is a beast! Anyway, the good news is that you've now got round-the-clock porn and it won't cost you a penny.'

'Mole, shut the fuck up. I've just spoken to Mac.' The silence on the other end told him that he'd either got Mole's attention or the signal had failed. 'Mole, you still there?'

'You've got my full and undivided. What do you need me to do?'

'When he phones back, can you trace him?'

'No problem.'

'And you can do that from my place?'

'Your abacus ain't worth shit, but it's good enough to get me into my computers back at Vauxhall Cross. I'll use the systems there to do the grunt work.'

'He'll phone me on the Batphone.'

'I'd appreciate it if you could buy me five minutes.'

'Mac'll phone when he phones – just be ready, okay?'

'Okay,' the hacker said. 'Remember: keep him talking as long as poss.'

Aston clicked off the mobile, dropped it in his pocket and pulled out the Batphone. He stared at the unlit screen, willing it not to flash until Mole got his act together. A quick glance to get his bearings, looking for the nearest tube station. There – the red, white and blue Underground sign for Bond Street a couple of hundred metres away on the other side of the road. He dashed out behind a black cab, the Batphone clutched tightly in his hand, making a suicidal bid for the other side. Motorists fired their horns, brakes squealed, and Aston kept going. He sprinted along the gutter then bounced up onto the pavement, pushing through the crowds, spinning shoppers out the way, ignoring their protests.

Twenty metres from the station entrance, the Batphone went. Aston pulled up and leant against the cool glass of a jeweller shop. The window display was a magpie's treasure trove of glitter and shine: watches, rings and pretty things. A deep breath before he connected the call.

'You ready to play?'

'Why did you kill all those innocent people?'

A long silence, and Aston was convinced Mac was going to hang up again. He listened intently, searching for clues to Mac's whereabouts. It was quiet. No traffic noise; no people noise. No planes, no trains, no construction work. Not a single sound to help him ID the location.

'Interesting opening move. Straight on the offensive.' Mac was back, using the professorial tone that wound Aston up so much, that condescending 'look how smart I am and how stupid you are' voice. 'But let's examine it, shall we? You said: "all those innocent people", which means you know about Leicester Square.'

Aston said nothing.

'I'll take that as a "yes".'

'So why *did* you do it?'

'Well, there's the thing. I didn't actually kill them, did I? Way I remember it, one of Allah's finest marched onto the platform and blew themselves to fuck.'

'Don't split hairs, Mac. How much did they pay you?'

'You think I did this for the money?'

'Well, what then? You did it because you wanted to get in Mohammed's good books? Bollocks, Mac!'

'Maybe I did it to get your attention.'

'Not buying,' Aston said. 'If you wanted my attention why didn't you just pick up the phone? Or how about this: why not shout at me? That usually works.'

'Ah, but these are the End Days, aren't they?'

'And what the hell's that supposed to mean?'
Got to keep him talking got to keep him talking doesn't matter that he's talking crap got to . . .

'Never read your Bible? Armageddon's just around the corner. The world's coming to an end and there's nothing any of us can do about it.'

'So you're a cynical old fuck,' Aston said. 'Tell me something new. Anyway, since when have you had religion?'

'Religion's got nothing to do with it. Does God need religion to exist?'

'So you're God now,' Aston said. 'Always knew you were arrogant but this takes it to a whole new level.'

'Let's face it, I can't do any worse than the current guy.'

'Okay,' Aston said. 'Let me get this straight: to get my attention you arrange to have a couple of hundred commuters blown up in an underground station?' His voice was calm but he was burning white hot, furious on behalf of the victims, their families, everyone affected by the atrocity. And Mac knew that, too. The bastard was playing with his head and loving every minute.

'That's about the long and short of it.'

'Kind of smacks of overkill, don't you think?'

'Got your attention, though, didn't it?'

'This isn't a game.'

'That's where you're wrong. That's exactly what this is. Life's nothing but one big fuck-off game. And like all games there are winners and losers. Some people win big; some people lose big.'

'People are dead. A lot of people.'

'Like I said: winners and losers. People die every day. Nothing I can do about that; nothing anyone can do. That's just the way it is.'

'That's a pretty cold way of looking at things.'

'No, it's a little thing called reality.'

'Give yourself up.'

A long laugh. 'Like that's going to happen. Anyway, time I was going.'

'No, wait!' Aston said. *Got to keep him talking got to kee . . .*

'What's this? Do I detect a touch of desperation? You any idea how pathetic that sounds?'

'You still haven't told me what this is all about.'

'I'm sure you'll work it out. I've got a ton of faith in you.' The phone went dead.

Aston swapped phones and called Mole, cursing how long it was taking to connect, praying that he'd kept Mac on the line long enough. 'C'mon, c'mon,' he muttered into the mouthpiece, eyes roaming the street, looking for anyone who resembled Mac. He wouldn't put it past Mac to be close by, watching him. It wouldn't surprise him if Mac had been standing right next to him all along. He really was that good. As quiet and insubstantial as a spectre, his Cold War codename PHANTOM had been chosen with good reason. Aston was already going through the next move in his head. Unfortunately, there wasn't time to mobilise The Increment, the crack squad of SAS and SBS personnel MI6 used for special ops. Aston was guessing that Mac was still in London; by the time The Increment got here it would be all over bar the shouting. That left the Met, and Aston could imagine the sort of a balls-up they would make. Mole would find out where Mac was holed up and the police would send in the boys with the guns, get the place surrounded. What then? A shoot-out to rival the end sequence in *Butch Cassidy and The Sundance Kid*? Newman and Redford going out in a hail of bullets? Aston hoped it wouldn't go that far, that they would manage some restraint. There had been too much death in his life lately.

'Hi,' Mole chirped.

'Well?'

'I got the trace.'

Yes! Result!

'But you're not going to like this,' Mole was saying. 'Not going to like it one bit.'

'Don't have time for this, Mole. Tell me what you've got.'

A long inhalation and Aston could see Mole sitting at the computer with his thick lips wrapped around a joint. 'Sorry,' the hacker said. 'Mac's at George's.'

28

Aston went into a flat-out sprint, barging past anyone who got in the way. He charged into Bond Street station and vaulted the barrier, his laptop bag slamming hard against his side. A ticket inspector saw him and shouted for him to stop. Aston accelerated, weaving through the crowd, easily outrunning the inspector who had to weigh a good eighteen stone. The protests grew fainter and fainter, and finally disappeared. Aston stopped a second, glanced at the overhead signs to get his bearings then headed for the Jubilee line. He took the escalator two steps at a time, three at a time, shouting for people to get out the way, ignoring their grumbles. Down, down, deeper and deeper. He jumped the last five steps, skidded on the polished floor and almost wiped out a busker who was hammering out an Elton John tune on a tinny portable keyboard. Running harder, harder, one thought going through his mind: *Please be okay, George, please be okay*. There was a train at the platform, doors closing. Lunging forward, he just managed to get his hands in the gap. A robot voice told him to 'mind the doors'.

There were plenty of spare seats, but he couldn't sit down. Hyped on adrenaline, heart rate going through the roof, he stood for a second, hands on hips, gulping oxygen and willing his breathing to settle down. He was puffing away like a forty-a-day man, a stitch niggling at his side. Laura kept trying to persuade him to go to the gym – she had even paid the membership fee, a birthday present as useless as the atrocious jumper she'd bought him for Christmas. Maybe she had a point, he thought as he stood there massaging his stitch and gasping for air. Getting fit had definitely moved up a couple of places on his mañana list. The train clunked forward into the dark tunnel and he paced up and down the carriage. There were a few worried looks aimed at him, people who probably had him pegged as a crack addict. He had the wired junkie eyes and the sweats. Dishevelled and desperate for the next fix, he'd obviously stolen the laptop and was planning to trade it for drugs.

Please be okay, George. Please be okay. Please . . .

Aston wasn't a praying man; he'd be hard pushed to say when he'd last been in church. In recent years there had been a couple of weddings, a funeral, the usual life stuff that necessitates a visit to one of those draughty old stone barns. But the last time he'd been to Morning Worship? That would have been when he was little and his mother had forced him out of bed each and every Sunday to go and sit on a hard oak pew and listen to a vicar who was as old as Methuselah droning on and on. The same hymns each week, the same dull sermon, the same pew. Aston had endured this torture until the age of fourteen when he'd finally persuaded his mother that he was able to make his own mind up about God, and sorry to tell you this Mum but He doesn't exist.

But right now he was praying to anyone who might be listening. The primitive gods of the Pagans, the animal gods of the Red Indians, the Father, Son and Holy Ghost, Allah et al. Even Buddah . . . he wasn't sure if the cheery fat guy was comfortable with this sort of attention, but that was tough shit because he was George's favourite and at this precise moment she needed all the help she could get.

He'd pieced some of it together, but that left him with a dozen more questions. George's mother wasn't ill and she sure as hell wasn't in hospital. Being a Saturday she was probably at the local synagogue, gossiping, no doubt complaining to the other matriarchs that her daughter still wasn't married while tactfully avoiding the touchy subject of her flirtation with Buddhism. The text . . . well, that presumably came from Mac. Which left two huge questions. Firstly, why hadn't she said anything to him? Secondly, why had she decided to handle this on her own? That was stupid. Then again, where Mac was involved nothing surprised

Aston anymore. He was a master manipulator – more than once Aston had joked that Mac was short for Machiavelli – and wasn't that what was happening here? Mac was manipulating him. That's what the phone call had been about. He'd hung up knowing Aston would get Mole to arrange a trace. It was the logical thing to do. Did Mac know that he was going in without any back-up? That as soon as Mole had given him the trace he'd go charging off like the proverbial bull? Probably. More than once Mac had crucified him for being impetuous. So he'd gone charging in with no back-up and no plan, but what else could he do?

It was only five stops to West Hampstead, ten minutes max, yet it was one of the longest journeys of his life. Aston couldn't get out of the carriage fast enough. He ran for the entrance, riding the slipstream of a middle-aged woman through the ticket barrier, hoping the inspector in the glass box wouldn't notice and cause a scene. Outside in the sunshine, he jogged while he rang George's mobile. Still on answerphone. He tried once more then broke into a run, muscles and lungs feeling the burn. And all the time one thought went around his head in time with the pounding of his feet.

Please be okay.

He stood outside George's for a moment to catch his breath. What now? Was Mac still inside? Was he armed? Aston bent down and felt under the stone rabbit for the spare key.

Gone. His heart notched up another gear as he got up, laid a hand on the front door and pushed. The wood had swollen, so there was a bit of resistance to start with. A squeak and it fell open. It was the final proof that Mac had been there. George always locked her door. Aston went inside, feeling as though he was walking into a trap, but knowing there was nothing else he could do. George was in there and she needed him. He tiptoed through the junk, slowly so as not to make a sound, keeping an eye out for anything that could be used as a weapon. A golf club was wedged between the wall and the rusty bike, a driver with a heavy wooden head. He picked it up and moved towards the lounge. He pushed the door open with the head of the club, peered inside. No one there. The kitchen and bathroom were empty, too. Just the bedroom to go. Left hand on handle, right gripping the golf club, he opened the door.

George was hogtied and gagged on the bed. Eyes wide, hair a mess, a thin layer of sweat coating her face. She was lying on her side, motioning with her eyes for Aston to untie her. No Mac. Aston relaxed and moved towards her. She blinked hard, eyes darting to the bedside table. That's when he saw the laptop. It was open. Facing the door. '4.00' took up most of the screen, a giant digital display.

He stood completely still, eyes taking in every detail. The bedroom was spotless, a complete contrast to the junk store vibe that permeated the rest of the flat. This was a place of stillness. Drawers and cupboards all shut tight; no piles of washing; linen and curtains in fresh yellows and white. A camera was set up next to the laptop, wires trailing from the back, a power supply and a thick grey cable.

The explosives were strapped to her stomach with thick gaffer tape. A bomb big enough to turn George into her constituent parts and leave a pretty sizeable crater.

After checking the floor for trip wires and booby traps, Aston put the golf club and laptop bag down and carefully moved forward. George was still motioning with her eyes, a gesture he now knew meant get the hell out of here. Mac liked bangs, the bigger and dirtier the better, and had drilled him extensively on explosives. The different types, different detonators, the way each bomb could be tied to the bombmaker through the techniques used in its construction, these techniques creating a unique fingerprint. Considered in a cerebral, detached way, it was a fascinating subject. The reality, of course, was that bombs were built to destroy. Lives or buildings, it didn't matter. Bombs were equal opportunity weapons.

The detonator was wired to the computer. There was a mercury tilt switch, which explained why George was communicating with her eyes. One wrong move and it would all be over. Ever so carefully, he leant over and peeled the strip of gaffer tape off George's mouth.

The numbers on the laptop started blinking down.

3.59, 3.58, 3.57 . . .

Aston froze.

Shit shit shit!

'Paul! You've got to get out! Now!'

'You okay?' Aston asked, surprising himself by how calm he sounded. He didn't feel calm. His insides were churning, palms sweaty; it felt as though the temperature had been turned all the way up. He stood stock still, not daring to move.

'Paul, didn't you hear me?'

'You okay?' he repeated.

'I've had fifty thousand volts shot through me and I've got a bomb strapped to my stomach. Yeah, Paul, I'm feeling fantastic. What the fuck do you think? I'm going to die and I've never been so scared in my life.'

'You're not going to die,' Aston said.

'Took your time, didn't you?'

Aston swivelled towards the voice. It was emanating from the small speakers built into the laptop. The sound was thin, telephonic like Charlie . . . no angels here, though. He stared into the camera lens. 'What the fuck are you playing at, Mac?'

'I'm helping with your education,' the tinny voice mocked. 'And now it's lesson time.'

'I'm not doing this, Mac.'

'Yes, you are.'

Aston glared into the camera and said nothing.

'Life's all about choices. And some of those are hard choices. Now, you've got two choices here. First off, you can walk out of there right now. Do that and I'll hand myself in. Of course, that's not going to help George out, is it? Choice number two: you ask nicely and I flick a switch and the bomb is disarmed.'

'What's the catch?' Aston asked.

'Well done! Looking for the small print.'

3.01, 3.00, 2.59 . . .

'Well . . . ?'

'No catch, just a simple choice. Do what's good for the many, or do what's good for the few? I'll be interested to see what you go for.'

Aston stared deep into the camera's nasty black eye. 'And you're going to hand yourself in?'

'You've got my word.'

'Yeah, right.' He glanced over at George, glanced over at the laptop.

2.40, 2.39, 2.38 . . .

'Anyway. I'll leave you to it. You've got a lot to think about.'

'Mac!'

Nothing more from the speakers.

Aston moved carefully around the bed, looking at the bomb from all angles. There was always a third choice, so what was the third choice here?

'You're not thinking about disarming it?' George said.

'Wouldn't know where to begin,' Aston admitted. 'It's not like you see in the movies. You know, do you cut the red wire or the blue wire?' He pointed to the cable that ran from the laptop. 'There are probably a couple of dozen wires running through there, all the same colour. The odds of picking the right one . . . well, they're not odds I'd bet on.' He looked at George hogtied on the bed. She didn't scare easily, but she looked terrified. A quick glance at the laptop. They were past the halfway mark now, the numbers marching relentlessly towards zero.

'You heard him, Paul. I die and he hands himself in. Do you think I could live with myself if I survived and there was another bombing, and I could have done something about it?' She looked imploringly at him, the side of her face flattened uncomfortably against the pillow, and it broke his heart. 'Come on, Paul, don't make this any harder than it already is.'

1.43, 1.42, 1.41, 1.40 . . .

'George, there's no way Mac is going to give himself up.'

'But—'

'No "buts",' Aston said. 'Can you imagine Mac stuck in prison for the rest of his life? What do you think? That he's going to march into the nearest police station and ask them to slap the cuffs on?'

George opened her mouth, closed it again. She looked so vulnerable tied up like that. He could imagine her muscles complaining, imagine the hopelessness she must be experiencing. The third choice. Think in straight lines and you're buggered, think around corners and the answer will be staring at you clear as day. The trick was getting your mind to bend far enough. And there had to be a third choice, Aston was certain of it. That was part of the game. The solution was out there, tantalisingly close. *Think then act.* He didn't have the expertise or steady hands to disarm the bomb; the tilt switch meant that cutting the bomb from George's body wasn't an option. It crossed his mind to drape something over the camera. He could sense Mac watching them, getting a voyeuristic kick from their terror, and that pissed him off more than anything.

1.18, 1.17, 1.16 . . .

'I want you to leave.' George did her best to put on a brave face, but her eyes betrayed her. They were damp and filled with a thousand 'if onlys'. 'Go on, Paul, get out of here.'

'What? So you get to play the hero?' He went for upbeat, but the illusion was obvious. 'I'm not ready to quit yet, George.'

They both looked over at the malevolent numbers on the laptop screen. Into the last minute now. In a lifetime made up of millions of minutes, billions of seconds, it was strange to think there might not be many more.

'Go, Paul,' George said simply.

'She's got a point,' the tinny Charlie voice

bleated. 'If I were you I'd get out while you can.'

Aston turned around so his back was to the camera.

'What's the matter? Not speaking, eh? Have I done something to offend?'

He ignored the voice. *The third choice* . . .

Aston reached out with his mind. The answer was out there somewhere.

'Better do as he says,' George was saying quietly, but he barely heard her. Somewhere in the distance came the faint whine of a siren.

The third choice. He pushed his mind hard, so hard he felt something snap up there, pushed it so far around the bend that it doubled back on itself. And that's when he saw it. A glimmer in the faraway.

22, 21, 20 . . .

'Paul, get the fuck out of here! Now!'

'Best do what she says. If you run, I reckon you can make it.'

16, 15, 14 . . .

The wailing siren was getting closer. And it had been joined by others. They seemed to be heading this way. Must have been Mole, Aston thought, calling in the cavalry. Bit bloody late, though. He moved around the bed, gently pushed a loose strand of hair from her face.

10, 9, 8 . . .

'You crazy bastard.' George looked terrified and radiant at the same time. She was smiling and crying. 'Thank you,' she whispered.

'You've fucked up big time,' Mac hollered, his voice a harsh electronic rasp through the speakers.

7, 6, 5 . . .

'Love you,' George mouthed.

4, 3 . . .

'Love you, too,' Aston whispered back.

2, 1 . . .

PART THREE

Babylon's Burning

If an injury has to be done to a man it should be so severe that his vengeance need not be feared.

Niccolo Machiavelli

29

Vienna, 1993

'You're so full of secrets, you know that, Robbie?'

He stopped walking, her hand small and warm inside his. Behind them, the Riesenrad creaked slowly around, the red gondolas swaying gently as the antiquated big wheel turned. The night air was filled with flashing lights and the noisy fun of the fair. Laughter and shouts of delight, hooters and muffled music, the smell of warm sugar and sweet treats and frankfurters. They'd finally made it out of the bedroom. Her idea, not his. The past couple of weeks had been a hurricane of frenzied fucking. Every spare second they'd spent in bed together; every second apart he'd been thinking about what they were going to do in bed the next time they met up. She was the teacher and he was more than happy to play the willing student. The things he'd learned, the things still to learn. He pushed her long hair to the side, cupped her face in his hand and kissed her cheek. Even that was enough to make him hard. He pulled her close, close enough for her to feel him digging into her thigh.

'Robbie,' she giggled in his ear. 'Don't you ever give it a rest?'

'What do you say we go find a hotel room? Book in as Mr and Mrs Smith . . . ?'

'Later.' She gave a flash of that peculiar little smile, eyes alive with the neon spraying from the nearby stalls. 'First, you're going to take me on the big wheel. Remember, we're doing things normal couples do for a change.'

'And the things we do, they're not the sort of things normal couples do?'

She flashed him a look, eyebrows raised: What do you think? Her mouth found his ear, her teeth found the lobe. She bit down hard and the pain was glorious. He closed his eyes, languishing in the sensation. 'Later,' she promised in a smoky whisper, sealing the deal with a kiss and sending his imagination into overdrive.

There were almost two dozen people queuing up for the Riesenrad, mostly couples since it was getting late. Two little girls hung onto their father's hand near the front, eyes darting excitedly in all directions, over-stimulated by the bright lights, noise and sugar. They joined the queue and she asked again. He'd hoped she was going to let it go, but obviously not. He sighed inwardly; this was one conversation he could do without.

'And?' she was saying.

'And what?'

'I don't know anything about you.'

'What's to tell?' he said. 'I've worked for the Foreign Office since I left university, and no doubt I'll be working there until I retire. I'm a boring old civil servant. It's as simple as that. Sorry. No big secrets, no conspiracies.'

'That's not an answer, that's an evasion.' She paused and the silence was stolen away by a scream from the roller coaster. A deep breath, then: 'You're not married, are you? You'd tell me if you were, wouldn't you?'

He laughed at this. 'No, I'm not married,' he said.

'What's so funny?'

'Nothing.'

They shuffled forward, edging towards the front. He could feel her gaze, studying every square inch, could see all the questions in her eyes. How much did she suspect? These past weeks had been intense. They'd spent a lot of time together. His cover was robust, but it wasn't designed for this. She wasn't stupid, far from it.

'Why so secretive?' she asked gently. 'What are you hiding, Robbie?'

'I'm not hiding anything.'

A sigh. She waited until he was looking at her. 'All I want to know is whether we've got a future together. And to do that I need to know who you are. Who you really are.'

'But you kn—'

'No I don't know who you are, Robbie. I want to but you make it so difficult.' She crossed her arms behind his head and pulled his face towards hers, tilting her mouth upwards to deliver the kiss. She laid her cool forehead against his. 'The thing is,' she whispered. 'I think I'm falling in love with you.'

And there it was, out in the open. A strange new feeling had been roaming through his heart lately, an *alien feeling he now had a name for. Love. His decision was made in a millisecond. It was a decision that went against the golden rule – the only person you can trust is yourself – but it felt right, and at this moment all he had to go on was instinct. The bottom line: this was the person he wanted to spend the rest of his life with.*

'I think I'm falling in love with you, too.'

The words felt odd coming from his mouth, odd but somehow right. She pulled back and her smile was wide and open, a smile worth a million pounds. She grabbed hold of his head and smothered his face with kisses.

'And you're definitely not married?' she said.

'Definitely not married,' he assured her.

Laughing, she broke away, pointed to the red gondolas spinning prettily through the night. 'Do you think they're safe?' she asked. 'They look a bit past it.'

'They've survived all these years. I'm sure we'll be fine.'

Hanging on his arm, she tilted her head and kissed him on the cheek. 'This isn't the time to tell you I'm scared of heights, is it?'

'Don't worry. I'll take care of you.'

The attendant looked as though she'd been selling tickets since the wheel opened. She held out an arthritic claw and he paid for two tickets, slipped a little something extra to ensure they got a gondola to themselves. Her leathery face lit up at this. She waved them into a gondola and slammed the door shut, sending them on their way with a wink and a gummy grin.

The gondola creaked into the night, metal struts and joints moaning softly. Below them, the city lights spread, twinkling into the distance, stretching further and further the higher they climbed. Toy trams snaked in and out of Praterstern station, taking the toy people to their toy houses. He pulled her close, running his fingers through her hair. She rested her cheek on his shoulder.

'Breathtaking, isn't it?' she said.

He had to admit the view was stunning. During his time in Vienna he hadn't done any sightseeing. All work and no play. Anyway, crowds of tourists really weren't his thing. Normally he would have done anything to avoid them – a DIY lobotomy with a blunt knife would be preferable – but it was different with her. Everything was different with her. She could make even the most unbearable situation tolerable.

'That old woman, the one who sold the tickets, she thinks you're going to propose.'

'Well, it is the perfect spot. I'm sure there have been hundreds of proposals up here, thousands even.'

'See,' she said playfully, 'you can be romantic when you want to be. So, are you going to propose?'

The simple answer was yes, but it didn't work like that, did it? Not when you worked for MI6. She had fallen in love with Robert Macintosh the civil servant. How would she feel when she discovered what he really did for a living? Because for this to work she would have to know everything. A relationship built on lies was a disaster waiting to happen, and this was one relationship he had no intention of screwing up. Being the wife of a spy was a tough one. She would be sucked into his secret world, forced to wear a mask. Was it fair to expect anyone to do that? His mother had lived *that life and what had her reward been? A late night visit to tell her that her husband had become another Cold War casualty, and a slow descent into madness. Was that a life to wish upon your worst enemy, never mind the person you love? He suddenly wished he could have one more conversation with his mother. Not even a whole conversation, just a single question would do. Given the chance to turn back the clock, would she have done it all again? He thought he knew the answer. A simple yes. His mother had loved his father, had loved her son. She wouldn't have given up either one. Anyway, you never knew what life was going to throw at you. You could have the most boring life in the world, then wake up one day, walk outside and get run down by a bus. Alternatively, you could take risks left, right and centre, smoke and drink, and live to be a hundred. There was no rhyme, no reason. So, what should he do? His head was telling him to walk away, but his heart didn't agree. At the moment his heart was shouting loudest.*

'Robbie, you've gone all quiet on me again.'

'Sorry.'

'I was joking,' she said. 'About you proposing. That would be ridiculous. We've only just met.'

'Actually, I don't think it's ridiculous.'

'You don't?' Her eyes were wide open, searching his face to see if he was making fun of her.

'It happens all the time. Whirlwind romances and all that.'

'And that's what this is? A whirlwind romance?'

'Well, it's turned my life upside down.'

She took a deep breath and met his gaze. 'You're serious, aren't you? You're going to propose.'

'Yes.'

'But . . . ?'

'But after you hear what I've got to tell you, I'm not sure you'd want me to.'

Her face darkened, worry wrinkling the corners of her eyes. 'It can't be that bad, can it?'

He answered with a long sigh.

'Well?' There was a note of apprehension in her voice, as though she wanted to hear what was coming next, but didn't want to hear.

'Everything you know about me is a lie.'

'Everything?'

'Okay, not quite everything. My name is Robert Macintosh and I do work for the Foreign Office . . . sort of.'

'Sort of?'

Another long sigh, the picture postcard view completely forgotten about now. He hated conversations where the other person made questions from your statements.

'I'm not explaining myself very well, am I?'

'Robert, you're making no sense whatsoever.'

It was the first time she'd called him Robert and he hoped it would be the last. The word sounded ugly coming from her lips.

A deep breath. This was harder than he'd thought. 'Let me try again,' he said.

'Please do,' she said.

'I work for MI6.'

She went silent a while, scrutinising him closely. He didn't flinch from her gaze, even though he wanted to. The gondola carried them higher, the age-old metalwork squeaking and weeping, the big wheel turning, turning, turning.

'Okay,' she said at last. 'That, I wasn't expecting.'

'No shit,' he said and tried for a smile.

'No shit,' she agreed and gave her strange little half-smile in return. 'Okay, Mr Bond, so what can you tell me? That's if you can tell me anything at all.'

He surprised himself by telling her everything.

He'd only just got started when the ride finished. The attendant pulled open the door and he slipped her some more Austrian Schillings to let them go around again. Her gap-toothed grin widened and she gave them what was perhaps her only word of English: 'congratulation!'. The couple at the front of the queue grumbled something in German and she silenced them with a fierce look. Another grin and a wink and they were sailing into the night sky again.

She was a good listener. Occasionally she asked a question to clarify a point, but for the most part she let him talk. It was easier than he thought, although this shouldn't have come as a surprise. He'd been trained in interrogation techniques and knew the hardest part was getting the subject to talk in the first place. That's why you always began with the simple questions: name, rank, serial number. Once they started talking that was it, the floodgates were open and everything just flowed out. And that's what had happened here. He'd initially intended to give her the bare bones, but once he'd started, he just kept going. He wanted her to know everything. To understand. It was easier than he'd imagined. Cathartic, even. After living a life built from lies it was good to be a real person rather than a shadow.

He had enough secrets to keep them spinning through till morning and on to the next day, but they couldn't justify going around a third time. The gap-toothed attendant had saved her widest grin for when they got off. 'Congratulation! Congratulation!' she shouted out as they walked away arm in arm.

They travelled back to her pension in silence. This wasn't the time or place for trivialities. And the back of a taxi wasn't the place for the type of secrets he was sharing; there were limits.

Back in her room, he told her all about his current assignment. They were sitting side by side on the bed sipping brandy, bathed in candlelight, shadows playing on the pitted whitewashed walls. The expression on her face told him that she didn't get it.

'Tell me if I've got this right?' she said. 'You went from heading up the Moscow station to being in charge of the Vienna station . . . isn't that a demotion?'

'Technically, no. The USSR is well and truly out of the game now. All the action is moving south, towards the Middle East. Strategically speaking, Vienna is currently MI6's most important station. It's perfectly placed to spy on the new Russian states and, more importantly, Iran and the Middle East. This is about as high up as you can get in MI6.'

'But . . .' she said, letting the word hang there.

He was once again struck by how sharp she was, how

different she was from the women he usually went for.
'But I was fucked over,' he said, and before he knew it
everything was spewing out, all that bile, all the hatred.
He told her about Kinclave, and in the candlelight, under
the austere gaze of that guilt-inducing Jesus, he confessed
his darkest thoughts, telling her how one day he would
get even, if it was the last thing he ever did he would
make the fucker pay. He felt naked when he'd finished,
stripped down to the soul. She now knew everything, his
darkest secrets. And that was the way it had to be. He
looked at her expectantly. Wanting her to say something;
not wanting her to say anything.

'If it was up to me I would have made you Chief,'
she stated simply. The tip of her tongue touched her
upper lip, emphasising the coquettish grin.

'So?' he said.

'So what?' she replied.

'About this proposal . . . ?'

She didn't reply, just raised an eyebrow.

'You're not going to make me get down on one knee,
are you?'

'The man who would be king bowing before me. Yes,
I think I might like that. Then again, maybe you'd
prefer it if I got down on my knees.'

She drained her brandy, put the glass on the bedside
table. She slid off the bed and unzipped him, slid a hand
inside his underpants and started stroking him. 'Now,
what was it you wanted to ask me?'

'Will you marry me?'

'Of course,' she said simply.

It crossed his mind that maybe he'd told her more

than she was ready for, that perhaps he'd come on a bit strong. But she had to know. They were destined to be together, and that meant no more lies, no more secrets . . . it really was that simple. And then she had him in her mouth and, much to his surprise, he found it really wasn't that important anymore.

30

Three big fat zeroes stared out from the laptop screen. 0.00. Still here. His entire body was pulsing to the rhythm of his racing heart: head, chest, fingers and toes. He inhaled a lungful of tired bedroom air, and air had never tasted so sweet. The police sirens were right outside the front door, a collection of random notes producing a grating black chord. Subtlety had never been the Met's strong suit. A strange sound filled the room and it took a second for him to work out what it was. Laughter. He looked over in the direction of the sound. George was shaking her head and muttering under her breath.

'That son of a bitch,' she said over and over in quiet disbelief. 'That fucking son of a bitch.'

She pulled against the rope binding her hands, preparing to do a Houdini. Shit, she didn't get it!

'No!' Aston shouted.

George froze, the laughter dying in her throat.

She looked at him as though he was some sort of lunatic, concern in her big brown eyes.

'Don't move,' Aston said. 'Not so much as a muscle.'

'What?'

'The bomb,' he said hurriedly, 'It's real.'

'Like fuck it is.'

Aston noticed she wasn't moving, the lack of conviction in her voice. She was hedging her bets, which, given the circumstances, was no bad thing. He was going on guesswork and hunches here, and so far he'd got lucky.

'It's real,' Aston repeated.

'Okay – if it's real, how come we're still here?'

'It's complicated,' Aston said. 'And I'm not sure I totally understa—'

The sirens in the street suddenly fell silent. 'Come out with your hands up!' The voice was distorted by the bullhorn, muffled by the front door, but there was no mistaking that this was someone used to being obeyed.

'We've got the place surrounded!'

Jesus, this was all he needed. He could imagine the squad cars in the street, fanned out in a semi-circle like Wild West wagons, cops in Kevlar crouched down behind them for cover, itchy trigger fingers at the ready.

'Come out with your hands up!' the voice repeated. 'We don't want anybody getting hurt.'

Aston ignored the voice as best he could. If his hunch was correct Mac had him trapped here for the foreseeable future. Time to blind him. Aston was worried that tampering with the laptop might set off the explosives, so he pulled a hankie from his pocket and draped it over the camera. If Mac was holed up watching somewhere, that would spoil his fun. Next he had to contact the police. Mobiles were out; if a mobile could bring down a jumbo jet then fuck knows what it would do to a bomb. Best not to take chances.

'Come out with your hands up!'

'You going out there?' George said, and her tone suggested that this was the last thing she wanted him to do.

'Afraid not. You're kind of stuck with me,' Aston said. 'Don't suppose you've got a phone in here?'

George motioned behind her with her head and Aston felt the colour drain from his face. 'The mercury tilt switch,' he whispered. 'Not a good idea to move. Not a good idea at all.'

'Sorry,' George whispered.

Aston found the phone and checked it out thoroughly before picking up the handset, making sure it wasn't connected to the bomb, that it wasn't booby-trapped. Satisfied it was clean he dialled 999. When the operator answered he asked to be put through to the officer in charge of the siege in West Hampstead before she had a chance to get 'police, fire or ambulance?' out. The operator told him to hold. A couple of clicks, static on the line.

'Come out with your ha—'

'What?' a gruff voice barked into the earpiece.

'Is this the officer in charge?'

'Yes, this is Detective Superintendent Fielding. Who's this?'

'Detective Fielding, I want you to listen carefully,' Aston said.

'Who is this?'

'Not important, just listen. I'm speaking from inside the flat and I need you to call the bomb squad immediately. No questions.'

Aston heard Fielding barking out orders, then he was back. 'They'll be here in five minutes, ten minutes max. Is the girl okay?'

'She's fine,' Aston said. 'Now get your men to a safe distance. And it'd be a good idea to evacuate the street, just to be on the safe side. I'm guessing here, but I reckon we're dealing with C4. Not enough to take out the neighbourhood, but enough to redecorate the flat Baghdad style. Oh, and try and keep the media at bay.'

Fielding disappeared for a couple of seconds. Indistinct mumbling in the background, then: 'Any more demands?'

Demands! How was that for a new definition of dumb? 'I think you've got this all wrong,' Aston said.

'You sound like a reasonable man. Nobody's been hurt yet. My guess is you'd like to keep it that way.'

'Listen, I'm not a kidnapper and I'm not a terrorist. Now, if I'm sounding a bit stressed it's

292

because I'm standing in a room with a bomb, and that bomb happens to be strapped to my best friend.'

'What did you say your name was?'

Brilliant. Fielding was working from the hostage negotiation handbook; either that or he loved Hollywood action movies. Step one: find out the subject's name. Step two: build a rapport. Handy tip: under no circumstances tell the subject 'no'. Aston had seen that film, too.

'I need to call you something,' Fielding pressed.

'If it makes you feel better, call me Larry,' Aston said.

'And how's it going in there, Larry?' Now he had a name, Fielding's tone had turned amiable. Here they were chatting away, one buddy to another.

'Fucking fabulous. I might have mentioned there's a bomb in here. That's got to be anyone's idea of a good time. Talking of which, any sign of the bomb squad?'

'They're on their way, Larry,' Fielding said. 'Look, why don't you come on out.'

'I can't come out.'

'Larry, I guarantee you won't be harmed.'

'Weren't you listening? I can't come out.'

'We can get a lot more achieved talking face to face. I'm sure we can find some way to resolve the situation.'

'Are you fucking deaf or something?' Aston shouted into the mouthpiece. 'I can't come out.'

'Relax, Larry.' A touch of anxiety had crept into Fielding's voice. Aston wondered if he was sweating yet. He hoped so. It would serve the stupid bastard right.

'And don't tell me to relax. All that's going to do is make me more tense. Turn to page eleven in the manual. It's all in there.'

'What?'

'Never mind,' Aston said.

'Why can't you come out, Larry?'

'It's complicated.'

'I'm listening.'

Aston took a deep breath. His patience was sorely lacking right now, and going around in circles like this was trying it to the limit. One more attempt at getting the detective to understand, then that was it. 'Detective Fielding, the situation is very simple.' Aston spoke as though he was talking to a very slow five-year-old. 'There is a bomb. That bomb is attached to my friend. If she moves or tries to remove the bomb it will go bang. If I leave the flat, the bomb goes bang. Is that what you want? To be left looking at a big smoking hole in the ground? Now let's be clear here. I am not a terrorist. I have not escaped from the local asylum. This is not a hostage situation. Do you understand?'

'It sounds as if we want the same thing, Larry. A peaceful resolution.'

Hallelujah! Finally the detective was seeing sense.

'Now,' Fielding continued. 'If this isn't a hostage

situation, then I don't see why you can't come out here so we can talk properly. At the very least, tell me your real name. If I'm going to help I need something to work with.'

'Jesus Christ!' Aston exhaled. 'Tell you what, phone me when the bomb squad gets here.' He hung up and shook his head.

'That went well,' George said.

'I'm starting to understand why Mac has such a low opinion of the police.'

Aston paced, trying to get the situation sorted out in his head. There was too much adrenaline in his system and it was stopping him thinking straight. Mole was the only person who knew he'd come here. So why had Mole not given the police the full story? Explained that this wasn't a hostage situation? He rubbed his face. This wasn't making sense. Then again, if you looked at it from Mole's perspective . . . Mole had no time for the police at the best of times. And he was prone to bouts of paranoia; the after-effects of too much dope, too much caffeine, and too much time spent in cyber-space. So Mole phones the police, gives them a false name, or better still, gives them no name at all, and then he gives them George's address, tells them to get over there pronto because there's some heavy shit going down. It was possible. And there was a certain logic there.

Of course, there was one other person who knew he'd come here. But what did Mac have to gain from calling the police in?

George's face suddenly folded in pain. 'Oh shit,' she hissed through clenched teeth. 'Fuck, that hurts!'

'What's wrong?'

'Cramp! Left thigh!'

Aston moved closer to the bed, closer to George, eyes fixed on the grey lump of C4. Ever so carefully he reached out and gently massaged George's thigh, keeping his movements to a bare minimum. Neither said a word. They breathed only when absolutely necessary.

'I think it's alright now,' George said. 'You can stop if you want.'

Aston stepped tentatively back from the bed. 'I really don't like this. I'm not sure how much more adrenaline I can take. You as scared as I am?'

'Scared doesn't begin to cover it, Paul.'

'We're going to get out of this.' Aston kissed her on the forehead.

'I believe you. And thanks.'

'Thanks for what?'

'Just thanks.'

Aston stared at the bomb, the zeroes on the screen. It was so small, yet it seemed to fill the whole room. And although it was small, he reminded himself, it was still plenty big enough to turn him and George into atoms. Chances were, they wouldn't feel a thing. A flash of light and that would be it. Welcome to the big nothing. Aston didn't subscribe to the idea of an afterlife. Spending eternity sitting on a cloud playing a harp didn't sound like much fun. Another glance at the C4, the tilt switch, the wires. It was so frustrating. He felt so useless. There was nothing to do except wait for the bomb disposal experts. And waiting was hard enough at the best of times, never mind when he was this wired. So where the hell were they? Fielding had said ten minutes max. They should be here by now.

The phone went and Aston snatched it up, expecting it to be Detective Fielding. 'Yup,' he said and was hit with a barrage of questions.

'Who's this? Is this the right number?'

I think it's your mother, Aston mouthed, hand over the mouthpiece.

All I bloody need, George mouthed back, *tell her I'm not here*.

'She's just popped out, Mrs Strauss.'

'And who are you? What are you doing in my daughter's flat?'

'It's Paul.'

'Paul . . . Paul,' she said, trying to place the name. 'Ah, Paul! So, she's out, you say. Is that another way of saying she doesn't want to speak to her mother?'

'Look, this isn't a good time.'

'Not a good time. I hear what you're saying. She never has time to speak to her mother these days. Always too busy. Well, tell her I phoned and tell her that when she *does* have time she knows where I am.' With that, the line went dead.

Aston carefully placed the receiver back in the

cradle. 'I think you've just managed to piss your mum off without saying a word. Pretty impressive.'

'Paul, my mother is constantly pissed off with me. And I rarely have to say a word. So,' she added, glancing over at the three fat zeroes on the laptop screen, 'how did you know Mac was going to disarm the bomb?'

Aston leant against the doorframe. The last burst of adrenaline had subsided, leaving him drained; the remnants of his hangover was lurking in the background like a shy poltergeist. Given the choice, he'd rather be crashed out on the sofa with a movie, black coffee and some aspirin. 'The third choice,' he said.

'What's that supposed to mean?'

'Something Mac keeps harping on about.'

'Still don't get it.'

'Not sure I do, either,' Aston admitted. 'Not all of it at any rate.'

'He only gave you two choices.'

'The third choice is the hidden choice. The one you've got to look around corners to find.'

'Still not making sense, Paul.'

'Basically, I figured that whatever he's planning next involves me . . . somehow.'

'And you based this bit of deduction on what exactly?'

'The one thing the two choices had in common was that I walked away in one piece.'

George fell silent for a moment then said: 'Let

me get this straight. You gambled your life on the basis of a . . . a hunch? And you did that to save my life?'

'Something like that,' Aston said.

The phone went again. Aston picked it up and said a cautious hello in case it was Mrs Strauss. Detective Fielding's gruff bark filled his ear.

'The bomb squad's here.'

'Well, what the hell are you waiting for?' Aston replied. 'Send them in.'

31

Like a giant black metallic tortoise, the bomb disposal expert eased slowly into the bedroom, lugging a large aluminium case behind him. He was entombed in heavy armoured body plating; BOMB SQUAD was stencilled in large white capitals on the front. The ensemble was topped off with a crash helmet and thick visor. The brilliant white teeth under the neatly trimmed moustache were a dentist's dream.

'My name's Stuart,' he announced with the reassuring confidence of an airline pilot, the accent pure Home Counties. Sharp eyes scanned the room, missing nothing. He looked at the bomb, the laptop, finally the bed. 'Hi,' he said. 'You must be Georgina?'

'George,' she corrected.

He turned to Aston. 'And you're Paul.'

A statement rather than a question, and Aston, ever the spy, wondered where he got his intel from.

'Paul, if I were you I'd make myself scarce.'

'I'm staying,' Aston said.

'Can't see any need for you to be here, so if you could—'

'I'm staying,' Aston repeated, more forcefully.

'For your own safety, I strongly suggest you go.'

'Or what? You'll have me removed? Quick update as to what we've got going on here, Stuart. We've got C4, a mercury tilt switch, we don't know for sure if the bomb's booby-trapped. Now, are you telling me your boss is going to give the green light for someone to come in here and drag me out? Put another person in the firing line unnecessarily? You've seen the size of this room. Three's already a crowd. So, they come charging in and start getting all heavy – because believe me I won't be going peacefully – the bomb gets knocked and . . . well, I think you get the picture.'

'Have you ever seen the aftermath of an explosion? It's not like the movies, you know.'

'Actually, I have. And believe me, given the choice I'd be as far away from here as possible. But that's my best friend lying on that bed, and right now she needs me here.'

Stuart studied him carefully for a moment. 'There's nothing I can say to change your mind?'

'Nothing.'

'For the record, I think you're crazy for staying.'

'I've been called worse.'

'Okay, I'd best sort you out with some body armour.'

'There isn't time. You saw the mercury tilt switch? George has already had cramp once. We got lucky that time.'

'In your own time, guys,' George called from the bed.

Both men turned towards her.

'If it's all the same with you,' she added, 'I'd really appreciate it if you got this fucking thing off of me.'

Stuart nodded. Without another word he flicked open his case and went to work.

While Stuart disarmed the bomb, Aston kept up a telepathic conversation with George. A smile here, a wink there, little gestures that said *I'm here for you*. George was putting on a brave face, but she wasn't fooling Aston. The stress was showing in every wrinkle and every line, a thin coating of perspiration making her cheeks and lips shine. *It's okay*, Aston said with his eyes, *you're allowed to be scared*.

He kept glancing over at Stuart; that car crash curiosity again. He didn't want to, but he was powerless not to. Stuart's eyes were completely focused behind the visor, his hands rock steady. Every now and again he'd straighten up and have a good look at the bomb. Then it would be back to work, moving with infinite care, every step thought out well in advance. Aston realised that his and George's lives were in this stranger's hands. He hoped Stuart knew his stuff; he certainly looked like he knew what he was doing. Aston felt sweat break out on his forehead as another surge of adrenaline fried his nerve endings. His skin tingled and his stomach turned over. A glance at his watch. Stuart had been working for only fifteen minutes, yet it felt like forever. The bomb disposal expert picked up a pair of snips and without hesitating began cutting wires. Aston realised he was holding his breath and forced himself to breathe. In, out, in, out. Stuart turned his attention to the laptop. He began clicking away, hit a few keys, nodding approvingly. Finally, he moved across to George, told her to lie still. Ever so carefully he extracted the detonator from the explosives, then he gently peeled away the silver gaffer tape.

'Okay, folks, you can breathe again,' he announced, straightening up. The lump of C4 sat in his steady hands. He put the explosives down on the bedside table and took off his helmet. His face was glistening with sweat and the moustache looked limp and damp. Even Superheroes got stressed, it seemed.

Stuart reached into the aluminium case, took out a Swiss Army knife and popped a blade. He cut the ropes binding George's feet and hands, told her to take it easy, not to sit up too quickly. George ignored the advice and sprung to her feet like a dog let off the leash in a field full of rabbits. She crumpled straightaway, but Aston was there to catch her.

'Didn't you hear the man?' he said as he guided her back to the bed and helped her sit down.

'Not the time for a told-you-so, Paul,' she said, but she wasn't angry. She massaged some life back into her limbs, her face alive with a huge childlike grin, the relief visible for anyone to see. Aston guessed he was probably wearing a similar expression.

'How are you feeling?' Aston asked.

'Pretty strung out, but glad to be alive.'

'Strange,' Stuart mused, casting the word out like a fishing line.

'What?' Aston said, taking the bait.

'The bomb was pretty simple – well, simple as these things go. That's not to belittle it. When you're dealing with bombs, they all demand respect. A little one can kill you just as much as a big one. No booby traps, very elegant in its construction. The computer program that controlled the detonator was particularly impressive. Whoever wrote that knew their stuff.'

'And?' Aston said.

'The mercury switch wasn't wired in,' Stuart said. 'It was attached to the detonator in a way that made it *look* like it was, but it wasn't. Whoever put the bomb together knew what they were doing, so what were they up to? It doesn't make sense.'

It does if you know Mac, Aston thought. Mac had wanted to play with them, had wanted them jittery and moving with the utmost caution. And it also reinforced his theory about the third choice. Mac hadn't wanted him to inadvertently blow himself up. Yes, it made perfect sense. 'You're right, it doesn't make sense,' Aston said.

'Can we get out of here?' George said. 'I need to taste real air again.'

'After you,' Stuart said.

Aston helped George to her feet and let her lean on him as much as she wanted, which turned out to be a fair bit. He could feel her trembling against his body, but he wasn't going to make a big deal out of it.

They headed for the hallway, Stuart in his bulky armour lumbering behind. The front door was wide open and the second they stepped through they were whisked away by two uniformed PCs, one male, one female. The WPC draped a blanket across George's shoulders, offered a few words of encouragement and support. A small posse of pressmen were already there, pushing up against the barrier that had been erected to keep them at bay, cameras pointed towards the front of the flat. Aston automatically raised an arm to hide his face and noticed George was doing a similar thing with the blanket. They were going to love this back at base, Aston thought. Lately, MI6 had had more media coverage than at any other point in its history. And the media still had no idea an MI6 spymaster was involved in the Leicester Square bombing. When that got out, the press would be baying for blood. Embarrassing didn't even begin to cover it. The fact that MI6 had been caught napping was bad enough, that one of their own was involved made it a catastrophe.

The Crisis Control Centre was housed in a large truck that had been parked fifty yards from George's. It gleamed whitely at the kerb, '*The Metropolitan Police*' emblazoned in large letters on the side, their logo printed next to it. Detective Fielding was waiting inside. Aston worked out who he was without being introduced; he looked as brusque as he'd sounded on the phone. Completely bald, his bullet-shaped head reflected the van's fluorescent strip lighting. His nose had been broken more than once and badly reset somewhere along the line. His neck was red, pinched by the tight collar of his shirt. The suit was navy blue and badly fitting, an Oxfam reject. With his saggy jowls, thick waistline and bald head, he reminded Aston of a cross between a bouncer and a butcher.

Fielding sat behind a cheap desk in the van's only seat. He didn't bother getting up. There was a computer on the desk, a map of central London fixed to one wall, a whiteboard on another. He dismissed the two PCs with an impatient insect-swatting flick of his meaty hand. There was a large gold sovereign ring on one finger, tacky as hell but no doubt useful for breaking teeth.

'So,' he said, 'one of you two mind telling me what the hell is going on here?'

Aston and George stayed tight-lipped.

'Like that, is it?' Fielding said. 'Okay, how about I tell you what I know and we can go from there?'

He gave them a hard stare. It was a stare usually reserved for murderers and rapists, Aston reckoned, a stare designed to extract confessions from even the toughest criminals. During the IONEC he'd undergone a lengthy interrogation; the Powers That Be needed to know how he'd act if he ever got captured by the enemy. His interrogation had gone on for two days and he'd coped admirably, not deviating from his cover once. George had also passed with flying colours. At the time, it never occurred to him that the enemy might be a thug-like detective from Scotland Yard. Fielding carried on with the hard stare and Aston had to admit he had it down to a fine art. Even though he hadn't done anything wrong, he'd never felt guiltier in his life.

'Okay, let's get started,' Fielding said. Used to things going his way, he flipped open a notebook and continued in his own time. 'At exactly 4.36 p.m. we get a call telling us there's a hostage situation in West Hampstead. The caller gave his name as Kevin Spacey . . . obviously not his real name. We mobilise and when we arrive we find you two inside. We intercepted the call from Mrs Strauss and she was most helpful. She was able to give us your names. And, rather interestingly, she mentioned you both worked for MI6. So that gets me thinking, and I'm wondering what a couple of spies are doing playing with bombs in West Hampstead.'

George chuckled and fluttered her eyelashes.

Aston kept schtum and let her get on with it. He'd seen her play this game before.

'Detective,' she said, moving a little closer to the desk, subtly demanding his attention. 'You'll have to excuse my mother, but she's getting on a bit in years. She has trouble separating fact from fiction, gets easily confused. All very sad. Just the other week she was convinced that she was Anastasia and was ready to jump on the next plane to Russia to claim her rightful inheritance. Like I said, it's all very sad. We're not sure what to do with her.'

'My heart bleeds, Ms Strauss. So, are you telling me you don't work for MI6?'

Another dry chuckle, another quick flutter of the lashes. 'Come on, Detective. Do I look like a spy?'

'You're not answering my question.'

'Are we under arrest?' Aston asked.

'No.'

'In that case, we'll be leaving.'

'Ah,' the detective said. 'I'm afraid it's not that simple.'

'Seems simple enough to me. We're not under arrest therefore we can leave whenever we want. I don't need a law degree to know that.'

'Yes, but if you did have a law degree you'd know that under the Anti-Terrorism Act I can hold you for two days for questioning. I think you'll find the facilities at Paddington Green are second to none.'

'You think I'm a terrorist? That's bullshit and you know it.'

'Mr Aston, all I need to hold you is the *suspicion* that you might be involved in terrorist activities,' Fielding said. 'You were in there with a bomb, you're not answering my questions – what am I supposed to think? Far as I'm concerned I've got all the suspicion I need. Now, either you two start co-operating or I'll drive you to Paddington Green myself. What's more, I'll keep you there until you start answering my questions. I'll get extension after extension after extension. I'll keep on going until we're all old and grey if needs be. But this I promise – you will talk.'

Aston and George looked at one another, sharing the same thought: this wasn't going according to the script. Two days getting cosy with the bullet-headed detective didn't sound like a bundle of laughs. And what sort of damage could Mac do in two days? But co-operation wasn't an option. The MI6 indoctrination went right to the marrow. *So what's the third choice here, Mac?* Even as Aston asked himself this, he already had the answer. If someone's going to bully you, then you make friends with the biggest kid in the playground and get them to beat the shit out of the bully. They weren't going to like this one back at Vauxhall Cross, but he was out of options.

'I take it I'm allowed a phone call,' Aston said. 'Those are the rules, right?'

While waiting for Aston to make his next move,

Fielding had taken off his blue Oxfam jacket and hung it over the back of the chair. Two dark sweat stains were painted onto the armpits of his wrinkled shirt. Fielding shrugged his massive shoulders ambiguously. The gesture could have meant fair enough. Equally it could have meant: that just proves you're hiding something so grab that shovel and dig your hole deeper. Aston couldn't be bothered deciphering the lexicon of Fielding's body language. Didn't have to. He knew his rights.

He pulled out his mobile, flipped it open, paused for a moment deciding how best to use his phone call. He scrolled through the phone book till he found the number he wanted. Mole answered straightaway. In the background Aston could hear people screwing, lots of high-pitched wailing and praising of God going on, the cheap bass thud and kinky guitars of a porno soundtrack. He made a mental note to get his living room decontaminated.

'Pau—'

'Shut up and listen, Mole.' Aston told him what he needed, aware of Fielding's hard eyes burning into the back of his skull.

'Quite finished?' Fielding said when Aston hung up.

Aston said nothing.

'Oh, the silent treatment, is it?'

Still nothing.

'I could teach a saint a thing or two about patience, Mr Aston. You want, we can do this all day.'

Five minutes of silence that seemed like a life-time until Aston's phone went. He connected the call and passed the phone to Fielding without a word.

'What's this?' Fielding said.

'It's for you,' Aston said simply.

The detective listened for a moment and then said: 'And I'm supposed to believe you're the head of MI6? Just take your word for it?'

Another pause then: 'Prove it.'

A longer pause. 'Okay you have my attention.'

For the rest of the call Fielding didn't speak. He listened in silence for a good minute, his face growing redder and redder. Aston could have sworn the sweat marks under his arms grew bigger, too. The only thing Fielding said came at the very end.

'I'll make sure that happens, Mr Kinclave.'

Fielding threw the phone and Aston caught it one-handed, biting back the urge to say something sarcastic. Fielding looked ready to explode and there was nothing to be gained from antagonising him further. The detective hollered, and the two PCs who'd escorted them from the house imme-diately appeared in the doorway.

'Please take these two to Mr Aston's, and make sure they get there safely. I don't want them molested by the press and I want you to wait at the kerb till they're inside.'

'Sir?' said the WPC.

'Got a problem following orders?'

'No, sir.'

As they descended the metal steps to the street Aston tried not to look back. He was convinced Fielding's stare would turn him into a pillar of salt.

Outside, George turned to the PCs and said: 'I don't suppose either of you two were involved with the evacuation?'

'We both were,' the WPC said. 'Why?'

'It's just that one of my neighbours is getting on a bit and I was wondering if he's okay.'

The PCs looked at each other and the policewoman said: 'You mean the old guy living in the house directly opposite your flat?'

'That's the one,' George said. 'What happened to him?'

'He said he was going to stay with his sister. He couldn't see what all the fuss was about. Kept going on about the war, and how there were bombs landing on this street all the time and nobody batted an eyelid.'

'Don't suppose you saw which way he went?'

The WPC shook her head. 'Sorry.'

In the back of the squad car, Aston whispered: 'Mind telling me what that was all about?'

'Clive lives opposite,' George whispered back, 'and he's a thirty-something ad exec.' She nodded towards the pristine red Merc parked on the hardstanding. 'I mean, come on, does that look like the sort of car a pensioner would drive? Three guesses who the old guy was.'

'I figured he'd want to stay close by, but not that close.'

'A bit risky, don't you think?'

'Depends how you look at it. As far as Mac's concerned, the best place to hide is right out in the open. It's when you start skulking in the shadows that people notice you.'

'Well, he got away, so I suppose he's got a point,' George said. 'You don't mind if I crash out at your place tonight? I really don't fancy being alone at mine. That'd creep me out too much.'

'Be my guest.'

As they pulled away, the driver asked where they wanted to go. Aston said he'd give directions on route. The barrier was moved and the squad car ploughed through the media horde. Photographers pressed cameras against the car window, forcing Aston and George to huddle together and hide their faces. Aston could feel her warm cheek against his, the whisper of her breath; he could smell the coconut in her hair.

'This must be what it's like to be famous,' George said when they were clear. Her head was going from side to side, presumably looking for paparazzi hidden behind cars and walls.

'I don't know how anyone could deal with that all the time,' Aston said. 'I couldn't stand the invasion of privacy.'

'Got anything to drink at your place?'

'Nope. On the wagon, remember.'

'That's your problem, not mine. After the day I've had I need a drink.'

As they approached the end of the street and the driver asked which way. Aston checked behind to make sure they were far enough from the vultures. 'Actually, you can let us out here.'

'Sorry, Superintendent Fielding was very specific about taking you home.'

Yeah, Aston thought, *so he can find out where I live*. 'Stop the car.' He spat the words out.

'No need to take that tone, sir.'

'Last time I looked it was a free country. Now, unless you're arresting us you'll pull over to the side of the road and open this door.'

The squad car moved gently towards the kerb.

32

The old barber chair is comfy and worn, and the thin red nylon cloth draped across my shoulders reaches my knees. Fogarty's hands are as steady as ever, but there are nasty red ligature marks circling his wrists. The bright lights surrounding the make-up mirror have turned his pupils to pinpricks. He's wearing this worried look, like he's not sure what to make of me anymore. That's good. I need him on his toes. Eager to please. Whenever he starts getting a bit too strung out I remind him of the money, and that seems to get him focusing again.

When I got back last night he was exactly where I left him. I'd half expected him to make some sort of bid for freedom. Not that it would have done him much good. Even if he'd managed to crawl across the living room, he would have still had the door to wrestle with. And even if he'd somehow managed to get into the hall there was no way he would have got out the front door, not with all those locks on there. And I'd cut the phone cord, so that wasn't a worry. He wasn't moving at all, and that got me concerned. For a second I was convinced he'd had a heart attack. That would have been a problem. And then he let out a snore and a grunt, and I knew everything was going to be okay. A couple of gentle slaps brought him back round. I hunkered down and removed the gag.

'Thank fuck.' His mouth sounded full of sand, the words like dry pebbles. 'You came back.'

'Like I was going to just leave you here.'

'I was beginning to wonder.'

My celebration dinner that night consisted of tinned corned beef, tinned potatoes and tinned peas, all washed down with a tin of piss-warm Foster's. I offered to share but Fogarty wasn't hungry. Skipping a couple of meals wouldn't be any great hardship. He has enough fat reserves to see him through till Christmas.

There was plenty to celebrate. The boy had come up with the goods, as expected. If I'm completely honest, there were a couple of moments where I thought he was going to screw up, but he came through in the end and that's what counts. Whoever says it's the journey that matters is talking crap. When you've travelled as far as I have you get to see that the destination is everything. The rest is wallpaper: boring and repetitive and of no real use to anyone. I finished my meal, lifted my can of Foster's in a toast. 'Here's to us,' I said. 'Nothing can stop us now.'

On the other side of the table, Sophia lifted her crystal wine glass. She was wearing wild flowers in her hair and her movements were flowing and easy. This was the Sophia I remember. Radiant and graceful and full of life. I blinked the moistness away and when I opened my eyes I was alone at the black marble-patterned Formica-topped table in Fogarty's cramped kitchen, surrounded by tins and holding my can of lager up to nobody.

Fogarty's working without his usual flair and exuberance. When he made me old you could tell he was having a ball, really getting into his work. He'd primp and preen, stand back fingering his lip, ponder over a quick puff of his cigarette then dive in to make a tiny alteration I couldn't see with my Philistine eyes; stand back and ponder then dive in again. His fat fingers moved quickly, expertly, as though they had a mind of their own.

Now he's working like a washed-up singer who's done one comeback tour too many. His performance is soulless. Mind you, Fogarty firing on two cylinders would still leave most make-up artists in the dust. He learnt his trade in Ealing during the Sixties and made a good living until the British film industry went kaput. That's why he opened the shop. Hiring out fancy dress costumes barely covered the rent so he started diversifying, providing alternative identities for people who needed to disappear and had the money to make it happen. For the right price he could get hold of passports, driving licences,

NI numbers – and of course there was that all-important new face. He takes another nervous puff, studies the photographs taped to the mirror, places the cigarette shakily into the ashtray. He picks up a pair of scissors.

'You'll be careful with those,' I warn.

'Yeah, Mac. Course I will.'

That's as much as he's said since I sat down in the big red barber chair. 'Relax,' I tell him. 'I'd hate you to slip.'

'Don't worry, Mac, I won't slip. You don't have to worry about that.' His smile is forced.

He starts trimming the wig, stopping occasionally to compare the style with the person in the photographs. I stare into the mirror and it's a surreal experience, even more so than when he made me old. This time we're rolling back the years. I'm looking through a window in time and seeing shades of the man I used to be.

Zoning out, I search for Sophia in the deep glass. She was here before, she'll be back again. I stare deep into the mirror and the person I'm becoming stares right back. I lose myself in memories: Sophia getting ready to go out and asking my opinion on a gorgeous black dress, whether it suits her or not, and her pretending to get mad when I tell her she looks amazing whatever she wears; Sophia, eyes closed, losing herself in a song; Sophia dressed in black leather and the crack of the whip; Sophia flashing that strange little half-smile, the look on her face suggesting she knows something

I don't . . . I want to prompt her back into existence, but it's not working, and the harder I try the further away she gets. I close my eyes, try to picture her in my mind, and my heart dies a little more when I realise I can't even do that. My God, I can't remember what she looks like! Panic grabs me. It's like I'm losing her all over again.

And just when I think she's gone for good, there she is in the glass. She was only teasing me. Even in death she can't help herself. I smile at her and she smiles right back, and that's how I know it's her. Nobody else on earth smiles like that. We're everywhere and nowhere able to exist in multiple times and spaces. Now we're back in Vienna, walking hand in hand through the Innere Stadt, humbled by the exquisite Baroque buildings; now we're outside a dirty block registry office on a rainy London afternoon, Sophia a vision in her blue wedding dress, the wildflowers in her hair mirroring the wild turbulent beauty in her heart; now we're in bed, losing ourselves in the moment, candlelight playing on her perfect skin, perspiration glistening in the cleft between her breasts; now she's singing for me, accompanying herself on the piano, a song she's written herself, and the words are in Italian because she believes it's the sexiest language on earth . . .

So many memories.

When did I realise what Sophia really was? A question with more than one answer. When I'm deluding myself, I like to paint myself as the victim in a grand conspiracy. In more truthful moments I'll admit that I knew from the second she sat down opposite me in that Vienna bar and told me her name. Subconsciously that is. My conscious mind wasn't really listening at that point . . . or, more accurately, it didn't want to hear.

Perhaps a more useful question is: When did I step over the line? Was it that fateful night when I spilled my secrets high above Vienna, spinning through the starry sky on the big wheel? Or was it that day, a month or so later, when Sophia came to me with the video. I knew something was up straightaway. She had this pained expression, like she was battling with some inner turmoil. 'I'm sorry, Robbie,' she'd said as she handed the tape to me. 'Please don't hate me.'

It's Sunday now, which means I've got six days. If you believe the hype, God got the whole universe up and working in that timeframe, so I reckon I can do what I've got to do.

'Finished,' Fogarty announces. He takes a cautious step back, his worried reflection plagued by shadows. 'See what you think.'

I take my time, turning my head this way and that. As I examine Fogarty's handiwork, I bombard him with questions about the best way to take the latex off, how to look after it, how to put it back on, how to make repairs. He answers reluctantly to start with but soon warms to his chosen subject.

'So,' he asks cautiously, 'what do you think?'

'Very impressive,' I say. 'Up to your usual standard.'

Fogarty's face sags with relief. 'So, Mac, how long are you planning to stay for?' he says, before adding hurriedly: 'Of course, you can stay as long as you want.'

'A couple more days,' I tell him.

'And the money?'

'I take it cash is okay?'

'Perfect,' he says.

He's acting nervous, like there's something he needs to get off his chest but doesn't know where to start.

'Spit it out, Fogarty.'

'It's just this tying up business . . . well, you don't need to do it. You can trust me.'

'And there you go again,' I say to his reflection, 'talking about trust. Do you know who I trust?'

'Who?'

'Nobody.' I reach under the red cloth, pull out the gun. A small dark hole appears in the middle of Fogarty's forehead, the sound of the shot swallowed by the silencer.

33

Vienna, 1993

She handed over the video and told him not to hate her. She suggested he watch it when he had a moment, and then she was gone. No kiss, no hug. No sex. She didn't even bother to take her coat off. In and out quicker than the SAS. He was left looking at the patterns on the back of the front door, clutching the video in his hand and wondering what this was all about. A redundant question. After he took a moment to think things through, it all became obvious. He poured himself a glass of wine, plugged the video into the machine, and sat back with the remote control.

Their sex life had quickly moved into increasingly darker territories. There were no boundaries, nothing was taboo. Whatever he wanted, she was more than happy to give. Pleasure and pain. Submission and domination. And it was all on tape, all of it shot in the room she'd rented. He smiled to himself when he realised where the camera had been hidden. The crucifix above the bed. Nice touch. Caught in the act by Jesus Christ Himself.

The picture was wide-angled and grainy, but there was no mistaking who the principal characters were. Nor was there any doubt in his mind what would happen if Kinclave got hold of this. A call back to London, a 'sorry old chap but I'm sure you understand', then shunted off to a desk in the middle of fucking nowhere. So how did he play this one? He took a sip of wine, paused the film. His on-screen doppelganger was currently tied to the bed, face frozen in mid-gasp as she dripped hot candle wax onto his testicles. Resigning was an option, but it wasn't going to happen. If he quit, then the bastards would have won, and he wasn't going to let that happen. Option two was to play along. See what she wanted and then work the situation to his advantage.

He hit play again and there was a crude cut to the next scene. She was on her hands and knees now, a dog collar around her neck, a mask covering her face. On screen his doppelganger jerked the lead and she yelped. God, she was good. One in a million. Now that he'd got over the initial shock of seeing himself on TV, he had to admit that there was a certain voyeuristic kick to be had here.

They met up the next evening and she was like a rabbit caught in the headlights. She wouldn't look him in the eye. Instead she kept stealing glances, like he was some sort of serial killer. She told him what she wanted in a stiff speech punctuated with lots of uhms and aahs. And when she was done, he burst out laughing and told her if she'd wanted something all she had to do was ask. Then he gave her some tips on the Dos and Don'ts of blackmail.

'You don't hate me, then?' she asked.

The question came straight from the heart and this surprised him. His answer really mattered to her. 'Why did you do it?'

A shrug. 'Why does anyone do anything? Money.'

It was as good a reason as any. And honest. He didn't doubt that for a second. There was nothing of the idealist about her. She was a realist, all the way down the line.

'So,' she said, 'do you hate me?'

'Why should you care?'

She hesitated, bit her lip. 'Normally I wouldn't. But you're different.'

'And why should I believe you? Why should I trust you? You've just tried to blackmail me.'

'Robbie, as a rule I don't think you should trust anyone. You start trusting and then you get hurt. But–'

'But I'm different,' he finished for her. 'So how do we play this one?'

Another shrug. 'This is new territory for me.'

'Me, too,' he said. 'How about we make it up as we go along?'

'Sounds good to me.'

She moved in closer, the scent of Opium following her. He buried his face in the dip of her shoulder, inhaling deeply, fingertips moving up her spine, up her neck. He got hold of her hair and twisted it around his hand, jerked hard. She exhaled sharply in his ear.

'Okay,' he said. 'Enough talking, let's fuck.'

Looking back, maybe it was that day with the video when he crossed the line, or perhaps it was that day *less than a week later when he passed her the slip of paper with the name on it. She took it without a word, looked at it, folded it and tucked it away safe. A few days later she handed him an envelope. Inside were the details for a Swiss bank account that held £50,000. A couple of weeks later he heard that one of MI6's informers in Egypt had mysteriously disappeared. Missing, presumed dead. After that first time it got easier. Not that he took risks. He was always careful about what he sold, making sure nothing was going to come back and bite him. And the rewards were spectacular. He was stacking up cash in hidden accounts like it was Monopoly money.*

He found out later that her background was far less glamorous than she'd made out. Her father hadn't been in the army; he was a pimp. Her mother had been one of his girls. There was no Austrian grandmother who'd told her romantic tales about Vienna.

It was only natural for her to end up in the family business. With her looks, and her willingness to do whatever a punter wanted, she'd ended up working for one of London's top escort agencies. Christopher had never been a customer, but associates of his had. When he needed a girl to carry out a very special job, her name came up. She was approached and a deal was struck. For her it was always about the money. She could never get enough. And she didn't spend it, just hoarded it away. For him the money was a big part of it, but not all of it. By accident or design, her timing had been perfect. She arrived in his life when he needed a new game to play, and the game she introduced him to was perfect. He got to take the piss out of the bastards who'd fucked him over. There he was right in the middle of them all, selling them out left, right and centre, and they didn't suspect a thing.

34

The bed bounced gently, nudging Aston from a surreal dream where he was running through a field filled with mannequins, all of them with his face. The bouncing moved closer and a hand touched his leg, fingers tracing a slow, sensuous path up the inside of his thigh. Through sleep-filled eyes he saw a hazy hump in the duvet hovering above his groin. Aston pushed his head back into the pillow, covered his eyes with the back of his arm. The tongue flicked up the side of his dick, slowly, teasingly, stopping when it reached the top. *No no no*, the alarmed thought ringing through his head. 'No,' he moaned sleepily, 'don't stop.' A pause where he thought she wouldn't continue, and then she had him in her mouth, working him expertly with lips and tongue, keeping him wet and warm with her damp heat. He was more awake now, awake enough to know he shouldn't be doing this, but too far gone to stop. 'Mmm,' he whispered, reacting to a change in her rhythm. She had a hold of the base of his dick, squeezing hard, and was massaging the head with her tongue. She kept up the rhythm, fucking him with her mouth, faster, faster, and he felt the orgasm building, did nothing to hold it back, edging closer and closer to the point of no return, the moan escaping his lips primitive, low and guttural, words forming from the groans, simplistic words, language at its most basic. 'God . . . George . . .'

She stopped so suddenly that his first instinct was to kill her. This wasn't funny. Not fucking funny at all. He grabbed the edge of the duvet and pulled it away with an angry flourish.

Laura was kneeling on the bed scowling at him.

Aston came completely awake in an instant, his penis shrinking, running for cover. Laura didn't seem to notice her own nakedness, didn't appear to be aware of anything except him, and her scrutiny was awful. He would have grabbed the duvet and pulled it over himself, or reached down the side of the bed for his pants, but he was completely paralysed. Laura wasn't saying a word and somehow this was worse than if she'd been ranting. She broke eye contact and looked around the bedroom, cataloguing the evidence.

'Well,' she said finally.

A single word had never sounded so cold, had never been delivered with such icy severity. How did you talk your way out of this one? Whatever he said would be the wrong thing. This was a classic lose/lose whichever way he looked.

'Well,' she repeated, 'what have you got to say for yourself?'

Aston rubbed his face, his morning whiskers scratching his palm, and prayed for a miracle. The only thing he could think to say was *It's not what you think*. But that would be like handing Laura a gun, curling her finger around the trigger and pressing his forehead against the barrel.

'Well,' she said.

'It's not what you think,' Aston heard himself saying.

'Would you believe I came here to apologise. Apologise! How's that for a joke? Ha-bloody-ha! I was actually going to apologise. To you. I'd had time to think, and I realised there was no way you'd have an affair with George, that it was me being all paranoid and pathetic. Just goes to show, doesn't it? I mean, how wrong can you get?'

Pleading the fifth he looked away, dragged the duvet carefully over himself, aware that any sudden movements might set her off again. With everything going on, that was the last thing he needed. Her timing couldn't have been worse. Mac was out there planning God knows what, and here he was having a domestic. It kind of put things in perspective.

'Jesus Christ, Paul, you are such a shit!' Laura picked up her clothes from the foot of the bed and dressed violently, wrenching on panties, jeans and T-shirt. The Salvador Dali print on the far side of the room was the most fascinating picture he'd

333

ever seen. The way those clocks melted over the branches – absolutely fascinating. Laura had run out of steam, but she wasn't done yet. He knew from experience that they'd drifted into the eye of the hurricane. This was a moment of stillness, a single calm moment where it was possible to believe that all was well in the world.

'How could I be so fucking stupid!' Laura exploded, punctuating each word with a jab of her trainer. She slammed down onto the edge of the bed, back to him, and put her shoes on, muttering to herself, winding herself up for the big one. She finished tying her laces and stood, pulled herself up to her full height.

'How long has it been going on?' she demanded. 'Come on, Paul. How long? You owe me that much, at least.'

Stony-faced, he studied the Dali, searching for hidden meaning in the brushstrokes. Disassociation was one of the tricks he'd learned during the interrogation phase of his training. Sometimes it was the only way to escape the pain, whether physical or mental.

'For Christ's sake, Paul, say something. Do you have any idea how much this pisses me off, you giving me the silent treatment like this? It drives me fucking nuts.' A pause and then she added in an eerily calm voice: 'Okay, that's it. And I mean it this time. There's no coming back from this one. We're finished.'

This was the point when he was supposed to

jump in and give her a hundred and one reasons why she should stay. They'd been at this particular junction before, many a time. He could hear himself offering all the usual platitudes, but it wasn't going to happen. Not this time. It was for the best, he told himself. Break-ups were sad, but life went on. The clichés seemed to sit comfortably enough. Too comfortably, perhaps. George had told him months ago that he should finish with Laura. Looked like she'd been right all along. He'd never admit that, though. George was an expert at the told-you-so.

'Alright,' he said.

'Alright?' Laura repeated. 'What the hell's that supposed to mean?'

'It means that I'm agreeing with you. You're right, it's not working.'

'Oh.'

'Come on, Laura, all we do is fight,' Aston said. 'I'm tired of all the fighting.'

Laura said nothing, just stared at him with big hurt eyes.

'It's for the best. Really it is. You've got to see that. If we carry on like this we'll wind up killing each other. I'm not happy, and if you're honest with yourself, you're not happy, either.'

Silence.

'I'm hoping we can stay friends,' he said.

'Friends!' Laura snorted. '*Friends!* I fucking hate you, Paul. You're such a bastard. I wish I'd neve—'

335

She was stopped in mid-flow by the sound of the front door opening and closing, footsteps in the hall.

'You gave her a key,' Laura hissed in disbelief. 'You gave her a fucking key to our flat! Our home!'

My flat, Aston thought, but this really wasn't the time for a territorial dispute. Another moment of stillness as the footsteps moved nearer, like the footsteps of the condemned walking across the gallows while a packed crowd held its breath.

'Come on, time you were up. We've got work to do.' George shouted out as she opened the bedroom door. 'The milk in the fridge had turned to cheese so I wen–' She stood in the doorway holding a pint of milk.

'You fucking bitch!' Laura spat. She turned to Aston. 'The two of you are welcome to each other. I hope you're really fucking happy together.'

'Laura,' George said. 'It's not what you think.'

'Funny, that,' Laura said, swiping her damp eyes with the sleeve of her sweatshirt. 'That's exactly what he said, too.'

'It's *not* what you think,' George repeated. 'I needed somewhere to stay and Paul said I could stay here.'

'You shared a bed,' she said, then added quietly: 'Our bed.'

'I slept on the sofa, Laura.'

'And I'm supposed to believe that. Do I really look that stupid?' Her tone was hard but Aston saw the tears in her eyes. She was only hearing what she wanted to hear, and what she wanted to hear were the words that cut into the most sensitive parts; like a nun whipping herself in penance for sins real and imaginary, she needed the pain before she could get absolution. Aston sat on the bed watching this sparring match with a kind of morbid fascination. He felt obliged to say something, but couldn't for the life of him think what.

'Laura—'

'You're telling me you spent the night with Paul and nothing happened?'

'For the last time, we didn't sleep together. Now, I don't know what the hell sort of fairy story you've got going around your head right now, but you're way off the mark.'

'Well, I don't fucking believe you,' Laura hissed. 'This is such bullshit!'

'I'm not going to argue with you,' George said. 'I think I'd better go. This is between you two.'

'No,' Aston said quietly and both women turned to look at him. 'George – you stay, we've got work to do. Laura, I think you should leave. I'll call you to arrange a time when you can pick up your stuff.'

Laura's face was a mix of resentment and hatred. Aston could see how much she was hurting but there was nothing he could do. It *was* for the best, really it was. She opened her mouth to say something, then thought better of it. She picked up her bag and without another word left the room.

George waited for the front door to slam, then

said: 'Would it help if I told you you're better off without her?'

Aston slumped back on the bed and pulled a pillow over his face, blocking out the big bad world. Obviously it was going to be another one of those days.

35

'How long have you been seeing Mac for?'

George looked up from her monitor and her expression was worth a dozen confessions. There were a number of questions that had been troubling him since yesterday. Why had she gone off to meet Mac like that? Why had she not said anything? And the biggie: Why had she gone alone? None of it made sense. It was during the short taxi ride to Vauxhall Cross that the solution occurred to him. When the lightning hit he'd been staring out the window, focusing on nothing and thinking about nothing. It was one of those stray thoughts he'd initially been tempted to ignore. No way George was having a fling with Mac. That was crazy. But the thought wouldn't go away, and the more it hung around the more plausible it seemed. If George was screwing Mac that would go a long way to explaining what she'd done.

'That obvious, huh?' she said.

'Not at all,' Aston replied.

'Are you surprised? Shocked?'

'Yes and no,' Aston admitted truthfully. 'I've always said your love life is a soap opera.'

George laughed.

'Want to talk about it?' Aston asked.

'Not really.'

'Will you talk about it?'

While she thought about this, Aston perched on the edge of the desk and looked around her pod. The Middle East controllerate occupied a large open plan office space on the fourth floor, and even though it was a Sunday, the office was still pretty busy. Since 18/8 it had been all hands to the deck. The partitions were high enough to offer a modicum of privacy without allowing too much; this was MI6, after all, a place where Big Brother was most definitely watching. Aston noted the little touches George had added to humanise the sterile. Pinned to the partition wall were a couple of family snapshots, a still of a blue-faced Mel Gibson from *Braveheart*, a child's painting. The painting was an abstract in bright primary colours: reds, blues, yellows and greens. Could've been a man, could've been a woman, could've been an alien. The artist's name was written in red biro in the bottom left corner: Liz. George's niece by the perfect older sister her mother constantly compared her to. The same perfect sister who'd lost her virginity at fourteen and used to smoke pot. Still, the painting and the photos were proof that, for all George's attempts to disown her family, it was all tough talk and bluster. Deep down she was a family girl at heart.

'I didn't mean for it to happen,' George said eventually.

'How long have you been seeing him?' Aston kept his voice neutral, non-judgmental. Softly, softly was the way to keep her talking.

'About six months.'

'That long?'

'Yup.'

'Well, you kept that a secret.'

George forced a smile. 'I work for MI6. I'm supposed to be good at keeping secrets.'

'Even still, it's not like you. Normally you can't wait to offload all the gory details. Usually I get more information than I can handle.'

'This was different. I wasn't sure how you'd react. What with it being Mac.'

'Don't see how that makes a difference.'

'Come on, Paul, you would have sulked for a week. Do you have any idea how territorial you are when it comes to Mac?'

'Am not.'

George replied with a raising of the eyebrows.

'Okay, maybe a little,' Aston conceded.

'Paul, no one can get to Mac without going through you first. Anyway,' she continued, 'he wanted the affair kept secret. Gave me some bullshit about how the Powers That Be wouldn't like it. Best to keep business and pleasure separate . . . that was another line he fed me. Jesus, Paul, how could I have been so fucking stupid?'

'Don't be so hard on yourself.'

'Don't be so hard on myself! Come on, Paul, I should have seen what he was up to straight away. It's all so bloody obvious now, isn't it? The reason he wanted to keep things secret was because he was bloody well married. Another fucking married man! How do I do it, eh? Am I some sort of magnet?'

'That wasn't the only reason, though, was it?'

'I'm getting there.' George almost smiled. 'I just need to beat myself up a little more first . . . if it's all the same with you.' A deep breath. She ran her hand through her crinkly hair, straightened out the scrunchy. Eyes closed, she moved her head from side to side and the bones in her neck clicked unpleasantly. Another deep breath. 'Okay, I'm done.'

Aston said nothing. He knew George well enough to know what was coming next. The best thing for him to do was to shut up and let her get on with it.

'That fucking two-faced cunt.' Her voice was low, but the words carried well enough for the agent three pods over to turn and look. She fired off a glare Medusa would have been proud of, sending him scurrying for cover. 'That bastard tried to fucking kill me. Can you believe that?'

Aston nodded, said nothing.

'I really thought I was going to die. I've never been so scared in my life. And what was it all for, Paul, eh? He was using me to get to you. For him it was just all some fucked-up game. He didn't give a shit about me. Bastard!' A sigh, a shake of the head, a weary smile. 'He used to tell me how beautiful I was. All the time. I didn't believe him to start with, but he kept saying it, over and over like he couldn't work out why I couldn't see it. You know what he's like, Paul? How persuasive he can be? Well, guess what? In the end I actually started believing him. How gullible is that? How fucking naïve?'

'You're not exactly ugly, are you?'

'Nice of you to say so, Paul. Thanks. You know how to make a girl feel special.'

'I didn't mean it like that. It sounded better in my head.'

George leant over and patted his hand. 'Don't worry. I know what you meant.'

'Why Mac? He's old enough to be your father. Maybe that's it, George, a father thing. You thought about that?'

'What's this, Paul? You been flicking through those psychology textbooks again?'

'Well?'

'I don't know. It's difficult to explain. He's got this presence, you know, that larger than life thing going on.' A long pause, then George said: 'I don't want to talk about this anymore. Let's not forget the bastard did try to kill me.'

George swung around in the seat and stared at the monitor. Conversation over. Aston took the hint and didn't press any further. She clicked open a file that held a number of emails all originating from the same address: blackbird343@yahoo.com.

'This is interesting,' she said. 'Looks like Blackbird's been a busy boy.'

'Who?'

George pulled up a file.

Aston looked at the picture on the screen. It was a typical surveillance shot, taken from a bad angle and computer enhanced. A handsome Middle Eastern face, lean and clean-shaven, black hair cut in a short back and sides, forty to forty-five.

'Got a name?' Aston asked, still looking at the picture.

'The name he's been using is Christopher Walker.'

'What's his story?'

'On the surface he's a born-again Englishman. Went to Cambridge where he got a degree in Economics, plays golf, drives a Jag, has a flat in Kensington. He has a harem of successful businesses, mostly in import/export.'

'On the surface . . .'

'When you dig deeper, things start to get interesting. The first thing you discover is that he's the son of a Saudi oil tycoon. Ahmed Al Fagih is as anti-American as they come, and there's a strong suspicion that he's linked with terrorism. Walker has been careful to distance himself from his father, but not careful enough. We've done some delving into his accounts and his businesses aren't doing as well as they appear to be doing. The general feeling here on the fourth floor is that dad's giving him a shitload of pocket money to keep him afloat. We've been watching him for a while now, and since Leicester Square we've been keeping a very close eye on him. He's a player, I'm convinced of that.'

'Why haven't you had him picked up?'

'We're waiting to see what he does next.'

Aston nodded. This was a common tactic. Because of the way terrorist groups were structured, cutting off the head rarely resulted in killing the snake. Cells worked independently and it often made more sense to leave a major player in the game to see where they would lead them.

George clicked on the latest email. It was short on specifics but interesting nonetheless. It talked of striking a massive blow against the Infidels. Blood would flow through the streets and the poisoned air would choke in their lungs, it promised. She opened a couple more emails and they all followed a similar theme. 'And it's not just Blackbird who's been chattering away,' George said. 'Overnight there's been a marked increase in email traffic on our flagged accounts. Something big's on the cards.'

'So where are we?' Aston asked. 'What do we actually know? Okay, Mac had something to do with the bombing. How deep that involvement is remains to be seen, but I think we can assume it's pretty deep.'

'Careful throwing assumptions around,' George

said, holding his gaze. 'All we've got is circumstantial evidence. He had that video clip on his laptop. So what? That doesn't mean anything.'

'He practically admitted the whole thing to me on the phone.'

'Did he admit it or not?'

'More or less.'

'More or less isn't good enough.'

'Well, it's good enough for me. Mac's up to his ears in this.'

'Why are you so quick to condemn him?'

'And why are you so quick to defend him?'

George went to say something, hesitated. 'Right now I'd be quite happy to see Mac crucified for what he did to me. Believe me, I'd be first in line to hammer the nails in.'

'But . . . ?'

'But I still can't get my head around the idea that he's involved in the Leicester Square bombing. It's just too much to take in.'

'I know what you mean, George, but we've got to face the facts. And the facts are pointing to Mac being involved. And if Mac is involved you can guarantee that he's a chief rather than an Indian. Mac's a control freak. When have you known him to play second fiddle to anyone?'

'Yeah, I suppose you're right. It's difficult to detach yourself from the situation, though. You can't just turn your feelings off.'

'But that's exactly what you've got to do in this business.'

'It sucks, doesn't it?'

'Yeah, it sucks,' Aston agreed. 'Okay, back to business. Mac says he's planning something that will completely overshadow 18/8. The first thing we've got to look for is motivation.'

'Well,' George offered, 'the usual suspects are belief, money, blackmail or revenge.'

'Scratch belief,' Aston said. 'I don't see him as a born-again Muslim, do you?'

'Not really.'

'And there's no way Mac would be stupid enough to get blackmailed. Next on the list is money.'

'Possible.'

'But you're not convinced,' Aston said.

'I can't see Mac doing this just for money. Money might be part of it, but it's not all of it.'

'What about revenge?'

'Revenge on who?'

Aston shrugged. 'Your guess is as good as mine.'

'If we're going to catch him, Paul, we need to know what motivates him.'

'Oh, so we're going to catch him, are we? Since when?'

'Come on, Paul, can you think of anyone better qualified? If anyone can suss him out, it's us.'

'My thoughts exactly,' said a soft, reasonable voice from behind. Aston turned and was surprised to see Kinclave hovering there. Aston hadn't heard The Chief sneak up and wondered how long he'd been standing there, how much he'd overheard.

George was looking as perplexed as he was, no doubt wondering the same.

'I want you two working together to find Mac,' Kinclave said. The Chief was keeping his voice low, making sure he wasn't overheard. His presence on the fourth floor couldn't have passed unnoticed, ears would be twitching. 'Until he's caught that's your number one priority. You know him better than anyone. Of course, it goes without saying that I want this kept as quiet as possible.'

'And how much longer do you think we can keep this quiet?' George said.

'This *has* to be kept quiet.'

'But how are we supposed to do that?' Aston said. 'After the stunt Mac pulled yesterday you've now got the boys from the Met sniffing around, and that's in addition to the questions the press must be asking.'

'I'm sure you'll find a way,' Kinclave said smoothly. 'I've got every faith in you.' He widened his gaze to include George. 'Both of you.'

'What resources have we got to play with?' George asked.

'In what sense?'

'Well, what about manpower, for a start?'

'Haven't you been listening? We need to keep a lid on this. A tight lid.'

'It's just the two of us,' Aston said, 'isn't it?'

'Jesus!' George said. 'You saw how many died at Leicester Square. You know what Mac's capable of. We should be calling in the police, MI5 as well.

If Mac isn't found, and found quickly, more innocent people are going to die.'

Kinclave swooped in close. 'Now listen to me,'
he said in a sharp whisper. 'You'll do exactly what
I tell you to do, and you'll do it because I'm giving
the orders around here. Now it might have escaped
your attention, but MI6 is currently facing the
biggest shitstorm in its history. I will *not* be remem-
bered as the person who was at the helm when
the ship went down. Am I making myself one
hundred percent crystal clear here?'

Kinclave stood up, and straightened the
Windsor knot in his blue silk tie. 'Find Mac,' he
said. 'Find him before this gets any more fucked
up.' He turned on his heels and marched off.

'Well, that's us told,' George said when The
Chief was out of earshot.

'Mind telling me what that was all about?' Aston
asked.

'Seems simple enough to me,' George said. 'He's
covering his arse, Paul. He wants Mac found, and
he wants it done quietly. Where do you think the
buck stops when it gets out that an MI6 man was
involved in the Leicester Square bombing?'

'But it won't work. It's got to get out eventually. Whichever way you look at it, Kinclave is
screwed.'

'I know that and you know that, but desperate
men do desperate things. Logic doesn't come into
it.'

'Desperate enough to let innocent people die.'

'Hey, I'm just trying to understand him. That doesn't mean I agree with him.'

Aston sighed and shook his head. 'This is getting more fucked up by the second.'

36

Call it training, call it paranoia, whatever, but I don't go straight to the meet. I travel the Underground for a while, enjoying the anonymity of my new face. Get off at one station, change line, get on another train, hurtle once more into the abyss. I go for the half-empty carriages; full enough to hide, not so crowded that you can't breathe. There are one or two frightened expressions, a couple of brave faces . . . if only they knew who they were travelling with. Little glances to check no one is following. Of course, nobody is. Why should there be? The face I'm wearing isn't on any Most Wanted list.

I get off at Bank and work my way through the maze of tunnels, following the signs to the surface. Above ground the sun is shining, the tall buildings casting slim noon shadows. I head for Cheapside, totally alive and in the moment, noticing everything. The roar of the cars and buses, the colour and bustle, the dirt and grime. I pass one of the Invisible Ones. She's rattling a tin cup and her eyes follow me. I'm suddenly convinced she knows who I am. Impossible, but it takes a moment to shake the feeling. I resist the urge to turn and stare, just carry on walking, heart beating faster. Cruising into the wake of a businessman with a mobile glued to his ear, I eavesdrop for a second, catching fragments. He's talking dirty, getting off on the fact that he's in a public place. His wife maybe? His mistress? Probably the latter. He looks the sort. A little too clean-cut, a little too good to be true. A final look-see; for this meet I need to be one hundred and ten percent sure I'm not being followed.

Out of the sunshine and into the sacred gloom; St Paul's Cathedral swallows me whole. My shoes crack against the hard floor, like pistol shots, echoing away to nothing in that vast cavernous space. I find a quiet seat in the shadows, a seat where I can see all the comings and goings, and wait for Nicholai. There are a fair few tourists milling about, mostly Japs and Yanks. Funny how you can tell so much about a person from the way they dress and wear their hair. The Japs are labelled up to their ears – Nike, Adidas, Sony, Panasonic – even the little ones have camcorders grafted to their hands. And these are definitely Japs as opposed to some other flavour of Asian. White eyes aren't supposed to be able to discern the difference, but I can. The Yanks are wearing baggy clothes to hide the excess weight: loud Hawaiian shirts and knee-length shorts, sweatshirts and sweatpants. A couple of the men have droopy San Francisco moustaches; some of the women have big Dynasty hair.

Nicholai is former KGB, old school. I've got a lot of time for him. We're a dying breed. When I was stationed in Moscow his job was to shadow me. He knew I was MI6, I knew he was KGB, but that was all part of the game. Basically, if they'd booted me out MI6 would have had to replace me, and the KGB would've had to go to all the trouble of tagging the new boy. Sometimes it's better to stick with the devil you know.

When the USSR went kaput, Nicholai went self-employed. He's made his money selling arms: guns, surface-to-air missiles, he can get hold of a tank if you've got the cash; all that good stuff was just lying around waiting to be picked up, and he got in there PDQ. Nicholai is currently living like a Tsar. He's got a luxury flat in Moscow, a small palace in St Petersburg, a luxury villa on the coast of The Black Sea, a second villa in Cyprus. His girlfriends are all under twenty, drop-dead gorgeous, bodies to die for. He's driven everywhere in a Rolls Royce Silver Shadow – armour plated, bullet-proof windows, red leather and walnut interior. It's amazing how easily he made the transition from protector-of-the-Commie-way to hedonistic capitalist. Mind you, principles won't put bread on your table – a conclusion I wish I'd reached sooner. It would have saved me a ton of heartache and wasted years. And I would have been a hell of a lot richer, too. Maybe even as rich as Nicholai.

Whenever we do business I always insist on the personal touch, and because of our history Nicholai is happy to oblige. When you're richer than God you don't get many opportunities to get out of the office; success is its own ball and chain, and my guess is that Nicholai sometimes misses the old days almost as much as I do. For all his roubles he doesn't mind getting his hands dirty – despite his griping, he enjoys it – and I can relate to that. There's nothing like rolling up your sleeves and getting in there yourself.

The old stones of St Paul's encourage gothic fantasies and I try not to look too deeply into the dark corners. I catch a ripple in the corner of my eye and I've got to smile. Only one person ever came close to getting up early enough to get one over on me. I swivel around and study the large shape in the shadows. Wondering how long he's been there, I get up and walk over, sit down next to him. He doesn't turn to look, doesn't acknowledge me, but I know he's already catalogued every single detail. We sit in silence for a while, both staring straight ahead.

'Still wearing that God-awful aftershave,' he says.

His English is excellent, polished and educated with a slight trace of an accent. He turns and smiles at me. The ruby imbedded in his front tooth is new; the good living has added another stone or two. He's dressed in the uniform of a Yankee tourist – grey NYU sweatshirt, grey sweatpants – the bad hair has to be a wig.

'Good to see you, too,' I tell him.

'Like the disguise, by the way. Fooled me . . . for a bit.'

'Fucking uncomfortable is what it is.'

Nicholai studies my face. 'Nice work,' he says admiringly. 'And not a facelift. At first I thought you'd had surgery. And then I'm thinking to myself that you wouldn't be so stupid.' He pats my latex cheek. 'Were we ever this young, my friend?'

Nicholai stands and I follow suit. He wraps his arms around me in a bear hug, hands checking for weapons. I do the same. A formality; neither of us is carrying. I'm not small but Nicholai dwarfs me. I recently saw a mandate stating that MI6 would no longer take on agents over six feet tall, some bollocks about them not blending into the background like good spies are supposed to. The moron who came up with that one had obviously never met Nicholai. He's still the best spy I know. If he wants to be invisible then he's gone.

'How was your journey?' I ask.

The laugh rumbles up from his toes. 'Always with the jokes, eh?' he says. 'A week stuck on that fucking boat drinking cheap vodka and being bounced around on waves as big as a house. It was no Caribbean cruise, I'll tell you that for nothing. I was actually pleased to see Ireland, can you believe that?'

'Beautiful country, Ireland.'

'The things I do for you, my friend.' A shake of his head, bulldog jowls wobbling. He pulls out a Pay As You Go mobile and waggles it at me. 'Shall we?'

We both sit together. I pass Nicholai a slip of paper with an account number and an international phone number on. The Russian makes the call and the banker on the other end confirms that the money has been transferred, all ten million. Nicholai clicks the phone closed, smiling. He reaches under the pew and pulls out a hold-all. Got to admire his sense of humour. It's white with heavy-duty handles and a map of the Underground on it. I unzip it, count seven 'I ♥ London' T-shirts stuffed in the top, one for each colour of the rainbow. Underneath I catch a flash of lead. The weight tells me the bag contains what I want. Nicholai hasn't diddled me yet, and I see no reason for him to start now.

'It might be a good idea if we avoid each other for a while,' Nicholai says.

'Embarrassed to be seen with me?'

'I'm serious.' He nods to the hold-all. 'I don't want this coming back to bite me.'

'It won't,' I assure him.

'I'm doing this as a favour.'

'Bollocks. You're doing it for the money.'

'That as well.' He smiles, the ruby in his tooth

glinting. 'The person I got this from is dead. The person he got it from is dead. And the person he got it from is dying from cancer in a shitty Siberian hospital, pumped so full of morphine that no one has a clue what he's on about. Nobody in my organisation knows about this transaction except me. *Nobody* knows about this except me and you. I would like to keep it that way.'

'You worry too much,' I tell him.

'Worry is the Russian way. We've been carrying the weight of the world since the beginning of time. That's why our shoulders are so broad.' He stands to leave, lays a meaty hand on my arm. 'Be lucky, my friend.'

I'm in no hurry to go and I sit for a while in that cool empty space, gazing around at the religious artefacts and paintings, staring up into the huge empty dome. The hold-all is sitting on the pew next to me and I shuffle a few inches further away, not wanting to get too close.

37

'You said it was urgent.'

'Maybe it is, maybe it's not.'

They were down in the Unreal, drifting in the twilight world of Mole's Hobbit hole. The overheads were out, the only illumination coming from the monitors, screensavers painting psychedelic patterns on walls and faces. Music was playing low in the background, Aerosmith going on about how the dude looked like a lady. Mole was coming to the end of his shift and a thick fog of cigarette smoke and patchouli filled the air. MI6's powerful air conditioners had met their match with the hacker. As soon as they pumped it out he was pumping it right back in.

'Well, is it important or not?' Aston asked.

'Put it this way, if I'd said I had something mildly interesting would you have jumped out of bed and come running to see me?'

'Of course not.'

'There you go. I rest my case.'

'What case? What the hell are you talking about?' George was standing with her arms crossed and Aston recognised the expression. This was not her happy face. George liked her beauty sleep and for her to drag herself out of bed at six in the morning there had to be a bloody good reason.

'Here's the thing, Georgie—'

'Don't ever call me that,' George snapped. 'You have till I count three. Get to the point or I'm out of here. One . . .'

'Dirty bombs,' Mole said in a voice that was barely a whisper.

That got Aston's attention. 'Where are you going with this, Mole?' he said.

'I think Mac's building himself one.'

'What makes you say that?' Aston said. His heart was suddenly tripping over itself, hammering too fast, but he sounded calm.

Mole waved George and Aston closer, hit a couple of keys. A news article appeared, spread across the three dressing-table monitors of Mole's main terminal. Aston skimmed the article, homing in on the main points and discarding the bullshit. It dated back to March 2002. According to the report, in December 2001 three Georgian woodcutters ended up with severe radiation poisoning while working in a remote forest in Abkhazia. They'd noticed a metal cylinder that had melted all the surrounding snow and decided to take it back to their camp, no doubt thinking they could earn a few extra roubles selling it as scrap. They got more than they bargained for: severe skin burns and liquefied internal organs. It turned out the cylinder was the power supply from a radiothermal generator, for all intents and purposes a nuclear battery. During the Cold War some bright spark had had several hundred RTGs built to power navigational beacons along the Arctic shipping lanes, and communication stations in remote locations. A good idea in the short term – low maintenance power supplies that would run and run – however, in the confusion following the collapse of the Soviet Union, the RTGs were forgotten; just another piece of Cold War junk. Unfortunately this junk was powered by a flashlight-size capsule of Strontium-90 . . . nasty shit that needs to be encased in lead to keep it safe . . . nasty shit that any self-respecting terrorist would love to get their hands on. And this stuff was just lying around waiting for someone to come and pick it up, Aston thought. The most worrying aspect was that because Russia was in such a mess nobody could say for sure whether all the RTGs were accounted for. They thought they had them all, but in a case like this 'pretty sure' didn't cut it.

Mole waited until he had both Aston and George's attention, then said: 'Remember I told you I thought there were more hidden files on Mac's laptop.'

'Yeah, I remember.'

'Looks like I was right. I recovered that one this morning. Now, it might mean nothing or it might mean something. The fact it was so well hidden leads me to suspect the latter.' Mole paused for a long thoughtful toke on his roll-up. 'For once in my life I hope to God I'm wrong. Can you imagine it. Mac let loose with a nuke. Doesn't bear thinking about.'

Aston's mind had been heading down similar pathways, and a quick glance at George confirmed she was moving in the same direction. The hacker was right. It didn't bear thinking about.

'Do you have any idea how easy it is to build a dirty bomb?' Mole continued. 'Any joker with access to the Internet can get hold of that particular recipe. All you do is get a lump of Semtex and a lump of nasty nuclear stuff, stick 'em together, light the blue touch paper and stand well back. Shit, you don't even need Semtex! I saw this programme once where they were going on about possible dirty bomb scenarios. The scariest was the one where the bad guys build a bomb using a firework. A *firework*! The bomb gets detonated in a quiet corner of an underground system, and the explosion is so insignificant that no-one's any the wiser until the bad guys phone in what they've done twenty-four hours later. By then the whole system is glowing luminous green. How scary's that? And from a firework? A *firework*, for fuck's sake!'

'Of course,' George said. 'Strontium's not the sort of stuff you can drop by Woolworth's and buy, is it? Without that you don't have a dirty bomb.'

'Remember,' Aston said quietly, 'Mac's been in this business for years. Who knows who he met while he was stationed in Russia. Then there was his posting to Vienna . . . I'm sure if Mac tried hard enough he could get hold of anything. I'm not saying it would be easy, but it is possible. And I don't mind telling you that right now "possible" is enough to scare the shit out of me.'

The three of them fell into a thoughtful silence. The only sounds were the hum and suck of the air conditioner, Mole drawing on his cigarette, and Aerosmith working through another case of heartbreak in one of their trademark power ballads.

'Mole,' Aston said finally, 'I've got a job for you. It's a biggie. Something that requires your particular skills.'

'Fire away. No promises, but I'll do what I can.'

'We need more info on Mac. Personal history, his personnel file, anything you can get your greedy hands on . . .' He noticed Mole looking at him peculiarly and stopped. 'What? Why are you smiling at me like that? Please stop.'

Mole turned back to the dressing-table monitors, pulled the wheelchair under the desk by grabbing the edge and rolling forward. His staccato fingers flew over the ergonomic keyboard and somewhere behind Aston a printer sprung to life.

Mac's life story took up twenty sheets of A4. Aston settled down at the nearest desk to read, using the monitor glow to illuminate the pages. A quick flick through to start with, then he went back and read properly the bits that caught his attention. Most of it was new to him. Mole had managed to get hold of Mac's personnel file. No surprises there. All MI6's records were on computer these days, and if it was on a computer Mole could get it. There were parts of Mac's story that read like a spy novel. Mac was always going on about how things were different back then, but until now Aston had never appreciated how different they were.

'This all kosher?' George said, waving the loose sheets at Mole.

'Of course,' Mole said, hurt. 'What do you think? That I made it up?'

She turned to Aston. 'Did you know any of this stuff about his childhood? His dad being murdered and his mum going Loony Tunes?'

'Not until thirty seconds ago,' Aston admitted.

'That must have been tough.'

'It would explain a thing or two.'

George flipped forward through the pages, eyes eating the words. 'And did you know Mac was involved in the Gordievsky defection, Paul?'

'Kind of. But I didn't realise he was *that* involved.'

Everyone at Vauxhall Cross knew about Gordievsky's defection; it was required reading during the IONEC. Like everything else at MI6, the story was shrouded in secrets and had been mercilessly embellished over the years, fact and fiction now impossible to separate.

For eleven years Oleg Gordievsky provided MI6 with top-quality information about the KGB. In an organisation that dealt in secrets on a daily basis, Gordievsky was one secret protected as though it were encrusted with diamonds; only the chosen few in the highest echelons were aware of Gordievsky's existence. MI6 went to extraordinary lengths to protect him. More than once they let operations run by agents who didn't Need To Know continue because, even though Gordievsky himself had got word through that the operations had been compromised, stopping them would have meant suspicion falling on their golden boy.

The information he supplied was so sensitive it was inevitable he would be burnt eventually. This highlighted the flaw at the centre of any high-level spying operation, a problem Aston was only too well aware of. The more sensitive the information, the more chance there is of the source being burnt. And therein lies the dilemma. To use or not to use, that's the question. If you use the information there's a risk of losing the source; if you don't use it what's the point in having it in the first place? It was a tough call, and the fact Gordievsky kept going for more than a decade showed how carefully he was managed.

His run of luck ended in 1985 when he was arrested and interrogated by the KGB. He was eventually released, but his passport was confiscated and he was suspended from work. At the time, Mac was MOS/1, the number two in Moscow. When Mac got word that Gordievsky was in trouble he set in motion the contingency plan to get him out.

Gordievsky's daily routine included an evening walk around Gorky Park, accompanied, of course, by a crack KGB surveillance team. The timing had to be perfect. There was only one place on his route where he was out of sight long enough, and close enough to a road. Cool as anything, Mac pulled up in a Saab 90 and Gordievsky jumped into the boot. Before the surveillance team knew what hit them, Mac was on his way out of Moscow, heading for Finland.

Risky though it was, the escape plan had run like clockwork and there were pats on the back all round. Shortly afterwards Mac was promoted to H/MOS, MI6's top field posting during the Cold War, with the promise of bigger things to come. And the Gordievsky defection was just one of the highlights of Mac's career, Aston realised as he flicked through the pages. Mac had been there and done it all, risked his life more than once. So where had it all gone wrong?

nasty nuclear stuff . . . fireworks . . . doesn't bear thinking about . . .

It was warm down in the Unreal but Aston could do nothing to suppress the shiver tickling his spine.

38

Three days and counting. By the third day God was halfway to building the whole fucking universe. I take the train out to the suburbs, watching the grim buildings pass by. The rising sun paints the bricks with fire, gold and orange and red. The shadows are still black, though. The carriage is empty and that's perfect. I've moved out of Fogarty's now. The fat bastard was really starting to stink the place up. It's only a matter of time before someone notices, and I want to be well out the way when that happens.

The train stops, the door dings open. I look out at the platform, keeping it casual. No jerky head movements, no eyes popping out on stalks. Nobody around. Good. The less people I come into contact with the better. The doors close and it pulls away with an electric buzz. I'm currently staying at a no-star place in King's Cross. The room is as basic as basic can be: a lumpy, single bed, cigarette burns on the chest of drawers, dark amoeba stains on the carpets. It's the sort of place where nobody asks questions, and right now I'll take that over a bidet and satellite TV.

I get off at the end of the line, High Barnet, and follow my feet through quiet streets inhabited by postmen, paper-boys and commuters who are chasing after the early worm. I'm comfortable in the skin I've chosen, comfortable in these shoes. Got to keep telling myself this; it's so easy to slip into paranoia when you're working undercover. It's good to be back in the field again. I'd forgotten how much I missed this. The adrenaline buzz is immense, every nerve end tingling. Not that you'd know to look at me. On the outside I'm completely relaxed, breathing normally, not so much as a single twitch or tic. But that's training for you. Training and years of practice.

The media hasn't got hold of my picture yet, but there's a possibility the police have. They won't have the face I'm currently wearing, but that doesn't mean I'm going to get complacent. None of the early birds pay me any attention, which is fine by me. I walk confidently, but not so confidently that I stand out. I'm someone who knows where they're going. I resist the urge to look over my shoulder every two seconds, stop myself staring too long at the people I pass. I am completely aware of everything around me, though. There's not a single detail that slips by.

I'd scoped the place out weeks ago, so I'm able to go straight there. Getting the key was a challenge. It's been a while since I picked a pocket, but it all came flooding back. Some things you don't forget. The fizz of adrenaline pushing up your heart rate, the quickening of feet, the bump and the 'ever-so-sorry', the hand dipping into the pocket and the cold kiss of metal, another 'sorry' and you're out of there. I left the keys in an obvious place in the flowerbed, making it look like they'd fallen out of his pocket in his hurry to leave the house. He probably spent most of the day wondering what the hell he'd done with them, and then cursed himself for the rest of the evening when he found them.

I'm being careful today. My real face is hidden behind latex and my fingerprints are hidden behind a thick layer of leather. I don't want to make it too easy for the forensics boys and girls. The house is airy and Mediterranean, whitewash and real wood, the work of a single man who's got the feminine touch. He's about the same height as me, same build, same colour eyes. Perfect for my needs. The fact he's a little fruity doesn't faze me. It's his identity that interests me, not his lifestyle.

He's snoring upstairs and I'm in no real hurry. I take a wander around the house, absorbing his essence, trying to get a feel for who he is. The Mediterranean theme carries through to the kitchen, more fresh wood and a terracotta tiled floor. The lounge is a conservatory: an upright piano pushed against one wall, a cello on a stand in the middle of the room. The Mediterranean theme has been abandoned here, darker serious wood dominating. His graduation certificate from Harvard hangs in an expensive frame behind the massive rubber plant.

Feathery footsteps on the stairs, sticking to the edges to minimise the squeaks and creaks. The snoring has stopped. Is he asleep or awake? Not that it matters. I pull out the gun, screw on the silencer. The bedroom door is open a crack. Wide enough to see the hump in the duvet. With the gloved tip of my index finger I ease the door all the way open, step inside. The bedroom is nice and soft, relaxing pastel colours – eggshell blue walls and pearl coloured curtains, a soothing mint green for the bed linen. Arty-farty Impressionist prints hang on the walls and a king-size bed has pride of place. The pine furniture seems to be particularly placed, everything just so, and I'm not surprised to see a couple of Feng Shui books in the bookcase.

I stand in the doorway watching, allowing him to wake up in his own time. He comes around gradually to start with, then all at once when he catches sight of the figure in the doorway pointing a gun. He does a backward crab crawl up the bed, dragging the covers with him. He'll settle in a second when he realises there's nowhere to run.

'Do what I say and you won't get hurt,' I tell him.

He's shivering all over, back pressed tight against

the headboard. This goes completely outside his frame of reference. The safe existence he's carved out for himself is one of music and cerebral flirtations, of good food and visits to art galleries with his latest beau. It doesn't include dark men with guns who turn up in your boudoir unannounced at the crack of dawn.

'What do you want?' He can barely get the words out.

'Do what I say and you won't get hurt,' I repeat. This is all new to him, got to give him a second to work it out. 'Now, what part of that statement gives you the go-ahead to ask questions?' I shift my weight, holding the gun with both hands now, sighting along the barrel, fingers relaxing then tightening, relaxing and tightening. He gets the message. 'I've repeated myself once, but I won't do it again. It's up to you to listen, and if I were you I'd listen very carefully. Don't make me repeat myself again.'

'Sorry.' The word is a mess of mushed, hurried syllables.

'Now,' I tell him. 'I need you to relax. I'm not going to hurt you, but I do need you to focus. Can you do that?'

He's nodding away like a nodding dog. Right now he'd agree with anything I say.

'Good.' A reassuring smile. 'See that wasn't so bad, was it?'

A frantic shaking of the head, looking at me with wide pleading eyes to make sure this is the right response, then a little nod, just in case, covering all the bases.

I tell him what I want him to do, stressing that he will be there on Saturday. Do you understand? You'll be fine for Saturday.

'B-b-but,' he stutters, digging deep to find the strength to get the word out. 'But there won't be anyone there till nine.'

'That's okay,' I tell him. I move the wooden chair from the bay window to the end of the bed and settle in for the long haul, the gun resting on my lap. 'I really don't have a problem with waiting.'

The minutes that follow must be the longest he's experienced, time stretching to infinity and back again. I don't take my eyes off him, and as I stare at that terrified face I wonder what he's thinking. Thoughts of escape, no doubt. Thoughts of retribution. During those long seconds he's had time to question the very meaning of his life, to weigh up the good and bad and see if he's come up wanting. Ironically, in these minutes before he dies, he's probably more alive than he's ever been.

Bang on nine I tell him it's time.

'Are you going to kill me?'

'Not if you do exactly as I say.'

He considers this. 'Okay, I'll do what you want,' he says eventually, as though he's got a choice in the matter.

'Have you ever heard of Stanislavski?' I ask.

He nods and shakes at the same time, head

spinning in a loose elliptical orbit, desperate to give the correct response.

'Konstantin Stanislavski was born in the mid 1800s and died in 1938.' I keep my voice warm, mellifluous. 'He was an actor and director. Russian, though you've probably already guessed that. He devised a process of character development called, funnily enough, the Stanislavski Method. This forms the basis of method acting, which you've no doubt heard of. Practitioners include the likes of Robert de Niro and the late Marlon Brando. All today's great actors owe Stanislavski a huge debt. He taught them what it means to really get under the skin of the character they're playing, to inhabit the same space and time, to breathe the same air. Someone else's skin, someone else's shoes.'

A quick glance tells me he doesn't have a clue where I'm going with this. That's okay. He'll understand soon enough.

'Dustin Hoffman – now there's an actor who'll always go that extra yard to inject reality into a performance. If a scene calls for him to slap a woman, he won't think twice about doing it for real. If a scene calls for him to be out of breath, then he'll run for half a mile before shooting it. Why pretend to be out of breath when you can have the real thing? He did draw the line at having his teeth pulled out in *Marathon Man*, although I dare say the thought crossed his mind. So, do you see what I'm getting at? Do you understand?'

He shakes his head, which is pretty much what

I expected. Enlightenment can sometimes be a painful process. I get up, walk over to the bed, place the gun on the bedside table. His eyes flick from me to the gun and back again, his imagination spinning Hollywood-inspired fantasies of bravery and redemption. I shake my head. Not a good idea. I sit on the edge of the bed, smile at him. Before he can register what's happening I'm behind him, my gloved hand over his mouth. I'm waving the flick knife an inch from his right eye. He struggles and I touch the blade to his cheek, drawing a thin sliver of blood. The clever lad he is, he soon gets the message. Stops moving. Holds his breath. He's trembling all over.

I stab him in the left thigh, twist the knife and rip it out. The gloved hand clamped over his mouth catches the scream. That's the thing with these terraced houses, paper-thin walls. He's whimpering into the thick leather, his spit glossing the glove. There are tears mingling with the blood on his cheek.

'I'm going to take my hand away,' I tell him. 'Not a sound, okay?'

I carefully remove my hand and he manages to keep quiet.

'The pain you're feeling is nothing compared to the pain you could be feeling. Do I make myself clear?'

A shaky nod of the head.

'Good. Here's what's going to happen. You're going to make the call now, and you're going to convince them you're sicker than you've ever been in your life. You're dying, right? Now, I want you to take your pain and use it.' I give him a playful slap on the cheek. 'Go on, make Stanislavski proud.'

'You're going to kill me, aren't you?'

'And you're not focusing.' I clamp my gloved hand on his mouth and squeeze his thigh. His face tightens with pain as I slowly increase the pressure. 'Alright,' I say. 'Listen carefully. Whether you live or die is the least of your worries. All that matters is what happens in the next second. If that second comes around and you're still alive, then, hey, that's a bonus. Give thanks to whatever God you queers pray to then get on with living the next second. Life's a gift and you've got to live like every single second is your last. Because that's all any of us can do. Take it one second at a time. Got it?' I grab his mobile from the bedside table and pass it to him.

The performance is stellar, worthy of an Oscar. Even I'm convinced. There's pain and suffering in every word. So sorry but I'll have to miss tonight's rehearsal, I'm not feeling so good. He assures them he'll be there Saturday, come hell or high water . . . I've always dreamt of doing this . . . No, there's no way I'm going to let you down . . . No, you don't have to get anyone else in. There are new tears in his eyes when he clicks the phone shut.

'You did good,' I tell him as I pick up the gun from the bedside table. Two quick squeezes of the trigger A double tap. The back of his head blows outwards, abstract crimson and black spattering against the eggshell-blue walls.

Before leaving, I slip off the leather glove and move closer. With the tip of my index finger I reach out and touch his tears.

39

'Thought I might find you here.'

Aston turned his bleary eyes from the monitor and saw George standing at the edge of his pod, two mugs swinging from the fingers of one hand, a bottle of JD in the other. He checked his watch. Almost midnight. Where had the day gone?

George cleared a space on his desk and sat down. She began pouring out drinks and Aston held his hand up.

'Not for me,' he said. 'Still on the wagon.'

'But it's Thursday night.'

'I don't care.'

George shrugged and added another splash to her mug. 'Ah well. All the more for me.'

Aston hated to think what he looked like, what he smelled like. He'd been at this since first thing, running himself ragged and getting nowhere. George, on the other hand, looked great. How did she do it? Some people thrived on stress, he supposed.

'How was the meeting?' he asked.

'Long. I tell you, if everyone would stop playing the blame game we might actually start moving forward. Anything new on Mac?'

'No.' There was nothing more to be said. They'd talked about nothing else for the past five days and had exhausted the subject. Going over the info they had again and again, remembering conversations and picking them apart, looking for the thinnest thread to grab hold of and finding that it wasn't attached to anything remotely substantial. Hypothesising, re-hypothesising, then hypothesising a bit more. It was hard to admit, but they didn't have shit.

Aston gave a long sigh and rubbed his tired eyes with the heels of his hands. Given the choice, he would have preferred to be at home staring empty-headed at the TV. He didn't have a clue what Mac was up to and that bugged the hell out of him. He had no idea of the what, no idea of the when, no idea of the where. No ideas whatsoever. And he felt he should. They hadn't heard from Mac since Saturday and Aston doubted his old boss was going to get in touch anytime soon. PHANTOM had disappeared into thin air.

'I think you should call it a night.' George drained her mug and got off the desk.

'No arguments here.' Aston stood and shrugged into his jacket. 'Come on, let's get out of here.'

The shadows were waiting outside. They'd been following him since Sunday, and they weren't very good. Either that or they wanted to be seen. Returning home from Vauxhall Cross on Sunday, he'd spotted the two-man tag-team straightaway. Tweedle-Dum had followed him to Vauxhall tube station, then it was over to Tweedle-Dee for the one stop tube journey up the Victoria line. For the short walk home, Tweedle-Dum had turned his jacket inside out. Aston had considered losing them, throwing a simple evasion – jumping on a tube train just as the doors were closing or doing the old doubleback – but it was more effort than it was worth. He'd called George when he got home and discovered she'd been followed, too. What pissed her off most wasn't the fact she was under surveillance. No, what annoyed her was that he'd merited a tag team when she'd only had a single watcher.

A big black BMW with tinted windows was waiting at the kerb outside Vauxhall station. As they passed, the back door swung open.

'Get in,' ordered a gruff voice. Fielding's bullet-head appeared out of the gloomy interior. 'About time the three of us had a natter, don't you think?'

'Are you arresting us?' In his peripheral vision, Aston saw the two shadows positioning themselves to block off any avenues of escape.

'If you want,' Fielding said. 'Or we could keep it casual. Your call.'

Aston looked at George and she shrugged. He slid into the BMW and she followed. One of the shadows stepped forward and slammed the door shut.

'Where are we going?' Aston asked, not expecting an answer. Fielding had gone into silent mode. The back of his broad shoulders angled aggressively towards them, the Detective stared at the ever-changing neon cityscape, the coloured lights creating dark kaleidoscopic patterns on his tough leathery skin.

In his own time Fielding turned and said: 'We got off on the wrong foot the other day. Everyone got a bit overexcited and things were said that shouldn't have been said. If memory serves, we were never properly introduced. I'm Detective Superintendent Harry Fielding. I'm with SO13, the Met's anti-terrorist branch.'

Aston and George already knew that. After their run-in on Saturday they'd got Mole to do some sniffing around. Know your enemy, as Sun Tzu would have said.

Fielding turned his gaze upon George and Aston in turn. 'You're Georgina Strauss. And you're Paul Aston. You both work at that fuck-ugly building on the other side of the river, where you spend your days chasing terrorists. Now, we could get into the finer details – hobbies, interests, bank account details – but I think we can put our time to better use, don't you?'

Aston noticed that Fielding made no move to offer his hand. It wasn't that sort of introduction. This was all about posturing, a flexing of muscles, albeit cerebral ones. Fielding was marking his territory, warning them it would be a mistake not to take him seriously.

'The only way to catch Macintosh is if we work together,' the detective said.

This got Aston's attention. How the hell had Fielding got Mac's name? A quick glance in George's direction told him she was thinking the same.

'He's not invincible, you know,' Fielding said. 'He's already made mistakes. Some really stupid ones. He's acting like we're incompetent and that means we'll catch him. We always get the arrogant ones.'

Aston said nothing. Nor did George. Fielding was gearing himself up for lecture mode. Aston had seen this often enough with Mac to know the signs.

'Take the Clive Denning murder scene, for example. There were prints everywhere. A ton of evidence. Even the most incompetent prosecutor would have to work bloody hard to fuck that one up. Still, I'm sure they'd manage somehow.' A sigh. 'That's the thing with this job, you work your bollocks off to catch the bad guys and then some fuck-up of a lawyer gets them off on a technicality. It's getting as bad as America, it really is.'

Fielding took a deep, calming breath before continuing. 'So we've got a murder scene with a ton of prints, prints that are also splashed all over your flat, Ms Strauss. We have a look on NAFIS, and come up with nothing. NAFIS is the National Automated Fingerprint Information System, in case you're wondering; we're into our acronyms at the Yard almost as much as you folks across the river.'

Aston knew what NAFIS was. If Fielding wanted to be a condescending prick, then fine. 'Look,' he said, 'are you going anywhere with this, because I've got better things to do.'

'Believe me,' Fielding replied, 'you don't. At the moment I'm the only person standing between you and prison. Thank the sweet Lord for the Terrorism Act. Those fuckwits at Westminster actually got something right there.'

Aston turned and stared out the window, wondering if the car was bugged. Probably. That's what he would have done if the roles were reversed.

'Do we understand one another?' Fielding asked.

Aston met his gaze. 'Perfectly,' he said.

'Good,' Fielding said. 'Anyway, I get in touch with MI5, see if they can come up with anything, and for once they come up trumps. They're able to give me a name and point me in the right direction. So, I had our computer guys do a bit of snooping . . . don't give me that look, Aston. You're always sniffing around our computers, only fair we repay the compliment.'

'You hacked into MI6's mainframe? Bullshit!' Looked like Mole was losing his touch, Aston thought. The hacker was going to throw a fit when he found out.

'So now, not only have we got a name,' Fielding continued, 'but our computer guys came up with a picture as well. A picture that is now in the hands of every editor of every daily in the land, a picture that has been forwarded to all the major TV channels. By breakfast Robert Macintosh's face will be one of the most famous faces in the country . . . or should that be infamous?'

'You *what*?' Aston said. 'You can't do that.'

'I can and I have,' Fielding said. 'Did I forget to mention that we want to talk to Macintosh in connection with the Leicester Square bombing?'

Aston felt his face drain. Fielding was dropping one bombshell after another. He'd completely underestimated the Detective. Kinclave was going to love this one. So much for keeping a tight lid on things. And how much did Fielding know? It was all Aston could do to stop himself firing questions at the detective. Give him the third degree. But he had to play this cool. Don't panic. Damage limitation was the name of the game. Who the hell was he trying to kid? If the media had Mac's picture then it was all over. By tomorrow morning he'd be looking for a new job; it was unlikely that Kinclave would be in a forgiving mood. And maybe that wasn't such a bad thing. If that happened then this shitstorm became someone else's problem . . . they were welcome to it! And the fact that Fielding wanted Mac in connection with the Leicester Square bombing was the final proof, Aston realised. Up until now he'd been holding on to the slimmest of hopes that Mac wasn't involved, that it was all some big mistake and there was a logical explanation. So much for that. Hearing the words coming from Fielding made it concrete.

'You'll like this,' the Detective continued. 'The explosives he taped to Ms Strauss matched the explosives used at Leicester Square. Top-grade military C4 originating in Russia. Contrary to popular belief, explosives are fairly easy to trace. For a start, there aren't that many places manufacturing them. Secondly, every manufacturer has to add a few inert chemicals so their explosives can be tagged. That way if any bad guys get their hands on it, forensics can at least trace it to the point of origin. Clever, huh?' Fielding's gaze shifted from Aston to George and back again. 'Of course, you two already knew Macintosh was involved, didn't you?'

Neither George nor Aston said anything. The question was rhetorical.

'Thing is,' Fielding said, 'I reckon I'm only getting half the story and you've no idea how much that pisses me off. So what do I do? I let you two run with the ball these last few days in the hope that you'll come up with something I missed. Needless to say, I've kept an eye on you.'

'We've noticed,' George said.

'I wouldn't expect anything less. After all, you lads and lasses on the other side of the river are the surveillance experts. Could teach us amateurs a thing or two, isn't that right? So what have you got for me?'

'Obviously we'd help if we could,' Aston said. 'But you seem to know as much as us. Probably more.'

'Ah, like that is it?' Fielding went silent. The road rumbled under the BMW's tyres. Aston watched the lights spin past the window, sensing the detective was holding something back. It was written all over his smug face.

'So,' Fielding said finally. 'Give me one good reason why I shouldn't just slap the cuffs on, lock you up and throw away the key.'

'That threat is starting to wear thin,' George said.

'Excuse me?'

'If you were going to arrest us, you would have done it already.'

Fielding glared at George, speechless, a man unused to having his thunder stolen. *Go girl*, Aston thought.

'So,' George added, all sweetness and light, 'what is this really all about?'

Fielding didn't say anything and Aston thought she might have gone too far. He was wondering what it would be like to spend the night in a prison cell when Fielding started speaking.

'We've found another body. Shot twice in the head, execution style. Macintosh did it, although at this stage we don't know why. Maybe he's got a taste for killing and is now targeting victims at random. What worries me most is that he has changed his MO.'

'And you're sure this was Mac?' Even though he knew the answer, Aston had to ask. With everything else that had happened lately this revelation didn't shock Aston. Mac was responsible for hundreds of deaths, what did it matter if he notched up another one?

'Without a doubt. He was much more careful with this one, but it was definitely him. The Denning scene was covered in prints. This time there was only one dab, a latent on the stiff's left cheek. The sick fuck couldn't help himself. He had to touch the victim after he killed him.'

Way off the mark, Aston thought, but kept this to himself. With his talk of 'MOs' and 'targeting victims', Fielding was trying to fit Mac into the profile of a serial killer, looking for what he wanted to see and seeing it. But that was too simplistic. Mac was no Hannibal Lecter. The only reason he'd touch the body like that was to let the world know he'd killed him. The question Fielding should have been asking was why would Mac do that.

'What can you tell us about the victim?' George asked.

'His name was Mark Parson. Five-eight, blonde and blue, thirty-three, medium build. A pretty boy, if you get my meaning.'

'What else?' Aston asked.

'He was American, moved here five years ago. No living relatives, here or in America. He worked in the city. Insurance. For Lloyds. In his spare time he was a member of the BBC Symphony Chorus. That's who tipped us off. Parson had phoned in sick on Wednesday morning, had to miss a rehearsal. When they tried to contact him this morning to check how he was doing there was no answer. He'd sounded pretty rough the previous day and they wanted to double check he was okay for this weekend. Saturday's the big one.'

Aston's stomach lurched as cold realisation sunk in. 'You're talking about The Last Night of the Proms, aren't you?'

'That's right. The late Mr Parson was supposed to be singing there.'

'Shit!' Aston muttered to himself, his mind going into overdrive. George looked as pale as he felt, obviously thinking along the same lines. Fielding asked 'what?' a couple of times, but Aston ignored him. It was worse than he thought, worse than he could ever have imagined. *'nasty nuclear stuff . . . fireworks . . . '*. Mac had promised something big and this would certainly qualify as big. And prestigious, too. A dirty bomb attack on one of London's most famous landmarks. It was too hideous to even contemplate. There would be thousands of people crammed into the Albert Hall on Saturday night. If a bomb went off there it would be a blood-bath. There would be bodies everywhere. Hundreds dead, thousands even. Then there was the radiation to deal with. How many more thousands would be exposed to that? Jesus, this had the potential to make 18/8 look like a non-event. Mark Parson was the same build, the same height. Was that what Mac was planning? He'd been made up to look old, he could just as easily turn the clock the other way; according to George, the person who'd done the make-up had done a hell of a job.

And then an even more worrying thought occurred to him. His mother was going to the concert. Aston reached for his mobile, hesitated. He looked at Fielding then George. Wrong time, wrong place. He'd call her later, the first opportunity he got. If she was hurt, or worse killed, he would never forgive himself. There were a ton of reasons why he shouldn't call her – the fact that if this got out it would spark a major panic being right at the top of the list; the fact that he could lose his job for doing something like this running a close second – but this was his *mother*. If he got fired, he got fired. Whatever happened, he had to stop her going to the concert. And he had to do it without panicking her. It wasn't going to be easy. She was already in a state because she thought the terrorists were out to get her. How would she react when she found out they really were out to get her?

'Alright, detective,' George was saying, 'how do we go about cancelling The Last Night of the Proms?'

'You're kidding, right?'

George shook her head. 'Never been more serious.'

40

From the bench I've got a wide-angled view of the Embankment, Cleopatra's Needle slap-bang in the middle, brown muddy water flowing in between. The Lego blocks that make up the Royal Festival Hall rise behind me, an uninspiring concrete monument that's just plain ugly. Off to my left, the London Eye turns lazy circles, climbing high into the sky and reminding me of the Riesenrad from that long ago night in Vienna when I told Sophia everything.

The weatherman had predicted rain. Looks like he got it wrong. The sky's blue, the sun a hazy orange, and there's a slight chill to the damp air blowing up off the river. I wrinkle my nose as a whiff of something unpleasant floats over. A glance at my watch. Still got twenty-three minutes before Christopher turns up. I settle back to watch and wait.

It finally happened: my name and face are everywhere. Staring out from the black and white portable in my hotel room, from news-stands, from the newspapers left behind on the worn seats on the tube. I'm not worried that my picture is plastered all over the place. I've got my new face and I'm more than comfortable with it. None of this getting jumpy every time I catch sight of my pic, or suffering a paranoia attack whenever someone looks at me for longer than a second. At this precise moment in time, Robert Macintosh no longer exists.

Slipping into someone else's skin is second nature for me. I've been doing it as long as I can remember. When I was small I'd always be pretending to be other people, anything to escape the humdrum. I'd sit for hours in front of my grandmother's bedroom mirror and lose myself in the glass. Sometimes I'd be a soldier fighting in the trenches, other times I'd be a spy fighting against the Nazis. And sometimes I'd be a millionaire with castles and flash cars and boats and beautiful women dripping off my arm. This fantasy was a million miles away from reality: a poky house on a council estate in Watford where there was never enough money for food because dear old Grandma drank it all away. Still at least when she was comatose she didn't beat me. I always promised myself that I'd kill her one day, when I was older and bigger. And I meant it, too. Shortly after my sixteenth birthday she came home pissed and passed out on the sofa. I broke her arm with a hammer. She told the doctor that she'd fallen down the stairs, and the lie didn't even merit an eyebrow twitch. A lot of women fell down the stairs in those days. After that I made her life hell. I was careful not to kill her, though. It was much more fun to keep her alive. Revenge is so much more satisfying when your blood is cold.

Christopher left details of the meet at the usual drop point in Paddington station. Of course, he wanted to meet in Richmond again. I left the chalk mark on the postbox in Kensington, left the return message at the drop point in Regent's Park. The venue for our tête-à-tête has been changed to Cleopatra's Needle. Sometimes you have to take charge of a situation.

The mood on the streets has changed. Fear replaced by hope. Even down in the Underground there's little sign of the fear that had taken hold after the Leicester Square bombing. The monster responsible for 18/8 now has a face and, according to the conversations that provided the soundtrack for my journey, it's only a matter of time before I'm caught. I wonder what they'd say if they knew the monster was walking behind them, sitting in the next seat, following them up the escalator. Would they be so brave then?

I've got a little over ten minutes till Christopher arrives. There's nothing on the water to make me suspicious. No river police, no one acting suspiciously, just the usual traffic: a couple of boats filled with sightseers, a river bus churning water in its wake. I turn my attention to the far bank.

Tourists mill around the monument, posing for pictures, laughing and joking. I can't hear what they're saying from way over here, but if I could I reckon I'd be tuning into a whole mix of languages. I let my eyes drift from left to right then back again, looking for anything out of the ordinary, looking for anything *too* ordinary. I don't see anything I don't expect to see.

I get up and walk over to the railing, stretching my legs, getting the muscles working again. I stand watching as the minutes tick by. Christopher turns up at 2:30 on the dot, not a second before or after. He's staring wistfully across the water, actually looking straight at me. Of course there's no way for him to know that. He's never seen this face before. Christopher is trying to play it cool, one hand resting on the railing, casual glances all around. The camera hanging around his neck is no doubt there to give him the look of a tourist. Nice try, but he looks uncomfortable. I have to smile when he lifts the camera and starts taking pictures. From where I'm standing it's obvious he's pointing and clicking at nothing.

It's a nice day to get out and see the sights, and there's a good-sized crowd around the landmark. A multicultural mix of faces, old and young, white and black and yellow. Cameras click and camcorders hum. People come, people go. It's a perfect place for a meet. One more surreptitious look around and then I start walking.

41

'There he is,' George said.

Aston followed George's finger to the face on the screen. A Middle Eastern man stared at them for a moment, then turned to look over the water.

'You sure?' Fielding said.

'One hundred percent. That's Christopher Walker.'

Fielding grabbed the mic, clicked the button. 'Okay folks, we've got a positive ID. Behind the monument, standing by the river. I want everyone to stay sharp, stay focused.'

They were in a surveillance van parked in Adelphi Terrace, a stone's throw from Cleopatra's Needle. With the three of them, a tech guy to twiddle the knobs, and a ton of hi-tech gear, there wasn't much spare room. Aston had drawn the short straw and was standing; Fielding and George had homed in on the van's two empty seats like heat-seekers. The van had come courtesy of Fielding. An uneasy truce had been struck with the Detective, the details hammered out as they'd driven around London in the back of his BMW last night. It made sense to work together, Aston told himself for the umpteenth time; to pool their resources, to at least put on a show of co-operation. Bullshit! They didn't have an option. Both Fielding and Kinclave had been very clear on that one.

Aston was feeling claustrophobic, stifled by the close confines of the van, hemmed in by Fielding's attitude. But Kinclave had ordered them to co-operate, and Kinclave was in the Big Chair. That had been one hell of a conversation. They'd got back to Aston's flat in the early hours and flipped a coin. Of course, it came up tails. He had clicked onto speakerphone and dialled. Kinclave had been pissed off about being woken up in the middle of the night, but that was nothing compared to the fireworks when he found out why they were phoning. The Chief was furious that the media knew about Mac's involvement with 18/8, livid that the police were involved. This was the Apocalypse as far as Kinclave was concerned, a PR fuck-up to end all PR fuck-ups, and there was no reasoning with the man. Because Aston was the messenger, most of the anger was directed at him. He felt Kinclave was being unfair; it wasn't his fault. George could have stepped in to help out, but hadn't. She had spoken when she'd been spoken to, and left it at that. As she had so often pointed out, he was big enough to fight his own battles. In the end Kinclave decided the only way to limit the damage was to show that the 'shiny new open-door' MI6 was doing everything possible to co-operate with the Met.

There were three cameras hidden around the monument. Another feed was coming from a camcorder operated by one of the undercover detectives playing tourist. Aston studied everyone who came into view, checking to see if anyone had Mac's movements, his build, his presence. So far, nothing.

'You really think Macintosh is going to turn up?' Fielding asked.

'Yes!' Aston didn't mean to snap, but he couldn't help himself. It was stuffy in the back of the van and this evoked unpleasant flashbacks: digging through those tunnels with his bare hands, the dirt scratching at the soft skin under his nails, the broken and battered baby in his arms. One moment it all seemed to have happened so long ago, to a different person in a different lifetime, the next it was immediate and real and he was reliving every single horrific second. It was something he was going to have to learn to live with, he guessed.

'What makes you think he'll turn up?' Fielding asked.

This wasn't the first time the Detective had asked. Wearing him down through interrogation, looking for holes in his reasoning, coming at him from different angles. That was the detective's way, Aston supposed, but it still pissed him off.

'Well, Walker's here, isn't he?' Aston said, eyes fixed to the screen.

'Why not arrange the money transfer by computer and mobile? That's what everyone else does these days. Ask me, this all seems a bit risky.'

'Mac loves all that cloak and dagger stuff. Clandestine meetings, dead drops, anything that gets the blood pumping, anything where he can show how clever he is.'

'You'd better be right about this.' Fielding's eyes narrowed, the pupils huge and black as they sucked at the dim light of the van. 'Remind me how you knew Walker was planning to meet Macintosh here?'

Fielding was fishing again. Aston had kept that particular card very close to his chest. Habit, he supposed. The information had come from George. Her cronies up on the fourth floor had recently discovered the bench in Regent's Park that Christopher used for dead drops. Any new messages turning up in the tiny magnetic holder hidden underneath the seat were removed, quickly copied and sent to the decryption team. The original was returned ASAP and Christopher was none the wiser. This had been news to Aston, but that wasn't surprising. MI6 was so compartmentalised it wasn't unusual for the different departments at Vauxhall Cross to have no idea what was going on elsewhere in the building. This was obviously something Mac didn't know about, either . . . and the reason Aston could be so certain of that was because the message had been in Mac's hand-writing.

'Need To Know,' Aston said.

'Do I need to remind you that we're supposed to be working together?'

'And do I need to remind you about the Official Secrets Act? You wouldn't want me to break any laws, would you?'

Fielding harrumphed and Aston smiled inwardly, keeping his face passive. The uneasy truce was holding. At least for now. He concentrated on the tourists on the screens, ignoring the faces; Mac could be wearing any face. If he was going to spot him it would be from his body language, the way he moved. Mac couldn't disguise that, he wasn't that good an actor . . . was he? Even as Aston had this thought he knew Mac was.

There were three undercover cops on the ground. George had wanted people from MI6 in there, too, but Fielding had won that argument on the grounds that Mac might recognise them. On one of the screens Christopher was still clicking randomly with his camera. Where the hell was Mac?

Fielding turned to George. 'If this fish is as big as you say then we should take him down now. Macintosh is obviously a no-show.' He reached for the intercom switch that would connect him to the undercover cops on the ground.

George laid a gentle hand on the detective's thick wrist, earning herself a get-the-fuck-off look. 'Not yet,' she said. 'A couple more minutes . . .'

'No way I'm letting this one slip through the net.'

'Neither are we. But this could be our best chance to catch Mac.'

A big sigh from Fielding. 'Okay, two more minutes, then we go in.'

Aston only half heard the conversation, his focus entirely on the monitors. Something caught his eye and he leant closer, resting a hand on George's shoulder. A man had wandered into shot, glanced briefly at Christopher. Another glance for one of the undercover cops and then he'd carried on walking, eyes staring straight ahead, moving as though he couldn't get away fast enough. He was Mac's height, Mac's build.

Aston launched himself towards the van door, wrenched it open, jumped out. Behind him, he heard Fielding shout: 'Go! Go! GO!' George was calling after him. Mac had been heading in the direction of Waterloo Bridge. Now he'd spotted the undercover cops he'd want to get somewhere crowded, somewhere he could blend in. Aston quickly discarded the Underground. It would mean Mac being out in the open too long. No, he'd head away from the river, lose himself in the maze of streets that wound up towards Covent Garden. Aston sprinted along the edge of Embankment Gardens, lungs and legs burning. He passed the extravagant facade of The Savoy and ducked into a side street, glanced towards the river.

There was Mac, standing by Waterloo Bridge,

trying to cross the road. Head turned away, trying to hide his face, Aston walked towards the bridge. Mac was in the middle of the road now, looking for a gap in the traffic. Behind him, Aston was aware of the commotion going on at Cleopatra's Needle. Mac made the other side and Aston broke into a run. Forty metres, thirty, twenty. Mac suddenly looked in his direction and started running. He sprinted up Savoy Street, moving fast. Mac reached The Strand, hesitated long enough for Aston to close the distance by another ten metres, then darted into the road in a suicidal bid for the other side. Brakes squealed, the crunching of metal against metal as a taxi smashed into a Porsche, another bang as a Ford rear-ended a bus. More screeching of metal as the street turned into a demolition derby. Aston just ploughed through the carnage, eyes fixed on Mac, who was on the other side now. Jesus, he was fit! Up Burleigh Street and Aston gave it all he had, aware that he couldn't keep up this pace much longer. He was dying here. Legs like jelly, lungs filled with white-hot ashes. The distance closed. Eight metres, seven, six. Aston reached out, fingers brushing the back of Mac's coat. His hand got a hold of the fabric, but Mac wasn't giving up that easily. He was shaking himself out of the jacket. Aston pounced, using his full weight to push Mac down onto the pavement. There was a thump and the stomach-churning sound of cracking bone. Aston lay there for a moment, breathing heavily. A small crowd gathered, but most people were walking past, pretending nothing was happening.

When the air stopped stabbing his lungs, Aston got off and flipped Mac over. His former boss's face was covered in blood, the nose broken. The mask was brilliantly done. So lifelike. He touched it. It even felt like the real thing. Mac was glaring at him through brown contact lenses.

'Sorry, Mac,' Aston said. 'This is the way it's got to be.'

'What the hell you talk about? Who the fuck Mac is?'

The words were barely intelligible, the fake accent from one of the Russian states. Aston stood and dragged Mac to his feet. 'You can stop acting.' Even as he said this he had a feeling something was wrong. Right height, right build, right shape, but . . . no, something wasn't quite right. Ignoring his protests, Aston patted him down. In the inside pocket of the long brown coat he found three wallets.

'I don't believe it,' Aston said. 'You're a pick-pocket!'

The man shrugged and made a confused face, evidently not understanding, or pretending not to understand.

Aston shook his head, pissed off with himself. He pocketed the wallets, then turned and headed back to The Strand.

'What? You no arrest me?' the thief shouted after him.

'Looks like it's your lucky day,' Aston called back, without turning.

'What a fuck crazy country is this.' Each word was infected by the pickpocket's grin.

'You said it, pal,' Aston muttered. Head down, cheeks burning with anger and embarrassment, he headed back to the surveillance van. How could he have been so stupid? He could already imagine Fielding's reaction. The detective probably wouldn't say anything, wouldn't need to. One smug look would be worth more than a thousand words. It was doubtful Fielding would ever take him seriously again. No great loss there. Aston doubted whether the detective had taken him particularly seriously in the first place. Then there was George to contend with. That was another matter altogether. How much mileage was she going to get out of this? That didn't bear thinking about. Then again, perhaps she'd be all nice and understanding. Stranger things had been known to happen. Aston thought about this for a moment. He wasn't sure which was worse. George taking the piss or George being sympathetic.

42

They were in Paddington Green police station, watching Fielding interrogate Christopher – although Fielding had made it clear he preferred the term 'questioning'. Same difference, thought Aston. Okay, so they didn't use thumbscrews and racks and hot pokers, but that was just splitting hairs. They were alone in a small grey office next door. There were two chairs, a table with a monitor and two Styrofoam cups on it. The sound and picture quality was excellent, the monitor of a high enough resolution to pick up every detail of Christopher's face, every line and pore. No crappy ten-inch monochrome screens where working out what was going on was on a par with interpreting Rorschach inkblots, and the sound was so lo-fi it may as well have been broadcast from a distant planet. No, this was the CCTV equivalent of a fifty-inch plasma widescreen with full Dolby Surround. And if that didn't do it for you, you could always watch what was going on through the large one-way mirror.

'What do you reckon?' George asked. 'Is he going to talk or not?'

'How the hell should I know?'

'Don't be like that, Paul. I was only asking. What's the matter?'

'Nothing.' Aston opted for answering in the code favoured by those carrying both X and Y chromosomes. Rough translation: everything was the matter, but the likelihood of finding words that even come close to adequately explaining were zilch, so I'd prefer it if, with all due respect, you'd let it drop and leave me the fuck alone.

'So you made a mistake,' she said. 'Big deal. Get over it.'

Easy for you to say, he thought, *but it wasn't you who ended up looking like a complete twat.* When he got back to the surveillance van and explained what happened, Fielding had shaken his head and given a glare of disapproval that matched anything Mac could conjure up. The other cops hadn't said anything, but he could tell what they were thinking because if the roles had been reversed he would have been thinking the same: *what a wanker!* Embarrassing didn't even begin to cover it.

'It really isn't that big a deal,' George said.

'Maybe not to you.'

'Come on, Paul, you're being too hard on your-self. We all make mistakes.'

'If you say so,' he snapped, and immediately regretted it. George was only trying to help. Aston turned and stared at the monitor in an attempt to end the conversation. 'Let it go, okay?' he added more gently.

'Okay,' George sighed. She paused then added: 'So what do you reckon? Is he going to talk or not?'

Aston studied Christopher's face through the one-way mirror as he sipped coffee from the Styrofoam cup a PC had brought shortly after they'd been dumped here. The PC had given him an I-know-who-you-are look as he'd departed, and this had pissed Aston off even more. As part of the truce, Fielding was the only one who was supposed to know they were from MI6. Of course, the reality was that everyone at Paddington Green knew who they were. When it came to in-house secrets the Met was as leaky as MI6.

Fielding and Christopher were alone in the room. Christopher had waived legal representation on the grounds that he hadn't done anything wrong, so why would he need a lawyer. The Arab's handsome face was emotionless and passive, unchanging as a statue. Here was someone who had been involved in the killing of hundreds, someone who was looking at spending the rest of his life behind bars, yet he was completely unfazed. Aston stared into the mocha-coloured eyes, expecting to be frozen by the ice creeping up from his soul. Surprisingly, the eyes were warm and soft, almost friendly. Christopher was clean-shaven, black hair cut short like a banker. He looked at least ten years younger than his official age. Pampering rather than surgery, Aston reckoned. Fielding was doing all the talking, coming at the terrorist from all angles. But Christopher wasn't talking. He just sat and stared directly at the camera as though bored out of his mind.

'So,' George prompted, 'what do you reckon?'

'He won't talk,' he said.

George sipped from her Styrofoam cup and they fell into silence. On the other side of the glass, Christopher was keeping his secrets. Fielding was asking leading questions about the Albert Hall but the terrorist was giving nothing away. There were no eyes darting towards the door looking for ways to escape, no excessive blinking, no sweating, nothing to show he was lying or stressed. There was nothing defensive in his posture, either: no folded arms, no hands in pockets. Nor were there any signs of aggression: no leaning forward into Fielding's space, no hands curled into fists. Christopher was sitting there completely chilled, leaning back in his chair, legs crossed, hands resting lightly on the table, smiling pleasantly and saying absolutely nothing. Somewhere along the line Christopher had been coached in dealing with situations like this. Aston recognised the signs from his own training. And that in itself was telling. Why would you need coaching unless you had something to hide? Christopher was acting far too cool. Even an innocent person thrown into this sort of situation would be stressed out, probably feeling a little guilty even if there was nothing to feel guilty about. It was only natural. Acting cool didn't cut it. If you wanted to come across as having nothing to hide then you had to give a little . . . the trick was knowing how much to give.

On screen Fielding said: 'We know how it's going to go down. We know all about Mark Parson.'

Nothing from Christopher, not even a flicker at the mention of Parson's name.

'That's it, isn't it? You get someone made up to look like Parson, they smuggle the bomb in. After all, the security surrounding the performers isn't going to be anywhere near as tight as that surrounding the punters, isn't that right? All the punters get searched before they go in, bags and pockets. But not the performers. I mean, who would suspect them, right? So the bomb gets smuggled in, the show starts, and then the big bang. Absolute carnage – hundreds dead, thousands dead.' An admiring nod and a smile from the bullet-headed Detective. 'You had it all worked out, didn't you?'

Still nothing from Christopher. He stared across the table at Fielding, his face unreadable.

Fielding kicked back in his chair and crossed his arms; his expression suggested he had finally discovered what made the universe tick. When he spoke, his tone was casual, relaxed. 'Incidentally, I forgot to mention the reason we know how this is going down is because we've got Macintosh in the next room and he's told us everything.'

And that's when Aston got the confirmation he was looking for. A brief moment of panic that lasted less than a millisecond. Blink and you'd miss it. Christopher's face had returned to marble, chiselled and unyielding, but Aston knew what he'd seen.

'Did you catch that?' Aston asked.

'I certainly did.'

'The bastard as good as put his hands up and admitted everything. I hate to say it, but Fielding's actually pretty good at this. It's the Albert Hall. Definitely the Albert Hall.'

43

They'd been arriving all afternoon, queuing patiently hoping to get the best places, Union Jacks of all shapes and sizes everywhere you looked. These were the hard-core Prommers, those who would later be crammed into the space in front of the stage, singing their hearts out and waving their flags, letting the whole world know what it meant to be British. Aston, who was sitting with George in a surveillance van parked at the edge of Kensington Gardens, saw only coffins of all shapes and sizes: big polished mahogany ones for the adults, little white ones for the kids. He'd been watching them all afternoon, staring at the screens till his eyes hurt, searching for Mac. Still no sign of him. Not even a whisper. Chaos all around: the noise of the crowds outside, police bustling in and out of the van for an update, radio transmissions crackling over the comms channels, and somewhere in the middle of all the commotion Aston was searching for the still point, the quiet at the centre

411

of the storm. Something didn't add up, didn't *feel* right, but he couldn't put his finger on what. His mind was whirling with a myriad of thoughts, but that was the one he kept coming back to. He needed to focus, to block out the irrelevant and concentrate on what really mattered.

The Albert Hall was crawling with undercover cops; they were everywhere. And Mac would spot them a mile away. Aston had pressed for a low-key operation, arguing it was the only way to catch Mac. There'd been hot words as he tried to get this through to Fielding, but the bullet-headed detective wasn't buying. He wanted a show of strength and had had every available man brought in; as well as the undercover cops there was an army of uniformed police in and around the hall. As far as Aston was concerned this was a cover-your-arse strategy, an MI6 special. If the shit hit and the bomb went off then nobody was going to turn around to Fielding and tell him he hadn't done enough to prevent it. Why look, he'd say, what else could I have possibly done apart from cancel the event, and let's face it that wasn't an option.

George had asked nicely for the event to be cancelled and the answer was still a resounding no. Aston could understand the reasoning, but that didn't mean he agreed with it. Cancelling a flight because there was a 'credible threat' was one thing. A couple of hundred people were inconvenienced and the press have a field day speculating whether or not there actually was a 'credible threat'. The big difference here was there was only one Last Night of the Proms; there were thousand upon thousands of flights each year, so one or two being cancelled wasn't that big a deal. Also, the Last Night was a celebration of all things British, an event where five and a half thousand flag-waving patriots got to shout about how wonderful their country was. Fielding couldn't cancel the event. His hands were tied. A couple of months ago, a bunch of terrorists who were planning to attack Old Trafford had been rounded up. That Saturday's match still went ahead, and the reason it went ahead was because, threat or no threat, the uproar would have been massive. And it was the same here. Aston could imagine the editorials: lots of references to the blitz and the indomitable Bulldog spirit. All well and good, but what if despite the fact that every spare cop in the city was currently at the Albert Hall, that every single person going in was being thoroughly searched, that the elegant old building had been given a complete going over by dogs trained to sniff out explosives, that every square inch had been searched by techies with Geiger counters, what if despite all the precautions Mac somehow managed to get a dirty bomb inside?

It was all wrong. To catch Mac they needed to get inside his head, find out what he was thinking. Instead Fielding was treating Mac like some dumb thug who'd wander into the Albert Hall with the bomb tucked under his arm. The detective probably thought that all they had to do was ID him, then it was just a case of rounding him up, slapping on the cuffs and carting him away. They didn't have a clue.

'Penny for them,' George said.

'What?' Aston replied.

'You're miles away. Again. Maybe you should take a walk. Go stretch your legs. I can hold the fort here.'

'No, I'm fine. I was just thinking about something Mac taught me. Association by disassociation, he called it. Whatever the hell that means. Basically you zone out from yourself and zone into the person you're after.' A tight wry smile. 'Get into someone else's skin, walk in their shoes.'

'Does it work?'

A shrug. 'Not sure. Can't do any harm, though, can it? Maybe you should give it a go. After all, you knew him pretty well, didn't you?' That last sentence hadn't sounded so abrasive in his head, but out in the thick air of the surveillance van it was dancing around like a malignant sprite. 'Sorry, George,' he added quickly, trying to repair the damage. 'That didn't come out how I wanted.'

She dismissed him with a tight 'whatever' and a blank look that could have meant anything. They both retreated into silence, studying the banks of monitors. There were cameras everywhere, inside

414

and out, the feeds leading to the two surveillance vans Fielding had acquired for the operation. Of course, the Met had the newer van, the one packed to the gunnels with the latest gear, while they had to make do with this one, which was ten years old, smelled like an old sock, and kitted out with equipment that had seen better days.

Fielding had left them here with instructions to watch the screens for Mac, and to contact him if they saw anyone who bore even a passing resemblance. That had been two hours ago and since then they hadn't seen the Detective. He was obviously out there rallying the troops, stressed to the max and praying that Mac had been hit by a bus or a stroke or lightning, anything. Their babysitter was a twenty-one-year-old PC with a neat uniform and fresh rosy cheeks who hadn't said two words. Whether this was a result of shyness or orders, Aston neither knew nor cared. The fragile truce was at breaking point. It was obvious they were being kept out of the way, their presence tolerated rather than welcomed. Fielding was giving them token co-operation here, keeping them around in case they came up with anything useful.

The police had had one major break. Around lunchtime, Fielding turned up clutching a brown manila envelope. Inside were pictures of a man who kind of looked like Mac, albeit twenty years younger, with black hair, a different nose and a different shaped chin. It was difficult to say how

Aston knew it was Mac, he just did. And then he worked it out. It was the eyes. The pictures were computer generated and brilliantly done – it was only when you looked at them closely you saw they weren't real photographs – all except one. The odd man out was a photograph of Mark Parson. The resemblance between Parson and the computer-enhanced younger version of Mac was staggering. They could have been twins.

Fielding had looked extremely pleased with himself when he told them how he got the pictures, and Aston had kicked himself for not thinking of it first. Mac didn't have the skills to create the disguises he'd been using, therefore he must have got someone else to do it. Fielding had gone out looking, and ended up at a little fancy-dress shop in the East End owned by Joe Fogarty. The late Joe Fogarty, as it turned out. His whale-like body had been stinking up the flat above the shop. The photos were tucked into the frame of the make-up table mirror, and Mac's fingerprints were everywhere.

The Prommers were filing inside now, an undulating stream of red, white and blue pressing through the entrances.

According to the experts, the dirty bomb was a weapon of 'mass disruption' rather than a weapon of mass destruction, a tasty soundbite based on speculation and hypothesis. Hiding behind science and statistics, the experts agreed that the likelihood of anyone getting radiation sickness or the Big C was negligible . . . as long as they were decontaminated quickly enough. However, Aston doubted the opinions of a few experts would stop the chaos and fear. According to them it was the environment that would suffer most. Once out of the box this stuff didn't just disappear; radioactive particles would merge with steel and brick and wood, and the only way to get rid of it was to demolish any buildings affected and bury the debris in the biggest hole you could find.

What the experts conveniently forgot to mention was that nobody had ever set off a dirty bomb, so there was no way of saying what the actual effect would be.

Then there was the fact that any sort of bomb detonated in the middle of the Proms would be devastating; the size and type didn't matter. The stampede for the exits after the explosion would kill more than the blast. Crude but effective. When he closed his eyes, Aston could visualise the carnage. The main lights going out and the red glow of the emergency lighting; bodies being trampled; the calls for calm drowned out by the screams of the injured and dying; children ripped from their parents' hands and crushed into walls; pensioners knocked roughly to the ground; everyone driven by the survival instinct with only the fittest surviving; the bodies piling up in the exits, mountains of flesh and bone that had to be scaled to reach the safety of the outside world; the screams and moans; the cracking of bones; the sound of complete and utter panic, and a crippling claustrophobia to surpass anything he'd experienced in those dark hot tunnels of Leicester Square.

The performance was due to start in little over an hour. There was still enough time to call the event off, to evacuate the hall and get everyone back to a safe distance. They would have to move quickly, though. The window of opportunity was shrinking with every passing second. He had to get Fielding to pull the plug, make the stubborn bastard see it was the right thing to do . . . the only thing to do. These were real people's lives they were playing with, innocent people like those killed at Leicester Square. If there was another 18/8 and he hadn't done everything in his power to prevent it, there was no way he could live with himself.

'Maybe I'll take that walk, after all,' he said to George.

She gave him a funny look, like she was reading his thoughts, made as if she was going to say something then glanced at the babysitter. 'If you find a coffee,' she said. 'I'd kill for one.'

44

'Fielding, we need to talk,' Aston said as he barged into the main surveillance van. The PC who had tried to stop him getting in was hanging onto his arm, and Aston shook him off. Suspicious eyes turned towards him.

'You've identified Macintosh!' the Detective said.

'No. Not yet.'

'In that case, what are you doing here?'

'We need to talk. Now.'

'Look, Aston, this is not a good time,' Fielding said. 'In case it's escaped your attention, we're in the middle of a major terrorist incident here.'

'I've got some new information,' Aston lied.

'Well, spit it out.'

'Not here. In private.'

'Jesus, Aston, I really don't have time for all this cloak and dagger bullshit.'

'Make time.' Aston stood his ground, staring the Detective down.

For a moment Fielding looked as if he was going to argue. Then he removed his headset, slapped it onto the desk, stood up. 'Two minutes, okay? Not a minute more.'

Aston stood aside to let the detective through, followed him down the steps. They found a quiet corner away from the crowds. 'Okay, Aston, this better be good.'

'You have to cancel the concert.'

'You're having a fucking laugh, aren't you?' He turned to leave.

'No! Wait!'

'I've got better things to do than listen to this crap.'

Aston grabbed the detective by the shoulder, spun him around. 'Look, Fielding, all I'm asking is for you to listen to me. You said two minutes. By my reckoning I've still got a minute left. Just hear me out, okay?'

'Get your hands off me.' Fielding shrugged Aston away, the colour rising in his face. 'We've already been through this a dozen times. The concert goes ahead.'

'If that happens, then thousands of people are going to die.'

'No, they're not. There's no way anybody can get a bomb into that hall. No fucking way.'

'There's no such thing as a hundred percent guarantee. You've been a cop long enough to know that. Even if there's only the slimmest chance of Mac getting a bomb in there, is that a chance

420

you're willing to take? Remember we're dealing with people's lives here.'

'Don't you think I'm aware of that?'

'Well, cancel the fucking concert then.' Aston was working hard to keep from shouting. It wasn't easy. What he really wanted to do was grab hold of the detective and shake some sense into him.

'I can't.'

Fielding spoke so quietly, Aston wasn't sure if he heard right. He studied the detective's face. He looked older; there was a glimpse of uncertainty in there, too.

'Can't or won't?' Aston prompted gently.

A long sigh. 'This is between you and me, okay? It goes no further.'

'Okay,' Aston agreed.

'Don't you think I would pull the plug if I could? This is a fucking nightmare waiting to happen. Maybe Macintosh is out there with a bomb, maybe he's not. But we have to assume he is. And like you said, there is a possibility he can get it inside the hall. A slim possibility, but a possibility nonetheless.' The detective looked over at the crowds still waiting to get in. 'All these people . . . I agree with you, Aston, the only way to ensure their safety is to send them all home.'

'Then why don't you?'

'Politics. This isn't my call.'

'So, whose call is it?'

'The Prime Minister. Only it goes higher than that.'

'Higher than the PM?'

'Think about it. Who's dictating our counter-terrorist policy at the moment?'

'America.'

'Got it in one,' Fielding said. 'And the party line is that we don't, under any circumstances, give in to terrorism. If we cancel then that's a point for the bad guys, and that can't be allowed to happen.'

'Even if innocent people die?'

'Well, that's why we're here, isn't it? To make sure that doesn't happen.'

'This is so wrong.'

'No arguments here. If we cancel it would make my life a hell of a lot simpler.' Fielding smiled a tight smile. 'You know who the scapegoat is if this goes tits up?'

'You.'

'Well, it's not going to be the PM, is it?' Fielding shook his head. 'This situation goes way beyond fucked up. All we can do is hope we get lucky.'

Aston watched him walk back to the surveillance van, shoulders slumped. He stopped at the bottom of the steps for a moment, straightened up, and climbed confidently inside.

'How did it go?' George asked as Aston entered the van and took the chair next to her.

'Sorry, couldn't find any coffee.'

'You know that's not what I meant.'

'What do you think?' Aston was aware of the baby PC's ears twitching, no doubt listening carefully in case they said anything Fielding needed to hear. The big boss had given him this assignment; make a good impression and it wasn't going to do his career any harm. Aston had been that ambitious once . . . seemed a long time ago now.

'That good?' George said. 'At least you tried.'

'Fat lot of good it did.'

'So what did he say?'

'He said he was just following orders.'

'Whose orders? I thought he was in charge.'

Aston glared at the babysitter until he turned away and pretended to get busy. 'The PM,' Aston mouthed.

'Oh,' George mouthed back.

'I've got a bad feeling about this.'

'You're not the only one.'

They stared at the screens in silence for a while, looking for Mac, then George said: 'All this waiting is killing me.'

'Me, too. I always hated waiting. I was the same as a kid.'

'Yeah, I can see that,' George said. 'I bet you went looking for your Christmas presents.'

'Found them, too,' Aston agreed.

'You've got your thinking face on. Mind sharing?'

'That easy to read, huh?'

'Only when you know what to look for.'

Aston smiled. 'One of the first things Mac told me was that I had to learn patience. When it comes to waiting, Mac could teach a Buddhist monk a thing or two.'

'Where are you going with this?'

'I'm not sure.' And that was the truth. The 'something' that had been bugging him all afternoon just wouldn't go away, but he still couldn't put his finger on what that something was. He tried coming from a different angle. 'Maybe we're concentrating too much on the now?' he said.

'And what's that supposed to mean?'

'Okay,' Aston said, 'think back to Leicester Square. It was an indiscriminate target. There was no warning. One big bang . . . job done. Now look what we've got here. The place is crawling with police.'

'You don't think he's going to show?'

'Of course he's going to show.'

'But there's no way Mac can get in there. The place is locked up tight.'

'Yeah, locked up so tight that five and a half thousand people just got inside.'

'But they're not carrying bombs.'

'And who says Mac's bringing the bomb in himself? That's what we're assuming, but that's not what he did at Leicester Square. Remember, he used a suicide bomber on that one.'

'Fielding's got it covered,' George said. 'Anyone who looks even remotely Middle Eastern will be thoroughly checked out. There's no way Mac can get a bomb in there. It's impossible.'

'Impossible is just an excuse for incompetence,' Aston said. 'Look what happened to the Titanic.'

Another glance at the computer-generated

photos of Mac/Parson. Aston snatched up the nearest one and studied it closely. Of course, it was possible Mac wasn't using the face in the photos; maybe that was a red herring, maybe he'd left the photos there knowing they'd be found and he had something else in mind, whatever that might be. Or perhaps his plan *was* to take on Mark Parson's identity. On Fielding's orders details of Parson's death were being kept quiet. The detective was still hoping Mac might turn up backstage disguised as Mark Parson. If that happened there were half a dozen cops waiting to take him down.

And what if both plans were genuine? Plan A and plan B. What if Mac was out there monitoring the situation, waiting till the last second before deciding which one to go for?

And what if there was a plan C . . . ?

Second guessing Mac made Aston's head pound. He stared in silence at the people on the screen. The hall was filling up and Aston could sense the excitement building. These people were expecting the night of their lives. He hoped they didn't get more than they bargained for. Aston stared at the screen with a hundred stray thoughts bounding through his head, wishing for clarity and finding none, and still he kept coming back to that one thought that niggled away at him in a sing-song voice, the idea that he was missing something obvious.

It wasn't the weapon, it was how you used it.

Hot on the heels of this thought came another,

this one whispering in a faraway voice. Mac's voice. It came from nowhere and was enough to send a shiver slipping across Aston's skin.

Don't assume. When you assume you make an ASS out of U and ME.

45

Victor Cope strides confidently across Vauxhall Bridge, comfortable in his skin, comfortable in his shoes. Up ahead, MI6's HQ rises from the riverbank, as imposing as any Orwellian nightmare. The Thought Police would be completely at home here, safe behind the bombproof windows and thick walls while they invented cruel and unusual ways to keep the proles in line. The official cost of the building was eighty-five million quid, but our friend Victor knows better; anyone who's worked for MI6 as long as Vic knows the building cost three times that. The final price tag was closer to the two hundred and fifty million pound mark. A quarter of a billion spent on bricks and concrete and glass and steel. Not forgetting the marble and all the other little touches designed to make the building more user-friendly, little touches that just emphasised what a disgusting shit-pit it was. What the hell did spies need with a squash court? In the old days spies sure as fuck didn't need squash courts. Back then they'd operated out of Century House, an anonymous, grimy 20-storey office block in Lambeth where the mirror windows reflected back the faces of curious passers-by, while protecting the secrets inside. In Vic's humble opinion this was a proper home for spies.

Vic marches straight up to the nearest pod, plugs the security card into the slot, types in the four digit PIN: 6-5-1-3. It doesn't cross his mind that the machine might reject it. After all, the computers know exactly who he is. Victor Cope, thirty-eight years old, a low-level grunt working for the Far East Controllerate. Nothing unusual about him being here on a Saturday night, either. MI6 isn't a nine to five option.

A green light flashes on, the door hisses open and he steps into the pod. The door closes behind him with a vacuum suck. A pressure pad in the floor confirms that there's just the one Vic. The door in front opens and he's in.

It's all so familiar, all so 21st Century. The hotel feel of the reception area, the soft light spilling from high above, the marble floors, slate walls and the bruised sky visible through the tall light wells. Of course, Vic has seen this all before and doesn't give it a second thought.

He makes his way towards the nearest of the two massive columns that dominate the area, hits a button and waits for the express elevator. A smooth hiss as the door sweeps open and Victor climbs aboard. He hits another button and gazes around nonchalantly as the elevator begins to drop. Anyone watching on the cameras will see someone who's meant to be here. It's all in the way you move, the way you carry yourself, the way you think. As long as you act like you belong, no one will hassle you. And that's as true in the heart of MI6 as it is anywhere.

Four floors down and the elevator stops with a soft bump. The doors open and he makes his way through the maze of identical corridors. There's no hesitating at any of the junctions; he knows exactly where he's going. The door opens when he's still six feet away. Vic walks into the gloom without breaking stride.

'And what can I do for you on this fine evening, Mr Cope?' Mole spins around in the wheelchair and smiles from behind a thick cloud of cigarette smoke. His face is illuminated by the monitors, a thousand streaked stars from a screensaver trapped in the thick bottle-bottom lenses.

46

'Okay,' George shouted above the siren, 'run this by me again. Why exactly have we stolen a police car?'

'Can you think of a quicker way to get across London?' Aston jerked the wheel of the Vauxhall Vectra hard to the left and swung over to the other side of the road, putting his foot down to get past a black cab and narrowly missing a scooter coming the other way. The glare from the blue flasher reflected in the shop windows as they flew past.

'Okay.' George dragged the word into a sigh. 'But that doesn't explain why you pole-axed that cute little policeman back in the surveillance van.'

'I needed his uniform,' Aston stated simply. 'You think they give the keys to one of these babies to any old Tom, Dick or Harry?'

Another indulgent 'okay' – then George said, 'Let me make sure I've got this straight, Paul. So far you've assaulted a police officer and stolen a police car. And we might as well throw in a charge of reckless driving as well, eh? How am I doing?'

'That's about the long and short of it. And don't forget, you're an accessory.'

'Believe me, I'm well aware of that.'

Aston executed another move that didn't figure in the Highway Code. This one involved using the handbrake to negotiate a T-junction. He stomped his foot down and the needle crept past fifty, shops and buildings streaking past in a blur. Out of the corner of his eye he noticed George tightening her seat belt. 'Don't worry. Mac had me take an advanced driving test. Passed with flying colours.'

He turned towards her and she let out a high-pitched squeal, five words coming out as one. *'Eyesbackontheroad!'*

'George, why has Mac continually managed to stay one step ahead of us? Think about it. All we've done so far is assume. Mole finds all that stuff about the dirty bomb on Mac's laptop so we assume that's what he's planning to use. Parson's body is found in Barnet and we assume he's targeting the Proms. After all, it fits really neatly, doesn't it? A high-profile target, hundreds dead and injured.'

'All a little too neat,' George agreed.

'And all built on assumptions. Where are the facts?'

'Well, Mac told us he was planning something bigger than 18/8. There's one fact for you.'

'No! That's not a fact, that's another assumption.

We're *assuming* he's telling the truth. Come on, George, that's a fucking huge assumption. Maybe he's planning on leaving the country and this is all a diversion.'

'Ah,' George said, 'but that's another assumption.'

Aston swung his head around. 'Now you're getting the hang of it.'

'*Eyesbackontheroad!*' George screeched again. A deep breath, then: 'So, do we have anything solid to work with? Anything at all?'

'Yes,' Aston said. 'The laptop.'

'Yeah, we got some pretty good stuff from that,' George said. '. . . oh shit! He wanted us to find the laptop, didn't he?'

'Basically, he wanted to lead us down a certain path, and we didn't just go running down that path, we sprinted. He's been leading us on from the word go.' A pause while he took a left turn, downshifting smoothly, one hand on the wheel. 'Okay, George, what's the biggest assumption we've made here?'

'No idea – but I get the feeling you're going to tell me.'

So he told her, and from the way her big brown eyes got even bigger he knew he was on to something. In his head, the idea had seemed crazy. Out in the open, breathing and taking on a life of its own, it sounded so obvious he couldn't understand how he'd missed it. The computer-generated photos had finally pointed him in the right direction. What annoyed him most was that he'd been staring at those pictures all afternoon and it hadn't clicked.

'Well, what are you waiting for?' George said when he finished. 'Put your bloody foot down.'

47

'Any problems?' I ask, slipping into more familiar shoes.

'Course there were no problems. Would I be sitting here if there were?'

The hacker has a point.

'And Mr Cope did the business for you?' he asks.

'Worked like a charm,' I tell him. Vic was dreamt up by Mole. Completely real to MI6's computers, but as insubstantial as a phantom in every other respect. 'So where is it?'

A nod towards the room's main desk where the laptop bag sat basking in the glow of the three dressing-table monitors. I walk over and carefully unclip the straps. Gently, I take the bomb from the bag and place it on the desk.

'I can't believe how easy it was to get it in,' Mole says. 'When you're in a chair, all anyone sees is the chair, know what I mean?'

I know what he means, but knowing and caring are two separate issues.

The hacker takes a drag on his stinking roll-up. 'Security don't even bother to check me out when I set off the metal detector any more. That's what I mean. To start with they'd be there the second I tried to get through the front doors, waving their magic wands over me, but they soon got tired of that. He's just a stupid cripple, what's the point? I tell you, I could come in here with enough guns and grenades to start a war and they'd let me through. Good evening, and can we help you with that bazooka?' He gives a rattling, phlegm-filled cough, takes another wheezy drag. 'As for the radio-active isotope scanners and the olfactory filters and all the rest of that whiz-bang hi-tech bollocks, give me a fucking break. Do you have any idea how much people trust computers?'

The hacker isn't expecting an answer. He's on a roll, talking crap, and I'm not listening to a word he's saying. He mimes flicking a light switch, dead ash drifting down from the roll-up dangling between his nicotine-stained fingers.

'Detector goes on, detector goes off.' He giggles, flicking in time to his words. 'On, off, on, off. Piece of piss. Isn't it great that everything's controlled by computers these days?'

'Yes,' I agree, sensing I should make a contribution. While the hacker's been up on his soapbox I've been staring at the bomb, completely hypnotised. Balls bounce across the screens, painting it with bright, friendly colours. It's smaller than I remember – a trick of memory. The colours make it look like a child's toy – a trick of the light. The flashlight-sized cylinder of Strontium 90 is encased in a thick layer of lead. Surrounding that, four bricks of military quality C4. None of that second-rate crap you usually get on the black market, either. Nicholai always makes sure I get the best. The timer is simple, taken from a bog standard VCR, the sort you can buy on any High Street. Of course the hacker had wanted to use a computer, but who gives a shit if a computer can control things to the nanosecond. Accuracy to the nearest minute is good enough. So long as it goes bang, that's all I care about. This bomb's as simple as you can get. The C4 detonates, destroying the lead casing, and all that good stuff just comes spewing out. The air conditioner gets hold of it and before you know it, you've got radiation from the basement to the penthouse. If the clean-up gets going straight away, it'll still be too late. Let's face it, even if the eggheads gave the all clear, said there was zero risk, would you want to work here? When it comes to radiation, our attitudes are mediaeval. We can't see it, can't touch it, don't understand it. Radiation equals cancer equals death.

'I take it the money's all sorted?' Mole says as he finally stubs out the stinking cigarette.

'Ah,' I say. 'Bit of a problem there, I'm afraid.'

'Problem?' he replies, his black caterpillar eyebrows undulating unpleasantly above the bottle-bottom glasses. 'Got to tell you, Mac, I don't like problems. Way I see it I've done my bit and I expect to get paid.'

'And you will get paid,' I tell him soothingly.

'I need this money, Mac.'

'Relax. You'll get everything that's owed you.'

'The only way I can get out of this shithole is by buying my way out. You know that. That's the reason I agreed to help. A new face and passport cost money, you know.'

The hacker reaches for his tobacco tin. I fire a look and he presses the lid back on, puts the tin down on the desk. I turn my back, reach inside my pocket. The plastic is cold. Smooth on one side, serrated on the other. I slip it out. This was a piece of piss to sneak in as well. The metal detectors didn't see it; not so much as a single click from the radioactive isotope scanners.

Mole is staring at the monitors lining the side of the room, lost in space, star streaks reflecting off his thick lenses. I walk over, place a friendly hand on his shoulder. *Don't worry, everything will work out fine*, my look says. I wait for him to relax, monitoring his mood by the feel of his shoulder muscles through the stained Aerosmith T-shirt. I move fast, my free hand whipping around his neck. A clicking as the cable tie ratchets tight. I jerk hard and get another half dozen clicks, spin the wheelchair into the middle of the room where he can't do any damage.

For a second he's caught in suspended animation, the puzzled expression indicating that it's taking a while for his brain to catch up with current events. And then he starts thrashing, a cartoon epileptic on amphetamines, arms flailing everywhere, strong piano player fingers grasping for the cable tie. It's odd the way his legs stay completely still. With a crash the chair topples to the left, spilling the hacker onto the floor. Flailing away like a beached fish, his desperate fingernails dig into the soft skin of his neck, scratching and tearing, leaving bloody weals. His lips are turning blue, stained red from where he's taken a chunk out of his tongue. The eyes, already magnified behind the thick lenses, grow bigger and bigger, as though he's decompressing too quickly. In time his struggles lessen. I can see realisation dawning. This isn't a video game where all you do is hit a key and you're up and raring to go again. No, this is Game Over for real. A twitch of an arm, a twitch of a leg, and it's finished. Mole's lying on his side, completely still now. Wide, dead fish eyes staring at nothing.

I search through the drawers and get lucky third time. Tools of all shapes and sizes. Mole was always a hands-on sort, as clever with hardware as he was with software. MI6 was always funny about sending its computers out to be fixed, worried that some unscrupulous boffin might accidentally come across something he shouldn't and sell it to the enemy. I tuck the screwdriver into my waistband. The handle is cold against my back.

I'm distracted by the sound of the door opening. A deep breath to compose myself, a shrug of the shoulders to work away any tension. I've waited a long time for this.

48

'Okay, Aston. I got here as quick as I could. What have you got?' The Etonian voice penetrating the gloom is sharp and authoritarian, a voice used to being obeyed. 'And can we get some lights on in here, please?'

A swish of the mouse and a click, and the room fills with bright operating theatre dazzle. Another click to seal the door. Kinclave looks at me, looks at the dead hacker, back to me.

'Who are you?' he says. 'What the hell's going on?' He moves towards the telephone.

'Don't.'

That stops him. He looks at me again, more closely this time. When he speaks he sounds calm, there's not a trace of tension. He's composed, super-confident, in charge. Got to hand it to him. He always was slick.

'Mac,' he says with a best buddy smile. 'You really pick your moments, don't you? Have you any idea the sort of evening I'm having? I'd much rather be out having a nice meal somewhere, or at the theatre. Instead it seems the world's gone mad.'

As he talks his eyes are everywhere, his brain ticking away at a million miles an hour. 'You could always drop by the Albert Hall,' I suggest. 'I'm sure they can squeeze one more in. An evening of patriotic chest pounding – you'd have a ball.'

His eyes lock on the bomb. 'The Albert Hall was never your target, was it?'

'No,' I agree.

'We can talk about this,' he says, and I detect the first hint of uncertainty.

'Talking's good,' I say. 'What do you want to talk about?'

'You don't have to do this, Mac.'

'Do what?'

'Jesus Christ, Mac!'

Kinclave is getting rattled, beads of sweat dribble down the side of his face. It's all going according to the script. I've had this conversation in my head more times than I care to remember. 'You seem a little stressed,' I observe.

'What the hell is this all about, Mac?'

I pause for a moment to contemplate. 'Where to start,' I muse. 'Well . . . how about we start with the fact that you completely and utterly fucked me over!' I try to keep my voice level, but it's not easy. I've spent many a year keeping my anger in check and now it can't wait to get out there and destroy.

'What are you talking about, Mac?'

'Don't come the innocent, Grant. You know exactly what I'm talking about.'

'I'm afraid I don't. You'll have to enlighten me.'

It's a good suggestion. In three steps I'm standing in front of him. Years of boardroom excess have made him soft, have dampened his reflexes. He's slow to react when I grab hold of the lapels of his suit jacket, still reaching for them when my forehead slams into his face. Blood spurts from his broken nose as he sinks to the floor. The first kick winds him; the second breaks a rib or two.

I roll him onto his back, wait for his breathing to settle. This wasn't part of the script, but who gives a shit? It felt good. And improvisation is the hallmark of any truly great performance.

'Feeling suitably enlightened?' I make to kick him again and it's a pleasure to watch him cringe. There's a dark, wet stain on the front of his Savile Row suit trousers, a hint of ammonia in the air.

'I don't understand.' His voice is weak and pathetic, the words muffled by his broken nose; there's a distinct wheeze when he breathes. With the illusion of greatness stripped away he really is a nobody.

'You will,' I say.

'What have I ever done to you?'

'You really don't know?'

'No. I thought we were friends.'

'Friends! In this business! Come on.' I hunker down, get in close. 'I should have been Chief,' I whisper.

In spite of his injuries he manages a weak laugh, the sort of laugh a terminal patient might make when he realises how pointless life actually is, how it's all been one big sick joke. His laughter sets something off in me. Before I know it, I've got hold of his jacket and I'm smashing my fist into his smarmy face, mangling his features into something even his own mother would recoil from. Somehow I get hold of myself before I kill him. He needs to live a little while longer. Kinclave rolls to one side and coughs, the sound wet and emphysemic. He spits out a tooth and looks at me with something approaching pity. It's almost enough to set me off again.

'I was supposed to be Chief,' I tell him.

'It was never going to happen,' he says, and it's an effort to get the words out. 'You were always too old school. All that cloak and dagger stuff might have worked in the Cold War, but the world moved on.'

'I had ideas. I was going to take MI6 into the next millennium,' I say and I hate myself for saying it. Kinclave has got me on the defensive, and that *definitely* wasn't part of the script.

'Mac, you were a good field officer, one of the best. But let's face it, you just didn't have what it takes. You weren't the right pedigree.'

And that's what it came down to. I didn't have the right school tie gathering dust in my wardrobe.

'It's not your fault,' Kinclave was saying, the words delivered with more pity than I can stomach.

He still doesn't get it, doesn't understand. Bruised and battered and bleeding, the self-obsessed wanker still thinks he's in charge.

I pull out the screwdriver from the back of my trousers and, despite the rage that's blinding me, my aim is accurate. His eyes widen and he gurgles a scream. I ram the screwdriver in deeper, give it a twist. He's still a way from death – about twenty minutes by my reckoning.

'Secrets,' I say. 'We've all got our secrets. Even you.'

For a second the fear in his face is replaced by understanding. And then the fear is back.

'Thought you'd kept that one quiet, didn't you?' I'm up close, so close I can smell the metallic shine of his blood. He doesn't answer because there's nothing to say. I can tell by his expression that he knows exactly what I'm talking about.

'Sometimes,' I tell him, 'life puts us in exactly the right place at exactly the right time. It was me who took the call from Whitehall. "Ever so sorry to bother you, old chap, but we've had this pretty young thing in asking to speak to Jeff Salter. He's not one of ours, so we're wondering if he might be one of yours." I told him I'd look into it, and I did.

'You know, Grant, it was a pretty callous thing to do, leaving her in the lurch like that. But I can understand why you did it. If the roles had been reversed I would have done the same. After all, it wouldn't have looked good on the old CV, would it? You never would have made Chief with something like that hanging around your neck. Best sweep it under the carpet and pretend it never happened, eh?'

A weak, bloody hand reaches out for my wrist. 'Please don't hurt him.'

'Unfortunately that's one promise I can't make, Grant.' I shake the hand away and turn my attention back to the bomb, set the timer for seven-thirty. That's when the concert starts. Might as well rub their faces in it. I bet it's chaos over at the Albert Hall.

I check my watch, then dim the lights.

49

'So, what's Mac up to?' George made a frustrated guttural noise, something primal that had too many consonants. 'This is doing my head in, Paul.'

'Don't ask me,' said Aston. 'I should've worked out what Mole was doing. Should've seen that one a mile off.'

'Yeah, you should've,' George agreed.

'Hey – that's the point where you're supposed to reassure me. Tell me it wasn't my fault, all that crap.'

'Just calling it how I see it.'

They bowled through the front doors, passes at the ready, and headed for separate pods. Both muttered a steady stream of colourful curses as the computer processed them, a task that took an eternity. Spat out on the other side, they sprinted through the vast reception area, heading for the express elevators. Even on a Saturday evening there were quite a few people milling around. Aston gave them all a perfunctory once-over as he passed, looking for Mac, knowing it was a long shot. There was no way Mac was going to be here. Breathless, heart racing, he reached the tall lift towers and hammered the button with his thumb.

'C'mon, c'mon, c'mon,' he muttered.

George stilled his impatient hand. 'That won't make it get here any quicker.'

Seconds came and went, a lifetime's worth passing before the lift arrived. The doors opened and they got in. Aston sent the elevator hurtling into the depths, his stomach lifted slightly as it stopped. And then they were running again, legs and arms pumping, George setting the pace. They reached Mole's office and George slid her card through the reader. The hydraulic door hissed open and they moved cautiously from the sterile glare of the corridor into the dim gloom of the Unreal.

It took a few moments for Aston's eyes to adjust. He stared at the shadowy shapes on the floor and when his mind and eyes finally synched up, his first thought was that the hacker must have had a heart attack. Given Mole's diet, lifestyle, and the excess weight he was carrying, it was inevitable. Then he saw the cable tie and any thoughts that Mole met a natural end evaporated.

George was down on her knees checking for a pulse. She pulled the wheelchair out the way, pressed her fingers to his neck, shook her head. Wrapped her hand around his wrist, shook her head again. No surprises there. For Aston, death was a face he was getting to know only too well.

One quick glance was all it took: Mole's wide un-blinking fishlike eyes, the thick glasses hanging from one ear, half on, half off, the shattered lens . . . death was in the details.

'Mac?' George asked.

'I think we're on safe ground with that assumption,' Aston replied.

'He's still warm, Paul. This only just happened.'

Shit, Aston thought, *Mac manages to stay one step ahead again*. Maybe they'd passed him on the way in – probably had – and he'd been so focused on getting down here he'd ran straight past him. Aston gave himself a silent bollocking that matched any that Mac had given him.

'Who's there?' The voice was weak, each word a strain. Aston turned and could just about make out the shape of a body lying on the floor; it was partially hidden by one of the desks. The hand-some face was smashed and bloody, but he recog-nised it straight away. He rushed over and crouched down, George at his side.

'It's going to be alright,' he said. 'We'll get help. Hang on in there, okay?' There was blood every-where. Spreading black and crimson, it bloomed out from the tear in Kinclave's silk shirt. A dark sticky puddle surrounded him. Aston was no doctor, but it was obvious the prognosis wasn't good. Carefully, George began unbuttoning the shirt. Kinclave pushed her hands away.

'It's okay,' she said. 'I need to see where you're injured.'

'Listen,' Kinclave whispered, the word whistling between his teeth.

'Don't talk,' Aston said. 'Save your breath.'

'You've got to listen to me, Paul.'

'I'm going to phone security,' George said. 'Get the doctor down here.'

'No.' The word was delivered with complete authority, stopping Aston and George in their tracks, demanding their attention.

'No,' Kinclave repeated more quietly. 'There isn't time.'

The Chief closed his eyes and breathed out a long exhalation. For a moment Aston thought that was it, Kinclave was dead, and then his chest rose and fell. When The Chief opened his eyes, there were tears there. One of them escaped and ran down his cheek, washed a clean line through the blood. And then he laughed quietly to himself, the cynical laugh of someone who's finally got the joke.

'I'm so sorry, Paul.'

'Sorry for what?'

'It's funny. You get a picture in your head of how things are going to turn out, but it hardly ever works out how you imagine.'

'I don't understand,' Aston said. Kinclave was talking nonsense, probably in shock. He was just about to tell George to phone for the doctor again when Kinclave spoke.

'I'm your father, Paul.'

Aston stared at Kinclave, bloody and dying.

There was no doubt he'd heard right, but although he recognised the words they didn't make any sense. 'What are you talking about?'

'Fucked-up old world, isn't it?' A brief smile flickered on his lips and then he was hit by a sudden coughing fit. His chest heaved wetly, blood bubbles dripped from his lips, his smashed nose. Aston lifted his head and cradled it in his hands, trying to make him more comfortable, trying to make it easier for him to breathe. The eyes flickered closed and his chest fell for the final time. Aston knelt there, stunned, cradling Kinclave's head. He was only vaguely aware of George's hand on his shoulder. She said something he didn't hear.

'Paul,' she said sharply, and that got his attention. 'Is that what I think it is?'

Aston followed her gaze, couldn't see anything. She was looking into the dark shadows under one of the desks.

7:26

The green numbers hung in midair, seemingly attached to nothing, evil and ominous. He laid Kinclave's head gently on the floor and wiped the blood off his hands. He got up and sleepwalked towards the numbers to get a better look.

I'm your father.

He tried to put The Chief's words out of his mind. There'd be time to worry about that later. Right now, he had to get his act together, needed to focus. It wasn't easy, but it had to be done. He closed his eyes and did a slow count to ten, concentrating on his breathing. When he opened his eyes the numbers were still there, glowing green and sinister.

So this was what a dirty bomb looked like. It was much bigger than the bomb that had been attached to George – big enough to make a hell of a bang. Mac had managed to plant a bomb in the heart of MI6. That must have taken some planning. MI6's HQ wasn't just any old office block, it was one of the most secure buildings in the country; a recognisable symbol of strength and security, like the Pentagon in the US. And this wasn't just any old bomb, either. There hadn't been a nuclear device detonated in anger since Nagasaki. When Mac said he was planning something bigger than 18/8 he hadn't been joking.

'Don't touch it,' George said in a panicked whisper. 'It could be booby trapped.'

'Don't worry,' Aston whispered back, uncertain why they were talking so quietly, and realising it was because of the bomb. It demanded that sort of respect. 'I'm leaving this one for the experts. This goes right outside my frame of reference.'

The numbers blinked to 7:27.

'So what now?' Aston asked.

'Contact security and get the hell out of here,' George said.

'Sounds like a plan.' Aston reached for the phone again, glanced at the numbers. Mac wasn't giving an inch. A countdown would be nice, but no, he couldn't even give them that. VCR clocks made perfect timers. Accurate and reliable and, because they were mass produced and available on any High Street, impossible to trace.

'How long do you reckon we've got?' George asked, reading his mind.

'No idea. But I think we should get out of here ASAP.' Aston put the phone down.

'What are you doing? Phone security.'

'And what if the bomb's set to go off in a minute or two minutes? Security gets down here and it detonates. No, there have already been too many people killed.'

'But, Paul, if it goes off . . .'

'If it goes off, some insurance company gets stung, but at least no one else dies.' A nod to the bomb. The green numbers showed 7:28, but not for much longer. 'My guess is that it's set to go off at half past.'

'And you're basing that on?'

'The concert starts then. It's the sort of thing Mac would do.'

'Okay,' she said, 'in that case, we'd best get a move on.'

George set the pace and Aston followed. For once there was an elevator waiting, and they jumped inside. Aston thumped the button for the ground floor and the lift hurtled upwards. According to his watch, there was one minute to go. He was suddenly aware of George staring at him.

'What?' he said.

'I don't want you doing anything stupid,' she said.

'Like what?'

'I'm serious, Paul . . .'

The doors slid open and then they were running again, heading for the entrance. 'Okay,' Aston said. 'I'm going after Mac, you go get security.'

George opened her mouth to argue; Aston could tell she was going to argue because of the set of her jaw, and the way her lips had tightened against her teeth. Before she could get anything out the ground shuddered beneath their feet and the alarms began screaming. Everybody in the lobby froze, heads up, puzzled expressions all round. The confusion quickly turned to fear; they'd felt the explosion, knew this wasn't a drill. Aston broke into a flat-out sprint and headed for the entrance.

'Get security,' he shouted over his shoulder to George. 'Mac's mine.'

50

Victor Cope passed through security without any problems. Comfortable in his skin, comfortable in his shoes, the computers didn't give him so much as a second glance, and because the computers were happy the security guards monitoring the CCTV cameras didn't give him a second glance, either; they carried on sipping their coffee, arguing about football, and bitching about the fact they'd pulled the Saturday night graveyard shift. He walked down to the river, found a quiet spot and stared over the water. All his awareness was focused on what was happening behind him. A tilt of the head to the left and he could see all the comings and goings at the entrance in his peripheral vision. He watched the dynamic duo rush inside like their feet were on fire, and had to smile. Oh, to be that young, that keen. And they must be feeling so pleased with themselves. Working it all out. How fucking clever were they? And then he waited. Of course, waiting doesn't bother our friend Vic; he's had plenty of practice. He was feeling safe in his borrowed skin and wanted to be nearby when it happened. Nobody had bothered him so far, and it was unlikely anyone would. He didn't look dangerous, didn't look like a terrorist, didn't look like a threat. He was just your average everyday nerd out on his own for a Saturday-night stroll, a Billy-no-mates with nothing better to do. His watch beeped once. A quick glance to see the big hand resting on the six. A second later he felt the dull thud beneath his feet. The alarms were barely audible, muffled behind tons of concrete, bricks and the bombproof glass.

With MI6's HQ rising behind him, our friend Vic walks away, resisting the urge to look back, the urge to hurry. A running man would draw attention, so he moves with casual confidence, a bounce in his step. Occasionally his head moves imperceptibly from side to side in time with his feet, nothing obvious, a little to the left, then to the right; enough movement to give him the full 360 degrees. He studies every passer-by, every passing car, giving them a careful once-over. When you run this close to the edge everything is either black or white; there are no shades of grey. Friend or enemy, win or lose, dead or alive. That simple. Shades of grey create doubt, and doubt gets you killed.

As he walks, he whistles one of Old Blue Eyes' tunes under his breath. *Come Rain or Come Shine*. Sophia used to love singing that, a cappella, her voice as sweet as honey. Appropriate, too; it has just started drizzling, the rain a light mist as delicate as gossamer.

Another quick look-see to ensure he's not being followed. Seems his luck is holding. Our friend Vic isn't particularly superstitious but right now a little luck wouldn't go amiss.

In the distance he hears sirens: police, ambulance, fire. Without missing a step, Vic disappears into the station and finds someone to buy a ticket from. With planning it's the small details that count. You've got to make sure those wheels within the wheels are well oiled and running smoothly. Whistling softly to himself, he heads for the platforms.

51

Aston slipped into Mac's skin, stepped into his shoes, and he asked himself one simple question. What would I do now? *I'd want to head into the city, head for the crowds, and that means getting across the river. Crossing Vauxhall Bridge by foot would leave me too exposed, so that's out. If I get trapped in the middle there'd be no escape. Jumping on a bus isn't an option, because that means hanging around on an open street waiting for one. Again, way too exposed. The Underground is the most logical option: plenty of shadows to hide in on the station, and once in the system I could go anywhere.*

Yes, I'd want everyone to think I was using the tube. I'd head for the platforms, probably using the barrier near the guard booth, maybe faffing around with my ticket to draw attention to myself, not being obvious, just dithering enough so my face would be clocked. I'd leave it a minute or two then head back outside, and this time I'd slip through the barriers like a phantom.

And that was why Aston headed straight for

the station's taxi rank. He found his own shadows to hide in and waited. He couldn't get close enough to see the taxi rank, but he managed to find a corner where he could hear everything that was going on: the bored cabbies talking about nothing, the rumble of trains pulling in and out of the station.

Footsteps. Aston pushed deeper into the shadowy crevice. The rainclouds had stolen most of the light, painting the evening sky a dull grey, water dripped from a rusty gutter. The footsteps came closer and he was able to discern two sets moving together with military precision. The tip-tap of feminine heels and the fat slap of male feet, someone carrying a few extra pounds by the sound of it. A taxi door creaked open. Seconds later it slammed shut; the chug of an engine that got louder as the cab passed by before slowly blending with the rest of the night noises.

The seconds ticked by without sign of Mac, and Aston was convinced he'd fucked up, put two and two together and got five. Maybe he'd overanalysed the situation. That was one of the many criticisms Mac had fired at him over the years; just one of the digs that had pissed him off so much because he'd been trying so bloody hard to get it right. He'd always given Mac one hundred and ten percent and it had never been enough. Not once. There was always something he could have done differently, something he could have done better. *Not good enough*. How many times had Mac told him that? He didn't even need to come out and say it. A disapproving look usually did the trick.

Out of the night noises came more footsteps, distant and light as air, soft soles caressing the ground. Aston pushed himself deeper into the shadows and held his breath. He didn't need visual confirmation that this was Mac. How many times had he been at his desk, head down and grafting, and heard those footsteps? Mac stopped and Aston could imagine him standing there, doing a quick 360 degrees, nostrils flared to catch the scent of danger. It was only when the footsteps started up again that Aston dared breathe.

He did a slow count to three then stepped into the archway, the rain falling in long threads behind him, the long well-lit tunnel stretching ahead. Above, a train rumbled by. The stranger stopped halfway along the tunnel, stopped long enough for Aston to convince himself he had the wrong person. A foxy grin, then Mac carried on towards him.

'Well, well, you must be feeling pleased with yourself. Managing to outsmart your old boss.'

There was no mistaking that lazy, smooth voice. Nor the sarcasm. Aston's brain told him this was Mac, but his eyes were having a hard time believing. This person didn't look like Mac, didn't move like him, didn't carry himself the same way. He didn't look anything like the late Mark Parson, either. This incarnation of Mac was twenty years younger than the original; the blond hair was black and streaked with grey. Mac had 20/20 vision but the man

461

standing in front of him was wearing heavy-framed glasses. The nose was a different shape, the chin, too; the forehead was wider and the eyebrows bushier. He looked like a computer geek.

It was definitely Mac's voice, though. This was the same voice that harangued Aston in his thoughts, the voice his conscience had adopted. And although his blue eyes were now brown there was no mistaking those, either. Sharp and watchful, they didn't miss a thing.

Mac marched straight up to Aston and gave him a couple of playful slaps on the cheek. 'Good to see you. Have you missed me?'

Aston said nothing, just stared as he took a step back, not wanting to get too close.

Mac held his gaze. 'I'm disappointed. Got to tell you that. Didn't you see me when you charged through the front doors earlier? Stupid question, really. You were a man on a mission, out to save the world. All you were seeing was what was directly in front of your nose, and I dare say even that was just a blur. I saw you, though. Had myself a nice little spot down by the river where I could watch events unfold. And you didn't see me. Didn't see that woman walking her dog, either. Or that gaudy, brightly lit restaurant boat cruising by. Didn't see a fucking thing, did you? Come on, Aston! Haven't you learnt anything from me? A hundred percent vigilance, a hundred and ten percent of the time. Those aren't just words, they actually mean something.'

Aston's tongue was frozen to the roof of his mouth. Mac had done it again, made him feel two inches tall. In his head he could hear the ghosts from his schooldays taunting him. *Loser! Loser*! He had an irrational urge to defend himself, to make Mac see that he wasn't a loser. It was pathetic and he hated himself for feeling this way, but he couldn't help it.

'So where's your back-up?' Mac said, studying Aston closely. 'Ah, you don't have any. It's just you and me, isn't it?'

A shake of the head, then: 'You really are a fuck-up. A complete waste of space. So, what? You thought you could bring me in yourself? Did you think that if you did that they'd make you some sort of hero? Get your face on all the front pages? Have the ladies falling at your feet? How's that for a new flavour of deluded? That's not the way it works. You work for MI6. You're a shadow, a non-person. You don't exist. Those fuckers over there will bleed you dry and when they're done they'll drop you in a heartbeat.'

'Is that why you did it?'

Mac grinned. 'That'll teach those bastards for fucking with me. Their nice new building turned into a no-go zone. A quarter of a billion quid down the pan. I can't wait to see the headlines. MI6 is going to be the laughing stock of the world. Let them try and keep this one off the front pages.'

'What about all the people who died at Leicester Square?'

'Every war has casualties. It's a fact of life. Very sad but, hey, what can you do?'

A pause, then: 'What about Kinclave?'

'That bastard got everything he deserved.'

'You knew all along he was my father.'

'Of course.'

'You used me.'

'You'll get over it.' Mac pushed past Aston, heading for the taxi rank. Aston went after him, put a hand on his shoulder to turn him. And then he was doubled up, struggling to breathe and Mac's lips were touching his ear.

'I can't remember the last time I had this much fun. You want to play, let's play. You think you're so fucking clever – let's see how clever you are.'

The blow stunned Aston, made his head spin. As he pulled himself upright, using the wall for support, he heard Mac's quick footsteps moving into the distance. He followed the sound to the taxi rank and saw the door of a black cab slam shut as he turned the corner. Aston ran towards the cab, but he wasn't quick enough. There was a sudden squeal of tyres as it pulled away, with Mac grinning behind the wheel. The driver was slumped in the passenger seat, his neck twisted at an unnatural angle. Aston ran to the next taxi in the line and pulled open the driver door. The cabbie turned, looking puzzled, and Aston flipped open his ID wallet and thrust it in his face.

'Police! I need to borrow your cab.' He snapped the wallet shut before the cabbie had a chance to have a proper look. The picture was his, but the only ID card he had on him was his MI6 one.

'You think I'm going to just give you my cab? Get real.'

No time for this. Aston grabbed hold of the cabbie and dragged him out. He was thin with bookish glasses, nine stone nothing and no real problem. The cabbie struggled and called out for help, but Aston easily wrestled him to the tarmac. He jumped into the driver's seat and slammed the door, aware that a couple of the other cabbies were heading his way, hard men who looked like they knew how to handle themselves. One of them reached out for the door handle and Aston slammed into first, jammed his foot down on the accelerator. The stink of burning rubber filled the air as the cab fishtailed forward, sending the cabbie spinning. He could see Mac; he didn't have that much of a head start. It was pissing down now and Aston flicked the wipers on full. He threw a right and accelerated along Albert Embankment, heading towards Lambeth, weaving through the traffic. He glanced to his left and saw a procession of blue and red lights parading across Vauxhall Bridge.

The needle crept higher, the distance closing. Holding the wheel with one hand, Aston grabbed the seatbelt and clicked it into place. Up ahead, Mac took a left onto Lambeth Bridge, skidding around the turn on the rain-slicked road. Aston downshifted to second, the engine screaming, the car leaning right as he took the turn. Mac slowed to take the roundabout on the other side of the bridge and Aston saw his chance. He hit the accelerator and careered onto the roundabout, praying for a gap in the traffic, and getting one. The Houses of Parliament loomed up ahead, grim and foreboding through the thick London rain. Aston was completely focused on Mac's cab, which was almost close enough to touch. Mac took a sudden left and Aston just made the turn, the back end of the cab swinging wildly. Eight metres and closing. Aston tugged the seat belt tight. He had to take Mac out before he got any deeper into the city. Following a black cab through the centre of London would be impossible.

They were bumper to bumper now. Across one crossroads, across a second, Aston braced himself and stomped the accelerator, looking for that last little bit. The two cabs collided violently, metal screeching and tearing. Aston didn't back off. He jammed his foot on the accelerator, driving his cab into Mac's. The needle flickered backwards from forty. Mac had hit the brakes; the one brake light that hadn't been pulverised glowing bright red. And still he kept his foot down, bulldozing Mac's cab closer and closer to the T-junction, the speedometer registering twenty then ten then five. Aston inched the cab across the junction, heard the screech of brakes as cars slammed to a standstill on either side. Horns blared and curses rang out. Aston wrenched his door open, noticed Mac was doing the same. He untangled himself from his seatbelt and by the time he got free Mac was disappearing down a side street. Aston was only seconds behind but when he reached the turning, Mac had vanished. Aston spun around, rain dripping from his hair, saw Westminster Abbey, saw the Houses of Parliament . . .

Aston didn't see Mac, didn't hear him. A tingling of his sixth sense and he moved without thinking, brought his arm up, turned his body. Mac's arm slammed into his with a heavy thump. Making the most of this small advantage, Aston bent into a crouch and swept his leg around. He felt it connect with something solid and Mac went down hard, an *oosh* escaping as the wind was knocked from him. The red mist was rising, filling his heart and head and soul. Mac was no longer a person. He was nothing. He tried to get up, and Aston stamped on his groin, driving his heel in. Mac let out a high-pitched animal wail and pulled himself into the foetal position. Before Mac could get his breath back, Aston dragged him to the kerb. He pulled his right leg straight, the heel touching the ground, and stamped hard on his kneecap. Mac howled and jerked his leg away, pleading through the pain. Aston wasn't listening. He pulled the leg straight again and held it in place while he brought his foot down a second time. It took three attempts to break the kneecap, the crack as it gave way clearly audible over the screaming. Satisfied Mac wasn't going anywhere,

Aston straddled him. Mac reached up and grabbed the front of his jacket with weak fingers.

'You don't have the balls to kill me,' he whispered, each word an effort.

'Who said anything about killing you? I just want to hurt you.'

He prised Mac's fingers away, pulled off the wig, tore away the latex. He grabbed hold of Mac by the hair and smashed his fist into his face. Soaked to the skin and oblivious of the rain, Aston punched until his knuckles were raw and bloody and he couldn't feel them anymore, until long after Mac had escaped into unconsciousness. He only stopped when a soft hand grabbed his arm. Aston turned and saw George.

'It's over,' she said gently.

She helped him up and he fell into her arms, burying his head into her shoulder and holding on tight. Her words rang in his ears – 'It's over' – but it would never be over; in every way that mattered this was just the start. And all around him the city turned darkly, moving to its own rhythm, calling its own tune: the insistent vehicle moan, the harsh grate of emergency sirens, the distant sound of a lone alarm going off, and filling in the cracks of this urban symphony, the whispers and shouts and cries of so many lost souls.

Epilogue

It was all George's fault. He'd wanted to do this over the telephone, take the easy way out, but she'd had other ideas. 'There are certain conversations you shouldn't have on the phone,' she'd told him. 'Believe me, this is one of them.' He'd tried to argue, but she'd already made his mind up for him. And to make sure he didn't bottle out she'd gone along for the ride.

They'd caught the 10.07 train from Paddington, arriving in Great Bedwyn an hour and twenty minutes later. It had been the longest journey of his life. Like waiting to be called in by the dentist, only worse. Throughout the journey he'd tried to think of what he was going to say, but his mind was blank. Numb. It was the only word that came close to describing how he felt these days, and even that was a long way off the mark. What he felt went way beyond numb.

The Last Night of the Proms had been a week ago, and already it seemed to have happened in a different lifetime. The cover-up was well underway. All the emergency personnel involved had been made to sign the Official Secrets Act. Of course, there were rumours, but these had been quickly dismissed. The official line was that there had been a small fire, which had been quickly contained. As far as the general public was concerned, the Vauxhall Cross bombing never happened.

Aston had been forced to take a couple of weeks off. Compassionate leave, they called it. A level of torture that contravened the Geneva convention was what he called it. He'd spent the past week in his flat, bouncing off the walls. One minute he was going to do a runner, catch the first plane out and become a surf bum in Oz or a Tibetan monk . . . or whatever. The thing was to get as far away from his fucked-up life as possible. It didn't work like that, though. Wherever he went, his fucked-up life would be following right behind. Running away really wasn't an option. So what should he do? The easy answer was to try to carry on as before. The problem was that he wasn't sure whether he could carry on working for MI6. Right now, his heart wasn't in it.

Aside from George, who'd practically moved in, his only visitor during the past week was MI6's strung-out shrink. Katrina had caught him napping on the Monday. The box in the hall had squawked and when he'd answered with a distant 'yeah', she'd introduced herself and he was trapped. Aston tried a couple of lines to get rid of her but she wasn't buying. He buzzed her in, cursing himself, and spent the next hour and a half evading her questions. If she told him once that she was only there to help, she told him a hundred times. In the end Katrina did most of the talking. He had no urge to 'explore his feelings' with her or anyone else, thank you very much. She might have visited a couple more times during the week, but he'd learnt his lesson and stopped answering his door; there was no one he wanted to see, anyway. She'd caught him on his mobile on Wednesday evening and he'd pretended he was in Spain. After that the visits stopped, which suited him fine.

George walked with him up the High Street. The day was gorgeous. Blue skies and sunshine all the way. Summer's last gasp. They reached his mother's house, a pretty little cottage with roses in the garden, and George leant across and kissed him on the cheek, straightened his collar.

'It's going to be fine, Paul.'

'Easy for you to say.'

'I'll be in the local when you're finished. Come and find me.'

Aston took a deep breath and pushed the gate open. His mother appeared in the doorway before he could knock. She reeled him in and gave him a huge hug.

'Paul, what a surprise. I wasn't expecting you. Why didn't you call? I haven't had time to tidy up or anything.' She pushed him away, held him at arm's length and gave him the once over. 'You've lost weight.'

'I've not lost weight, Mum.'

'So how come you're thinner? You're obviously not eating properly.'

'I am eating.'

'You'd best come in and I'll make you a sandwich.'

'I'm not hungry, Mum.'

'Ham or cheese?' she called over her shoulder as she headed for the kitchen.

Aston ignored her. He pushed open the door to the lounge and made himself at home. The cottage was tiny, but it was plenty big enough for Roy and his mother. It was immaculate, no dust anywhere. The ceiling was low, the beams exposed, flowery fragrances filled the air. There were lace curtains over the windows and every spare surface was filled with ornaments and framed photographs. It made him cringe how many of the photos had his face smiling out. This wasn't the house he'd grown up in, that was on the edge of the village, a big old rambling affair probably three times the size of this cottage. As far as he was aware, Brian still lived in that big old house. Brian was another subject she didn't talk about.

'You've just missed Roy,' his mother said as she came back in carrying a tray. She placed a plate of sandwiches on the coffee table. The tea was served in the best china.

'Shame.'

'Don't say it like that.'

'I didn't say it like anything.'

'Anyway, I've got a bone to pick with you.'

Aston had a pretty good idea what that bone was. She'd left him a couple of answerphone messages during the week, calls he hadn't returned because he didn't want to get lured into a conversation with her.

'I watched the concert on the telly, but it's not the same as being there, is it? And to think we had tickets.'

'What did you tell Roy?'

'Exactly what you told me to tell him, Paul. That I wasn't feeling well enough to go because I had an upset stomach. He was so disappointed.'

'I'm sure he'll get over it.'

'But that's not the point, Paul. Nothing happened.'

'And you'd prefer that it had.'

'Of course not.'

'I'd love to tell you what really went on, Mum, but I can't.'

'Because of your job.' She said this as though it was something to be ashamed of. She'd always wanted him to be a doctor.

'Because of my job,' Aston agreed. 'Look, I went out on a limb to warn you. I shouldn't have done that, but I couldn't risk you getting hurt.'

'I know, Paul.'

'You can't tell a soul.'

'My lips are sealed.'

'Not even Roy. I could lose my job over something like this.'

'I heard you,' she said. 'You're not eating your sandwich.'

'I told you, I'm not hungry.'

'But I made it specially.'

Aston shook his head and picked up his tea. He took a sip, wondered how to start the conversation, wondered again what the hell he was going to say.

'Something's on your mind, Paul.'

'What makes you say that?'

'Well, you didn't come all this way to drink tea with your old mum, did you?'

Aston took another sip, put the cup and saucer down on the coffee table. 'I want you to tell me about my father,' he said. 'And this time I'm going to sit here until you tell me everything. No changing the subject, no lies. I want the truth.'

'Oh,' was all she said, the colour draining from her face.

'I have a right to know.'

'But, Paul, that was all so long ago. What good is it going to do?' She got up and headed for the door. 'I'm going to put the kettle on. Do you want some more tea?'

'Sit down!' Aston said, the words coming out more harshly than he intended.

'Don't shout at me, Paul.'

'I'm not shouting.' He was working hard to stay

on the right side of reasonable. 'Look, please sit down.'

She dropped into the armchair, shoulders sagging. 'But why now, Paul? Why can't you just let it lie?'

'Because I know who my father is.'

She let out another long 'Oh'.

'Is that all you've got to say?'

A long pause, then she said: 'So, who is he?'

This wasn't the answer he expected. He hesitated, studying her carefully, then said: 'What do you mean: "who is he"? Are you telling me you don't know who my father was?'

'It's not that simple, Paul. I wish it was. You want things in black and white, and I wish I could give you that, but I can't.' She was on the verge of tears, her words tumbling out in a rush.

'Calm down.'

'But it's so embarrassing. I feel so ashamed, so stupid.'

'I need to know the truth,' he said gently.

She pulled a tiny lace handkerchief from her sleeve, dabbed her eyes. 'You're right,' she said.

When she eventually got going, there was no stopping her. She bared her soul, talking with an honesty he never imagined her capable of. He was the priest, she was the sinner, and this was a confession. She hadn't worked in a trendy clothes shop in Carnaby Street, instead she'd been a dancer in a club in Soho. Aston didn't ask what sort of dancer. She'd been young, only eighteen, but that was no excuse, not really. Jeff was good-looking and charming with money to burn. He worked at the Foreign Office, and there was nothing suspicious about that because they got more than their fair share of civil servants at the club; it was quite an upmarket place, really. The dancers weren't allowed to date the customers, but Jeff was persistent and in the end she'd agreed to go out with him on the condition that they kept it a secret. One date led to another, and another. He promised the moon and the stars, and she'd lapped it up. They were going to get married and have a big house and a family, the whole deal. And so she'd let him . . . well, you know, and because everything was so perfect she hadn't been as careful as she should and the next thing she knew she was pregnant. She'd been so happy when she told him because this was all part of the happy-ever-after. Okay it was a bit sooner than they'd planned but that didn't matter because they loved each other. He'd hugged her, told her again that he loved her so much, and she knew everything was going to be so perfect . . . and how bloody stupid was she?

That his mother had said 'bloody' barely registered; the fact she was swearing was small change.

Shortly afterwards, Jeff Salter vanished. She'd contacted the Foreign Office, but no one of that name had ever worked there. His flat had been abandoned and the landlord was just as anxious to find him because he owed rent. In the end she decided he must have been married, a story she clung to because it was better than nothing and it gave her somewhere to focus her anger. And then the baby arrived and there was no time for hate, no time for wondering what might have been. There were more important things to worry about.

'And you never saw him again?' Aston said.

'No.' A pause. 'How did you find him?'

'I didn't. He found me.'

'And how is he?'

'Dead.'

She put a hand to her mouth, inhaled sharply. 'When? How?'

'The official story is that he had a massive stroke.'

'The official story?'

'I'm sorry. That's all I can tell you.'

'And don't I have a right to know what happened?'

'One day,' Aston promised.

'Why not now?'

'You know why.'

'You can at least tell me his real name.'

Aston thought for a moment, shook his head. 'Sorry, Mum,' he said gently. 'I can't.'

'You're not being fair, Paul. You have to tell me.'

The tears were back, and Aston knew that if he stayed he was just going to get angrier. That wouldn't do either of them any good. He got up in a daze, said he'd call her when he got home. The tearful 'oh' told him she was expecting something more, although what that might be he didn't know. Absolution, perhaps? Forgiveness? What the hell did she expect? That if she went and said a couple of Hail Marys everything would be alright? Because it wasn't alright. Listening to his mother's confession, he'd been forced towards the realisation that the one person he'd known his entire life was a complete stranger. She'd told him most of it, but he sensed there was a lot she wasn't telling, and for that he was thankful. There was only so much emotional napalm the heart could take.

George had taken up residence in a window seat, a half filled tumbler of JD and coke in front of her. Aston sat down opposite her. His glass had a double in. He took a long drink, straightened up the beer mat on the table and put the glass down, ice cubes tinkling.

'My guess is that isn't just coke in there,' she said. 'It went that well, huh?'

'Absolutely peachy,' Aston replied. 'What do you think?'

'I think I should drop the subject.'

'One of your more astute observations.'

'Well, when you do want to talk, you know where I am.'

'Yeah, living on my sofa.'

'Someone's got to look after you, Paul. Anyway, if you want me to leave, say the word and I'm gone.'

'Stay as long as you want. The truth is I kind

of like you being there.' Aston took another sip. It was the first alcohol he'd had in weeks and Christ did it taste good. He put the glass back on the table. 'Anything new on Mac?'

'Nothing you don't already know.'

'Humour me, okay? Right now all I'm looking for is a distraction. Just talk at me for a while. You're good at that.'

'Well,' George said. 'The rumour mill at Vauxhall Cross is working overtime. So far Mac's responsible for Lord Lucan's disappearance and there's a good chance he helped kidnap Shergar. Oh and get this, it was Mac up on the grassy knoll.'

'Stick to the facts, please.'

'Okay, he's still in Belmarsh and I can't see them letting him out any time soon. The shrinks had another go at him on Friday, but the general consensus is that he won't be able to pull off an insanity plea.'

'And you need a fancy degree up on your wall to work that one out? No way is Mac insane. If you ask me, any time Mac does should be hard time – the hardest time. I hope the bastard spends the rest of his life in Belmarsh. For what he did it's the least he deserves.'

'You'll get no arguments from me.'

'How much money have they found?'

'So far, a couple of million. But there's more where that came from, a lot more. According to the gossip, he could have anywhere between ten and a hundred million stashed away.'

'You know, I wish I'd seen his face.'

'Me, too.'

'Never assume,' Aston said in a reasonable imitation of Mac's voice.

'Or you'll make an ASS out of U and ME,' George finished, although her 'Mac' was a little too high-pitched and lacking in the bass end. 'There was nothing inside the lead casing. Don't you just love that, eh? He *assumed* there was something in there, but there wasn't.'

'The bomb still caused a ton of damage, though.'

'Yeah, but it could have been so much worse. If it had actually been a dirty bomb Vauxhall Cross would have been a no-go zone for the next century or two.' George glanced at her watch. 'Ten minutes till the next train. What do you think?'

Aston looked at the half full glass on the table, decided he'd had enough. 'Let's go.'

Outside the pub, George linked her arm in his. 'It will get easier, you know,' she said as they headed for the station.

'Yeah?'

'Trust me on that one.'

'It's a fucked-up old world . . . that was the last thing he said to me. As fatherly advice goes it's kind of lacking, don't you think?'

'Not really. You've got to admit, he had a point.'

'It's not quite up there with "neither a borrower or lender be", though.'

'And what sort of advice is that? I'd say being a lender is a pretty good occupation. You can earn a hell of a lot more than you do working for MI6.'

'You always have to disagree with me, don't you?'

'It's my God-given right, Paul.'

Aston stopped and smiled at her. 'Thanks,' he said.

'Thanks for what?'

He leant in, flicked a stray hair from her face then kissed her on the forehead. 'Just thanks.'

Afterword

I began writing *The Mentor* way back in July 2003. Betty Schwartz, who was working for Hodder at the time, had got in touch to see if I had any ideas for a Big British Thriller. Back then I was just another unpublished writer struggling to get noticed, so when someone from the big league comes knocking on your door, you jump to it.

Every novel needs a 'what if . . .?' to kick-start it. And the 'what if' that suggested itself here was straightforward enough. What if there was a 9/11 attack in Britain? Would that premise be powerful enough to drive a novel? I thought so. I needed an event to get the novel going. Something big; something chilling. Most of all, it had to be plausible. A suicide bomb attack on the tube in the middle of rush hour seemed to fulfil this criteria. It never occurred to me that it might actually happen.

Fiction writing is make-believe. At the end of the day it's just words on a page and nobody really gets hurt. Part of my job is to venture into the dark places and report on what I find there; we all have a primal fascination with the monsters living in the shadows. So, I'll take you into the mind of a serial killer; I'll whisper a running commentary as we share a murder victim's last moments; I'll take you down into an Underground station and show you the aftermath of a terrorist explosion. And it's okay for me to do that because it's make-believe and nobody gets hurt.

But what if fiction becomes fact?

Fast forward to July 7, 2005 . . .

The day started like any other: a bath, breakfast, boot up the computer and get to work.

And then the phone call.

It was Karen. She told me to turn the news on, something had happened on the Underground. At that point the reporters were still convinced it was a massive power failure; nobody had mentioned terrorists yet. As events unfolded it was like the worst case of déjà vu ever. The pictures coming up on the screen, the things the reporters were describing, it was all so familiar. I'd spent months writing about this and now it was coming true. I watched in stunned disbelief, completely horrified. Tom Clancy must have experienced something similar on 9/11 – in one of his books a 747 is flown into the Capitol building.

The story played out, and it was worse than anything I could ever dream up. These were real people who died. Innocent people whose only crime was being in the wrong place at the wrong time. It didn't bear thinking about. There's a scene near the start of *The Mentor* where Aston is flicking through the 24-hour news channels and decides the reporters don't 'have a fucking clue' because they weren't actually there. They're reporting on events from a distance; all their information is second-hand. I could relate to that.

I avoided the novel for a good few months after 7/7. I needed to distance myself from it; needed space. When I eventually re-read it there was obviously work to be done. Originally the book was written from the point of view 'what if the unthinkable happened?' In the final version I change the angle slightly: what if it happened again?

We live in uncertain times; terrorism is a part of our lives. As long as there's a lunatic out there with a bomb and a cause, we can't change that. However, what we can control is the way we view that threat. A couple of months after 7/7 I visited London. What struck me most was that nothing had really changed. Yes, there were the posters on the tube warning people to be vigilant, the announcements about unattended baggage, a more visible police presence, but apart from that it was business as usual. And that's the way it's got to be. Business as usual.

Steve Jackson
January 2006

The Double Eagle

James Twining

In Paris a priest is murdered, the killers dumping his mutilated body into the Seine. Only he has taken a secret with him to his death. A secret that reveals itself during his autopsy and reawakens memories of Depression-era politics and a seventy-year-old heist.

Jennifer Browne, a young and ambitious FBI agent is assigned to the case. This is her last chance to kick start a career that has stalled after one fatal error of judgement three years before.

Her investigation uncovers a daring robbery from Fort Knox and Tom Kirk, the world's greatest art thief is the prime suspect.

Tom, caught between his desire to finally get out of the game and his partner's insistence that he complete one last job for the criminal mastermind Cassius, faces a thrilling race against time to clear his name. A race that takes him from London to Paris, Amsterdam to Istanbul in a search for the real thieves and the legendary Double Eagle.

0-00-719015-8

Dark Justice

Jack Higgins

It is night in Manhattan. The President of the United States is scheduled to have dinner with an old friend, but in the building across the street, a man has disabled the security and stands at a window, a rifle in his hand.

The assassination doesn't go according to plan, but this is only the beginning. Someone is recruiting a shadowy network of agents with the intention of creating terror.

Their range is broad, their identities masked, their methods subtle. White House operative Blake Johnson and his opposite number in British intelligence, Sean Dillon, set out to trace the source of the havoc, but behind the first man lies another, and behind him another still. And that man is not pleased by the interference. Soon, he will target them all: Johnson, Dillon, Dillon's colleagues. And one of them will fall....

'Open a Jack Higgins novel and you'll encounter a master craftsman at the peak of his powers . . . first-rate tales of intrigue, suspense and full-on action'   *Sunday Express*

0-00-712723-5